D0115949

# Just Your Local BISEXUAL DISASTER

# Just Your Local Bisexual Disaster

ANDREA MOSQUEDA

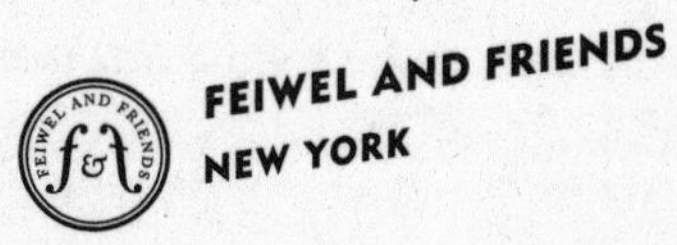


FEIWEL AND FRIENDS
NEW YORK

A Feiwel and Friends Book
An imprint of Macmillan Publishing Group, LLC
120 Broadway, New York, NY 10271 • fiercereads.com



Our books may be purchased in bulk for promotional, educational, or business use. Please contact your local bookseller or the Macmillan Corporate and Premium Sales Department at (800) 221-7945 ext. 5442 or by email at MacmillanSpecialMarkets@macmillan.com.

Library of Congress Cataloging-in-Publication Data is available.

First edition, 2022
Book design by Liz Dresner
Feiwel and Friends logo designed by Filomena Tuosto
Printed in the United States of America

ISBN 978-1-250-82205-5
1 3 5 7 9 10 8 6 4 2

*For my little sister.*
*Thanks for being my built-in best friend*
*and for never taking me too seriously.*

*For the 956 and all the stories it has yet to tell.*

# 1

In the Rio Grande Valley, a quinceañera was the most important party a kid could ever have. Not even weddings were treated with such a militaristic approach. Planning my little sister Alyssa's quince was quickly turning into a three-ring circus, and she was more than ready to be the star of the show.

Today's act: the first try on of the dress.

"Should we have a theme?" Alyssa asked as we sat in the back seat of our mom's Altima on the way to the Sewing Box. It was the tried-and-true dress shop in San Benito, smack dab in the middle of Sam Houston Road near the railroad tracks; both my older sister, Veronica, and I had gotten our quince dresses there, so of course Alyssa had to get hers there too. She must have tried on a dozen of them before settling on this one, and now she was going to get to see it, fancy turquoise beading and all, for the first time.

Our mom was driving, so Veronica turned around to face us. "Shouldn't you have thought about that before you bought the dress?" She raised a perfectly plucked and filled eyebrow; she was twenty-five going on forty and went to the University of Cosmetology Arts and Sciences, the cosmetology school in Harlingen, one town over, so her looks of disapproval were often accessorized with sharp winged liner and flawless lash extensions.

I paused the new Cuco album I was listening to and took out my headphones. "Themes for quinces are sooo tacky though."

"I thought your cousin's theme was kind of cute," Mom noted defensively, tilting her head to glance at us in the rear-view mirror.

"Her theme was 'pink,' Mami. A color can't be a theme," Alyssa insisted.

The rosary hanging from the mirror swung a bit as our mom changed lanes, the glint of the cross shining into my eyes and making me squint. I rubbed at them a bit, yawning. I'd been dragged out of bed at 9 A.M. on a Saturday for a dress try on that didn't involve me. Alyssa hadn't even picked out a dress for her damas yet, so Veronica and I were just here to be the family peanut gallery.

The damas' dresses would surely be a debate all their own. Everything about Alyssa's quince was turning into a spectacle, and it was just getting started. Alyssa had her court picked out. Her group of friends had already been suitably ranked so only her closest friends got to be a dama or chambelán (or just escort) and be paraded around with her on the day of her quince.

I shuddered just thinking about all the dresses Alyssa was going to make me try on when it was actually time for me to step into the dama role, zipping myself into the supportive middle sister suit that I'd worn my whole life.

"What would your theme even be?" I asked.

Alyssa shrugged, tossing her head to flick her too-long bangs out of her eyes. "I don't know, Mardi Gras?"

Veronica stared at her incredulously. "Mardi Gras? You've never even been out of Texas, much less to Louisiana—"

"Not true! We've all gone to Mexico—"

"Does that even count as travel if all we do when we go there is see the doctor and go school shopping?" I asked.

"Te gusta la doctora," Mom reminded me. "And things are too expensive here. Eighty dollars for a backpack. Pinche—" Our mom shook her head, catching herself, and I tried not to laugh as she continued, "And there was that time we went for a few days when your grandma was sick. That was kind of like a vacation."

Alyssa squinted. "I don't know if I'd call a rosary and a burial a vacation."

"Well, we all took a big family photo after, so—"

"The point is," Veronica said exasperatedly, "that you don't need to have a theme."

"Yeah, and what do you know about Mardi Gras?" I asked.

Alyssa glared at me. "I know we can wear masks, which would definitely be a great look for you."

I swatted at her, and she whined, "Maaa, Maggie hit me!"

"You're both being rude right now. Apologize to your sister, now, both of you." Our mom couldn't turn away from the road to glare at us, so Veronica did it for her; it was almost *worse* since she had Mom's eyes and our dad's thick eyebrows, the most intimidating combo imaginable.

I sighed and turned to Alyssa, who was slumped in her seat sulking. Baby. "Sorry I hit you."

"Sorry I called you ugly."

"It's fine." I shrugged. "We're all ugly deep down inside."

"Facts," Veronica said, looking down at her phone. She was texting her boyfriend, CJ, judging by all the hearts in the message thread, so I leaned forward, craning my neck not so much to peek at the messages but just to invade her personal space. It worked, and she glared at me and pushed my head back, sending my beanie toppling off my head in the process. I slid it back on and reclined in my seat, smiling. "Seriously though, isn't Mardi Gras culturally appropriative?"

"We're Catholic." Alyssa thought about it as we pulled up to the Sewing Box, our mom parking by the curb. "I don't know. Besides, if we don't have a theme, then the default theme is me, and honestly, can any of you think of a better theme than that on my birthday?"

Veronica looked over at me, and we both tried to hold in our laughter as Alyssa hummed, satisfied with our lack of answer, and undid her seat belt, jumping out of the car as soon as Mom unlocked it, yelling, "Come on!"

Alyssa might have been all jokes in the car, but in the Sewing Box, her gaze was trained sharply on the seamstress, more serious than I'd ever seen her in her almost-fifteen years of life. Alyssa hopped up to help her as she approached with the enormous garment bag. I probably should've helped, but I was very comfortable curled up on one of the chairs at the rickety, magazine-covered table in the showroom, phone in my lap.

Hey, it wasn't *my* quince. I did my time, thank you very much.

As Alyssa disappeared into the dressing room with my mother, I turned back to the text debate I was having with my best friend, Amanda, about whether brand-new Converse could count as formalwear. I sent her a pic of the room.

**Amanda:** OMG exciting! I wish I could have my quince all over again

**Maggie:** Ew I could never. It was so much work

**Amanda:** You looked so hot tho

A grin crept onto my face. Amanda was straight, so I knew she meant it in the most platonic of ways. But that didn't change the fact that it made me feel warm inside whenever she said something like that.

Veronica flipped through one of the magazines on the table. It was full of bridesmaid and dama dresses, and she held the magazine out, pointing to a strapless number in the corner. "What do you think about this one?"

I peered at it and winced. "It's good for *you*. My boobs could never hold that shit up."

Veronica laughed. "I'm sure your escort would *love* that. Who are you thinking about asking?"

"Ugh, I don't even know. I'll probably just ask Jordan." Jordan Estrada had been my best guy friend since first grade, when we took the same bus to Sullivan Elementary and Jordan had a CD player along with one of those album books with the little slipcovers for holding the discs.

As though summoned, a message from Jordan to the group chat popped up on the screen. Helpless Children Support Group (name given proudly by Amanda: "we're a bunch of babies who need help") had started when we all got smartphones in ninth grade, but the maturity level of its content hadn't risen much since then. It was just a dumping ground for memes and digital proof of our pendejadas.

I opened the picture Jordan had sent. It was the poster for the Screamin' Summer Showcase, where he and his weird indie pop band Key of Reason were performing tonight. Thank fuck because the concert was soon and I'd already forgotten where in Harlingen it was supposed to be.

**Amanda:** Cute poster!!
**9565559870:** Thanks, I designed it last week!

For a minute, my mind blanked at the unsaved number before I remembered and saved the contact as Dani Mendoza. Dani was new here, having transferred from Harlingen High at the beginning of the school year, and Jordan had met her in art class. Riding his skateboard into the classroom, he'd nearly run over Dani's feet, and rather than get angry, Dani had faked an injury to get them out of class. Jordan had been bouncing with excitement when he introduced Dani that day at lunch.

I didn't know a ton about Dani so far, since she'd been in my life a grand total of three seconds, but Dani paired light, breezy dresses with beat-up Converse and had her ears stretched, with a tragus piercing and a hoop in her cartilage, so I was willing to accept her application to our island of misfit toys just based on aesthetic alone.

**Matthew:** Catch me on keyboard
**Jordan:** He's not half bad, y'all
**Amanda:** I'll believe it when I see it

"Maggie!"

Alyssa stood in front of me, ponytail lopsided and hands on her hips. Her ruffled baby hairs made it look like she had a brown halo, and it took me a second to realize she was in her dress, fully zipped in and laced up for the first time. "What do you think?"

Mom was talking excitedly to the seamstress and her assistant in Spanish, too fast for me to hear, and Veronica motioned her pointer finger in a circle to get Alyssa to spin like she was on *Say Yes to the Dress*. I just stared at the turquoise dress, taking in the spaghetti straps and picking up the skirt to examine the flower-patterned beading. The back was laced with ribbon, tied with a bow at the bottom. I knew this whole thing was supposed to be about her becoming a woman, but to me she still just looked like my little sister, playing dress-up. "It looks really good, Al."

Veronica nodded, starting to untie the back. "Time to think about the damas' dresses to match."

My phone buzzed, and I looked down to see a message from Amanda.

**Amanda:** Can you tell your ex not to bring his gf to the show? She's so exhausting to be around and she always brings her gross friends

**Maggie:** He has a name and so does she. But yeah i'll tell him

I rolled my eyes, bringing up Matthew's text thread. Despite the fact that Matthew was *my* ex, it seemed like Amanda sometimes hated him more than I did. Part of it was for breaking my heart, probably, but the other part was that I spent a lot of my time with him and not her when we were dating, and now she could finally take her aggression out on him. Whatever the reason, I hated when I had to get between them.

**Maggie:** Can you tell tori not to bring her friends to the show tonight? I don't want Amanda to start shit

**Matthew:** Too late. They're already coming. Her lack of impulse control is not my problem

**Maggie:** Oh god fine whatever i tried.

"Maggie, let's go," Alyssa urged, nearly decapitating me with the end of the garment bag. I had been so absorbed in Matthew's texts that I hadn't noticed Alyssa had already changed. She shifted the garment bag to push her bangs behind her ear. "Time to take this bitch home and stare at it for a few weeks."

My phone buzzed and I resisted the urge to check it. "Can't wait."

I didn't get my phone out again until I was buckled in the back seat, forgotten as my family chattered on around me about quince stuff and The Story So Far blared in my earbuds.

**Matthew:** Shouldn't we be the ones fighting
like divorced parents over hangouts?
Not my girlfriend and amanda lol

**Maggie:** Do you want to fight with me?

**Matthew:** It was one of our favorite hobbies.
I'm sure it would be like riding a bike ;)

A warmth tugged low in my belly, making me shift in my seat and look around to see if anyone had noticed that another aftershock of our earthquake of a relationship had just left me shaken. This happened way too often for my liking—consequences of dating one of my only friends and not having the heart to kick him out of the friend group because Jordan got attached to him.

A notification popped up, this time a message from Jordan:

Sam and i broke up. Like for real for real.

My mouth dropped a bit before I frowned, my surprise passing and giving way to an annoyed relief. Sam and Jordan had been on and off for months, but this time the ax must have finally dropped.

**Maggie:** Yikes. Sorry my dude.
Do you need anything?
**Jordan:** I have an extra ticket to homecoming and a matching shirt. Be my plus one and shit?

It was an absolute no-brainer. When Matthew and I broke up the second time in sophomore year, we had already bought matching shirts for MORP (SBHS's version of the quintessential Sadie Hawkins dance), but like the phenomenal friend he is, Jordan dutifully took Matthew's shirt even though he was swimming in it and went to the dance with me anyway. I owed him this.

**Maggie:** Um YEAH ofc. What would you do without me?
**Jordan:** Die of melodramatic mortification probably

---

That afternoon, I needed Veronica's help: Jordan's concert was in two hours and my bangs were obnoxiously long. I desperately needed a trim, so I came downstairs from our apartment to the store, waving to our mom at the counter before heading out the door to the backyard, toward the sound of my sisters' laughter.

Veronica was already on the back porch, with Alyssa in the swiveling desk chair that Veronica used as a barber's station. In between helping our mom with the store and going to UCAS, Veronica was always trying to get extra practice by running a makeshift hair salon out of our house, but Mom had banished her business to the back porch in the name of easy cleanup.

Alyssa loved to be the guinea pig for her more experimental ideas, always happy to set trends at school, whether it was with a braid crown peppered with sprigs of plastic daisies or a purple streak through her bangs. That one had caused her to be sent to in-school suspension, but Alyssa had insisted that the disciplinary infraction was worth it, if only because it bolstered her reputation among the other ninth graders. She changed her mind later though, after Mami found out she'd been in suspension and yelled so loud, the noise carried down into the store and sent a pair of teenage boys fleeing for the door without buying anything.

It was unfair how much cooler my sisters were than me. Being the middle child *sucked*.

Veronica saw me first, shears stilling as she pushed a strand of sweaty Pravana-red hair out of her face. "Sit down. I'm just trimming Alyssa's bangs. Then I can do yours. They're getting too long."

I dropped my camera bag on the concrete and sat in the decrepit lawn chair near the back door, putting my feet up on an old ice chest. "Do you have time to do it before I leave with Amanda for the concert?"

Veronica looked up at me, the hand with the shears coming up to rest on her cocked hip. "Have you finished all your homework? You know you're not allowed to go anywhere until it's done."

I scowled. The unfinished AP Calc assignment in my backpack seemed to glow like an infrared beacon of shame. Veronica waved her shears. "That's what I thought. Get started. You know that NYU isn't going to accept anything but As."

I sighed, taking out my folder and my school-issued

calculator. "Yeah, fine, you're right. So will you be able to do it in time?"

"Personally, I think you should go with your bangs like that. Then you can do that emo skater boy hair flip all night like all the bands," Alyssa quipped.

She wasn't wrong, but I stuck my tongue out at her anyway.

Veronica waved a hand, already looking down at Alyssa again. "Don't worry, I'll get it done before your School of Rock crowd even packs up their roadie van. You just focus on your schoolwork."

I tried not to roll my eyes and got to work on my problem set. "Focus on your schoolwork" had been my family's mantra since I first started taking photos in ninth grade and said I wanted to go to NYU. They had dismissed it as a phase until I started taking school seriously and pulling all As, and since then, they'd gotten a little *too* supportive, if that was possible. They even gave me less shifts at the store so I could get involved with extracurriculars.

I appreciated it. I really did. But it was hard to feel the same about NYU when I had looked up the cost and actually thought about what it would mean for my family if I were to go.

Now I wasn't so certain, but I sure as hell wasn't going to tell them that.

Something prickled on my forearm, and I swatted it, my hand coming away with a smashed mosquito the size of a nickel. "Nasty." I snagged a tissue from Veronica's workstation and wiped the mosquito guts from my skin before grabbing another to wipe the sweat off my forehead. The Rio Grande Valley was on the southernmost Texas border, so it was hellishly hot most of the time, but something about fall, with school starting, football season, activity happening all around, made the Texas heat absolutely boiling. I glanced longingly at the rusty metal fan beside me, fingers itching toward it, before I looked at Veronica to make sure she wouldn't be thrown off by the air. "Can I turn on the fan?"

Without missing a beat, or looking up from Alyssa's bangs, Veronica said, "I don't know, can you?"

I scowled before flipping the fan on to the highest setting. "Rude. That's the last time I try to be considerate."

"It's not like you ever tried that hard in the first place, baby crier."

"Yeah, baby crier," Alyssa echoed, swinging her feet back and forth. I gave her the stink eye, and she retaliated by sticking out her tongue. "So what's up?"

I shrugged. "Nothing. Homecoming is tomorrow. Sam broke up with Jordan, so we're going to the dance together."

Alyssa and Veronica both stared at me, wide-eyed. "You're going on a date with *Jordan*?"

"Ew, gross, no! He just didn't want Sam's friends to talk shit about him, so I offered myself as a shield."

Veronica narrowed her eyes, scanning my face before whatever she saw there convinced her I wasn't lying. "Good. I was about to lecture you for hooking up with a friend."

"Matthew was my friend," I pointed out.

"Yeah, and look how that ended up," Alyssa reminded me.

"Ugh, fine. You're right. Whatever. I'm not about to make the same mistake with *Jordan* of all people."

Veronica and Alyssa both nodded, resuming their former activities. "So why didn't you already have a date?" Veronica asked, combing out Alyssa's wet bangs and studying the length.

"Didn't ask anyone." I shrugged, busying myself with chipping away at the remnants of black polish on my nails. "You know I'm not really looking for a relationship right now."

"A date isn't a relationship," Veronica pointed out.

"A date leads to a relationship."

"Not necessarily. A date is like testing out a new person, before you really jump in. Besides, didn't you break up with Matthew the last time?"

I stared at her. "Yeah, so?"

"So shouldn't you be the one with no trouble dating again?"

"Not if I don't want to date right now. Even if I did, everyone gets out there at their own pace," I muttered, still looking down. "Isn't that what all those self-help Instagrams say?"

"Yeah, but I don't even think you've liked anyone since then," Alyssa pointed out.

"It's not my fault I'm not interested in anyone."

"There's a difference between not being interested and forcing yourself to not be interested," Veronica said.

"You know I'm not great at relationships. I mean, look at how all of mine turned out." I cringed at how pathetic my voice sounded. But this was something I could only really talk to my sisters about, since they'd seen the aftermath of my failed relationships and it was impossible to keep secrets in our tiny apartment. I shared a room with Alyssa, so she'd heard enough nighttime sobbing to know exactly what I felt at all times.

Veronica put down her shears. "How are you supposed to get better if you never even let yourself try?"

I didn't know. Just the idea of trying to date someone again and putting all that effort into something that would ultimately fail made me want to fall over and take a nap right on this concrete floor.

Alyssa nodded eagerly, her crooked bangs swaying with the movement. "Dating isn't all bad, but I *did* break up with Josh last week, so I get needing a break from all of this love stuff."

"You're not allowed to date yet," Veronica dismissed her, still looking at me. "Just think about it, okay?"

I waited for her to look away, but she didn't, so I just sighed, relenting. "Fine. I'll think about it. And only if I see someone I'm semi-interested in."

Satisfied, Veronica nodded and turned back to Alyssa's bangs. "That's all I'm saying."

"This was solid advice, by the way." I nodded at her textbook, balanced on the cheap set of drawers next to Veronica that housed her tools. "Do they teach you psychology over at UCAS or do you just learn this shit as you get older?"

Veronica finished trimming, and Alyssa hopped off the chair and grabbed the small hand mirror as I took her place. "It's in the textbook, before *ombre* and after *how to raise your delinquent sisters*."

Alyssa examined her new bangs, turning this way and that as she pouted at herself in the mirror. She handed down her verdict indirectly, but we all knew the power she held, even if it was just about a haircut. "I don't know what you're talking about, I'm awesome."

---

Sometimes I helped Amanda get photos for yearbook, and yeah, it was a great addition to my résumé and portfolio for college, but I preferred a photo shoot with a little more edge. Luckily, two of my favorite local bands to photograph were on the roster for the Screamin' Summer Showcase.

I had been snapping photos for Key of Reason since the band's formation, but my client list had grown since then to include Ire and Vines, a screamo/rap band from the upper Valley. The drums were loud and rollicking, the drops were sick, and the lead singer was a beast on stage, so I could always trust them to give me all the cinematic shots I needed.

The crowd was screaming behind me, jumping along with the beat of the thumping bass, and for once I was grateful for the metal barrier that separated the crowd from the stage as I stood in that space, snapping picture after picture of the band. I'd been hitching rides to concerts since I was Alyssa's age, and I'd always thought the best place to be was right in front, smashed up against the gate and sprayed with the sweat of a rotating cast of musicians.

But now I knew there was a better one: right here, just beyond the gate, in that space where only bodyguards and crowd-surfers returning to the human sea could enter.

The lead singer, Malcolm, was singing into the microphone, veins popping and cheeks red. I snapped a photo, in awe but distant. I was not a fan or a band member. Right now, I was here to observe, to capture, but my mind was always behind that gate, on stage, everywhere there was music and someone to appreciate it.

The first time Amanda and I went to a concert, in eighth grade, we'd skipped school and gotten one of Amanda's cousins to drive us to the Pharr Event Center, forty minutes away, to be first in line for a Bring Me the Horizon show. Smashed up against the gate, with a thousand screaming fans pressed up behind me trying to get impossibly closer to Oliver Sykes, I walked away with bruised ribs and a huge smile on my face, and a ringing in my ears that had moved to my heart and never left.

The Screamin' Summer Showcase had been planned by local bands themselves, held on acres of open fields just outside Harlingen heading toward McAllen. Even though these were local bands, I was more than happy just to be an instrumental blip on their radar. Ire and Vines's fan base had been growing exponentially since I'd started, and I hoped that one day I'd get to tell someone, "I knew them before they got big."

Every band or solo musician had their own style of performing. Some were more dedicated to the vocals, others to audience participation. Whatever the artists loved about themselves, it was my job to capture it.

A ripple resounded through the crowd to the right of me, and I broke away from the viewfinder to see golden limbs flailing above the crowd, moving on the sea of hands to the gate, and a security guard rushing past me. I knew what that meant. I moved quickly to the left to give the crowd-surfer enough room to drop over the fence next to me. I craned my neck, searching for the brave soul who had decided to ride the moshing crowd.

Dani Mendoza, cheeks red and French braid half undone, came sailing out over the audience. She was wearing a Dashboard Confessional T-shirt and a pair of ripped black shorts, but what stood out was the humongous smile on her face, remaining even when the crowd almost missed the waiting arms of the security guard as they dropped her unceremoniously over the fence. Dani winked at me and gave me a two-finger salute as the security guard pushed her in the opposite direction.

As I picked my jaw up off the ground, Dani rounded the gate and disappeared back into the crowd. The band ended their last song, and I jolted back into my body, scrambling to get backstage.

As the band came offstage, I waved, pushing a sweaty strand of hair out of my eyes. "That was fucking great."

The lead singer, Malcolm Morales, greeted me with a side

hug as the rest waved and sat on the ground, chugging bottles of water as they went. "Glad you had fun. Get anything good?" he said, motioning to the camera in my hands.

I grinned. This was always my favorite part, seeing their reactions in person. "Lemme show you."

We flicked through the first few, with Malcolm humming approvingly over my shoulder, but I knew what shot would stop him dead before we got to it. It was a photo of Malcolm himself, bent backward in an *Exorcist*-like bridge, mouth in midscream as he gripped the mic in one hand. You could see every drop of sweat sliding off his straightened hair, every muscle taut.

I wanted to pump my fist in the air like some airhead jock when Malcolm shouted, "Fuck yeah, dude!" and motioned for the others to come and see.

Pride welled up in my chest. Artists are narcissists but also painfully insecure and in need of validation, and I was no exception to this rule, so anytime I managed to get one of them to feel good about themselves, it was a win for both of us.

"Why are you monopolizing the photographer?" Jordan asked as he sauntered over from backstage. He and Malcolm had met a few years ago, and when he'd mentioned needing a photographer, Jordan had referred him to me. In the future, when I became a legendary tour photographer for the rock stars of tomorrow (*when*, not *if*), I'd forever remember the Valley bands that filled the first pages in my portfolio.

Malcolm gave him a fist bump. "Might have to snag her for Ire exclusively if she keeps taking shots like this." He gestured for Jordan to look at my Canon, and I got to bask again in the brief pride that came from seeing Jordan's eyes widen with approval as he peered at the tiny screen.

After they said their goodbyes, with me promising to edit

the photos and send them over later, I turned to Jordan. "Did you know Dani was here?"

Jordan's brow furrowed. "Um, yeah? I invited her in the group chat, remember?"

Right. I flushed. "Well, it just took me by surprise when I saw her crowd-surfing." I couldn't say why it would have helped to have some prior knowledge of Dani's presence, but whatever. I was going with it. I narrowed my eyes at him.

"Why do you care if she's here?" Jordan asked, bemused.

I didn't. At least, I didn't think so. "I was just surprised—I don't—"

I was relieved as we approached the space behind the stage that Key of Reason had claimed as their makeshift green room, tuning their instruments and warming up their voices. I nodded at them before I saw Amanda, perched precariously on a nearby amp. She looked out of place among the ripped jeans and flannel, the stink of cigarette smoke; she'd tied her hair back neatly in a smooth, shiny ponytail, and she'd matched her sundress to her Michael Kors bag, the shiny gold buckles complementing the metal bits on her sandals.

I nodded at her outfit as I motioned for her to scoot over and share better. "How're you supposed to mosh in a dress? I mean, I know flashing the band is a punk tradition, but—"

Amanda rolled her eyes and smiled. "You know my moshing days are over. My mom almost killed me that time I broke my nose. I've been standing in the back this whole time."

I remembered that. At a Story So Far concert three years ago, a crowd-surfer landed directly on Amanda's face. As fun as the concert was, I kind of hated that memory, just because I wish I'd paid more attention to what it felt like to be there with Amanda, how safe the mosh pit felt with the person I trusted most in the world. Sometimes I missed the years we'd spent in our shared scene phase: straightened hair teased to high heaven, ears stretched wide, and band T-shirts from Hot Topic with horrifying drawings that got me whacked with a chancla by my mother. I went through all that with Amanda, heavy eyeliner and Bath and Body Works Vampire Blood–scented body mist because we were still *deep* in a vampire phase too. My taste for the obscene had faded into a rather tasteful pop-punk facsimile (I hoped, at least), but Amanda had grown out of it entirely, preferring Charlotte Russe sandals to Vans, A'Gaci to Hot Topic.

I loved my best friend, but sometimes I missed that version of her.

Matthew was the sometimes-keyboardist of Jordan's band, and I waved at him from where he stood leaning against the cab of his truck. He smiled before looking past me, his smile erupting into a grin, and the sinking feeling in my stomach announced the arrival of Matthew's new girlfriend before I even heard, "Hey, babe!"

Matthew stood up and reached for Tori, the senior from his theater class that he'd recently become Instagram official with, as she strode into his waiting arms. Tori eyed me over Matthew's shoulder.

Tori was a tall, willowy fair-skinned brunette whose expressions were often as cool as her skin tone. She was the kind of girl that it hurt to look at because you both knew you'd never measure up. Even now, I could see her sizing up Amanda, and when Tori's stony stare settled on me again, I made an effort this time to stand taller and not avoid her eyes.

Under Tori's critical gaze, I felt every imperfection, saw my too-small breasts and my cheeks that hadn't yet lost their roundness, my olive skin still peppered with remnants of last week's menstrual breakout and scars of older zits. Tori with her perfect skin, designer clothes, and the first boy I ever loved in her arms.

I had to remind myself sometimes that Matthew and I were broken up, and for good reason. I didn't need to torture myself by looking at him with his latest girlfriend any more than necessary, especially if she would be around all the time now.

Her lackeys, Letty and Jackie, were standing just off to the side, eyeing Jordan's band with open disdain. Jordan watched them warily, body just a little tense.

Even happy-go-lucky Jordan, beloved by all, knew to be careful around them. Catty, gossipy, and petty, I'd only been mostly saved from their wrath by my proximity to Amanda, whose reputation as an all-around Good Girl as well as teacher's pet rendered her untouchable, simply because this town was way too small. Still, even that didn't prevent them from sending us dirty looks in the hallways. Maybe it was my proximity to Matthew, or my tendency to let my disgust show on my face.

"Anyone have a water?"

Dani approached us from the back of the crowd, red-faced and sweating but grinning broadly, the sleeves of her T-shirt pushed up to show her lean but strong biceps. I handed her a water bottle from the ice chest.

"Thanks." Dani popped the cap off, tipping her head back and guzzling. I traced the path of a stray bead of sweat as it rolled down her neck, my mouth suddenly dry. I could feel Amanda watching but didn't dare turn to face her as Dani started talking again. "That crowd was crazy. I had to get out of there."

"Saw you crowd-surfing earlier. You looked like you were very comfortable up there."

Dani smiled wistfully. "I've been going to concerts for a while. It's familiar territory."

"Yeah, I get that," I agreed. The concerts I'd been to always felt familiar, even though they were for different bands, and that was really comforting, especially when the world outside the venue was confusing and scary and strange. "I bet you have stories—"

"Tell me about it! Maggie and I go to shows all the time, right, Maggie? Since, like, middle school. It was kind of our thing," Amanda interrupted with a hard nod, her voice too loud and high-pitched to be casual.

I shrugged, turning to Dani. "Yeah, so there's always a ton to go to—"

"Yeah, we usually have to leave pretty early to get good places in the crowd. It's not always for everyone," Amanda said too casually. "But if you feel like you can handle it . . ."

Amanda's voice was tight and hard, and I had never heard it that way before. She was staring at Dani the way she looked at Matthew, with a cold politeness that could cut you with its sharp edges at any moment. I didn't get it. Was I not allowed to go to concerts with other friends? It's not like she was falling all over herself to go with me. What did it matter to her if I had other friends who did?

Jordan's brow wrinkled in confusion as he nodded in a discreet "What the fuck?" gesture toward Amanda. I shook my head a bit. I didn't have time to dissect Amanda's mood right now because the last band had started leaving the stage. "Time to go, guys."

I didn't have time to fixate—it was time to step into photographer mode again.

---

Later that night, Alyssa fast asleep in the bed across from me, I squinted at my laptop screen, a beacon of light in the room's darkness. Editing the photos was always the most annoying part, but I was lucky to find something that made it just a little better.

I'd let Malcolm take a few pictures with my camera, most of which were funny shots of Ire and Vines, but there was also a picture of us: Matthew, Jordan, Amanda, Dani, and me. *Hey, we never get Maggie in pictures! Take one of us,* Jordan had begged, and Malcolm had.

It was actually a really good picture. Jordan's head was thrown back, mouth open in laughter at something Matthew was saying, and Amanda was sitting on the amp and had her arms around my waist, resting her head against my shoulder. I hated being in pictures, but I had smiled for this one when Amanda had tugged me into her, tripping over my own feet to get closer to her. Dani was close to us, but a little ways away, like she didn't quite know where she fit. She had a small half smile on her face, secretive like she wasn't sure if she trusted us but felt the need to be close nonetheless, and one hand was tucking a strand of her hair behind her ear, her piercings catching the light of the setting sun.

A smile tugged at my lips as I saved the picture to the cloud. It wasn't a perfect picture by any stretch of the imagination. It was a little blurry and the composition sucked, but it didn't matter. This picture was just for me, and I thought it was a really good place to start.

# 2

I knew exactly how Matthew looked when he was angry.

I couldn't forget it, no matter how much I tried. We'd shared a lot of firsts when we were together, and those moments left their mark. Now, it was like every memory we'd made had stuck to my brain and never left. His smile, his laugh, the way he looked when he was nervous.

That's how I could immediately tell something was wrong when he stalked up to me as I sat in the library during lunch, eating a mediocre cafeteria sandwich while I edited photos for the yearbook. I could see his anger simmering under his skin, recognized the firm line of his lips and the dent between his brows. Interesting. Nothing particularly controversial had happened lately, so it was kind of nice to know I could still get under his skin just by existing.

"Heard you're going to the dance with Jordan tonight," Matthew said, his eyes burning into mine. His shoulders were tight, and I could see the bulge of his fists from where they were shoved into the pockets of his jeans.

As much as I wanted to look away, I refused to, and stared back at him. "That's none of your business. Stay in your lane."

"It *is* my business when my ex-girlfriend is going after my best friend," he accused, the sharpness of his hiss cutting through the silence of the library.

The people at the tables turned to stare at us, and I flushed, equal parts embarrassed, pissed, but also . . . curious? I turned to face him fully, and his face dropped to the V of my black T-shirt. A rush of indignance flared up to push out the rather lust-colored thoughts threatening to take over. "Lower your goddamn voice. And besides, *your* friend? If I recall, *I* introduced *you* to Jordan, not the other way around."

Matthew shrugged. "All the more reason to not complicate our group like that."

I scoffed. "That's rich coming from you. Bringing your new girlfriend around your ex and her friends is really nice and not complicated at all."

It was his turn to be skeptical, glaring. "What, jealous?"

"No, but you sound like it." I raised my eyebrows.

He scowled. "Just think there are some lines you shouldn't cross."

"Then don't draw them." I took a deep breath and let it out before continuing, "We're going as friends. He and Sam broke up, and he had an extra ticket and no one to go with. Not that it's any of your business. I just don't want you to go around spreading lies."

Matthew froze, his eyes roving over my face like he was trying to catch me in a lie. I held still, trying to keep my expression fixed so he couldn't see that his examination was making the hair on the back of my neck stand up. When he finally spoke, his shoulders loosened and he gave an apologetic smile, his voice noticeably calmer. "I thought maybe that was it. Just, ya know, had to be sure. Sorry for freaking out."

I blinked. I didn't really know how to react to this sudden

shift, so I just said, "Yeah, whatever. Why were you freaking out?"

It was Matthew's turn to blush. "It was just weird to hear. That's all."

I perked up and scanned his face. "Weird because it's Jordan or weird because it's me?"

Matthew lifted and dropped one shoulder. "Both, I guess."

"Well, again, it's none of your business who I date. You're dating Tori."

"I don't know, Mags." Matthew sat down in the chair next to me. "I guess it just never occurred to me that you would eventually date someone else."

A flare of annoyance shot up my spine, and I gritted my teeth. "Why? Is it that hard to believe that someone would want to date me?"

That dent formed between his eyebrows again, and he frowned. "How can you say that? I dated you. I know how incredible you are."

"Yeah, and eventually someone who isn't you will."

I watched something flash across his face, replacing the annoyance with something sad and soft. "I know that. Trust me, I know that." He reached out suddenly and laid his hand on top of mine on the table. "It just . . . reminds me of how fucking lucky I was to get to date you. Thinking that someone else will eventually get the chance to start something with you reminded me of how badly I screwed up mine. Just because I'm with someone else doesn't mean I've forgotten what we had."

I stared at our hands, frozen, too shocked to pull away. Where was this coming from? "Isn't that exactly what being with someone is supposed to do, make you forget the last one?"

His gaze was heavy, pinning me to the chair, and my brain was racing, trying to decipher the look on his face. "I couldn't forget you, Maggie. Not even if I wanted to. Believe me, I've tried."

I opened my mouth, about to respond, but the only thing that sounded was the bell ending the lunch period. I looked out the library's big window to see students rushing in from all directions to get to their classes, then turned back to Matthew, who pulled away from me and blinked a bit, shaking his head. "I gotta go meet Tori, but I'll see you later, okay?"

Before I could respond or process anything, he was up and heading toward the door. Outside, I saw him meet up with Tori. He put his arm around her, leading her away. I watched until he looked back at me, holding my gaze a little too long.

---

"Sounds like he was jealous."

I looked at Jordan in surprise, but he just shrugged, continuing to drum his fingers on the steering wheel. I had told him about my Strange Encounter of the Matthew Kind as soon as he'd picked me up for the dance that night, but I hadn't expected him to actually agree with the suspicions I couldn't even voice out loud.

"Why would he be? We're over," I muttered darkly, but for some reason my words sounded hollow, even to me.

The light changed to green, and Jordan pressed on the gas, making a right on Williams Road. The purple high school marquee came into view, illuminated by the streetlights. "It's not completely unreasonable to believe that he might not be over you—or you him, for that matter. It's not like your breakup was squeaky clean."

"It should have been." Then again, maybe some part of me didn't want it to be. Not then, and maybe not even now.

Jordan pulled into the long line of cars leading into the student lot. The homecoming dance took place in the cafeteria, immediately following the Battle of the Arroyo, the annual football showdown between San Benito and Harlingen. Unsurprisingly, San Benito had lost, and I expected Dani to look prideful all night.

The dance had a history of being a flop since it took place right after the game with no time to go home and change into clothes *not* soaked in football stadium grime, but this year, under Amanda's watchful eye as junior class president, the dance was surprisingly not awful. Walking in under a huge purple-and-gold balloon arch, I could see face painting and a pie-throwing booth where students could pay money to hurl pie tins piled high with whipped cream at Vice Principal Sosa. People were actually dancing, bodies writhing in the center of the cafeteria to the reggaeton the DJ was blasting.

"You guys made it!" I turned to see Amanda and Dani at the ticket table by the cafeteria door in the main hall, waving.

"How's it going?" I asked, casting a glance at the long line forming behind us.

"I hate our classmates," Amanda said with a crazed smile.

"I don't know anyone so I don't hate anyone yet," Dani added.

"When do you guys get done here?"

"Megan and Bobby are going to take our place in, like, an hour," Dani said helpfully.

"Yeah, and Jaime was supposed to be here before we started our shift, but you know he can't get anywhere on time for shit." Amanda rolled her eyes.

"Your boyfriend needs a watch." I frowned, pointing out, "He's always late to everything. He doesn't respect your time—"

"All right, I've had enough of this conversation," Amanda said, rolling her eyes and waving a hand to dismiss my—very legitimate—criticism of her on- and off-again boyfriend. "Get out of here and go participate in school-sanctioned shenanigans."

"Time to go shenan-again." I smiled before turning to Jordan. "Let's go hit Mrs. Sosa with a pie for every time she took away your skateboard."

Over the next hour, Jordan and I made the rounds. I had been assigned the dance for the yearbook, so we ran around the cafeteria getting shots of everyone enjoying the booths. I even got shots of Jordan—yes, firing pies at our vice principal.

Later, Amanda and Jaime joined us, Jaime just out of basketball practice judging by his shower-wet hair, so I was relieved that I didn't have to hear about his inattentiveness anymore tonight. Dani was following them, leading Matthew and Tori and smiling at me when she caught my eye. I grinned back, giving a small wave, but my hand fell when I saw Amanda and Jaime standing at least a foot apart, Amanda rigid with her arms crossed. It was clear Amanda was upset, eyes shiny and lips pursed. Jaime kept reaching for her hand, but she studiously ignored him, staring into space.

I looked away from them when I heard Tori trill, "Hi, Magdalena."

I resisted the urge to flinch, just countered with "Hi, Victoria. How are you? You look great." I gestured to Tori's dress.

Tori gave me a too-sweet smile. "Thanks, I love to put in *effort* for things like this. You know how it is, right?" she said, giving a very obvious once-over to our matching football spirit shirts and my worn grey beanie and ripped-up black jeans.

I nodded, turning to Jordan, whose lips were pressed tightly together. He shrugged and struck up a conversation with Matthew about some video game, which I tuned out. I couldn't help but think about that blank space in my head next to "escort for Alyssa's quince." Ever since Matthew and I had started our on-off thing in ninth grade, we'd been each other's dates to everything. This was when I felt his absence the most, when I knew that if things were different, he would be here.

"Is it always like this?"

I turned to Dani, surprised. She was smiling, bemused, as she tilted her head to the side to nod at the chatting group. "You and Jordan third wheeling?"

I chuckled. "More like fifth or sixth wheeling, but yeah, sometimes. Did you enjoy the show last night?"

Dani gave a toothy grin, her eyes lighting up. "Yeah. I haven't been to a concert since I left Harlingen, so that was really nice."

"Did you go to a lot before?"

The light in Dani's eyes dimmed a bit, and her smile turned sad. "Not as many as I would've wanted to. Not as many as I should have."

I bit my lip. I wanted to ask her about it, but I didn't know how, so I just blurted, "There's more around here. I go to a lot 'cuz I take pictures, so we could . . ."

The corners of Dani's lips perked up. "We could."

I nodded, feeling like one of those bobbleheads that fries to death on the dashboard of your car in the summer. "Yeah, I mean, we all could, you and us and . . . There's more concerts around, is what I'm saying."

Dani gave a breathy laugh. "I heard that, yeah."

I felt light-headed and warm, could feel the flush creeping up my neck. Luckily, I was saved from that *dangerous* turn of emotion by Amanda snapping, "Fuck off, Jaime, don't touch me."

I whipped around to see Amanda stalking out of the cafeteria. I turned to Dani, who was wide-eyed, and gave an apologetic nod. I gestured vaguely in Amanda's direction before following my best friend.

The main corridor was dim, the only light coming from the wide windows looking out toward the faculty parking lot. The darkened halls were supposed to discourage students from wandering off, but every once in a while, you'd hear the giggling of some couple bounding through the darkness, looking for some privacy in the abandoned wings.

I found Amanda sitting by the front windows, wiping her cheeks frantically and sniffling.

"Hey," I greeted softly. Amanda turned around. By the glow of the streetlights outside, I could see the tears on her cheeks. "What's going on, friend?"

"Jaime's a fucking dick, is what's going on," Amanda spat, sniffling some more.

I came closer, rubbing her shoulder. "What did he say?"

Amanda shook her head wildly. "Nothing, he just . . . he's going to college next year, and he's acting like it's happening tomorrow. Like his whole damn life is changing tomorrow and that includes me." She looked at me, big hazel eyes wet and gleaming with sadness. "We've been together so long, I never really thought about what'll happen after."

I shrugged. "We've still got time. Graduation is a long way off. You guys still have time."

"Not the way he's talking." Amanda sighed, staring up at me through thick lashes. "I know we still have a year here after this one, but . . . promise me you won't leave me, when we get out of this town? Everything is going to change one day, but I don't want this to change." She gestured between us.

I frowned. "Amanda, I'm not—"

Amanda shook her head, and she surprised me by taking my hands in her own, holding on tight. "No, I just—I just want to make sure that no matter what happens, we'll still be best friends. Relationships end, whatever, but it would kill me if we weren't friends anymore. Boys are whatever, but how am I supposed to live without you?"

The heat of Amanda's palms burned through my skin, and all I could do was nod stiffly. "You don't have to. I'll always be here for you. Time won't change that."

Amanda nodded, sighing. "I'm just really, really glad we're going to college together. I don't think I could handle the rest of my life if you're not with me."

My stomach dropped a bit. Amanda and I had been talking about going to New York for college since ninth grade, and it had always been a done deal for her, even if it had never quite felt signed and sealed for me.

To be fair, how could she know that, if I'd never actually told her?

"Yeah, well. We'll be in a long-distance friendship anyway since Morningside Heights is so fucking far from the East Village."

Amanda smiled widely, fondly, at me before yanking me into a tight embrace and burying her head in my shoulder. "I don't care. You and me, we're endgame. Always and forever."

My chest filled with warmth. And that right there was why I had never told her I was having doubts about NYU: because it made her so fucking happy to think about the rest of our lives, and I always wanted to make Amanda happy.

I squeezed her back, reveling in her warmth, until all of a sudden I felt the light press of lips against my neck. As quick as it appeared, it was gone, taking anything I might have said along with it.

*We're endgame? Always and forever?* A neck maybe-kiss? What the *fuck?*

I was having trouble stringing words together to make a coherent question, so I was grateful when I heard the sound of rolling wheels against the tile. "There you guys are," Jordan called, riding his skateboard in circles around us. "I got bored. Am I interrupting?"

I shook my head wildly as Amanda let go. "Nope."

Amanda wiped the last of the tears from her face before beaming at me. "Nope, just needed some one-on-one time."

My face was on fire, and I looked back at Jordan, willing the ground to open up and swallow me, Vans and all. "So, are we getting Whataburger now or . . . ?"

Sitting in Jordan's car, the memory of Amanda's lips on my neck was a branding iron, and I found myself lightly stroking the spot on my neck where she had burrowed so enthusiastically. Her touch had shaken something loose inside me, the remnants of a feeling I had all but forgotten, and it reminded me of the last time I'd felt like this: the night I'd come out to her.

Amanda was the first girl I ever loved, in that middle school way that you do when you're a budding bisexual who doesn't know why one friendship feels more intense than others. Of course, I'd never told her that—not even when I had the chance, when I thought that maybe she might like me too.

It was the night of my quince, in September of ninth grade, and Trish Martinez kissed me in the parking lot while we were waiting for her mom to pick her up. She left a piece of notebook paper with her number scrawled on it in my palm. It was my first kiss with a girl. I had always suspected that my romantic preferences, whatever they were, weren't exclusive to boys, but the press of Trish's lips and the grip of her hands on my hips flooded my stomach with a warmth that was impossible to ignore. I felt a part of myself slide into place on that sidewalk, under a streetlight moon, like a record finally spinning at the right speed.

So naturally, I reacted the way any fifteen-year-old would after a life-changing event: I texted my best friend.

**Maggie:** SOS
**Amanda:** WHERE
**Maggie:** BATHROOM BEHIND THE STAGE
**Amanda:** HOLD ON I'M COMING

I had been picking anxiously at a loose thread on my dress, my leg bouncing up and down. It wasn't that I thought she'd be mad about it. I was just worried that maybe, with this new revelation, she'd finally guess at what I'd been hiding since we first started being friends a year earlier. We had started out as enemies at the beginning of eighth grade, fighting over grades and who could run the fastest mile in PE, but by the end of the year, we'd both grown bored of competing and actually discovered we had more in common than just our drive. We'd spent the rest of the year joined at the hip, and that's when I'd finally started to realize that being obsessed with her had nothing to do with hate and everything to do with a crush I couldn't admit, not even to myself.

Until now, when I was finally about to tell her what had been brewing inside me all along. As I waited for her, I recalled every moment when we'd held hands at school, when she'd jokingly called me her wife to anyone who made snide comments about how close we were, when she would sit on my lap like it was the most natural thing in the world when we were outside in the courtyard at lunch and there were no more available seats.

Maybe she felt something too, and that made me all the more anxious for her to get there so I could find out.

The door opened, and Amanda burst into the bathroom in a flurry of purple taffeta. The strap of her dress had slid off her shoulder, and I studiously ignored it. I already couldn't feel my hands from my nervousness, and if I let myself get distracted, I might actually combust. "Hey."

Amanda slumped in relief. "Oh, thank god, I thought you were getting murdered by that ghost that people claim to see in this event hall."

"Sadie would *never*." I gave a nervous laugh, not taking my eyes off her. Chewing on my bottom lip, I blurted, "I have to say something."

Amanda's eyebrows rose. "Huh. What is it?"

I dug my fingernails into my palm to try to quell the shaking. This was my best friend. I could tell her anything. This was Amanda. It had to be okay. I didn't have a backup plan if it wasn't. "I'm bi. I like girls, and guys, and basically everyone who is my gender and not my gender." I had looked up this definition of bisexuality on the internet, and the detail in the description felt like it fit me just right. A label of one's own. "And I kissed Trish Martinez. Or, she kissed me."

Amanda froze, then her brow furrowed. Her face twitched, going through a million micro-expressions, and I watched, holding my breath, as I looked for one that could look like love, or jealousy, or relief at me having confessed to something she felt too. She didn't speak for a moment that felt about seven thousand years long, and when she did, all that she said was, "The strangest part of that was Trish. Everything else kind of makes sense."

I made a mental note to bookmark that Trish comment and circle back later, but for now, I felt a tiny bit . . . disappointed. I had hoped that me coming out would spark something in Amanda, maybe even a confession of her own. But I couldn't let myself hope that Amanda could see me that way. For now, I just hoped that—"You're not mad?"

"Why would I be? This isn't the nineties."

"It's still Texas," I muttered, staring at the shoes I'd stolen from Veronica.

The sound of heels clacking against the tile echoed around the bathroom, and I looked up just as Amanda hugged me. She smelled like hairspray and her favorite perfume, the Marc Jacobs one that had a stopper shaped like a daisy, and I let the scent comfort me as she hugged even tighter, even though I wanted so much more.

"You're my best friend. Nothing could ever change that, especially not who you want to kiss." Amanda chuckled weakly. "I don't blame you. Girls are great. Sometimes I wish I liked girls too."

*Then why don't you?* I wanted to ask, but I couldn't bring myself to, not when she'd told me—at least indirectly—how she felt. If she'd liked me, she would've said something, wouldn't she? It seems like now I had my answer.

Amanda's hair fell into my face, and I closed my eyes. I sighed just a little, and I hoped it didn't sound as sad as I felt. Amanda didn't like me, and I couldn't bring myself to confess to my feelings knowing that what waited on the other side of my courage was probably just rejection.

Now though, I realized that maybe I hadn't been direct

enough. All the signs had pointed to her maybe feeling more for me: holding my hand, playing with my hair, always inviting me over for sleepovers and cuddling with me late into the night. Now, as we all drove to Whataburger, the car loud and chaotic, I replayed the memory of Amanda's lips on my neck, and the warmth of her body through my dress in that bathroom two years ago, analyzing the two situations for any indication that Amanda may have felt more for me than she let on. Had I made a mistake two years ago, not explicitly telling her I had feelings for her?

Thinking about this now, I couldn't help but remember Alyssa's quince, and the fact that I still had to find an escort for it. My brain automatically placed Amanda in that role now, as though champing at the bit for a placeholder to plan the night around. I was sure she'd go to the quince with me if I asked. It would be fun, comfortable. I felt safer with Amanda than I ever did with anyone else. Maybe at Alyssa's quince, something could . . .

No. I was getting ahead of myself. I couldn't bring myself to hope yet, not until I could figure out if it was actually possible for her to feel something for me too.

After we were done eating, Jordan drove me home and walked me to the front door of the store. He stopped outside the door and leaned against it, looking at me expectantly. "What's up with you? You're all silent and it's weird."

I ground my bottom lip between my teeth, using it to anchor myself so I wouldn't be swept away by what I was feeling. "I feel like I'm about to get into some deep shit."

"If this is about Matthew—"

"It's not about Matthew! Or . . . I guess it's not just about Matthew."

"Dude, what?"

I wrapped my arms around myself, trying to contain all of the confusion that swirled inside of me. The Valley wouldn't get cold until maybe Thanksgiving, but at night you could feel its chill. I opened my mouth to say more but was interrupted by the sound of Veronica banging on the door. "Mom said your not-date is going past curfew. Get in here."

I sighed. Never any privacy in this house, especially not after dark. "Come to the store tomorrow. We'll talk then."

# 3

That Saturday was so sweltering, the raspas were melting in my grasp, leaving sticky rainbows on my hands. Lupe's, the snack stand next door, was only a few feet from the store, but it felt like miles walking across the shimmering asphalt. Taking my spot on the curb outside, Jordan, who had been idly hopping barriers in the parking lot, rolled to a stop in front of me.

"So let's see if I've got this right: Your long-forgotten feelings for Amanda are back?" Jordan said, gliding to the left.

"Yup." I took a scoop of my leche raspa using the weird straw/spoon tool that came with it. Cold ice chips and sweet sugary syrup, exactly what I needed before I committed the rest of my afternoon to the store.

"Amanda, who is probably straight and with Jaime." Jordan skated back to the right.

"Mm-hmm."

"Anyone else I should know about?" Jordan said. I knew it was just a joke, but then I remembered my conversation with Matthew and the weird, very familiar chemical reaction he had sparked in my body.

"Now that you mention it, I've been getting some pretty strange vibes from Matthew lately."

Jordan nodded. "And now Matthew, despite having a girlfriend, is giving you weird signals that might be an indication of his feelings for you." Back to the left.

"Which is super confusing."

"And you're developing an interest in Dani. Sexuality unknown."

"Yup." I hung my head and groaned gutturally at the ground. "Jordan, how the fuck did I become a bisexual cliché?"

Jordan rolled to a stop in front of me, and I watched as he popped the skateboard up with his foot and stepped off. "Dude. This has nothing to do with you being bi."

"Doesn't it? Like all those stereotypes say, like I can't decide or whatever." I sighed, stirring my raspa around, trying to evenly mix in the syrup. The top layer of ice never had enough syrup. Jordan plopped down next to me. His elbow knocked into my side as he picked his raspa up off the curb, almost knocking my cup out of my hand. "Watch it."

Jordan punctuated his comment by shoving his bony shoulder into mine, causing me to yelp. "No, it doesn't have anything to do with that, homes. This coulda happened to anyone if they had all that stuff that you have with them. It's not like these are just random feelings for random people. Yeah, Dani is basically a stranger, but Matthew and Amanda are people you have a history with, people who your heart is hardwired to love because you've done it before and it's familiar and shit. Like muscle memory."

I sighed. Not only did I feel like a cliché, but I also felt *bad* about feeling like a cliché because I was perpetuating a biphobic stereotype. I felt like my brain was going to start leaking out my eyeballs. "Yeah, I guess. And on top of all this, I need to find a date for Alyssa's quince, and I can't help but think about how good each one of them would look in the outfits."

Through a mouthful of ice, Jordan garbled, "So what's the move then?"

"What do you mean?"

He gave a "duh" look and waved his hands. "I mean, what are you going to *do*?"

I took another bite and syrup dripped onto my bare thigh. I wiped it away with a napkin, and for good measure, I wiped the cup too, decidedly not looking at Jordan. "About what?"

Jordan scoffed, and I looked up at him finally, raising an eyebrow.

"*About what,* she said," he mocked. "About the fact that you're in love with three of your best friends!"

"No one said anything about love." I stabbed into my raspa with more force than necessary, pushing the rapidly melting slush around. "I think you think I told you because I'm looking for some help here. I'm not. There's no solution. Hell, there's not even a problem. I'm not going to do anything but wait for it to pass. That's all."

"There's not even a problem—" Jordan spluttered, pulling back to look at me in disbelief. "Maggie, I don't know if you know this, but this is a problem. You're already pining."

"I am *not,*" I snapped. "I'm fine."

"You're pining and you're not even doing anything about it."

"What is there *to* do, J? Amanda is straight—" *Even though she is saying some strange things and kissing places that friends shouldn't kiss.*

"You don't even know—"

"Matthew and I are just—" I broke off into a short whine.

"Matthew is just Matthew." *A beautiful guy who's been such a great friend and seems to get cuter and sweeter the longer we're broken up. Who might still have feelings for me.*

"But what about—"

"Dani *just* got here. I don't want her to think I'm only trying to seduce the new girl." I sighed, then put my raspa down on the asphalt. I lost my appetite and just looking at it made me feel sick. "I don't even know her really. What if I just like her because she's cute and likes concerts and she turns out to be a real dickbag?"

I ran a hand through my hair, combing out a few of the waves. "Look, I've already thought of every possible way this could ever work, and bottom line is it wouldn't."

"You can't just keep not dealing with it."

I laughed despite the fact that none of this was fucking funny. "Watch me."

Jordan shook his head, looking disappointed. "If you really wanted to bury your head in the sand, you would've just asked me to be your escort and been done with it. You know I look great in a tux."

"That's true," I agreed. I pulled my knees into my chest, then dropped my chin down onto them. "But I don't know. It just didn't feel right. I think . . . I think I just want this one to feel special, ya know? When you escorted me to my own quince, that was fine, but I just want more for this one. Which feels ridiculous because it's not even my quince."

Jordan's smile was small and sad. "That doesn't mean you can't wish for it to be special. Quinces should be magical for everyone involved." Jordan shrugged. "How can it not be, with cool dresses and cake and centerpieces that your abuela is gonna take home? It's okay to want a little bit of that magic for yourself."

I chuckled, kicking at the gravel. "Yeah, I guess you're right about that. I just want it to feel different. Matthew and I were broken up during my quince, and yeah, Trish kissed me as she left, but you know how that relationship turned out, and . . . I just want this one to be good. You know?"

Jordan nodded. "Then you have to make this one special. In whatever way you can. Just give yourself a chance."

"How? Say 'Hey, Amanda, I know you're straight and my best friend, but I'm gonna throw away four years of friendship just for the chance to make out with you.'"

"Well, it's a start. Could use some editing—"

But the words kept tumbling out before I could stop them. "Or 'Matthew, hi, it's me, your ex-girlfriend of a thousand times. Let's try to make this time work and hope it doesn't explode in a ball of flames the way it's done every time before.'"

"Okay, now you're being dramatic. It wasn't *that* bad—"

"Or 'Dani, I know we just started being friends and I don't even know if you like-like girls, but I already think you're the coolest person ever and I just want to hold your hand . . .'"

I trailed off, my gaze dropping to the ground. "And this is exactly why my strategy before all this was so perfect. It was so much easier to just decide not to have feelings for anyone."

Jordan was quiet. I chanced a glance at him to find him staring at me, a shocked look on his face.

"Maggie," he said softly. "How long are you going to do this to yourself?"

"Graduation isn't too far off, I guess." I sighed. "Half of this is just happening in my head, which is the issue. I don't know what any of them are feeling or thinking, and at this point, I'm too afraid to ask."

Jordan hummed thoughtfully. "Well, since it's happening in your head, maybe you could work that to your advantage."

"What do you mean?"

"Okay, hear me out." Jordan waved his hands in the air, as though gesturing to an imaginary whiteboard. "What if you could, like, follow this train of thought for each of them all the way to the end and get off at whatever decision station you come to?"

I blinked. "What are you talking about? Did you smoke something before you came here? Without me?"

Jordan shook his head. "Nah, nah, listen. It could work. You just hang out with them like normal and study them as if you were dating them. Like a dating simulator. Except you're not dating them. So it's basically all in your head, and therefore"—he waved his hand like he had presented me a gourmet meal instead of a half-baked idea—"no consequences. Look at that. I'm a genius."

I shook my head. "That will never work. It's not like there's anything to evaluate. None of them are even options."

"Aren't they though? Matthew seems to be giving you strange signals, and so does Amanda. And Dani is a fresh start."

I waved him off. "Amanda has Jaime and Matthew has Tori."

Jordan thought for a moment. "If they were committed like they say they are, they wouldn't be giving you these signals. People in happy relationships don't develop a weird fascination with their ex's love life or go around *kissing* their best friend."

He had a point. "Still, I can't—I can't wreck their relationships. I'm not that person."

Jordan shook his head. "You don't have to. You're just, like, rating them in your head and measuring them up against each other. You don't have to act on anything."

Jordan took a bite of his raspa before continuing through a

mouthful of ice. "You gotta actually think about what it would be like to date them. Look, I've had a *ton* of hopeless crushes that just burned out in my head once I actually thought about what it would really be like to date them. Believe me, once you get past the manic pixie dream girl, Zooey Deschanel fantasy part of it, it's pretty damn easy to not have feelings for someone anymore."

That was certainly true. I'd had enough celebrity crushes that petered out soon after I heard they'd started a death cult or tweeted something racist. "So it's possible that I can think myself out of my feelings?"

"I don't know, but the mind is a powerful thing." He poked my temple. "Or whatever it is you have in there that seems to be just bisexual flags and emo music."

I smacked his hand away, and he laughed. "I just want a little bit more time so I can figure out how I really feel. Ya know, before I mess everything up the way I always do."

"Not always." Jordan shook his head. "I'm sorry, my dude. I wish I had more ideas about how to fix it."

"I'm pretty sure no one but God Themself could fix this."

---

Jordan's mom came to pick him up soon after that, and I waved goodbye from the curb, watching her Honda turn left at the light before disappearing behind the expressway. I was grateful he'd left. I was tired of running circles in my own brain. I needed a distraction.

I wandered back into the store, where Mom was holding open the back door. Leaning against the counter, I looked around. There were only a few customers right now, but I was paranoid.

"Thank you, Junior," I heard Mom say. Veronica's boyfriend

of about a billion years, CJ—Cesar Junior—was hefting two boxes full of Marlboro cartons through the door and onto the counter, probably part of the shipment we got on Thursdays.

"Of course." CJ beamed as he searched the drawers behind the counter for a boxcutter. I handed him one from the Folgers can next to the register that doubled as a pencil holder, and he gave me a cheery, grateful grin before slicing into the box.

"Vero is on the porch with Minnie from La Especial, and Alyssa's upstairs. Call me if you need anything."

"I got it, Mom. CJ will be the muscle in case we need to kick people out."

CJ lifted a sinewy tattooed arm in agreement; he wasn't scrawny by any means, but we all knew he couldn't hack it as a security guard, especially because he had the personality of a golden retriever.

"Mm-hmm." Mom narrowed her eyes skeptically but headed to the staircase anyway. The need for sleep after waking up at the asscrack of dawn to open the store was probably greater than her doubt about our ability to not burn shit down while she was gone.

CJ began taking cartons of cigarettes out of the box as a few teenagers about Alyssa's age came to the counter with bottles of Gatorade and packages of Pulparindo. They lived in the neighborhood. I always saw them around, walking the length of Sam Houston or going to McDonald's a few blocks up, even during the summer when it was hotter than hell outside. I bagged their stuff and watched them go, laughing and pushing each other as they walked through the parking lot. There weren't really sidewalks in San Benito, at least not many that had been completed. They started and stopped like a stutter, thrown haphazardly around some places in town, only walkable for a few yards before the broken concrete disappeared and you were forced to walk on the side of the road, navigating deep-ass holes hidden in the overgrown weeds.

The town of San Benito didn't care much for appearances, for fancy infrastructure or neighborhoods where all the houses looked alike. Aesthetics weren't a huge priority when you were a city as poor as ours was. Most people were barely scraping working-class status, if that. At times it was easy to forget that the rest of the world wasn't like that. It was impossible to feel ostracized because of your poverty when everyone was in the same rickety hand-me-down boat. We were just out here trying to survive, and the abandoned grain factories and open fields, all the cracks in concrete where wildflowers grew, those were the scars we all shared. It was real in a way I'd never been able to capture with my camera, though it never stopped me from trying.

The city was humble. It wasn't magical, but something so much more tangible. It was real, and strangely regal, the way its chin was permanently set in defiance of a world that would happily swallow it down and consume it entirely.

We would not be ignored. We would not be forgotten. We would always find a way to survive.

The back door swung open, and I recognized the woman who worked at the bakery near the resaca. She was wearing leggings and a T-shirt, and her hair was freshly blown out and colored a deep mahogany. "Muchas gracias, mijita," Minnie was saying to Veronica, who followed her in from the back porch. "Siempre me encanta como haces mi cabello." She pressed a wad of bills into Veronica's hands.

I watched Veronica count it quickly and frown, handing some back to the woman. "This is way too much, Herminia."

Minnie shook her head, refusing to take back the money. "Es la propina. Tienes mucho talento."

I had never seen Veronica blush so hard, and I wanted to pay Minnie just for making it happen.

After Minnie and her fresh cut had left, Veronica slumped against the counter, holding her cheek out for CJ to kiss. "Hard day at the office, Ronnie?" he asked.

"Nah, it's just fucking hot out there and I'm tired." Veronica fanned herself with the bills in her hand.

I snickered. "LOL I'm dying. You look like a low-level mobster."

"Yeah, keep laughing. One day you'll be in this capitalist hell with the rest of us, grinding all the time for petty cash."

Alyssa bounced down the stairs, catching sight of Veronica with her money and immediately jumping into the chorus of a Megan Thee Stallion song. She was still singing as she disappeared down the freezer section and came back to the counter with a cherry boli in her hand, already tearing open the plastic.

"Did you pay for that?" Veronica said sharply, Alyssa noisily slurping the juice out of the packet before hopping up to sit on the counter. I made a note on the list we kept on the counter of stuff Alyssa had eaten without paying for. I added "boli" beneath "Maruchan shrimp" and "that pink Brisk, the small one."

"Whaddup, tiny G?" CJ waved, then held his hand up.

"Ceej!" she trilled, high-fiving him.

"How was your Spanish test?" Veronica asked.

Alyssa shrugged coyly. "Mi nombre es Alyssa y no hablo español."

"Obvio," I agreed.

"You both sound like a buncha gringas," Veronica pointed out unhelpfully.

Both of our accents were terrible, of course, because none of us knew Spanish all that well. Veronica knew more than the rest of us because our parents spoke it a lot when our dad was alive. But when he died, he took our Spanish with him; Mom just didn't have the time or the energy to teach us after that, so we never learned. Our tongue was just another thing the state trooper took from us when he killed our dad.

"At least they're trying," CJ offered, patting Veronica on the back like *she* was the one trying instead of the one ragging on us. "DF wasn't built in a day."

Alyssa beamed. "See? We're just fine."

Veronica smiled, shaking her head ruefully. "I guess."

CJ grinned at her fondly before kissing the top of her head. That made me smile because I rarely got to see Veronica look so *soft*.

"What do I want to be when I grow up?" Alyssa asked, pouting as she drummed her hands on the counter.

I screwed up my face. "Why are you asking us? Isn't that supposed to be *your* decision?"

Alyssa whined, "But I don't want to. How am I supposed to make a decision about the rest of my life right *now*? I still have to raise my hand to go to the bathroom."

CJ winced. "Ah, yes, you're in ninth grade. They're doing that thing where they're trying to funnel y'all into career paths like Camp Half-Blood cabins."

"I don't know what that is, but yeah, I guess."

CJ and Veronica both groaned, and I laughed. "Ha, you guys are old."

"Shut up, you read them too," Veronica reminded me.

That was fair. "You're still old."

Veronica flipped me off. "So are they still giving you the same three career pathways they gave us when I was in ninth grade?"

"Yeah, just engineering and medicine and being a lawyer. I'm bad at math, and the legal system is trash, so what am I supposed to do?"

"You know there are more jobs out there than that, right? I mean, I'm not in any of that," Veronica pointed out.

"I'm in medicine technically," CJ said, "so I can't speak to that."

"I liked taking pictures, so I just called that a career to make them leave me alone."

Alyssa shook her head. "At least you knew *that*. You wanted to go to NYU since you were in ninth grade. I don't even have that."

"It was just a thought I had. Just one, and it grew into something bigger." Something life-changing, something my family latched on to like a life raft in a storm, something that could steer my life in the right direction if I let it.

Or derail it with a mountain of student debt and years spent away from the Valley, away from my family, away from my *home*.

"You're so lucky that you knew what you wanted to do so early on," Veronica said. "You don't have to stumble around trying to choose a life path and then wonder if you chose wrong. You're the first Gonzalez who won't have to rush into a job. That's a big deal."

Her eyes were sad, and I bit the inside of my cheek as a stab of guilt prodded at me. Mom and Veronica hadn't had the luxury of being able to choose a lofty goal. Mom had to take over the store after our dad died and raise three kids by herself, and Veronica had to step up. That meant choosing a post–high school plan that allowed her to stay at home to help Mom with me and Alyssa.

I couldn't help but remember that whenever they got on my case about school, and every time I felt lazy or tired or scared about NYU and everything it meant, the guilt kept me in line. The last thing I needed was for them to think their sacrifices were in vain.

My phone buzzed, and my pulse picked up when Matthew's name appeared on the screen. It was just the distraction I needed. Swiping my finger across the notification, I waited for the picture he sent me to load.

It was a close-up of Matthew, his signature half smile and brown eyes lit up in the low light from his bedside lamp. He had a tiny red teddy bear pressed to his cheek, and my stomach fluttered when I recognized it as the bear I gave him for our first Valentine's Day.

**Matthew:** Just found this little guy in my closet. Remember Georgie?

**Maggie:** How could I forget? We named him after we watched the second *It* movie.

**Matthew:** No wonder we were together for so long. Who else would put up with our weird obsession with horror movie remakes?

I grinned. It seemed I wasn't the only one thinking about the past lately. Maybe it wouldn't be the worst thing in the world if he knew I was still an option.

**Maggie:** Do you think Georgie is sad about our divorce?

It was a gamble, but if I was going to do this, I might as well go all in. I waited around at the counter, half listening to my sisters chattering for an agonizing five minutes, until my phone dinged again.

**Matthew:** Probably. I know I still am.

Hope flared to life in my chest, along with a healthy dose of confusion, a cocktail of curiosity. It was the tiny potion bottle that led Alice further down the rabbit hole, and I was ready to follow it down.

---

That night, despite my conversation with Matthew, I dreamt about Amanda.

All I could see was her, grinning as we drove around in her car, her laughter filling the space until there was no air but her. The memory of her lips on my neck pushed its way into my dream, and I swore I felt it, as if time reached back through my sleep to remind me of what happened. I saw her body hovering over mine, and I couldn't see her face, but somehow I knew it was her. I wanted to commission a poet to write lines that felt like her curves, a painter who could do with a brush what her touch did to my skin.

But then I woke up, and I was only a photographer, and you cannot capture a dream with a camera. You cannot capture a memory. You cannot capture a ghost. But maybe that was all a dream was sometimes: a ghost of a memory, haunting your sleep with what could've been and what never would be.

---

All roads lead to the Sewing Box.

Or so it seemed, since I'd been yanked out of bed on yet another Saturday and dragged to the seamstress. At least Alyssa seemed to be having more fun with it than I had with my quince; knowing she was actually legit excited about this made it easier to deal with her general exuberance around the whole thing.

"Maggie? Can you do something for me, beautiful big sister of mine?"

Except when she involved me.

I looked up from my phone, where I'd been sending selfies with the big smile filter from Snapchat to Amanda on Instagram. "What do you want?"

Alyssa batted her long eyelashes at me, a pleading look on her face, as she pointed to the seamstress's assistant, who had just emerged from the racks with an armful of turquoise dresses. "Can you please try these dama dresses on? I need to get a feel for the aesthetic. There's only a few."

"Really." I eyed the stack reluctantly as the skinny assistant struggled to hold them all.

"Please?" Alyssa wheedled.

"Ugh, fine." I pushed myself up with an exaggerated groan. "Bring on the tulle."

I went about trying on all the dresses, coming out after each one. Each one was horrendous, and with each passing dress, Alyssa and our mother got more creative with their critiques.

A short, cap-sleeved monstrosity with a curly ended petticoat that poofed in all directions: "It looks like you should be wearing tap shoes and curls like Shirley Temple."

A tight tube dress that clung to everything: "Your abuela won't speak to me anymore if I let you wear that."

A sweetheart neckline with a skirt that curved like a bell: "Oh, mamita, that's not bad."

"Mamá, she looks like a Barbie doll they put on those birthday cakes at HEB."

Finally, I slipped on the last dress in the dimly lit dressing room. Zipping it up, this one felt different than the others, and when I looked in the mirror, I was surprised to find that I even liked it a little. It had a tasteful V-neck with a built-in ribbon at the waist and a skirt that flared just enough, and I found myself smiling at the mirror, swishing the skirt around a bit so the satiny fabric could catch the light.

"Mamita, you look so beautiful!" my mom trilled when I came out of the dressing room.

Alyssa beamed, putting her hands on her hips triumphantly. "I have great taste! You look hot. Wait until your escort sees you."

My smile faltered at that. "My escort," I said, monotone. "Right."

Veronica was going to be a dama with CJ as her chambelán, and I was expected to be a dama as well. I'd been idly considering escorts and had drawn a blank up until this point. Now I had three possibilities, and maybe if I could figure out which one was *actually* a possibility . . .

"Do you know who you're gonna get? I need to know, like, soon."

"It helps to have all the measurements in early," the mousy assistant interjected from where she was taking notes.

Alyssa gestured toward her. "See? Confirmed. So who's it gonna be?"

"I haven't thought about it." I swallowed. There were three people I could see standing beside me at my little sister's quince, but the best answer I could give Alyssa at this point was "Crap."

---

**Maggie:** *picture of her in the dama dress*

**Maggie:** BDE=Big Dama Energy

**Amanda:** OMG you look hot *fire emoji* *heart eyes emoji*
**Jordan:** YEEEESSSSS
**Matthew:** I feel like as your ex i'm not allowed to comment but NICE

---

"You know my quince pics are totally gonna add something to your portfolio," Alyssa mentioned in our room later that night. She had been on Mom's laptop since we got home from the Sewing Box, looking at party mood boards on Pinterest; from where I sat on my bed, I could see her scrolling through an endless sea of dessert table motifs. She didn't look up or even pause her clicking as she said, "If you think about it, I gave you an opportunity to help your career when I asked you to do them."

I had been staring at Matthew's and Amanda's responses to the picture all night. My mind was turning, searching for whatever hidden meaning they could give me that would help my situation, so I was grateful for a chance to look up from my phone—especially if only to point out the flaw in Alyssa's logic. "I don't think performers who dance and sing and play instruments and such are going to be looking at static photoshoot shots, Al. But more photos don't hurt."

Mom had hired a cousin to do the photos on the actual day of the event, but Alyssa had asked me to take the photos that would be included with her invitations—and included on the wall next to Veronica's and my quince portraits. I agreed out of obligation, but also kind of out of arrogance. I didn't trust any photographer in the Valley, or the entire world, really, to photograph my sister as well as I could.

Alyssa shrugged, unbothered. "That's what I'm saying. I'm bulking up your résumé."

"Well, thanks for hiring me to do work for you for free, I guess?"

"You're welcome. I live to serve."

I wanted to be a tour photographer almost immediately after I started paying attention to music that wasn't on the radio. The bands we liked never came to the Valley, and Amanda and I always struggled to get rides to concerts whenever they did deign to come here, since they'd usually come to McAllen, forty-five minutes away. I lived vicariously through Instagram live feeds and YouTube concert diaries, Twitter feuds and TikToks, my tiny phone screen a window to the world I craved.

Being in an area like the RGV, so close to the border, meant superstar artists didn't come here. It was too small an area, too far a trip, with too big of a (cue eye roll) perceived safety risk. I'd lived here my whole life. I'd grown up with the border in my backyard. The news said it was dangerous, that *we* were dangerous, but the Valley had always been my home. I had lived alongside "danger" my whole life but never felt its sting until there were white billionaires and rich politicians, who had never set foot here, telling me to be afraid of the only place in the world that was safe for people like me.

I wanted to bring the outside world to kids in the Valley who, like me, could only watch adventure from afar, could only access it on a phone screen, because the world decided it was far too good for us. It felt like a torturous contradiction, that I had to leave the Valley to help it, but I couldn't see it any other way, not even if I wanted to.

And I really wanted to, sometimes.

My phone buzzed, and my mouth went dry when I looked at the screen.

**Dani:** That was an amazing dress.
You looked so gorgeous!!
**Dani:** Heard you and Amanda talking about *She-Ra* yesterday so I started it and now I can't stop. Thanks for taking away my entire weekend.

I sat up straight on the bed, staring down at my phone. Dani had never texted me outside of the group chat. What was this? I considered the message, being careful not to type until I was ready in case Dani could sense I was a fumbling mess from the annoying three texting dots. And bringing up *She-Ra*? That's like the cartoon version of "Do you listen to girl in red?" Does this mean she's queer? Oh god. What if she's actually queer?

I forced myself to relax, then replied.

**Maggie:** You're welcome. Catra is EVERYTHING and Entrapta is my favorite person in the world

A response came in almost immediately:

**Dani:** Yes I love them so much *crying emoji* Adora is the biggest himbo in Etheria. Idk how she's survived up until this point.
**Maggie:** It's all Bow. She and Glimmer have only survived bc of Bow
**Dani:** And Bow's croptop. We owe it all to Bow's croptop

I grinned. Okay, I got this. I could hold a conversation. Whether she was gay didn't even matter because I was killing it—

**Dani:** Catra needs to get her shit together and date Adora. If she doesn't, I will.

Well, that answered that question. I pressed my phone to my forehead and groaned. So it seemed she was queer *and* a conversationalist with great taste in TV shows. This little thought experiment had grown a mind of its own, and if I didn't adapt, this whole thing was going to evolve into an even bigger mess than Catradora and their five-season arc.

I was in dangerous territory. I needed to tread lightly. Taking a deep breath to center myself, I swallowed my fear and started to reply.

# 4

Mrs. Lozano was young and a little free-spirited, with jet-black hair that she kept in a choppy bob and a sleeve of tattoos hidden under her neat cardigans. She was content to just let us draw or paint or work on assignments for other classes (or gossip about people in the back of the room while eating Hot Cheetos and charging your phone as discreetly as possible by hiding the charger cord behind your backpack). But when I entered the classroom on Monday, Mrs. Lozano had a suspicious gleam in her eye that told me my AP English essay wasn't getting done in this class today.

Mrs. Lozano leaned against the whiteboard. "What do you want out of the rest of the semester?"

Confused silence permeated the room. "Miss, what does that even mean?" asked one of the girls who had really nice manicures and perfect makeup and sat at the back of the class eating Hot Cheetos.

Another spoke up too, saying, "Yeah, miss, just be straight with us!" Those girls really were the bravest of us all.

Mrs. Lozano just smiled and said, "What are you trying to discover about yourself? What journey are you on now? What are you trying to find? That's what I want you to tell me with twelve works of art, one for each week in the next semester. The last one should tell me the result of your journey."

Adela from the soccer team piped up. "So, like, pictures?"

"I suck at taking pictures," Jordan called out.

Mrs. Lozano shook her head. "It doesn't have to be photos. You can draw, sketch, or make GIFs. Whatever way you choose to be creative is your decision. I'm not looking at your technical skills, although that's a bonus. I'm just looking at how well you tell your story.

"Whether it's some sports game you're trying to prepare for or a choice you have to make about college or a job or some other personal decision, I want to hear about it. Whatever medium you're using to process your life, I want to see twelve works of art by the end of the semester."

A choice?

I raised my hand immediately. "Do we have to share it with the class?" I could feel Letty's and Jackie's eyes boring into my back, but I refused to turn around.

"You don't have to share it with anyone you don't want to. Well, except for me. And that means"—Mrs. Lozano paused to give a sharp look to the class—"no nudity or other inappropriate content, please. I'm giving you a lot of creative rope here. Don't strangle yourself, or each other, with it."

My mind was reeling. All those photos I took of the group, at Jordan's concerts and outside of that . . . could they really help me figure out what I was feeling? Was I seriously considering using a school project to understand my love life?

As ridiculous as it sounded, it made some sense. Photos were how I understood the world, understood what was right in front of me. If there was any way I knew how to work through my shit, it was from behind a lens.

Only now I was going to get graded on my ability to understand myself. Yay. Fun.

---

"This isn't even going to work. How am I supposed to blab about my feelings to my teacher? It's embarrassing," I complained after school, shoving the snare drum just a little too hard into the back wall of the stage. It crashed into the hi-hat, making both wobble precariously as it clanged.

Jordan winced. "Watch it, drama queen. The after-school program isn't rolling in cash."

"Sorry." I cringed. "I'm just mad. And clumsy."

"I know both of those things, and yet I still let you do this with me. I'm the king fool."

I rolled my eyes as I finished putting the bass drum against the wall, then sat on the stool. The after-school program had officially let out fifteen minutes ago, but I could still hear the students lined up outside the cafeteria, their laughter and Spanglish floating further and further out of range as they walked to the buses. "Thanks for letting me. I need volunteer hours for NHS."

"As long as you don't get me fired for breaking the instruments, we're even. I hate moving this shit by myself." He leaned the bass guitar against the wall and slid down to sit beside it, wiping sweat from his brow.

Jordan runs the rock band part of the after-school program at Fred Booth Elementary, since he agreed to work for a pittance compared to the actual certified instructors that worked the rest of the program, so whenever I needed volunteer hours for National Honor Society, I just hung around doing homework in the back of the room while he taught the kids, then helped him clean up afterward. It was a system that worked for both of us.

"What are you doing for your project?" I asked.

"I'm going to draw the kids as superheroes prepping for their recital. Two birds, one stone," Jordan said with a shrug and a bright smile. "I don't have time to do anything else. I need a new guitar, and I don't wanna ask my parents for money, so I'm gonna start running errands for people. Ask your mom if she knows anyone who needs pet-sitting or lawn-mowing."

"You got it. I don't know how you have the time for all that."

"My parents are never home," Jordan reminded me, "and I'm not like you and Amanda, hoarding extracurriculars because you're going to fancy, expensive schools. I've got time."

I frowned. "You know you can come over if you're lonely, right?"

Jordan rolled his eyes but smiled. "You couldn't stop me if you tried."

I knew that was true, at least. His mother, Reneé, was a nurse at Valley Baptist Medical in Harlingen and often worked nights and slept during the day, and Jordan's dad Marco's work schedule as a security guard was just as hectic. I knew Jordan was used to being alone, and that he usually spent most of his time at Matthew's house if he wasn't at mine, so at least I could count on him to come over a couple times a week to eat my mom's cooking.

On the ride back to my house, I still hadn't come up with an idea for my project, so I was going back through my Instagram, trying to get ideas. Switching accounts, I went to my long-forgotten finsta, full of dark, oversaturated photos of half-lit girls in profile captioned with melodramatic lyrics from early 2000s emo music. I wanted to punch my ninth grade self for thinking bad black-and-white photography was the solution to all her problems. Everything about this profile was cringe-inducing, but at least it was private—

WAIT A FUCKING SECOND.

"There!" I said suddenly, shoving my phone in Jordan's face as he came to a red light.

"I'm driving!" he yelped, rearing back in surprise and hitting the brakes as he peered at the screen. "Why am I looking at your weird emo finsta from seventeen years ago? I thought you'd deleted that."

"Nope, and I'm glad I didn't." Jordan looked confused, so I continued, "What if I create a finsta for my project?"

Jordan tilted his head, squinting. "Isn't that kinda the opposite of keeping it a secret?"

I shook my head. "Not if I make it private and just share it with Mrs. Lozano. No one else will know about it. No paper trail for anyone else to find. Besides, you know no one our age actually takes Instagram seriously anymore. No one is going to go looking for my profile."

"That's true." Jordan nodded in understanding. "It would just be—"

"Like an online photobook . . ." I deleted my old profile and started a new one. I lingered on the name, but I knew the opinion I'd had of myself for years, the phrase that had been running around in my head for so long, since Matthew maybe, but probably since birth.

@yourlocalbisexualdisaster

Maybe it should've been more clever, less on the nose, since I was going to give this to Mrs. Lozano as a *school assignment*, but maybe the lack of creativity spoke to how much of a disaster this whole thing really was.

Maybe this assignment would give me the answer. I pressed Confirm, and it felt like a prayer. "The journey, or whatever, for this class. What if whenever I hang out with Dani and Amanda and Matthew, I take pictures and just write about how they make me feel?"

Jordan's eyes lit up. "Dude. That's fucking genius. Like, poetic and shit."

As if in response, someone behind him honked, and he jumped and hit the gas when he realized the light was now green.

I barely noticed, opening up my notes app to write my thoughts as they came. "I could make each person have a theme, so it's clear there's three people and three separate bonds. I can edit them differently so they look really distinct from each other."

"You could use different color filters," Jordan offered helpfully.

I nodded, my fingers flying across the keyboard to keep up with my thoughts. "And I'll use the captions to talk about my feelings, like I'm narrating almost. Do you think that could work?"

"I think it has to. Otherwise this is going to end really awkwardly."

I bit my lip. "What if they find out?"

Jordan screwed up his face. "How? Our assignments are private; Mrs. Lozano said so."

"I know, but Dani is in this class. What if she finds out somehow, like looks at Mrs. Lozano's computer or—"

"You're going to what-if your idea into the ground, Mags."

I sighed. "I know. I just . . . I really need this to work. I can't believe I'm turning finding a date for Alyssa's quince into a school assignment."

"Honestly, it's very *you*. Ya know, avoiding your feelings and having to be forced to deal with them."

I glared at him. "Gee. Thanks."

He beamed at the road ahead. "Happy to help."

---

That night in my room, the blank black space had never looked more menacing, and it had nothing to do with targeted ads or starving influencers promoting detox tea.

These posts weren't going to be photos as much as windows; I needed them to be a look inside my brain, my heart. All I had to do was capture it so that someone, other than me, would know what it meant. Matthew, Amanda, and Dani were all so different, and they all made me feel something distinct. I didn't know why they all made me feel the way that they did, but I could sense the different colors and sounds and moods in my head. No matter how confused I was, their aesthetics had always been clear to me, and that was enough to start with.

When I thought of Matthew, I pictured him in black and white. The artful mess of dark hair and the hard, precise edge of his jaw belonged on an old-timey movie screen, all James Dean bravado. His mouth tasted like cigarettes and sparked against mine like hazy summer stars. When we were dating, I always wanted to photograph him pinup-style, a red Corvette and a leather jacket, comb in the pocket, all chiseled profile and strong hands. I remembered him blurry, like first love and first times and the stain they leave on your heart.

He sounded like Jeff Buckley, like Patti Smith, like Robert Mapplethorpe's last stuttered breath. I heard slow acoustic melodies when he talked, pictured Bob Dylan's hands on the strings of his guitar and the confession that ripped from Johnny Cash's throat.

This project needed music. After all, what was a story without an epic soundtrack?

Outside my room, Alyssa and Mom were arguing. Alyssa wanted McDonald's; Mom was fervently arguing "hay comida en la casa," which was followed by the low sounds of Veronica trying to mediate. Shaking my head to clear it, I picked up a pen and started scribbling in the notebook open next to me at my desk, deciding to pick a song for each post before continuing on to my next two subjects.

Amanda had always been the bubblegum pop to my emo trash self. She was soft, a Monet painting with her pastel clothes and delicate silver jewelry, soft curves and neatly pressed lines on a designer blouse. I wanted to paint her that way, with all the soft floating brushstrokes. She was pink and orange and yellow. She made me feel rosy, as fucking corny as that sounded, like the color of the sky in the Valley before sunset. For the ways Amanda blurred boundaries, I decided to make the pictures a little ethereal and faded at the edges, and I'd edit them to have a soft rosy pink hue like the one Amanda emanated when she was around.

She was the electropop interlude to my angsty punk paradise, the neon sign shining outside the seedy bar, cutting through the dark. I knew what she sounded like too: Top 40, sadgirl techno-pop, every earworm hit that burrowed into your psyche and invaded your daydreams no matter how hard you tried to ignore it. CHVRCHES, Billie Eilish, Becky G, Lizzo, and Chloe x Halle.

Dani was more difficult simply because she was still a mystery to me, and one full of contrasts at that. Sundresses and stretched ears, soft smiles and the hard impact of people shoving you into the mosh pit. All her jewelry was gold, and she was always in warm, earthy tones with this cool eclectic bohemian style that would've looked pretentious on anyone else our age but somehow looked just right on her. She was gold the way the sun would backlight a concert stage just before sundown. Gold. That's Dani. Music: god, she made me feel like a fuckboi, but it was such a sappy love song–type shit with her.

Or just a sad song because you never know.

A finsta held the key to my freedom from this Feelings Hell, possibly forever. I stared at my phone, at the blinking cursor in the open text post. My thumbs were at the ready, but they hesitated at the keyboard.

I wasn't ready to deal with the mess this might cause, but the idea of spending more time trapped in this romantic purgatory was unbearable. Now I had the chance to get out, to let go of everything—all the feelings I had never dealt with, all the fear I'd run from, all the things I was unsure about—and I couldn't pass up that chance at peace.

Resolved, I pushed my laptop to the side and sat up, hunting around the room for something to photograph. A roll of turquoise tulle sat in front of Alyssa's dresser, a swatch of the material she was going to use for her centerpieces at the event hall, and my scribbled-on Converse were buried under it. Scrambling across the room, I nearly busted my ankle arranging the tulle so it draped over the shoes. Juxtaposed with the scribbles, you'd almost think my shoes deserved to be somewhere magical.

My little sister's quince is probably going to make her feel like an adult, but trying to find an escort for her quince, I still feel like a child, fumbling around in the world, made to adore everyone who's nice to her, who shows her kindness. Is it so bad that I have three paths for my heart to travel down? Is it bad that I'm going to use this project to figure out which disaster should be the end of me?

Simple, direct. Click and post.

---

"Mom, *listen,*" Alyssa insisted the following Sunday as she, Veronica, and our mom pored over dress catalogues at the rickety kitchen table before church. I was doing the dishes with half an ear tuned in to their conversation because I was more useful here than I was discussing color swatches and what the church-appropriate height for a heel would be. "I don't *want* to add straps to my dress. I want to go strapless. It's my *quince*. I'm a *woman* now. And I want to take the photos today so I can put them on the invitations. I don't have time to wait for her to add straps."

"No me importa. You're not a woman and you're not even fifteen yet." My mom glared.

"Not fair, Veronica and Maggie got to go strapless and nobody protested!" Alyssa pointed accusingly at the living room, where both Veronica's and my quince portraits stared at us from above the couch.

"I *did* protest. Loudly. In English and broken Spanish." I cringed looking at the picture. The overexaggerated sweetheart neckline and fluffy skirt looked like it belonged on top of a lemon meringue pie, not on my barely pubescent body.

"That's why nothing came of it. No entendí tu español." Mami smirked, and I glared at her until she laughed.

Alyssa sniffed. "You and Veronica got to wear strapless dresses. How do you think I feel, knowing that Mami loves you guys more than me?"

Mom tsked, rolling her eyes. "Ay, mamita, why are you so dramatic?"

"See?!" Alyssa thrust a hand in her direction. "She didn't even deny it!"

"Watch where you put that hand." Our mother raised an eyebrow and gave her The Look.

Alyssa immediately shrank back, pouting as she sulked in her chair. "I'm just saying."

"Veronica and Magdalena didn't have as many boyfriends as you, so *they* could wear strapless."

"Did she just slut-shame our baby sister?" I asked Veronica, who nodded. "Not cool, Mom."

Mom rolled her eyes. It was always spooky to see her do that because she looked exactly like Veronica in all her annoyance. "You know what I mean."

"I don't even *have* a boyfriend anymore!" Alyssa protested.

"Look," Veronica said, "do the photo shoot today and we won't make you add straps if we can add, like, a sheer jacket-type thing to the dress for the church service. It's always cold in the church anyway."

"But what about—"

"You can take it off at the event hall, whatever." Veronica looked at our mother. "Right, Mami?"

Mom gave a world-weary sigh. "Fine."

"I guess," Alyssa agreed reluctantly.

"I'm only saying yes because you don't have tetas."

"Mom!" Alyssa whined, crossing her arms in front of her A-cups.

"Pues, it's true."

"Speaking of dresses," Veronica said, effortlessly steering us away from a conflict like always. "Maggie, who's gonna be your escort?"

I bit my lip. Alyssa snapped her head around to look at me. "Yeah, dude, I need to know, like, soon. So I can order the outfit or rearrange it so you can stand solo like a loser."

"Hey!"

"*Soooy un perdedor,*" Veronica sang, grinning.

"I hate all of you." I narrowed my eyes but didn't say anything else. I knew in a pinch, I could ask Jordan to do it as a friendly favor, but part of me wanted the romance of wearing a pretty dress and dancing the whole night with someone I *like*-liked. The project was due the Friday before Alyssa's quince, so what better way to light a fire under my ass than to have a family-oriented deadline for this project?

"Since the quince is on the twelfth, I'll need to know by the fifth. Don't make me choose for you," Alyssa warned. "I'll pick cousin Leonardo, and you know he always gets drunk and puts his boxers on over his clothes because he thinks it's funny. Don't try me. I'll do it."

So I'd need a road map to my heart before November fifth. Certainly no big deal.

---

Alyssa's quince photoshoot was planned for this afternoon, and honestly, any other photographer would've walked right out after Alyssa's *America's Next Top Model*–level bullshit.

"Ugh! I'm just not feeling it, ya know? You guys aren't

giving me the right feeling here," Alyssa said, resting her hands on her hips, making an audible rustling sound as they landed on her fluffy turquoise ball gown.

I sighed, lowering my camera from my face to give her another exasperated glare. This was the fourth time she'd stopped the shoot. We were at the lake near the Harlingen Public Library because Alyssa had demanded an outdoor shoot with water and, for fuck's sake, ducks in the background. It was nearing sundown, but the heat was still causing beads of sweat to roll down my back. "We're going to lose the light if you can't get into this."

Alyssa squinted. "You're the photographer, you're supposed to help me get into this!" Alyssa stuck a hand out at the ducks, who were swimming off frame. "See, you're even losing the models."

"This shit's for the birds," Veronica interjected from her seat on the folding lawn chair she'd brought, grinning and fanning herself with a piece of junk mail she'd grabbed from her car. I turned my glare on her. She wasn't helping, even if that pun was dad joke gold.

"I need ambiance," Alyssa said. "I can't work this way. Someone needs to create an atmosphere."

An idea dinged in the back of my head, and I smiled. "I know what to do. Hold on."

I wandered a bit away from them, scrolling through my phone because they were going to give me *so* much shit for what I was about to do. I found the number I wanted and hit Call. "Hey, are you busy? Does your cousin still run that photo place in the mall . . . ?"

A half hour later, Matthew's truck pulled up in the parking lot, and I handed Veronica the camera and said, "Be right back. Help is here."

She squinted in suspicion at the sight of the familiar truck, and she opened her mouth, probably to ask me why the hell I'd invited my ex-boyfriend here, so to avoid the questions I didn't want to answer, I booked it to the empty parking lot of the library next door. Matthew was getting out of the truck when I reached him, and he gave me a smile and a one-armed hug. He smelled exactly like I remembered, like laundry detergent and Old Spice body wash, and I had to stop myself from pressing my face into his shoulder and taking a deep breath. I pulled away and smiled as I followed him to the bed of the truck. "Thanks so much for doing this."

"It's nothing, just like old times." Matthew unlatched the back and hefted a large metal fan off the truck. "Drama queen needed some help?"

"As always." I grinned as I picked up the small generator that was next to it. We began walking toward the lake. "Yeah, I figured she needed something a little more professional than I could give her."

Matthew chuckled. "Fuck professionalism. You don't need fancy equipment and shit. I know these pictures are gonna be sick because they're *you*, ya know?"

I didn't reply because I didn't trust myself. The setting sun was making me nostalgic in that way that endings do, and his scent was making me dizzy. God, I was pathetic.

Alyssa screeched when she saw the fan, almost smashing the bouquet of plastic flowers in her hands as she clapped. "Oh my gosh, that's perfect! Matthew, hurry and set it up!"

Veronica glared at her. "Don't be rude. Say thank you to Matthew for coming out here."

"Yeah, yeah, he broke Maggie's heart. I don't have to say thank you to him."

I grimaced, flushing. "Hey now—"

But Matthew took it in stride, smiling ruefully. "Hey, Maggie broke my heart too, let's not forget."

"Elephants don't forget, and I don't either." Alyssa narrowed her eyes.

Matthew reached into his back pocket and took out a wireless speaker, and my eyes widened. "I also took the liberty of bringing a speaker so you can model to some music. You still like Fifth Harmony even though now they're basically Fourth Harmony?"

Alyssa dropped the glare and smiled, hopping up and down. "Normani is the only person from them who deserves our streams right now. Play 'Motivation.'"

I would've started hopping too, had I not been so busy staring at the triumphant grin on his face, the light in his eyes. Not only had he procured a fan and driven out here on such short notice, but he had taken it a step further without me even asking, remembering what Alyssa liked without being told. It was new, this thoughtfulness.

And there it was, that seesawing of my telltale heart. This was the Matthew I'd fallen for, over and over again. The Matthew that dropped everything for his friends, who remembered little details and made you feel special. I couldn't tear my eyes away from him as he set up the generator and the fan, looking right at me as he straightened up. "Ready to make some magic?"

I nodded, breathless, and Veronica hit the button to blare the music.

The shoot was quick after that, Alyssa in her element as she posed to the upbeat pop melodies. Tossing her hair back with her dress fluttering in the breeze, she looked like some kind of superhero princess. She was living out her music video, *Teen Vogue* fantasy, and it showed in every picture I snapped.

My eyes kept drifting to Matthew between shots no matter

how much I tried not to, and he smiled innocently at me, unaware. The pit of my stomach burned with desire. This was supposed to make the decision easier, but all I'd done right now was play myself.

Sounds about right.

But as the shoot came to an end and Matthew and I were loading the equipment into the truck, I decided to just bite the damn bullet already. As Matthew closed the cab of the truck and turned to look at me, the words spilled out before I could talk myself out of it. "Can I buy you dinner? Ya know, since you saved my ass and all."

I punctuated the sentence with a laugh that I hoped sounded genuine and shoved my hands into my pockets because they were shaking. I could not show weakness. I could not act like this was anything other than being friendly.

Matthew was quiet for a beat, just looking at me, but then he smiled softly, the kind of smile that used to be reserved just for me. I tried not to think about how many people he might have given it to since he had stopped loving me. Finally, he said, "Yeah, let's do it. Why not?"

I could have listed several reasons, but I wasn't about to cost myself an opportunity.

The Pizza Hut in front of the San Benito Wal-Mart was holy ground, sacred and haunted by the memories of first dates and post–football game celebrations. My friends, and probably everyone else in San Benito, had all passed through that space at some point or another. Cheap pizza and a quiet atmosphere, with free refills on soda, made it a haven for broke teenagers looking for a place to hang out that wasn't hot and filled with tiny annoying bugs.

Even now, as we sat down at a corner table, the maroon-and-beige-checkered tablecloth had that same sticky film I remembered from the last time I'd come here, on a date with Matthew. I glanced across the room, my eyes pulled toward a booth near the window. At the beginning of last year, Matthew got his license and he'd picked me up in his dad's Range Rover. He'd handed me a bouquet of rainbow-dyed daisies from HEB, the tips of his ears turning red, and we'd split a pizza sitting on the same side of the booth, eating one-handed so we could keep holding hands through dinner.

I could see all of this now, the memory projecting itself onto the booth, laughing and talking and sneaking kisses.

We ordered our usual: two Pepsis (one of them Diet) and a large pineapple-and-pepperoni pizza to share. I usually ordered it with jalapeños as well, but Matthew didn't like spicy things so we'd never ordered it when we were together. One of the perks of being broken up: total agency over my own pizza toppings.

It was easy, when he leaned toward me with a smile after the waitress left, tilting his head and asking, "So how have you been, Maggie?"

"I've been okay. Start of the school year and all. AP Art is turning out to be more of a bitch than I thought."

"Yeah, I know. Theater has been kicking my ass, shockingly enough. I really didn't think it would be this hard, but I was so fucking wrong." He shook his head in disgust.

"I still can't believe you're in *theater*, of all things, but you do love the spotlight, so—"

"I do not! You wound me, Mags." He put a hand on his chest, rearing back dramatically.

I laughed. "You do too! Why else did you even join?"

He narrowed his eyes at me. "I'll have you know it's good career practice."

"I didn't know lawyers needed to know how to recite Shakespeare."

"'The lady doth protest too much' is totally something you can say in court!"

"You should jot that down in the Notes app where you keep all your witty one-liners and smooth pickup lines."

"So you admit they're smooth." He raised his eyebrows, his eyes twinkling.

I rolled my eyes. "Well, they got me to date you, didn't they?"

"Here I thought it was my good looks and charming personality."

I suppressed a laugh and felt a blush creeping up. "He's right, Your Honor," I said.

"Lawyer-ed." He grinned. "Seriously, though, it's like that phrase where the world's a stage or whatever. Court is like that, I think. You have to perform, make people believe what you want them to believe. You have to be convincing, captivate a crowd and shit. What better practice ground than a low-budget version of an Oscar Wilde play?"

All I knew about court was what I saw in *Lucifer* and *How to Get Away with Murder,* but I believed him. "Since we're not dating anymore, I'm allowed to say that I think the law is total crap and I don't get why people dedicate their lives to defending it."

He shook his head, a good-natured smile on his face. "I'd never expect you to stop busting my balls just because we're not dating."

"Someone's gotta keep you humble." I shrugged. "And I do it better than anyone else."

"That's still true." He was serious, no trace of his earlier humor, and I didn't know what to make of it. I didn't have time to ask him about it because he continued, "So how's your sister? Is she liking high school so far?"

I smiled. "Yeah, she's enjoying herself, I think. She already has more friends than Veronica and me combined. Her quince is in November, and she's had her court decided from, like, the first week of the school year."

Matthew nodded. "Yeah, when you called me to go over, it got me thinking about *your* quince."

It did? "Really?"

"Yeah, really." His half smile was sad. "I'm sorry for that, by the way."

"You mean the way you left me without an escort? Yeah, you should be." I frowned. "Whatever, I've forgiven you. Sort of. Mostly."

He rolled his eyes. "Well, how about I make it up to you, huh? Do you need an escort?"

My heart leapt up into my throat, and for a moment, I panicked. Had he found my finsta? Was he trying to badger me into admitting my motives?

But my suspicion vanished as soon as I took in the earnest look in his eyes, the small and genuine smile on his face, and I asked, "You'd really do that for me?"

He shrugged. "Mags, I've known you for a long time. There's not really anything I wouldn't do for you."

*Except maintain open and honest communication with me in order to build a healthy relationship*, a nasty little voice whispered in my ear, but I shoved the thought away. I couldn't let doubt ruin this moment. If we had any hope of doing this again, I had to look at him like someone I had never dated before, like someone who had never broken my heart.

"Even now?" I murmured. His cheeks flushed as he rubbed the back of his neck, and butterflies erupted in my stomach.

"Especially now," he said, that crooked smile just a bit softer, weighted down with something I couldn't place. Was it nostalgia? Grief? Regret?

Or maybe I was just projecting everything I felt onto him.

Here it was, the escort that I needed, on a silver platter in the middle of a Pizza Hut. If I said yes right now, where would that lead us?

But then I remembered Amanda and Dani, and *Tori,* so I chose indecision. It seemed to be the only thing I could rely on these days. "I might take you up on that offer. I'll let you know."

"You do that. I have a lot to make up for, and it's about time I start." He shrugged lightly, like he hadn't just thrown kindling onto the bonfire in my chest.

His phone buzzed on the table, and we both jumped a bit. He reached for it, looking down at the screen and scowling.

"What's wrong?" I asked.

He shook his head, pocketing his phone. "It's nothing."

I wanted to roll my eyes. Ah, his fatal flaw: anything even resembling vulnerability. Getting this out of him would be like pulling teeth, if I remembered correctly, so I broached it carefully. "Didn't look like nothing."

Matthew sighed. "My dad canceled on his weekend with us. It's the third time."

"Really?" I blinked, surprised. He never shared how he was feeling, and here it was, so easily unearthed. Usually it was a lot of him silently stewing before he snapped at me to relieve his frustration. Now, it had taken less than thirty seconds, a stark contrast to the thirty minutes that it used to. What other ways had he changed since we broke up?

Matthew nodded, his face dark. "Yeah. Said he has to work. Last week he said he was sick, but I saw on Facebook that he went dove hunting with my tíos."

"Matthew—"

"I knew something was up," he said. "My mom was yelling

at him about something yesterday—I guess this was it." Matthew shook his head. "It's whatever. It's not a big deal."

"Why do I feel like that isn't quite true?" I asked quietly.

"It's *fine*, Maggie." Matthew ran his hand through his hair. "It's just, there's a lot going on. Jesus and I are used to our dad treating us like crap, but Abel is only ten. He doesn't know why his dad doesn't want to see him."

"Do *you* know why?"

"If I knew why, maybe I would know how to fix it by now. Figured out a way to fit into his life better." He scoffed. "Maybe I could give Abel some lessons on how to make our dad pay attention to him."

I frowned. "You shouldn't have to 'fix it.' Your father should want to see you because you're *you*. You should be teaching Abel how to not give a shit that his dad is being an asshole."

"To do that, I'd have to know how to not give a shit. And I still haven't learned yet." He paused. "Why do I still care about this? Why do I still want him to . . . to . . . ?"

"Love you?" I swallowed around the lump that had risen in my throat. I didn't know why this made me so sad. It's not like I had a dad anymore. Not a living one anyway. "I think we'll always want the people we love to love us back, and maybe we'll do anything for it."

Like sitting in a Pizza Hut recreating your first date with your ex when he has a girlfriend. My stomach roiled at the thought.

"Some things aren't worth chasing." He slumped back in his chair, drummed his fingertips on the gingham tabletop. "I just wish I could tell Abel that."

I thought about it. "Maybe he needs a distraction. Has flag football started yet? I know you said he wanted to do that this year."

Matthew looked over at me in surprise. "You still remember that?"

I shrugged, my cheeks warming. "You told me about it, and I love Abel."

Matthew grinned. "Little shit misses you. He doesn't like Tori all that much, keeps asking me to get a nicer girlfriend."

"So why don't you?" I blurted before grimacing. "Sorry, that was rude. Tori's not that bad."

It was a lie, of course, and a bad one, and from the sound of Matthew's skeptical chuckle, he knew it too. "Well, I guess I asked for it when I said you shouldn't stop busting my balls."

"You know what, you're right. This is all your fault."

He laughed again. "I guess so. Tori's all right. She's just a little . . . prickly is all. Doesn't know how to make friends. She's cool when you get to know her. Besides, she'd probably cut my balls off if I tried to leave her before Halloween. She wants to do a couples costume."

"You should go as Sid and Nancy. It matches the hostile vibe she has going on."

"So am I Nancy?"

"Duh."

Matthew laughed and shook his head. "She's fun to hang out with, and she doesn't take my shit, which is cool. I know you guys don't really vibe, but I'm hoping that'll get better eventually." He rubbed the back of his neck, cringing. "I'm not really great at this whole thing, well, you know."

He looked at me, and his gaze was loaded, intense. It threw me for a bit, because I couldn't tell what he was seeing, or what he was feeling, or what I was supposed to be feeling in return. "Same. For the same reasons, I guess."

"Well," Matthew reasoned, "we both have similar scars. So neither of us knows what the fuck we're doing."

I nodded. "Damn straight. Good at life but bad at love."

Matthew tipped his head to the side with a shy smile. "I don't know about that. You've always tried your hardest. It's what I . . ."

"What?" I said a little too quickly, hope filling my body despite my constant commands for it to please calm down.

Matthew's gaze pinned me in place, and I couldn't bring myself to look away. "I loved that about you. You always fought for me."

*I always did. Still do.*

I wanted to kiss that smile, to leap across the table and erase the last few months of moping and start again. But I just reached over hesitantly and patted his hand. "Hopefully we'll both get better at this."

"I hope so too."

After the meal, the waitress brought the check over. Eyeing us, she said, "I hope y'all had a nice date."

Matthew's face was red, and mine was flushing too. I stared at him helplessly, waiting for him to speak because I sure as hell didn't have any words right now. "Um, yeah, well, uh—Thanks?"

I gulped and dropped my gaze to the check, busying myself with counting out my money to avoid looking at him. When the waitress left with the money, I finally turned back to him, raising a questioning eyebrow. "Don't look at me like that," he said finally.

"Why did you let her think that?" I demanded.

He arched an eyebrow and gave me a sly half smile. "I thought 'No, we are not on a date, we're exes who are trying to be friends and hang out one-on-one even though it's tense because we're both fuckups who don't know what we're doing' would take too long to explain."

He was probably right. I needed a detailed timeline and our astrological charts to fully understand our situation myself, but the hesitancy in his eyes and the acknowledgment of the weird place we were in made me feel a little better. At least we were together in this confusion, trying to figure out what we were to each other. "Maybe one day we'll find a way to talk about us without having to explain all the baggage."

"I sure hope so." His eyes lingered on mine for a second more before he averted his gaze, then stood up from the table. "I'm gonna go use the bathroom, okay?"

I watched as he left, and the waitress brought the receipt. My eyes widened when I saw the heart at the bottom and a smiley face, and if that didn't feel like a sign . . .

I knew what my post had to be. Positioning the receipt tastefully crooked against the checkered tablecloth, I angled my phone and snapped a photo. I prepared the photo for another post, and checking to make sure Matthew hadn't returned, I started to write:

> M, you're as deceitfully sincere as you are beautiful. Honest as you are cruel in your inherent temptation. Some days I wonder if you're a different person now, a person who fits with me. Or would your anger, your hatred for your father, your vices eventually turn you back into the person you were when we broke up, sending us spinning out in different directions once again?

I didn't read it over because I knew if I did, I'd want to edit out the sharp edges, the harsh lines of judgment I couldn't keep from escaping, so I just hit Post and put away my phone as Matthew came out of the bathroom. He gave me that charming half grin, no sign of his earlier nervousness, as he asked, "You ready?"

I smiled, nodding, and put down a tip before following him out of the restaurant. I felt lighter, like the post had been a release valve and I'd opened it for just a moment to get some relief. Even if no one could see it, I knew what I had written, and writing down exactly what I was feeling in that weird moment with Matthew was strangely cathartic. Huh. Writers really were onto something.

Matthew drove me home after that. When he pulled into the parking lot and cut the engine, he looked over at me and said, "This is so fucking weird."

I felt it too, but I wanted to hear it from him. "What do you mean?"

Matthew shook his head, a wistful smile on his face. "Remember we used to sit out here for hours when I'd bring you home?"

I smiled as the memory reached me, the two of us so small and sitting in a car that was way too big for our tiny love. "You did that before, when we were friends too."

Matthew looked over at me, a lock of his dark hair falling onto his forehead. My hand twitched on the console, aching to brush it back, but I was afraid. "Would your mom come at me with a chancla if I walked you to the door?"

The night was so quiet, I could hear the sounds of people in the store, and I hovered off to the side of the doorway. Matthew slowed to a stop in front of me, turning slowly to face me. The fluorescent lights buzzed above us, and the air between us felt heavy, electric with all the things I could not say.

"Thanks for dinner," Matthew said, hands in his pockets as he glanced at me. I wondered if he'd also forgotten how to say goodbye to me without a kiss; I knew I had. Most of the time, I tried to avoid being the last one in the car with him; it hurt too much to pretend I didn't remember the days when our whole world used to be just me and him, parked in that Range Rover next to my house with nothing to do but each other.

"I know it's been a really long road and stuff, and there's still stuff we're not good at, but . . . I really like having you in my life. A lot. So I'm glad we—you . . ." He trailed off, rubbing the back of his neck. "Ya know."

I smiled. I did, more than he'd ever know.

And then Matthew smiled and opened up his arms, and I couldn't resist, even if I wanted to. I stepped into them and wound my hands around his back, trying not to breathe a sigh into his T-shirt. He had filled out since we broke up, the muscles of his back firm against my arms and his chest hard against my cheek. His arms were strong, holding me in a way that felt familiar but not friendly, and when he looked down at me, his eyes burning into mine, his lips parted like he had something to say, or to do. I stared at him, not dropping my gaze, nervous but curious to see what he would do next.

If he did what I thought he might do, this little game I was playing might change completely. Matthew pulling ahead in the running . . . Who knew what that would mean for us? Maybe I would have a quince escort and a new chance at a relationship that I'd never felt was truly done, all before November.

But then I remembered Tori, and my feelings for Dani and Amanda, and I looked away, and he did too.

We pulled apart, said good night, and I let out a shaky, stubborn breath as he drove off into the night.

I went into the store, and Veronica and Alyssa were there, Alyssa perched on the counter with her legs hanging off and Veronica hovering over one of her textbooks. They were both looking at me expectantly. "What?"

"How was Maaatthew?" Alyssa said, her voice nasally and goading.

I rolled my eyes. "Why do you have to say it like that?"

"You know why," Veronica said. "What did you do?"

I shrugged. "We went to Pizza Hut."

"Sounds like a date," Alyssa said.

"Yeah, doesn't he have a girlfriend?" Veronica raised her eyebrow at me. "Mami didn't raise you to be a homewrecker, or be with someone who doesn't mind making you a homewrecker."

"Chill, Vero. No one's home is getting wrecked. Nothing happened."

Veronica gave me a look before shaking her head. "Whatever. I trust you. If only because Matthew came in clutch today."

"Yeah, that fan practically *made* the photo shoot."

I gave them both a sour look. "Excuse you, but I was the one *actually* taking the photos. Where's my credit?"

"Yeah, but I already know you're a good photographer. He was the one who had to prove himself."

"And did he?" Veronica wasn't looking at Alyssa. She was looking at me. "Prove himself to you?"

He had dropped everything to drive twenty minutes to another town to bring me a fan and a generator. And the way he'd looked at me . . . I wanted to believe that he had changed, and that I had too, and that it was enough. "I guess we'll see."

Veronica sniffed. "Well, I think you should stay away from him. There will be plenty of people for you to date at NYU. People who aren't toxic and will actually be worthy of you."

"And who might have a lot of money so you won't have to work!" Alyssa said.

I smiled, but it didn't feel quite right. Veronica was right, but the idea of starting over with someone in a completely different state—someone who didn't understand my family, didn't know my culture, had never heard of the Valley—was terrifying.

Getting back with Matthew would give me another reason to consider staying here. Matthew had been my shelter for so long that now I couldn't tell the difference between heartsick and homesick.

Maybe there wasn't one. When home had a heartbeat, how could you not surrender to its rhythm?

---

**Amanda:** Saw Alyssa's IG story and I'm LIVING for these photos. YOU ARE A PHOTOGRAPHY GODDESS. She looks so good!

**Amanda:** Also why was Matthew at the shoot *side-eye emoji*

**Maggie:** He brought the fan. It was nothing. Just friends helping friends.

**Amanda:** Don't even. *girl with arms crossed over her face emoji*

# 5

Alyssa's meticulous quince preparation hadn't yet been proven physically dangerous, but that was sure to change today. Her court, made up of six damas and six chambelánes, were coming over for dance practice for the first time.

The doorbell rang, and Alyssa almost knocked over the kitchen chair she'd been sitting on with how fast she flew to the front door. The sound of her wrenching open the door was followed by squealing. The lower voice accompanying hers could only mean it was her best friend, Christina. "Mom, we're going to the backyard. Bring the food!"

The door slammed. Footsteps thudded down the stairs, Alyssa's and Christina's voices growing lower and more giggly. Mom was following behind them, probably suspicious of a bunch of rowdy kids in her store; she didn't really trust any of our friends that much.

Except for Jordan, but that was mostly because my mom had a soft spot for kids whose mothers worked a lot, like she did.

The door opened again, followed by Amanda calling, "Is it safe, or are there more kids coming to trample me?"

"All clear!" The HEB bags I was rooting through on the counter were bulging with snacks for Alyssa's friends, and

I had just unearthed a box of Fruit Roll-Ups I was considering stealing when Amanda entered the kitchen, still in her running shorts and SBHS marching band T-shirt, flushed and sweaty from Saturday band practice. Amanda was a drum major in the band, meaning we had very little time together from August until December and we'd never actually sat to watch a football game together, which was fine by me because football games were for jocks and popular kids and I wasn't either of those things. I'd rather take photos than sit in the overcrowded stands anyway.

I always took the time to stop and watch the halftime show, though, because Amanda was a fucking *great* drum major. She lost herself in every performance, a passion in her eyes that I didn't see when she was doing things with the billion other clubs she pressured us to join. She was in total control, her spine always straight and each wave of her hand confident and without hesitation, and it was absolutely mesmerizing.

Okay, maybe I was a little biased. The fact remained that she was good at what she did, and it showed. They went to state every year. And so what if I had a thing for strong powerful women who were good at what they did?

"Is anyone here?" Amanda said, heading back out to the living room.

I followed her. "Nope, everyone is outside. Why—"

And then she was pulling her top off in the middle of my living room.

"What are you doing?" I demanded. I could only watch as she peeled her sweaty shirt off, using it to wipe her forehead. "Dude, seriously?"

Amanda just stared at me, gesturing with her shirt. I was incredibly distracted by the hand that rested on her popped hip, the soft plane of her stomach, and the stretch of creamy skin that led to her boobs, snug in a purple-and-pink sports bra. My mouth was dry, and I looked at her face again so I wouldn't look anywhere else. She'd never done this in front of me before. Why now?

"I forgot the extra shirt I keep in my car, and I cannot be in this sports bra anymore because my tits can't breathe in this thing. Do you have that shirt I left here last week?" With that, she marched down the hall in her socks, and panic sparked in me.

"Dude, my room is messy—"

"You know I don't care about that."

I knew she didn't, and I also knew my room wasn't messy, since she found the shirt sitting on top of my laundry basket. It was washed and everything; Mami must have snagged it before I could toss it in with my laundry.

The minute she was in my room felt like a thousand years, and I bounced from foot to foot in the doorway waiting for her to tug on the shirt. She looked out of place in my room, a puzzle piece that didn't belong, and I didn't know why. Something about her perfect salon-dyed hair and flawless skin just didn't match up with the shabbiness of my room, the scuffed walls and old furniture, Alyssa's things encroaching on my side of the room because of the lack of space.

I was grateful when we went back to the kitchen and Amanda peered at the quince magazine on the table. "Oooh, what is it, two months from now?"

"Yeah, you're coming?"

"Duh." Amanda reached out and twirled a bit of my hair around her finger, tugging lightly. The pull jerked around something inside of me. God, was I literally just her puppet? "Gotta support my best friend."

"Support your best friend by taking the snacks to the

rugrats," Veronica said, entering the kitchen and grabbing a handful of grapes out of the fridge. "I'm going to go replace Jason in the store. I'm pretty sure he steals cigarettes."

"Maybe it was me," I offered. "I could have a life you don't know about."

Veronica shoved my head a bit as she left the room. "We both know you're not hard enough for petty theft."

I watched her go before turning to Amanda. "I'm tough, right?"

Amanda, already opening a pack of Oreos, nodded solemnly. "The toughest."

We went to do homework on the back porch, trying to be subtle about keeping an eye on my crafty little sister and her weirdo friends. Alyssa and Christina had their work cut out for them trying to teach a bunch of awkward barely teens how to do the choreography they'd picked out on YouTube as the group dance. They were using the random concrete slab in the backyard, which had been there since before I was born, as a makeshift dance floor.

"Maybe they should've started on this earlier than two months before the day," Amanda observed as a tall gangly boy almost took a girl's eye out with a flying elbow.

I was doodling on my AP Physics notes. Amanda and I were sitting cross-legged on the floor so we could use the ice chest as a table to do homework, but our attempt at being productive had mostly devolved into us eating Takis and talking.

"I don't think they could've pulled this off if they had two years, so I guess the odds were never in their favor," I said.

Amanda raised a hand in the *Hunger Games* salute, not looking up from her five-subject notebook.

I craned my neck to look over at Amanda's worksheet. "What did you get for number six?"

"I got eighteen point seven."

"Fuck, how did I get six point four?"

"Because you're bad at physics?"

"You're bad at friendship."

Amanda patted my cheek, and I felt the burn of it even after she took her hand away. "It's okay. Fuck math anyway. You're great at other things. Like photography. And being pretty."

"How is being pretty going to help me with physics?"

"It's not—why do you think you're bad at physics?" Amanda shrugged. "Wanna come to my house after this? I bet I could get your mom to let you sleep over."

"Yeah, right," I scoffed. "And I bet her exact words to me will be 'esta casa no es un hotel.' She hates when I come and go."

Amanda waved me off, already turning around to march into the store. "I'll risk the Spanish backhand."

I didn't know what brujería Amanda had done to get my mom to say yes—probably called her own mother to talk Mom's ear off with a wine-fueled rundown of her day until she was so annoyed that she said yes just to get off the phone—but soon enough, I was in Amanda's car, pulling into Liberty Estates, where Amanda lived with her parents in a big house with a pool and more space than they'd ever really need.

The wealth gap between Amanda and me was jarring, but then again, it mirrored pretty much every other gap in our friendship. Since my father died, right after Alyssa was born, the store had been the only thing keeping our house—our whole life—afloat. Even then, it's not like we were rolling in money. Amanda's dad was a lawyer, and her mom helped run his law firm. She even had a college fund, for fuck's sake. We might as well be from different planets.

"My parents are working today, so you can just make

yourself at home. Go nuts. I'm going to shower, I smell gross from practice," Amanda said as we took off our shoes at the door, padding across the tiled living room in our socks.

The central air conditioning always made the house feel like heaven when you stepped into it from the boiling heat, and everything inside was coordinated, from the curtains to the decorative pillows. She even had a TV in her room, which reminded me once again of how fucking poor I was compared to her. Insecurities aside, though, she had the most comfortable bed ever, so I snuggled down into it, dragging a throw over me and sinking into the pillows. "You go, I'll be here."

I didn't know I'd fallen asleep until it was time to wake up; I was jerked from sleep by the sound of the door opening. "Have a nice nap?"

I lifted my head from the pillow and rubbed my eyes when the light hit them. "Your bed is soft, fight me."

When I focused back on Amanda, I wanted to look away just as quickly because I was afraid I'd never look away again. She was standing in the doorway in just her towel, dyed-caramel hair dripping and water droplets peppering her skin.

My mind suddenly blank, I raced to fix my face, to make sure it wasn't making unintended boner faces, imagining neutral faces for reference so I didn't focus on the way the towel was just a stitch too short on Amanda's long legs.

Falling back into the pillows, shrouded by sweet, innocent darkness, I said, "Sooo tired," as I prayed Amanda didn't notice the way my brain had just twitched and short-circuited.

God really thought They were funny, didn't They?

I heard Amanda cross the room and open her dresser drawer, and I determinedly refused to emerge from my pillow cocoon until the bed dipped. I pulled myself out to glance at my best friend, and yes, Amanda's tank top and pajama short combo didn't leave a ton to the imagination, but it was at least *something.*

"What do you wanna watch?" Amanda grabbed the TV remote off the nightstand, scooting toward me until she was pressed into my side, every inch of her bare thigh pressed against mine. "I was watching *Love Is Blind* last night."

"We can just keep watching that." Amanda's nearness was making me overly conscious of my body. Oh god, what if I smelled? Fidgeting, I grabbed one of her zillion yellow and pink decorative pillows and held on tight, hoping it would ground me for a bit.

After a few minutes, it was obvious Amanda was distracted. She was texting a lot, so eventually I just lowered the volume on the TV and looked her in the face. "Do you want me to leave? It's barely started and you sent whole paragraphs in three different message apps already."

Amanda shook her head, sighing and handing her phone to me. "Can you put it on the charger please? Maybe then I won't be so fucking rude."

"Don't be fucking rude." I parroted the meme in a high-pitched voice, dropping her phone onto the wireless charging pad on her nightstand.

Amanda, of course, was right on cue. "Oh my GAWD."

I giggled. Amanda and I had seen enough old Vine compilations together to be able to quote any and all memes with perfect timing, and it was nice to know it was still true—even if nowadays there was more boyfriend talk than meme quoting.

"I'm just getting so many texts about band. Mr. Menendez is becoming more and more of a dictator the closer we get to Pigskin." Amanda sighed, lowering the volume of the TV. "I hate football season. I just want to keep watching TV with you here for the rest of our lives."

I smiled. "I don't think Columbia would like it if you ditched your schoolwork and extracurriculars to watch reality TV with me."

"Probably not, to be perfectly honest." She shifted on her pillow pile so she was on her side, looking at me. "I just wish it was like it used to be. Just us, no responsibilities, no school or boyfriends or—"

"No boyfriends?" I couldn't help but ask.

Amanda chuckled. "I just know we don't hang out as much anymore because I'm with him a lot of the time. And I kind of miss having time with you." She tilted her head to the side, smiling ruefully. "It's almost like you're my best friend or something gross like that."

I rolled my eyes, poking her cheek until she laughed. "You're so sappy. It's fine. We're just . . . I don't know, growing up? Is that what this is?"

"Having no time for anything fun ever? Sounds a lot like growing up." Amanda pulled back, stretching. "Is there anything new in Maggieland that I should know about?"

Um, the fact that the middle school feelings I tried to smother with a pillow of repression had resurfaced and were wreaking havoc?

But I was prepared for this; I learned a long time ago that I had to rehearse before I lied to literally anyone, so my anxiety led me to have a lot of imaginary conversations with people when I was in the shower. "I've just been stressed about this art assignment." It was technically true. This project—and the reason behind it—was driving me up the wall.

Amanda nodded. "I heard Dani talking about it the other day at lunch. Mrs. Lozano is a whack job, but it seems pretty dope. Instagram and everything. If anyone could get an A on this, it's you, Gunner Stahl."

I smiled. Of course Amanda would remember one of my favorite music photographers. "I hope you're right."

"Duh. Are you sure that's all that's bothering you?"

I nodded. Still not technically a lie.

"Good. I hate thinking there's some secret part of you that you're hiding from me. It was hard enough when you came out. I hated the idea that you had been all alone, listening to emo music in your room—"

Leave it to Amanda to make my coming out about her. "Hey—"

Amanda ignored me. "Going through this really hard time and you couldn't even talk to me about it." I had drawn my legs up to my chest at some point in the conversation, and I jolted when Amanda reached out and put a hand on each of my knees. We were close now, too close. I could count each one of Amanda's freckles, every fleck in her hazel eyes. I bit my lip, afraid to breathe, as Amanda said, "You know you can talk to me, right?" Her voice was low but gentle, a hushed assurance.

But that was the thing. The number of things I couldn't talk to her about was increasing. I couldn't tell her about how uncertain I was about the future we'd so carefully planned together, and I couldn't tell her about my feelings for her. She was the only person I wanted to talk to about any of these things, but now I couldn't, and how fucked was that?

Amanda continued, serious, eyes steady on me. "And if it's, like, a bisexual thing, you can also talk to me about it. Boy, girl, person, whoever . . . I'm here for it."

I bit my lip. Why did she have to add that? I wanted her to be my girlfriend, not just my best friend, and that was the biggest secret of all.

"Yeah, I know," I lied.

"Even if it's someone totally sus like Trish and Matthew

were," Amanda said, cracking a smile and running a hand over my curls. I leaned into her hand instinctively.

When we were younger, Amanda had been my safe place, my constant, especially once my mother started to rely on me more to help with Alyssa. My indecision about NYU, my crush on her . . . it was opening a chasm between us that widened by the day, and I didn't know how to stop it.

Well, I had an idea.

My eyes lingered on Amanda's lips. She was so close. I could find out once and for all if she felt the same way as I did. I could close this distance, reach across it and bend the earth to my will to bring us together, if I was brave enough, and if she was willing. I scanned Amanda's face, looking for any sign of discomfort, anything that could prevent me from leaning in and—

Amanda's phone dinged. Amanda reached for it, the bubble bursting, and I pulled back, shaking the last few seconds from my head. Her eyes widened as she read the text, and she grinned before feverishly typing away.

"Wait, Josh Ortega is having a party and Jaime wants me to go." Amanda was up off the bed, immediately rummaging through her closet.

Of course. Jaime. "I don't really wanna go anywhere right now."

Amanda looked up at me, two glittery bodycon dresses in her hands. "Come on, pleeeease," she wheedled, her eyes wide and pleading. "I'll owe you, like, a zillion."

I sighed loudly, nodding. I'd never been able to refuse her anything—for better or worse.

When Amanda went to do her hair in the bathroom, I wandered to her vanity, examining the bottles of beauty products. The last of the sun's light was being filtered through the dark pink curtains, tingeing the bottles rosy. Fumbling with my phone, I snapped a picture, enhancing the photo so the bottles looked extra pink, editing them to look slightly blurred and ethereal, like something you would see in a fairy's private chambers or a Hayley Kiyoko music video.

The return of my feelings for you scares me, A. I thought I was over this, but you still have the power over me. What if now I'm going to spend the rest of our friendship pining after you, avoiding looking at you whenever you wear something revealing or memorizing every touch like it's the last one we'll ever share? You've been my best friend for so long. I never thought that you could ever be anything more, but now that I have even a trace of hope . . .

---

The party was being held in El Ranchito, the rural middle ground between San Benito and Brownsville. A poorer area near the border fence, the neighborhoods were sprawling, with acres of open space separating one tiny house from the next, making it the premier party destination.

Speeding down a winding, dimly lit country road, Amanda swerved to avoid a pothole. There was a horse tied up on the side of a ditch, and the streetlights made everything a warm brown, moving back into the black as soon as we were out of the halo of light.

I clicked through Spotify; Charli XCX was the only way to start a night out. "Next Level Charli" filled the car. Pulling up the group chat, I scanned the messages.

**Amanda:** ROLE CALL who is going to Josh's?!?
**Dani:** *girl raising her hand emoji*

**Matthew:** It's ROLL call
**Jordan:** At least be accurate when you're yelling at us
**Amanda:** Fckn nerds
**Maggie:** ANYWAY
**Jordan:** I can't go, church in the AM
**Maggie:** Okay say a prayer for us bc we'll be busy sinning thx

"Who else is going?" I asked, rolling up the window so I wouldn't have to shout.

Amanda shrugged. "The usual, probably a bunch of the football team and the cheerleaders. That group of artsy burnouts that's friends with Josh's older brother."

My phone buzzed, the group chat its own private party.

**Dani:** Omg there are so many people where are you guys *side-eye emoji*
**Matthew:** Yeah it's lit pull up *fire emoji*

"Tell them we're here," Amanda said.

We had turned onto Joines Road, and Josh Ortega's house was lit up with rainbow lights that pulsed with the bass of the music blaring from inside. There were already cars piling up in and around the driveway, parked precariously on either side of the ditches in front of the house. Amanda pulled over and parked in the field next to the house, cutting the engine.

The house looked out of place, a loud and colorful oasis against the dark rural night. I hesitated as I watched people exiting and entering, tripping over each other, laughter cutting through the night.

"Wait, before we go in," Amanda said, holding up a hand.

She stopped in front of the house and said, "Put your skills and your three cameras to use and take a picture of my outfit for Insta."

"So bossy." But I took out my phone anyway, opening up the camera. "Switch places with me, you're backlit like this."

We switched spots, and Amanda smoothed her hair back, flipping it as she turned to look over her shoulder, ass in full view. I bit the inside of my cheek. My eyes tracked Amanda's form on the tiny screen because it was safer than staring straight at Amanda as I took it all in: the black bodycon dress that left no curve hidden, the hoop earrings and red heels she borrowed from her mother every time we went to a party, even though she barely knew how to walk in them.

I snapped the picture, swallowing shakily. "Sending it to you now." I busied myself with sending the photo so that Amanda couldn't see the blush raging on my cheeks.

The little house was packed with people, lights and thumping bass guiding us to the living room, where Justin Resendez, one of the football players, had set up his DJ equipment in a corner. People were grinding on each other in the middle of the room, so crowded I couldn't tell where one body ended and another began. Couples were making out on the couches, along the walls, anywhere with a flat surface and a shadow for "privacy."

Amanda leaned in to call over the music, "Wanna get a drink?"

I nodded. I'd need it if Amanda was planning to be here for a while, and especially if—

"Hey!" Amanda trilled, her voice going up an octave as Jaime met us in the hallway, sliding a hand around her waist in a one-armed hug. Amanda smiled at him, putting a hand on his chest.

If Amanda was going to be hanging off Jaime the whole time.

"Wassup, girl? Maggie, what's good?" Jaime said, not looking away from Amanda, who beamed under his gaze.

"Hey." My chest felt hollow. I looked away, but of course Jaime wouldn't let me go that easily.

"How've you been?" Jaime smiled at me then, like he actually cared what I said, and I wanted to groan because he'd always been nice to me throughout the entirety of their relationship, even during the few times they'd been broken up.

*How have I been?* Shitty since I realized I wanted to kiss his girlfriend. "Good. Hanging in there."

"That's what it's all about." He nodded, and I nodded, and really, what else was there to say? The most we had in common was that we were both in love with the same person, and that wasn't exactly party-appropriate small talk.

"Mags, Amanda, y'all made it." Matthew was wearing a navy button-down, his hair still wet from a shower. He had a standing game of one-on-one with his little brother Abel every Saturday. Was that where he'd come from?

It was weird to know all these little things about the people I loved, even if my relationships with them had changed or, in the case of Trish and my dad, ended completely. My mind felt like a graveyard where memories laid themselves to rest: Karina, one of my best friends in first grade, broke her first bone falling from the monkey bars, Amanda's favorite song in eighth grade was "I Miss You" by Blink-182, and my dad used to grill once a month and would burn the carne asada every time, but he never gave up. My mom made fun of him but still ate it because she didn't want to waste money, and she thought it was funny anyway.

What could I do with these pieces, the love I had, if there was no one to give them to?

"Yeah, it's great to see you," Tori said in a tone that said it definitely *wasn't*. I ignored the barb as I saw Dani across the room and waved her to us. Dani's smile opened up as she noticed and started walking over.

When she emerged from the crowd, it was impossible not to notice how much more relaxed Dani looked outside of school. Casual in a black tank top, ripped jeans, and strappy black sandals, with sweet-smelling brown hair fresh from the shower and beginning to curl, she looked completely chilled in the crowd. She looked as peaceful here as she did when I'd seen her at the concert. Fascinating. I was super on edge, because *crowds*, so it was nice to know that someone else, at least, felt at ease here.

The group moved to the kitchen for drinks. It was calmer there than in the living room, as the lights were on and people were lounging around the counters and chatting.

I had always been the smallest one of our group—consequences of being a preemie—but that meant I was always the speediest too. I was also the one least concerned with elbowing people out of the way, so I was the first to the cooler on the floor, haphazardly digging cans of Modelo and Natty Light out of the ice.

"Come get your beer, I'm not your mom," I called out to the rest of the group.

We passed the cans around as Josh Ortega emerged from the back hall, booming, "Whaddup, y'all?"

Huge but not a football player, country but not a Future Farmers of America kid, Josh didn't quite fit into any group. He floated from clique to clique, friendly with all of us, and his easygoing nature combined with the fact that his dad was never home made him the ideal host of our underage hijinks.

"Glad y'all came. Matthew, Jaime, what's going on?" he asked, fist-bumping all of us with his beer. "It's Dani, right?"

Josh was looking at Dani, eyes gleaming hungrily. Narrowing my own eyes, I moved closer to her.

Dani didn't notice, just said, "Yeah, we have Dual Economics together."

"I have that third period," I jumped in. Best to play offense here. "What did you guys think of the test?"

Josh and Matthew immediately started complaining about it, so it was a suitable distraction. I didn't know why Josh looking at Dani made me so on edge, but then again, did I really need a tangible reason to be afraid of men?

As if to prove my point, some guy crossing behind me decided to cop a feel.

I had practiced these kinds of imaginary conflicts in my head before, but I still surprised myself when I didn't hesitate, whipping around and dumping my beer on him, shaking it until every last drop fell out of the can. He swore, the string of expletives slurred, and I spat, "Don't fucking touch me" and threw the can at his face for good measure.

Like a shot, Matthew was in front of me, shoving the guy in the chest until he banged against the stove. I stepped back to rest against the counter and just watched as Josh leapt into action, grabbing the guy by the shirt.

"Get the fuck out of my house, now," Josh ordered, tugging the perv's collar hard as he and Matthew crowded him against the counter.

"What the fuck—"

"Now." Matthew's voice was calm but forceful, the threat of thunder without the loud clap.

The guy swore again, spitting at Matthew's feet before Josh

half led, half hauled him out of the kitchen. Matthew glared after him before turning to me, his face softening.

"You okay?" he mumbled.

I nodded. The tremble of my chin was embarrassing, but then I saw that concerned frown that had always made me feel safe when we were dating. It still did. "I didn't need you to fight for me."

"You did that perfectly well on your own," Matthew said, that damn crooked smile emerging on his face.

Matthew's eyes were gleaming with pride and a little adrenaline, and I could've combusted on the spot. How easy it would be to sink into his arms again, how no one would think it was strange if I hugged him after a scene like this—

"Nice hustle, babe."

No one except his girlfriend.

I felt the bubble bursting, the golden hero's gleam extinguished by Tori, striding into his arms and giving him a deep kiss. Matthew waved sheepishly back at us as Tori dragged him out of the kitchen and down the darkened hall. I turned to Amanda and Dani.

Amanda made her distinct retching sound, which never failed to make me laugh, and it worked. "I can't believe they have the audacity to do that in front of you. You good?" she asked me, putting her hand on my arm and squeezing. I gave her a weak smile.

Dani simply looked alarmed by the whole thing, eyebrows reaching her hairline and her mouth screwed up in disgust as she said, "Do you need to get out of here?"

Amanda nodded, watching me.

I shook my head. The whole thing had just made me want to be distracted tonight anyway. "I'm good. Let's not let it ruin our night, yeah?"

"All right. Well, I'm going to go check out the backyard, maybe get some air," Dani announced, looking around at everyone before her eyes lingered on me. "It's getting kind of stuffy."

"I'll go with you," I immediately volunteered.

Jaime and Amanda looked at each other before Amanda said, "Nah, we're gonna go do something somewhere else. Have fun, though!"

She tugged Jaime's arm, and he grinned as they exited the kitchen, wandering off into the living room. Looking at Dani, I suddenly felt shy. We'd been texting steadily since our conversation about *She-Ra*, about school and friends and music and which taqueria in San Benito was the best (trick question: Brownsville had *the best* tacos, and I'd been so relieved that Dani agreed),but in-person interactions still made me a little jumpy. Oh geez, I was so bad at this.

Dani just smiled. "Lead the way."

We went out the back door to the patio area, where people were smoking cigarettes or joints and chatting quietly. The fields stretched out all around them, the sound of everyone's conversation drowned out by the quiet of the night. Even through the haze of smoke, I could count every star. I know this area wasn't the best, but it was my favorite, and as far as I was concerned, San Benito didn't have areas much better than this, wide open spaces with a black sky studded with stars.

I enjoyed being so far outside the city, especially at night. The openness of the fields and the winking stars felt holy in a way that my years going to church never had. My eyes swept the backyard before I pointed to a picnic table off to one side, where a group of people were leaving.

When we were situated on top of the table, I drew my knees in, as Dani stretched out beside me, leaning back on her elbows. Fishing something out of her pocket, she asked, "Do you smoke?"

"I'm not big on tobacco." I despised the smell of cigarettes. My mother used to smoke them when I was younger but had quit ten years ago. Still, the smell lingered at the edge of my memories.

"Me either. This is a joint. Unless you don't smoke that either, then I have nothing to offer you, and I won't smoke this in front of you."

I smiled, relieved at both the fact that Dani didn't smoke cigarettes and that she knew to ask for my consent. "Then yeah, I'll split that with you." Dani offered me the joint, but I shook my head, saying, "You first."

Dani flicked the lighter and lit the joint, the tip glowing an orange that was almost violently bright against the blue night. Inhaling steadily, she took the joint away, holding it delicately between her slender fingers as she released the smoke after a few seconds, forming a perfect O with her pretty, rosy lips.

I watched, hypnotized. *Wow.*

"Cool trick, huh?" Dani grinned, holding the joint out.

Still starstruck, all I could do was nod dazedly, taking the joint. Disgusted with myself at how grossly objectifying I was being, I took a big hit. I really needed to calm the fuck down right now.

We passed the joint back and forth between us a couple more times until Dani said, "I'm sorry that guy was such an asshole. Really, though, are you okay?"

I smiled at her gentleness. "Yeah, just a little shook, but it'll pass. It happens. It's not right, but like—" I shrugged. "Toxic masculinity ruins everything."

"Tell me about it." Dani blew out smoke, tapping off ash on the side of the table.

"Josh seemed to like you, though."

"Sucks for him. I'm into girls," Dani said. "As my choice of favorite characters might have given away." She smiled ruefully as she passed me the joint.

All I could do was stare as I took it, the end smoldering uselessly as I tried to process what she said. She was queer. Gay? A lesbian? I didn't know. The point was, she liked girls. That meant she could like me, maybe. The idea of that was fucking terrifying.

"Huh. Well, that explains the fact that your all-time favorite character is Villanelle. How else could I possibly take that?"

"I'd hoped that would give it away," Dani said, giving me a half smile.

My heart jumped. Talking to a new person over text is one thing, but actually confronting someone with the reality of your shit is different, so I understood the need for code-switching and subtlety, and I smiled at her. "You could've just asked me if I listened to girl in red, and I totally would've known what you meant."

Dani laughed. "Ugh, you're so right. I completely forgot. I'm a terrible lesbian."

Ah, so that answered *that* question. "You're allowed a pass maybe, but I'm not a lesbian, so I can't say. I'm bisexual. In case you couldn't tell by the cuffed jeans and the flannel."

Dani smiled shyly. "I suspected, but thanks for confirming. Makes things a lot easier."

What the fuck did *that* mean?

Maybe it was the joint that had made my tongue looser, or maybe it was the half-moon hanging above us, clear as fucking day. Or maybe it was just Dani herself, the way she leaned in to listen to me as though there was no one in the world with a sweeter voice.

"Why did you leave your old school?" I realized I had said that out loud, and I cringed. "Sorry if that was too personal."

Dani's face darkened a bit, and fear seized my chest. Had I asked too much, been too intrusive? But Dani looked pensive, as though she was thinking about how much to divulge. "My dad got a new job here. But I think it was also just good timing."

"Why is that?"

"I had a girlfriend. She was . . . She wasn't always good to me, and I didn't really react to it well." Dani looked at the ground. "By the time it was over, she'd taken all my friends and spread rumors about me to everyone. It just got really unbearable. I had to quit cheerleading because we were on the team together. That's why we moved."

Dani had looked so familiar when we'd first met, and that must have been why: I'd seen her face on a sponsorship poster on the wall at Las Vegas Cafe in Harlingen, where one of my tías worked and often gave us free food when we went there for dinner once a week. The click in my brain was satisfying.

But the story seemed to weigh down her shoulders, making her hunch in on herself. Pushing past the careful distance I'd put between us, I reached out and touched Dani's hand, which rested on the table, patting it twice.

"Well," I offered softly, "you have friends now. And no rumors here. I don't even know anything about you, really."

"Do you want to?" Dani asked, uncertain.

"Yeah." I thought about it for a moment before amending, "But whenever you want to tell me. No rush. We have time."

There was a pause, and then a wide smile bloomed on Dani's face, and damn if the look in her eyes didn't make me feel like all the stars in the sky had some competition. "I appreciate it," Dani said softly.

The sound of glass shattering disturbed the night air, followed by a burst of wild laughter. We both turned to the sound before seeing no one was hurt and losing interest. Dani's gaze swept around us. "It's beautiful out here. I'd love to draw this."

That was news to me. "You draw?"

"Yeah, for pretty much my whole life. You do photography, right?"

I nodded. "What do you like to draw?"

Dani smiled. "Everything. Landscapes, people, things. Sometimes just stuff I see in my head. I mostly use graphite or charcoal. I've drawn some of my cousins' tattoos, which is pretty cool."

That was *so punk*. "Do you have pictures? Can I see?"

Dani grinned, proudly bringing out her phone and flipping through her photos. I drank in the stream of sketched doodles of cities and flowers and space, as well as fleshed-out drawings of hands and eyes and lips. I was struck by the intricacy of her designs, especially when she showed me the ones that had been used for tattoos.

"I didn't have a lot of time to dedicate to it at my old school because of cheer, so quitting and moving here improved my art at least. I'm trying to get into RISD, so . . ." She shrugged.

That was interesting. I hadn't met another person in our grade, besides Amanda, who wanted to leave Texas for college. People didn't often leave the comfort zone that was the Valley, which is why Amanda and I had always stuck together.

So Amanda and I did extracurriculars and studied our asses off, and we kept each other sane in the process. Knowing Dani wanted to go to RISD made it clear how we ended up in all the same clubs and extracurriculars. We were all chasing the same dream.

Even if I wasn't quite sure it was mine anymore.

"I'm trying to get into NYU. Glad you could join me in my suffering."

Dani laughed, but the statement sat at the bottom of my stomach like I'd swallowed the pit of an avocado. Why did it feel like a lie? I was *technically* still trying to get into NYU, even if I wasn't sure about it. I was covering all my bases, laying down the foundation for the life I wanted. Had wanted. Wasn't sure I still wanted.

But I liked having that dream in common with Dani, and if it was *technically* true for the moment, maybe it didn't matter that this connection we shared was a bit more fragile than she realized. Even if it *did* make me feel like shit.

"Yeah, so I guess something good did come out of my breakup: I figured out that I'd totally neglected my own life to make that relationship work. So now I'm just trying to focus on school and art and trying to get into RISD." Dani shrugged one shoulder. "Since my last relationship was a garbage fire, I'm not exactly rushing to get into a new one right now, so that makes it easier to focus on the rest of my life."

My stomach plummeted to my feet, and guilt crept into my brain. My feelings for her would only complicate her plans for her life, and after learning so much about her . . . I couldn't help but want the best for her, even if it meant breaking my own heart in the process.

Maybe that was what it took, though. Sometimes you had to break a bone in order to set it right again, and I was more than willing to crack myself open if it meant we'd both have a better chance at healing.

Dani kept showing me more photos of her art, and by the time she was done, I had to pick my jaw up off the floor to say, "These are incredible. You're *really* talented."

"Thank you." Dani gave the shyest smile, and my stomach dropped like I'd missed a step on the stairs. There was something so intimate about showing people your art, like you're cracking your chest open and turning your heart inside out to show them what's inside. That vulnerability, that honesty, shone on her face like the sun on the surface of the ocean, and it was impossible to look away.

With the art, Dani looking like *that*, and my low tolerance for weed, I knew it was only a matter of time before I did something that would ruin everything, like ask to kiss her or confess my undying love and offer to run away to Mexico with her, and that would be really, really inconvenient for both of us. "I need to find a bathroom."

At least in the house there would be more people and fewer chances of us being alone together.

We braved the throng of thrashing bodies on the dance floor to the kitchen, tiptoeing down the hall, which split into two smaller hallways. Dani offered to check the left one while I went down the right. I fumbled for the knob and found it, not bothering to knock before walking in.

The first thing I saw was the king-sized bed. The second was the porcelain skin of Tori's bare back, peeking out through her unzipped dress, from the center of the bed.

I wanted to run, but I was rooted to the floor, even as Tori whipped around, searching for the cause of the sudden intrusion, and Matthew came into view, his head craned to look over Tori's shoulder. His eyes widened at the sight of me standing there. "Shit, Maggie, can you—"

"I had to pee," I blurted, my face burning. "Sorry!"

Without waiting for a response, I scrambled for the door, yelping as I banged my knee against the frame in my haste to leave. I slammed the door, tripping down the hall. Through the darkness of the house, I couldn't quite see where I was going, but anywhere was better than the tiny glimpse of hell I had just been subjected to.

The need to pee had been shocked out of me, so I lingered at the end of the hall, brain swimming as I tried to process the scene I'd walked into. I knew I should go find Dani or at the very least some vodka to pour into my eyes. Anything to erase the image of tall, slim, perfect Tori straddling my ex-boyfriend.

Tears pricked at my eyes. I leaned against the wall, tilting my head up toward the ceiling and trying to blink them away. The haze of my high had vanished, and now I was left with all my emotions in full force, the pain of what I'd just seen carving a hole in my chest.

It had once been me and Matthew who had slunk away from parties and other group hangouts, finding excuses to meet in bathrooms or to find the one corner of someone's yard where the floodlights didn't reach. Stealing kisses in cars, on back porches, behind tool sheds and under bleachers. The memories came one by one, weighing on my windpipe like stones.

And what was I to Matthew, really? Just a girl to vent to over pizza?

I couldn't think about this anymore. I needed to get out of here, get away from it, from *him*.

"Maggie!" I whipped around to find Amanda hurrying down the hall toward me, Dani on her heels. "I don't want to be here anymore," Amanda complained. "Let's go. This party is lame anyway."

Trying to shake the green monster climbing up my back, I gave Amanda an expectant look, waiting for her to explain why she looked so sour after going off to make out with her boyfriend of a billion (six) years. "Ookay, what happened to you? Are you drunk? Where's Jaime?"

"No, I'm not drunk and I *don't* want to talk about him," Amanda snapped before looking at Dani. "Do you need a ride home? I'll drive you."

"Yes, that would be great." Dani bit her lip, looking between both of us. "If y'all don't mind."

Amanda looked at her like she had three heads. "Don't be like that, we're like best friends now, so it's cool."

I sent a quick shout-out to God for giving me a distraction from my own melancholic inner monologue. "Great, then now we have the whole ride home to talk about what's got you all fucked up."

After making sure that Amanda hadn't had anything to drink, we started driving, and Amanda started venting.

"Look, I'm not the kind of girl to be like 'What are we gonna be in ten years?' But he keeps being so wishy-washy. It would be nice to at least have something to say when his ex-girlfriend verbally attacks me in fucking AP Calc," Amanda ranted.

I nodded, remembering when Amanda had gotten into a near-smackdown with a sophomore on the varsity soccer team when she said that band kids shouldn't get letter jackets. Her temper was legendary. "That was awful. Who does that?"

"Boys are just so infuriating. You can't just make out with me and then get all fucking clammed up when I wanna talk about something real." Amanda turned to me now that we were at a stoplight. "I wish he was more like you. At least I understand where I'm at with you. Girls are so much easier to talk to. You're lucky that you have twice the options."

I caught movement in my peripheral vision, and I turned to see Dani eyeing me from the back seat, her brow raised at the vaguely insensitive statement. I had no words for her, so I just grimaced in return. "Stop gendering communication. Him not wanting to talk about shit with you is because he's a dickbag, not because he's a guy. Don't make excuses for him."

Amanda grimaced. "What the *hell* is a dickbag?"

"A bag where you keep your dildos?" Dani suggested.

Amanda groaned. "Then I *wish* he was a dickbag. At least then I could get off without feeling morally compromised."

I caught Dani's eye, and we both looked at Amanda, who kept a straight face for point-five seconds before breaking out into a snorting laugh, and so did we.

Later that night, while Amanda snored beside me, I flicked through the photos on my phone. I was tired but my brain wouldn't turn off, so I looked through the few pictures I'd taken of the party. My mind *and* my phone played images of Dani, Matthew, and Amanda on loop, a Möbius strip of romantic torment.

If these issues were going to keep me up at night, I might as well get a good post out of it. The Matthew and Tori sighting had certainly been the most heartbreaking of the evening, the most dramatic, but I didn't want to relive that moment right now. Looking through my profile, I realized I still hadn't introduced Dani, so I got to work.

I found a picture I'd taken of the backyard, golden floodlights illuminating the shadows of partygoers, bobbing like specters in the night, and I edited it a bit so the lights glowed like stars against the dark sky. I added the caption, and the words flowed easily, even though I'd never been much of a writer.

I talked to D for the first time alone tonight. We were in neutral territory, someone else's house, someone else's party. In a way, it felt like I was someone else entirely. Sharing myself with a new person was nerve-wracking and much harder than I expected. It's easier to talk to A or M because I know exactly who I am with them. To D, I'm almost nothing, no one, and I like that. I don't want to jeopardize this new friendship that we have, and she's not looking for anything romantic, so . . . maybe this project will help me get over this so we can be actual friends with nothing else in the way.

As the post appeared on the grid, Amanda's body made the executive decision to roll over, her arm falling heavily across my torso. I froze, locking my phone and sliding it under the pillow hurriedly. I watched Amanda's slumbering form anxiously, trying to see through the dark if her eyes were open. But they weren't, and her breathing hadn't even shifted.

I breathed a sigh of relief and moved to pull out of Amanda's grasp, but her hold tightened, locking me in place for fear of waking her up. I tried not to sigh in exasperation.

To spill your heart on the internet about your feelings for someone while someone *else* you had feelings for was currently trying to spoon you in her sleep made me feel dirty. I should be able to figure out my own feelings by now. Was I just the slutty bisexual I felt like I was?

I was so fucking tired of the mess that was my life right now, but the only way out of this was through it. I locked my phone and pulled the sheets over my head. Hopefully sleep would come soon.

Cupid or Aphrodite or whoever had chosen to inflict me

with the disease of love owed me a few hours of unconscious bliss.

---

Jordan came over for lunch after church the next day. My mom knew about his family situation, so she had made it her personal mission to overfeed him whenever he came over. He always repaid her by helping to set the table and wash the dishes, so it was an arrangement that worked for everyone, really.

It was only after Jordan had inhaled three servings that he asked, "Mrs. G., can Maggie hang out with me after lunch? I'm going to get groceries for my neighbor. We're just going to HEB."

This was news to me, but still I looked at Mom eagerly. There were only ever a handful of opportunities to go out on Sundays, but it was early in the afternoon, so I was going to lobby hard for this. Veronica and Alyssa were silent too, knowing the fragility of the request. "Please, Mami? I'll be back early, I promise."

Mami leaned back in her chair, her brow furrowed in concentration as she deliberated. I pressed my lips together as her eyes flicked down to Jordan's empty plate—good on him for remembering her fondness for his black hole of a stomach—and back up to his puppy dog gaze. "Just to HEB?"

"Yes, ma'am."

Mami cleared her throat. "Hm. Well, fine. Let me get my list."

In Jordan's car, I folded the sticky note with my mom's grocery list and put it in my pocket. "Not that I don't appreciate the invite, but why exactly are we going to get groceries for your neighbor?"

"News of my errand-running business has spread like a disease. I'm rolling in requests." Jordan beamed as he turned onto Sam Houston.

I grinned. "Nice. Look at you, making progress."

Jordan did a little dance with his shoulders. That GIF of Elmo doing a happy dance while sitting on the toilet came to mind. "I'm an entrepreneur, just like that guy that invented Hot Cheetos. Watch me go full capitalist. I might invest in stock and destroy the Wall Street facade."

"A worthwhile mission. Dream big."

As usual for a Sunday afternoon, HEB was bustling, the midday post-church grocery rush in full swing. Just finding a parking spot was difficult, and Jordan had to haphazardly brake every few feet to avoid hitting carts—and the people who steered them—as we crept down the aisles, looking for a spot.

"Time to keep a tally of how many people we see that we know," I said as we secured a spot and got out.

Jordan's head bobbed over the car as he circled it, pushing a cart with, as expected, a squeaky wheel. "First one to five buys food."

"You're on."

The walk to the front door was long enough that sweat beaded on my skin, but the blast of air-conditioned wind as the sliding doors whooshed open chilled me to the bone, and I shivered as we walked down the produce aisle. I fished out my list, scanning the few items my mom wanted, all in the dry goods aisles. "I'm gonna go take care of this."

Jordan scrutinized the list in his hand and ripped it in half. "Dope. Can you get these while you're at it?"

I frowned, taking it. "What do I get out of this? You're the one being paid."

"I'm the one tasked with being your emotional support friend through your lovesick project. Consider this compensation."

"You really are turning into a capitalist."

Jordan grinned, pumping a fist in the air. "Sweet, I'm already on the come up."

Weaving through the aisles of HEB is like a real-life game of Minesweeper. I'd barely gotten through half the items on our combined list and I'd already spotted two kids from school and one teacher, all of whom I'd avoided by immediately doing a one-eighty and leaving the aisle the way I'd come. Dramatic? Maybe, but HEB had a magical way of trapping you in ill-timed conversation.

But as I turned to leave the canned goods aisle with the last few items I needed, I realized the universe wouldn't let me out of this without a fight.

My torso collided with the corner of someone's approaching cart, knocking the wind out of me, and I yelped.

"I am so sorry!" I heard, and the familiar voice made me snap up.

Dani's bright brown eyes froze me in place, and her lips split into a grin mid-apology. "Maggie, hi."

My cheeks were burning, and my brain was blank, so the only thing I was able to spit out was "I'm sorry."

Dani laughed, shaking her head and leaning over the cart. She was the picture of calm and collected in her olive-green Henley and worn high-top Vans, chestnut curls in a messy, loose bun. It wasn't fair how pretty she looked on a routine grocery trip. "I think this is one of those chicken-egg situations where it's either neither of our faults or both, so I'm sorry too."

"A conundrum indeed." I rubbed my stomach a bit and shifted the basket I was carrying to prop it on my other hip. "So what are you doing here?"

Dani cocked an eyebrow, her lips twitching. "Getting groceries?"

I rubbed the back of my neck. "Oh, um, I mean, yeah, that makes sense."

Dani chuckled again. "I'm here with my mom. She's arguing with the guy at the carnicería, so I left before things got too heated."

"Things are getting spicy in the meat department fandom."

"Exactly. You get it. How are you?"

"I'm good, just here with Jordan actually. He's off, somewhere, I think—"

"Right behind you," Dani finished, nodding past me.

"Beep beep," I heard, and I turned to see Jordan rolling up, feet up on the bottom bar of the cart as its momentum propelled him toward us. "Dani! Fancy seeing you here."

"Hey! Maggie and I just ran into each other. Literally."

Dani beamed like it was the most amusing joke in the world, and I laughed. "Come on, that pun was practically handed to you."

She grinned. "Still made you laugh though."

I flushed. "Shut up."

I looked at Jordan for some relief from the depth of her gaze but almost groaned at the look on his face as he glanced between the two of us. "Say, Dani, I can't help but think this is fate."

I threw him a look. Where was he going with this?

"Maggie and I were going to hang out after this, but after having hung out with her for ten years, I'm pretty bored of her—"

"What the fuck, Jordan?"

Jordan waved his hand. "You know what I mean."

"No, I don't—"

"So I could use some fresh friend blood," he continued. "Do you wanna hang out with us after this?"

I stared at him, trying to suppress a glare but still send the message that I was *not* okay with this. Dani, however, seemed oblivious. "Really? That would be great, if y'all don't mind driving me home after. I just need to ask my mom and we'll probably finish up in a bit."

Jordan nodded, beaming. "Yay! You can just meet us at the front, and we'll go from there?"

"It's a plan." Dani clapped her hands and waved as she turned the corner, out of view.

I waved back until she was out of sight, then smacked Jordan with the back of that same hand, glaring at him. "What the fuck is wrong with you?"

"Ow, stop. You're so violent."

"Why did you do that? I didn't even have time to do my hair before we came!" I groaned, gesturing at my frizzy waves and ripped jean shorts, my worn Mayday Parade T-shirt. "I'm not ready for this."

"That's why it's perfect! Maggie, the HEB gods have presented you with a miracle!" He gestured up at the ceiling, as though there were angels flying around instead of stray grackles that had flown in from outside. "You can get to know her outside of school, just like you know the rest of us."

"I already talked to her at the party—"

"This is different, it's one-on-one."

"Then what are you doing here?"

Jordan snorted. "I'm your courage *obviously* since you're such a chicken. I'm the third wheel so you don't psyche yourself out."

I pouted. As much as I hated to admit it, this was kind of

brilliant. "Fine. You're right. But if I totally humiliate myself in front of her, it's on your conscience."

"Oh, you *definitely* will. I can't wait to watch." He gave me a toothy grin, and I smacked him in the shoulder again, continuing down the aisle as he squawked.

My hands were shaking as we gathered the last of the groceries and paid, and I half expected that Dani wouldn't show, but there she was, smiling by the curb, and despite the change in plans, I felt at ease. She was my friend, after all, and that mattered more than any crush.

"Everyone ready?" Jordan asked.

Dani grinned. "Let's have an adventure."

We had to drop off the groceries to Jordan's neighbor first, and then to my mom (who thankfully only gave me a moderate amount of shit for going out after the grocery run). After that, we made our way to the trail.

The Heavin Resaca Trail was a broken-up three-mile loop around part of the resaca, which cut through San Benito like a winding rattlesnake. The large park, surrounded by neighborhoods on all sides, was one of the only things about the town that had changed drastically in my short life. When I was a child, the trail had only been a broken asphalt path that looped unevenly around the water. The city got so many complaints from people who endured broken ankles and bike accidents on it that they had to have the whole thing repaved, so the asphalt was stark black and smooth as glass. It threw me off every time when I could walk across it without rolling an ankle on a crack.

The afternoon sun was as bright as ever when we pulled up to the abandoned grain factory, but the slight breeze was enough to trigger that special fall feeling, the one that told you things were changing, ending, maybe even beginning if you got the timing right, despite everything looking mostly the same. We crossed the street warily, checking both ways. A teenage girl, a junior at San Benito, had died a few years ago crossing this same intersection on a run, hit by a careless driver, so now we were careful, the anxiety making us look both ways multiple times before we walked. We passed families with children, having barbecues at the picnic tables, and some teenagers canoodling on a bench.

And yes, I meant our table. I ran my fingers over the many sets of initials carved into the wood, finding Jordan's, and Amanda's, and mine and Matthew's, dated last fall. Jordan, who of course never left home without his skateboard, skated up ahead as we sat down, and Dani and I studied the carvings and Sharpie-scribbled initials and dates scrawled across the chipped wood.

"Wanna add your name?" I asked her.

Dani tucked her hair behind her ear, fiddling with the strand when it caught in her piercings. "Are you sure? I know y'all don't know me that well . . ."

Romeo might have had the right idea: to be that hand, so close to that pretty face.

Oh my god, I was a creep.

Jordan skated back to us, his eyes lighting up when he saw us looking at the carvings. "Oh, are you adding Dani? We should! I mean, we liked you enough to add you to the group even though we didn't know you in middle school."

I frowned. "What does middle school have to do with it?"

Jordan shrugged. "I feel like after we met Matthew and Amanda at Miller, we just stopped having the capacity to tolerate anyone else. Matthew and Amanda are *a lot*, especially after Matthew got his hooks into Maggie. We didn't get any peace after that."

I blushed and shoved him, and he laughed. "You're so rude." I took out my house key, handing it to Dani. "Your choice. Just a hint though: We reeeeally want you to choose us as friends."

*Me. Choose me.*

Dani smiled, and god, it was blinding. She took the key and carved her initials into the wood, and as soon as I looked at the batch of initials, an uneasy feeling settled in my stomach. Now it was permanent, her addition to the group. What if something happened that drove her away? This picnic table was a witness, practically a contract, and if things went sour, I'd always have to look at it and remember what could have been.

I didn't want to mess this up. Why couldn't my heart just let go of these pesky feelings? I wanted more than anything to leave her alone, to not complicate her life with my shit, but every time she did something, all I could think about was how much I wanted her, how much I wanted her to want me.

But I wanted her to be happy more, so I'd hold myself back, even if it hurt.

We walked along the asphalt until we were on the other side of the trail at the amphitheater, the area lit up in gold.

Jordan skated up and down the asphalt, around the ramp of the stage, and Dani pointed to the large concrete steps serving as bleachers beyond the stage.

"Wanna sit?" Dani asked, and I nodded eagerly.

"I'm going to skate along the water so I can test these out," Jordan said, gesturing at the new lime-green wheels as he skated past us. "Be back in a few!"

"Fine, just dump the old for the new. Whatever, Jordan!" I whined at his retreating back.

Hopping expertly over a crack in the sidewalk, he gave me the finger without looking back, and I laughed. Had my oldest friend just set me up on a trial date without even discussing it with me?

As Dani turned to face me with an adorably small smile, I was glad he had.

"I like this trail. It's nice. Ours is too big; I always feel like I'm going to be murdered when I go through there alone."

"This piece-of-junk land? It's okay. But you guys have that park out by the HEB. That's waaaay bigger than this. And you have an actual set of walking trails, not a barely there circle."

Dani considered this before shrugging. "McKelvey is nice and all, especially at Christmas. But other than that, it just feels empty. Look at all those people over there. They're together, and they're happy, and we can see them having a good time. It almost makes me feel like I'm a part of that happiness."

She pointed, and I saw the family that had taken their kids out to the basketball court, some of the kids running, shrieking, toward the playground. Laughter boomed from the area, clear even from all the way over there.

I thought about McKelvey Park with its elaborate series of walking trails that looped around a playground on a hill, overlapping one another, and sloped toward the Rio Grande River. There always seemed to be new hiding places popping up and new roads to explore, but sometimes those parts took you too far from the whole. Here, there was almost a built-in community in that every part of it was laid out in the open, looping in on itself. It was an open, almost honest, space, not hiding in the slightest.

It almost made me want to be honest too, about the secret I held right now, but then I looked at Dani and remembered what exactly I was hiding, and why I was hiding it, and how much I really didn't want to say anything and ruin this fragile bond we'd created. So I just said, "I see what you mean" and hoped she couldn't hear what I was holding back.

Dani nodded. Next to her, the amphitheater lit up her profile. From this angle, the light gave Dani an ethereal golden glow, and I couldn't help but long for my camera.

"Can I, um—" I blushed. I hoped this didn't sound creepy. "Can I take a picture of you right now? There's really good light, and I like to, ya know—"

Dani broke out in a smile. "Yeah, of course you can."

I was relieved. Any more awkward bumbling, and I probably would've fainted. "Okay, cool, hold still." I took out my phone, opening the camera and zooming in.

"Should I smile, or . . . ?"

"Hmm, just do what feels right, I guess. Either way, you look great." The words fell out of my mouth before I could remind myself not to be creepy, but Dani didn't look put out by it. She just smiled that soft smile that I was starting to crave, like when you haven't had water in a while and remember how much you need it.

Everything else fell away as I looked at the screen. The way Dani gazed into the lens made the whole situation feel intimate, as though there was no one else but us in this stretch of dark. My finger hovered over the shutter button, knowing that as soon as I pressed it, this moment would be over.

I comforted myself, silently promising to find the next one. I hit the button.

"Wow," Dani said, nodding when I showed her the photo. "I saw you taking pictures at the show that time, but I forgot to ask if I could see them. You're *really* great at this."

I stood up a bit straighter, smiling shyly. "Thanks. It's fun, and I like showing people at their most honest, or at their best. Or both."

Dani smiled. "Are you doing photography for your art assignment?"

I nodded. "Yup." I really didn't want her to ask any more questions about my project, so I decided to take the spotlight off me by asking, "What are you doing for yours?"

Dani smiled and said, "I'm documenting my first semester at a new school, but I'm drawing stuff, not taking photos, so I can imagine your project must be a whole different beast."

I let out a short, wild laugh at that. "You could say that."

The sound of Jordan's board meeting the railing jerked my gaze away from Dani, and I was relieved as we watched him, quiet for a moment.

I looked out at the water, at the fountain in the middle of the canal, and past it, to the swings, the children riding bikes and scooters and skateboards. Now that Dani had mentioned it, the park did have a certain charm. The playground equipment and benches looked less run-down and more worn and loved, and the perpetual screams of children's laughter made you feel like you weren't alone, even if you were.

"We've been coming here for years," I said. "It was the first place we were allowed to hang out on our own, away from our parents."

Well, not completely alone. Our parents had eased their grip on our lives a little bit when we reached eighth grade, but my mother was the most reluctant, so she often sent Veronica—then a senior in high school—to tail us subtly. I had distinct memories of hanging out with the group at the trail and seeing Veronica and CJ, posted up on the dilapidated swing set or eating McDonald's at a picnic table, always a respectable distance away.

Dani smiled. "We usually went to the movies."

"Ah, right. Y'all had money." I tried to inject as much humor into my voice as I could, but it still sounded bitter. My childhood had been spent scrounging for every last penny, and

Harlingen was two times the size of San Benito, with more white people and money than people in San Benito had seen in their life.

Dani raised a brow. "Wow, is that what you think?"

"Well, I mean . . ." I trailed off, feeling the acidic bite of instant regret on my tongue.

Dani sighed. "I had friends with money, yeah, but also, six-dollar Tuesdays are a thing for us too. And I know you guys go to the movies sometimes. Amanda told me y'all went to the midnight premiere of the last Marvel movie together."

I cringed, knowing she was right. "Yeah. I'm sorry."

Dani's smile was impish. "It's okay. Most people just assume everyone who went to Harlingen is white and has money, which is most of the time true but not always."

"Fair. So you hung out at McKelvey often, then?"

Dani nodded. "Of course we did. It was big enough to get lost in, and sometimes that's what we needed. And after everything that happened, I took walks there myself a lot. I must have mapped that whole place twice over, from beginning to end."

Dani's stray curls were falling from her bun, her face tilted serenely into the breeze. The heaviness that Dani hinted at didn't show in her expression, in her eyes, and I wondered how hard she had worked to not let the world harden her.

"Weren't you afraid? To be out there all alone?"

Dani shook her head. "If there is anything Harlingen taught me, it's better to be lost and alone than to know where you are and wish you were anywhere else. I think that learning that has helped me a lot in my singlehood. I think I like it too much now, to be honest."

My throat squeezed, and I hated that I wanted to cry at that because I couldn't do anything to make myself feel better about it. It was what it was: Dani wanted to be alone, and I wanted to be with her, and there was no getting around that.

Dani didn't seem to notice my internal conflict. She just swept her arm out, changing the subject. "I bet you get some really good pictures out here."

"I do actually." In my head, I flipped through my memories of summer, shots of the group hanging out here at sunset, close-ups of birds and flowers, one huge aerial shot of the whole trail that I took when Matthew swiped his older brother's drone. "I guess I've never thought about it before."

I had never thought of the photos I took here as extraordinary, simply because I got similar shots all over the Valley, but then I remembered that not many places in the world had this kind of access to nature, the chance to just exist alongside its magic and capture it with the press of a button. Would I be able to find this when I left for college, or would I always be searching for that beautiful backdrop, the perfect sunset, everywhere I went?

The thought put a lump in my throat. The choice between staying or leaving was already difficult, and it felt even more impossible now.

"Yo, can we get ice cream? I'm dying," Jordan said, skating up to us. I swam to the surface of consciousness. I was grateful for Jordan in that moment because if I thought too hard about the future, I was going to start crying, and I didn't want to ruin this moment with tears.

That night, though, the sadness was far from my mind as I looked at the picture I'd taken of Dani. The golden light of the amphitheater enhanced the color of her skin and hair, the shine of her smile, and I knew what Dani's theme would be. I cropped the photo, making it a close-up of the lower half of her face, the line of her neck and the stray curls that were falling out of her bun, all shining gold in the light.

D makes me see things in a different way. She even added another dimension to the way I thought about my future. Everything that had looked mundane before suddenly seems injected with light, illuminating even the darkest corners, and now I'm more undecided than ever about where I want to go to college. I wonder what else I'll learn about myself the longer I'm around her. Will I like what I see or will it just make me even more afraid?

# 6

The following Wednesday, the band director called the marching band together for double-practice after school. Amanda complained the entire walk to Stripes, where we were going to get an afternoon pick-me-up.

"It's because the drumline doesn't know how to work together, which is the whole *point* of this choreography," Amanda ranted as we crossed the street. I waved to the crossing guard, who waved her sign in response.

"I want a corn dog. Or should I get a burrito? I definitely want Hot Cheetos though," I thought out loud.

"They're supposed to be in a V like a flock of geese, but they just look like confused pigeons—"

"What are the pigeons confused about?" I squinted behind the sunglasses I'd stolen from Veronica's room that morning as we walked over the uneven patches of asphalt and grass.

"I don't know, I didn't ask them. I just wanna know why Gabriel can't get his section together," Amanda whined, shaking her head as we entered Stripes.

I followed Amanda down one of the savory snack aisles as she picked up a Clif bar and a bag of Limón Lays. I got my Hot

Cheetos and a bottle of Mountain Dew before going to find Amanda at the ICEE machine.

"After Marcy and Jennifer broke up, the whole section broke into a civil war." Amanda shook her head as she alternated the blue and yellow flavors.

"Who is Captain America and who is Iron Man?" I asked.

Amanda thought about it as we got in line to pay. "Marcy is definitely Captain America. That girl is too nice, and Jennifer cheated on her, so yeah. You also don't have to stay for practice, ya know. It's probably going to run long, because it always does, because Mr. Menendez is a fucking asshat—"

"You're my ride home."

"Jordan is still here."

I shrugged as we walked out of the store and began crossing the street back to the high school. "I don't mind waiting for you, and I like the band's show this year anyway. Plus I need pics of the band for the yearbook."

Amanda smiled, and I was taken by surprise when she reached out to hold my hand. "Why are you always so supportive of me?"

"I'm your best friend, duh."

She squeezed my hand in response. "The bestest."

Amanda didn't let go the whole way to the stadium, and every step made my heart bob like it was floating on the surface of a river.

The metal bench set up on the track that surrounded the field had turned into a grill after roasting in the sun all afternoon, so I sat on my flannel to prepare my camera. My mom was totally wrong about my flannels; they served a multitude of purposes, even in hot weather. It was punk as well as functional.

Satisfied that my ass probably wouldn't catch fire today, I white-balanced my camera on the back of an English assignment and stood, beginning to mill about the track taking shots of the band readying themselves for practice. Mostly though, I just watched Amanda, standing with her hands on her hips on the platform as the band director moved people into position. With the extra height, she towered over the band, and her voice, yelling at the stubborn drummers from the fifty-yard line, carried over the whole stadium before the band director came over to speak to her and she quieted, listening.

The band director gestured, and Amanda nodded before he walked to the track and yelled, "Places!"

Amanda snapped to attention almost immediately. It was one of my favorite things about her, the way she seamlessly shifted from student to leader in seconds. She faced the band, taking their places on the field, and with a wave of her hand, the formerly chattering band went still and silent. The sun was hitting Amanda at just the right angle, making her look regal as she lifted a hand, and I had pressed the shutter at the moment right before she waved and the band went silent.

Then, with another gesture, the music began.

The band's show was a strange story that I only understood because Amanda had explained it to me so many times, and even then, I only knew it was something about a girl entering a parallel dimension. There were mirrors involved, and also clowns.

This band director was a little strange, but oh well. The band always received the highest scores at district competitions, so I assumed he was doing something right.

I eventually grew bored of watching, even as entertaining as Amanda's gesticulating was, as the band ran through their show a few more times. I had all the pictures I needed, so I decided to move to the bleachers so I wouldn't be so close to the noise of the band's performance, where I finished my AP

English essay. Soon the music stopped, replaced by the metallic thuds of footsteps coming up the bleachers. I pushed my hair out of my face and looked up to see Amanda walking up to me, a red Solo cup in her hand. "What's up?"

"We're on a water break, but I thought I'd bring you some Gatorade," she said, perching herself next to me before hissing. "Jesus, you can fry an egg on this bitch."

My spot on the bleachers had cooled down enough, so I got up and offered her my flannel. She gave me a grateful smile as she sat down on it.

"You good?"

She nodded, and I applauded myself for my own foresight. Maybe I could do this romance thing right after all. I took the cup from her and peered inside at the purple liquid. "Is this grape?"

Amanda shook her head. "No, I know that you don't like red or blue by themselves, so I mixed them because you do that sometimes."

It shouldn't have felt like such a big deal. We'd been friends for a long time—of course she'd remember my preferred combination. So why did this ordinary cup of purple liquid flood my insides with warmth?

I looked back at Amanda, hoping she didn't sense the internal freak-out I was having, but she was gazing out over the field, at the band milling about like ants on the turf. "It looks so pretty from up here. I've never noticed."

It was. Streaks of blush pink and bright orange were fanning out in the sky above the stadium, the clouds clearing like afterthoughts. "Never noticed from on top of the riser thingy you stand on?"

"It's called a drum major podium. Put some respect on her name." Amanda put her elbows on her legs and plunked her chin down into her hands, balancing on them as she gazed out over the field. "I don't get a lot of time to stop and look at the sky when I'm trying not to fuck up my conducting. Can't be distracted by clouds."

Don't say it, don't say it, don't say it—"Yeah, I guess you have to *conduct* yourself accordingly—"

Amanda gave a barking laugh, pushing my shoulder with hers and hitting my knee. I grinned and took a sip of my Gatorade. Just right. "Oh, come on, I practically gave that to you." She left her hand on my knee, letting go with a squeeze that made me jump and blush. She didn't seem to notice, just continued, "It's like the whole world doesn't exist when I'm up there. The world is just the band and me and the field and whatever time is on the clock." She shrugged, smiling gently. "That's why I love your photos of the band. You always make it look like the way it makes me feel. And the fact that you can do that is just . . ." Amanda shook her head. "Maggie, you don't know how cool that is."

I didn't know what to say. Amanda was looking at me with such fondness, an admiration I'd never seen from her. I was always the fuckup friend, the late friend, the messy friend. To see Amanda Guevara looking at me like I was magic felt like a dream. "Thanks. That means a lot."

Amanda nodded at my camera bag. "Can I see the pics?"

My face burned. I had taken so many pictures of her at this practice that she would have no trouble making a yearbook spread for herself if she wanted; I couldn't let her see them. "Camera's dead," I lied quickly. She pouted, so I said, "I'll show them to you in yearbook tomorrow, they're really cool" just to get her to stop frowning.

It worked. Amanda broke into a big smile. "I'll hold you to that. I'm going to miss this a lot when we go to college, working together on stuff like this. At least we'll be in the same city though."

And there it was. The future of our friendship seemed to hinge on New York, and every reminder of that was a punch to the gut.

Before I had time to think about it, the shrill screech of a whistle erupted from the sidelines, and the little ants on the field started darting around frantically. Amanda's spine straightened, and her hawklike gaze searched the field for the band director. Gone was the peace of the water break, and so was my best friend Amanda. In her place was Drum Major Amanda, who smiled at me as she stood up.

"It shouldn't be too long now. Just hang on for a bit longer, and then we'll go."

I looked after her longingly as she walked away, then exhaled, wondering if my feelings would get any less confusing. And damn if people wouldn't keep making it hard on me.

"You need to pick an escort for my quince," Alyssa announced, when I found her and Veronica on the back porch after Amanda dropped me off. Veronica was arranging Alyssa's hair into a mop of curly ringlets on her head.

"You need a hairstyle that makes you look less like a poodle."

Alyssa fumbled for the hand mirror and glanced at herself in it, making a face. "I think she's right, Veronica."

Veronica sighed, glaring at me and blowing a sweaty strand of her red hair out of her face. "Fiiine, we'll try again later."

"Anyway," Alyssa said loudly. "I need to know in time, or I can't get the dress or tux or whatever."

I sighed. "I'm working on it."

The deadline had been ticking in my mind, a taffeta-wrapped bomb. I was no closer to my decision than I had been when I started this, and I had to kick things into high gear. All I needed was a way to jumpstart it.

"Work harder." Alyssa glared. "Remember cousin Leonardo. Don't try me, I'll do it."

That night, as I was sorting through the band pictures in my camera, I saved a shot I'd taken of the band from the back, facing the setting sun at an angle. The sky was now a gorgeous mix of purple, pink, and orange, and the band was gazing up like they could see the crowds at halftime, still with anticipation. I bumped up the saturation just a bit to enhance the pink and posted to my finsta.

> Watching A during practice today felt like stealing a moment with someone in their element. She's always looked so put together, but especially so when she's conducting. We started out the same when we met: teenage hellions with a plan, us against the world. She's going to be so mad at me if she discovers I'm flaking out on our plan, and I want to keep it from her as long as I can. That means keeping my feelings a secret for a little longer too.

But as I stared at the photo, Alyssa's threats came back to me, and I couldn't help but feel the pressure of time ticking away, each second pulsing in my veins, a visceral reminder of everything at stake.

---

"Maggie, can you hang back after class?" Mrs. Lozano asked a few minutes before the bell rang in art the next morning.

"Yeah, sure." She continued walking to her desk, and my stomach clenched. I ran through my last few posts. Did I say "fuck" in any of them? Did I somehow post a nude without realizing it? I didn't even *take* nudes.

Then again, the whole project was a little sus, so maybe she had a problem with it in general.

I approached her desk as the bell rang, trying to gauge her expression, but she just smiled sweetly. "You needed to talk to me?"

"Yeah, I just wanted to talk to you about your project." My face probably confessed my anxiety because she shook her head quickly. "You did nothing wrong. Don't worry."

I let out a breath. "Oh, thank fuck." Mrs. Lozano frowned, and I winced. "My bad. Sorry."

Mrs. Lozano smiled and shook her head good-naturedly. "I just wanted to tell you that I'm really enjoying your project so far. I imagine you're not enjoying the conflict there."

My face burned. "Yeah, well. I'm glad you're having fun though."

Mrs. Lozano laughed. "I just wanted to talk to you about further down the line. You and I both know that you're trying to go to NYU"—ah, yes, yet another person expecting the world from me—"but I noticed some hesitancy in your captions."

Oh, shit. I had forgotten, sometimes, that in being honest in my posts and captions, I had turned them into a confessional about not only my feelings but my plans for the future as well. "Oh. Yeah. Well, I mean, I'm not a senior, so I haven't, like, made any plans yet."

"But you're working like you're trying for NYU. Your grades and your extracurriculars speak for themselves." Mrs. Lozano smiled. "That's a good thing. It's good to be prepared for anything."

"Why do I feel like there's a 'but' in there?"

"Because there is." She drummed her fingers on her desk, her eyes focused steadily on me through her glasses. I felt pinned to the spot. Was this a trick all teachers learned to intimidate their students? "I can't help but feel like you're not taking your choice seriously. You have agency in this. It's your future, your college experience. Just because something is what's expected for you, doesn't mean it's the right choice."

"But it was *my* choice. At the beginning anyway. It's what I told everyone I wanted." I bit my lip. "What am I supposed to tell people, that I just don't know if I want it anymore?"

"You tell them that. Or you don't. Like you said, you don't have to make any decisions right now, but I don't want you to be all alone in this and have no one to talk to about it. I also really don't want you to decide something this big based on what you think everyone else wants for you. What do *you* want for you?"

No one had actually asked me that before. I opened my mouth but nothing came out. "I, um . . ."

What did I want anymore? I didn't know. I didn't even know who I had feelings for. How was I supposed to decide what to do with my *future,* for fuck's sake?

Mrs. Lozano shook her head quickly. "You don't have to answer that right now, Maggie. Just think about it. And keep doing what you're doing with your project. Can't wait to see how that pans out." She grinned.

I smiled, but it felt more like a wince.

---

**Matthew:** Who's coming to my play??
**Amanda:** All of us unfortunately
**Maggie:** We're bringing tomatoes

**Dani:** ^^and spinach to make a nice salad. That's what she means.

**Maggie:** I said what I said.

**Amanda:** @matthew your gf better stay away from me she just elbowed me in the hallway.

**Maggie:** *side-eye emoji*

**Jordan:** I wouldn't call it deliberate but kinda

**Matthew:** Maybe if your ego didn't take up so much space . . .

Matthew's theater class had been working on their first play of the year for only a few short weeks, which is why, Matthew warned us, it would probably be a disaster.

Still, we filed into the black box right after school on Thursday, ready for any chance to support/terrorize Matthew as we took seats in the back row. The black box was San Benito High's theater classroom, so called because it had black tile floors and the walls were covered floor to ceiling in black chalkboard, so the crew could draw the scenery in chalk on the wall behind the stage instead of spending money on actual backdrops. It was claustrophobic, but at least it gave the room an appropriately dramatic ambience.

"The theater kids are as pretentious as yearbook kids, but they're more in your face about it," Jordan said, adjusting his beanie and setting his skateboard down, resting his feet on it and pushing it from side to side.

"Do *not* compare my yearbook staff to those—" Amanda said, adjusting her poster to balance perfectly on her lap as she pulled her perfectly straight hair into a ponytail.

"Some of them do seem to have an interesting aesthetic," Dani jumped in, placing the plastic flowers we had bought ironically for Matthew under her seat. She gestured to one of the theater kids, who wore a rainbow tutu and black cat ears with her hair teased half a foot tall.

"Amanda just thinks it's weird whenever people don't dress like they're ready for a job interview at all times. Amanda is preppy, they're scene kids. It's oil and water, or whatever that phrase is. And Maggie's got that emo thing going, which is a totally separate thing," Jordan added, jerking a thumb at me.

I gave him a look as I unpacked my Canon from its case. "Leave me out of this."

"At least all Maggie does is wear Converse and complain a lot in her band T-shirts and wear too many flannels even though it's hot as balls all the time," Jordan said.

"I swear to God . . ." I was about to say more, but then Amanda put a hand on my thigh, presumably to calm me down, but it just made it worse. I could feel the heat of it burning a hole in my jeans. I didn't even have the presence of mind to snap back, just flipped my middle finger at Jordan.

Amanda glared at him. "How dare you insult my Maggie this way, and at least my staff provides something to this ungrateful school—"

*My Maggie?* My face flamed, and I looked down at my camera, busying myself with clearing the memory. After all, I needed to have plenty of room for photos for the theater class's yearbook spread, and no one needed to see my face turn beet red because of a pretty girl.

"Gee, tell us how you really feel, Amanda. Don't hold back."

I looked up to see Matthew approaching, and smiled. "Well, if it isn't Jack Worthing." I paused, thinking it over. "Or Ernest. Whatever your character's name is. This play is confusing."

"Don't you be tryna to kiss up after Amanda is over here

running her mouth." Matthew shook his head. "You're just mad because of whatever hallway incident you made up in your head."

Tori was also in eighth period theater with Matthew, and I spotted her from across the room. She gave me the stink eye before ducking into one of the dressing rooms with her group of fawning lackeys.

Amanda sniffed. "Well, Tori is just here because she got kicked out of choir, it's not like she has talent—"

Matthew looked like he was about to retort, but Jordan jumped in, asking, "Sooo if it's *The Importance of Being Earnest*, why are only, like, half the people in weird old-timey costumes? All old-timey costumes or bust."

This distraction was successful, as Matthew launched into an explanation of the school's budget problems, and how they only had a few costumes from other old-fashioned plays, until the seats were mostly full and the lighting techs flickered the lights.

"Looks like that's my cue," Matthew said, glancing over his shoulder to see the theater teacher, Mr. Martinez, gesturing at him. Matthew turned around to toss me a grin. "If you get my good side, I'll buy you dinner."

"I don't have to do anything for you," I said, looking down at the camera so he wouldn't see me blush.

"Maybe I just want to buy you dinner."

It was embarrassing how quickly his words shifted something inside me, the way my hands itched to reach out for his. I distracted myself from it by saying, "Maybe you should go before I hit you with my camera. Break a leg, you arrogant ass."

Even the shit-eating grin on his face as he walked away was beautiful. Actors: snake charmers, every one of them.

I was out of my seat for most of the play, shooting photos. I was forever rushing around, trying to predict every shot before it happened so I could be in the right position to capture it.

When I trained my lens on Matthew, I paused over the shutter release as I stared at his face through the viewfinder. For a moment, I was free to stare at him unabashedly, taking in his smooth brown skin, his dark eyes, the way emotions flashed across his face at every turn. I could play this off as the simple action of a dedicated photographer, waiting for the right shot.

Which found me, as it always did.

Matthew suddenly peered directly into the camera, and it was as though he looked straight through the viewfinder and into my eyes. He smiled then, no sarcasm or arrogance or quick wit, just a huge smile that, at that moment, was just for me. This was Matthew, plain and simple, the way I had always loved him the most.

I pressed the shutter.

The late afternoon sunlight was blinding as the group exited the black box after the play, and I squinted into it, sliding on Veronica's sunglasses. I walked toward the student pickup area outside the band hall, where my mother's Camry was already idling by the curb. "All right, well, I'll see you guys tomorrow."

"Wait, you're not coming to Wingstop with us?" Dani asked, frowning.

"Yeah, Mags, tell her I'll drive you home," Matthew urged.

"She's in the parking lot, and she doesn't like you anymore, dummy," I reminded him. "Breaking my heart that many times didn't win you any points, even if we're still friends."

"You broke my heart too, ya know—"

"She likes me, I could ask her," Jordan suggested.

I scoffed. "Shit, you'd all have to ask her for her to let me go out on a weeknight."

The group looked at each other in silence for a moment before Amanda said, "Let's go," and took off for the car. The rest of them, except for Matthew, followed.

"Guys! I didn't mean—for fuck's sake," I spluttered, running out of energy. My friends were the unstoppable force to my immovable object, after all.

Matthew chuckled. "You have a lot of people who care about you."

"Or people who want me to get yelled at," I muttered, craning my neck to see what was happening as my friends surrounded the car and were probably giving my mother hella anxiety.

"The group's not the same without you. You know that. You're the core," Matthew said.

I smiled. "Someone has to keep y'all in line sometimes. You can be pretty big douchebags. I'm the brains of this operation."

"We both know that Amanda is our resident brain." Matthew smiled softly. "You say a lot of shit, but I know how much you love us."

"Yeah, whatever." But I smiled. "Is Tori coming to Wingstop?"

"Why, would that be an issue?" Matthew raised an eyebrow, and I knew it was a challenge.

From my time as a Professional Ex-Girlfriend, I knew what my lines were: "Of course not. Tori's fine."

Matthew smirked, shaking his head. "Nah, she's got plans with her family. We might link up later, but I don't know. We're kind of in a fight right now, so . . ."

That got my attention. "What's going on?"

Matthew looked like he was about to say something, but then there was a loud whoop, and Amanda was running back up to us, shouting, "Maggie!" and waving her arms.

I went to investigate, if only to not be alone with Matthew anymore.

That was how I ended up in the back of Matthew's truck between Dani and Amanda on the way to Wingstop, listening to Jordan and Matthew argue about music in the front seat with Dani interjecting. Amanda was texting, frowning at her phone every now and then before setting it down, dejected.

"I'm not saying that Vampire Weekend isn't great," Jordan was arguing, "but I just mean that there are *better* bands. Like, a lot of them."

"Can we at least agree on Weezer, or Bleachers?" Dani suggested cordially. "This ride is going to be over before you even pick a song."

Amanda gave an annoyed grunt, still looking down at her phone, so I decided to bite. "Okay, what's up your butt?"

"Jaime is still being a dick. He's playing FIFA with his boys right now and can't even take a two-second break to text me back."

"Video games make you all one-track-minded. For someone who plays sports, he's bad at multitasking," I said, picking at a loose thread on my jeans. "A lot of guys are, I think. That's why they suck at texting. And sex. Wait, why do we date guys again?"

"I heard that," Matthew said over his shoulder.

"You were supposed to," I sang before looking back at Amanda and jerking a thumb at him. "See? You're better off single."

Amanda laughed brightly, sinking a bit in her seat until

she could put her head on my shoulder. "Yeah, probably. I'd be better off with someone like you, to be honest. There needs to be a guy version of you."

Frustration made my chest feel tight, and I wanted to snap that there was a perfectly good girl version of me who could give her everything if she only wanted it. But I just clenched my jaw and took a deep breath, picturing the words escaping as I exhaled. The visualization helped, and the fresh oxygen had me breathing easier for the moment.

I could get through this, and I would.

Dinner was loud and chaotic as usual, with Jordan and Matthew competing to see who could eat more Atomic-flavored wings and Dani, Amanda, and I complaining about the upcoming AP Calc test. The meal was cut short when Jordan won their competition and promptly ran outside to throw up in the parking lot. All in all, it was a typical night for us.

Matthew dropped everyone else off first, since my house was on the way to his own.

Jordan waved back at us as he walked to his front door, and we waited for him to go in. Matthew checked his phone and grimaced, tossing it into the cupholder with more force than necessary.

"You okay there, bud?"

He sighed. "I don't really feel like going home right now. Would it be weird if . . ."

I smiled at the windshield. "It's always weird. Let's just go."

With Sam Houston stretched out before us, streetlights like an airplane runway, Matthew put the car in drive.

---

**Jordan:** You and Matthew going home alone? *side-eye emoji*

**Maggie:** Stahhp

**Maggie:** He just wants to talk. Nothing to write home about. Probably.

**Jordan:** Idk about that. Good luck!

# 7

Everywhere I look, I see us, M. I mean, not us exactly, but the kids we used to be. It wasn't that long ago, but it feels like lifetimes. We're scattered all over this town, pieces of us hidden in the Pizza Hut where we had our first real date and in the back row of the Cinemark on five-dollar Tuesdays. What would happen if I gathered them, put them together like a puzzle? Would they be a map back to us?

The 1975's newest album was playing as I hit post on the photo I'd just taken. It was a picture of the road ahead of us, Sam Houston lined with palm trees and dimmed streetlights. I edited it for black and white and added the caption, hitting Post before putting away my phone. Matthew was leaning back coolly in the driver's seat with one hand on the steering wheel, as if there was no place he was more comfortable. This moment alone with Matthew had just dropped into my lap with no warning or prompting, so I had to make the most of it. It was eight at night as we rolled down Business

77, and the sun had set on our side of town. The traffic had come and gone, and we headed down to the trail.

Matthew was quiet, but I knew what he was waiting for, so I didn't mind the silence. The darkness of night was a peaceful companion, and after a few minutes, we parked on the side of the main road.

We started walking on the side that was lined with play equipment. The crowds of children on the playgrounds were thinning, but the tiny old basketball court was still full of neighborhood boys shooting hoops and heckling each other in Spanish, loud old-school rap blaring from someone's portable speaker.

The trail was a regular spot for our friends now, but it had been mine and Matthew's originally. The old playground where we'd been each other's first kiss had long been torn down, a safety hazard even then. Even so, as I looked at the shiny new play structure that stood in its place, I couldn't help but mourn.

Matthew, skinny and short, and with braces, and me with my bruised knees and acne, clasped hands, shaking as we pressed our lips together. The memory was a ghost before me, our former selves shimmering in the glow of the streetlights.

It was much simpler then.

Matthew gestured at our picnic table, which was empty tonight, thankfully, and we climbed on top of it. I folded myself criss-cross-applesauce and rested my hands in my lap, waiting.

"Mind if I smoke?" Matthew said, taking a pack of Marlboros out of his back pocket.

I grimaced but didn't say anything as he fished out his lighter.

Matthew inhaled, then blew the smoke out to the side. There was a breeze, though, and I wrinkled my nose as some of the smoke blew my way. This was definitely one thing about him that I did not miss. Matthew sat back on his elbows, looking out over the water.

"Who were you texting earlier, when you looked all put out?" I asked.

"I wasn't put out," Matthew muttered. "Who even says 'put out'?"

"You only smoke when you're upset."

Matthew had started smoking because he thought it looked intense, like Bogart and his pretty shades of grey. But it had quickly become a crutch when things in his life, and our relationship, had taken a turn.

I didn't want to think about that right now. Not when we were alone and he looked beautiful, even with the plume of smoke blooming from his mouth.

"Maybe I just like to smoke. Have you considered that?" he said, his words steely like the door of a cage slamming shut.

I had had a feeling this would happen when he drove me out here. Another fight, another conversation that ended up nowhere. Geez, we weren't even dating anymore, and it had already come back around to this. I wasn't surprised. This was just how it was with Matthew. In the end, it was always me against his anger, his walls.

But for years, Matthew had been my knight in shining armor—at least, that's how I thought of him in my head, my last memory of him: his russet skin and black hair, his muscles and the steel in his brown eyes. I had hidden behind him for years, behind guys with wandering hands and girls with narrowed eyes and sharp tongues. I had been able to face it because I had Matthew to take the brunt of it.

But I wasn't fourteen anymore. I didn't need Matthew to speak for me. So why was I still here? Dating him had taken so much energy from me in the past, and right now I had bigger things to think about than his emotional development. He took too much of me, and I didn't get enough in return, so in the end, the one left lacking was me.

And I deserved more than that.

Resigned, I laid back on the table, staring up at the leaves on the tree branch looming overhead. I tried to see through the leaves, but it was too dark.

We sat in silence for a while, tension heavy between us, the lump in my throat and the secondhand smoke making it hard to breathe, before he put the cigarette out on the table, fidgeting with the end between his fingers. "Tori and I are fighting."

*DING DING DING.*

I pressed my lips together tightly to keep a sigh from escaping. He and Tori were fucked up, so of course he would come back to his ex. Why was everyone so predictable—

"She wants to meet my family."

My eyes widened. Now that was interesting. "Really?"

Matthew nodded.

I forced myself to look at him and not the ground. "So what's the problem?"

"I don't know, it's too soon?"

I raised an eyebrow. "Um, I met your family, like, a month in. My *mom* met your family. I feel like you're lying."

Matthew was silent, staring out at the water, so I waited until he finally spoke. His voice was low and heavy. "She wants to meet everyone. My dad too. How am I supposed to bring her to my dad's house and introduce her to his twenty-three-year-old girlfriend and their kid?"

I whistled through my teeth; that was something that had definitely thrown me, so I couldn't blame him. "Yeeeah, that's a hell of an introduction."

Matthew nodded, eyes on the ground. "My family is a fucking mess, and what if she doesn't want to be a part of something so intense? We've been having fun and stuff, and I really like her, but what if she finds out how fucked up I am and doesn't wanna put up with it?"

"Well, what's the alternative, not telling her and just letting her think that you don't like her or—or that you don't trust her?" My voice was small, echoing those awful feelings I hadn't thought about in so long. "Tori doesn't strike me as the type of girl to put up with your chain-smoking, brooding self for very long. Eventually she's going to make you talk."

"You didn't. You let me deal with things at my own pace."

I paused at that, taking the time to examine his face. His words didn't hold any malice, or bitterness, and his expression didn't either. He was just questioning. "Yeah, and I was enabling you," I said quietly, weighed down by the undeniable truth of it. "And look where we ended up."

"It wasn't that long ago," Matthew said. "What if I'm the same person?"

I shrugged. "You probably are, but at least you're finally talking about it. At least you realize you have a problem."

It was true. That he was even here right now, asking for help and trying to sort through his feelings, was not something the Matthew I had dated would have ever done. And here he was, doing it for someone else. I'd be lying if I said that didn't sting. *Why wasn't I worth it?*

Matthew sighed. "So how do I fix it?"

"I don't know. You need to talk to Tori. Not me. No offense, Matthew, but I'm done fixing your shit." I needed to figure out who *I* was, and I could only do that if I wasn't focusing so much on helping him figure out who *he* was.

I expected some pushback, but instead Matthew just exhaled heavily. "Yeah, I've put that shit on you way too much. I don't wanna be stuck making the same mistakes. I'm tired. I wanna do better."

Something clicked inside of me then, tectonic plates shifting under my skin, like the last few pieces of a puzzle sliding into place. Matthew was open and vulnerable, trying to be a good boyfriend, a good partner. He was *trying* for Tori, in a way he never had with me. There was a hollowness in my chest, but I didn't know what from because it wasn't malignant—just mournful.

He wasn't mine. Not anymore.

"You're doing better right now, at least. You're trying, and that's really cool." I could hear the way my own voice sounded, sure and gentle, and I almost couldn't believe what I was saying. Each word felt more honest than the last. Hesitating, I put caution aside and patted his hand lightly. "Now you just have to talk to her instead of me."

"What if I'm not clear or—or she doesn't get it or . . . ?"

"Trust me. She'll just be grateful that you tried. After all, it was all I ever wanted when we were together."

"I . . . I'm really sorry I was so bad at being your boyfriend." Matthew was shy, and for once, I wasn't powerless in our relationship; now I had the power to decide how hard he beat himself up, how much regret he would carry into the next part of his life.

But I just smiled. "I forgive you. I'm sorry too. Let's just be better at being friends, okay?"

"I like the sound of that." He grinned. "You know, I think this is my favorite of our fresh starts."

I had to agree. "The very best."

---

That night, I sat in bed scrolling through the photo library on my phone. I had one last thing to do before I closed the Matthew chapter of my life—and my project. I reached the folder labeled "DO NOT OPEN" and said fuck it to my past self, opening the folder. There were countless photos, milliseconds from every phase of our relationship, every step of our growth. In every one we were a little taller, and a little sadder, but smarter too, the lights in our eyes changing their meaning from shot to shot. Photos from dates, holidays, birthdays. He'd been beside me at every family gathering since we'd gotten together right before high school. I took a deep breath and, with shaky hands, deleted picture after picture.

But there was one I kept: the first one. It was a picture of our picnic table, taken on a spring afternoon in the park the first time Matthew and I had ever been alone together, the first place he'd held my hand and kissed me. I kept that photo but changed it to black and white. This was the end of Matthew in my assignment, but not in my life. The Matthew who had been my first love, my first real heartbreak, was gone, but now here stood Matthew the Friend in a way he hadn't been able to before. Maybe this is how it was meant to be all along. I needed a post to commemorate this moment.

M and I were these crazy, scattered kids. We didn't know what to do or how to treat love gently, and we broke everything more often than we fixed it. We weren't that much younger, but it feels ages away from us now. Everything was so difficult. He was everything I wanted at the time, but he's moved on and goddammit I want more too.

---

I woke up that Saturday to Alyssa yelling unintelligibly, squatting in front of my bed. I ducked under my pillow, but it was too late; my little sister had already taken a flying leap and landed splayed across my torso, knocking the wind from my chest. "Do you know what day it is?"

"Saturday, and you're supposed to be sleeping," I groaned, pushing her off to the side and trying to pull the covers over my head. I felt her roll off the bed before the covers were dragged off of me and the pillow was lifted from my head. "You piece of—"

"It's one month and one week until my quince, and Mami says you *have* to help me with my invitations. I have my debate competition today, and those invites have to go out this week, so I can't do it."

I squinted at her. She was already fully dressed, hair straightened, at—I checked my phone—eight in the morning. Jesus Christ. "You could have just started with that. Why did you put off the invites so long if you *knew* you had debate this weekend?"

"Because I have the best big sister in the world who is so helpful and has better handwriting than me?" Alyssa batted her mascara-covered lashes at me, smiling sweetly.

Ugh, I hated my weakness for compliments. "Fine, that's fair. Has Mami made breakfast?"

"She made chorizo and egg, and she said she's giving yours to the stray dogs next door if you don't get up."

That was how my sorry ass ended up rushing to the kitchen counter, scooping chorizo and egg from the pan on the stove into a flour tortilla in my Scooby-Doo pajama pants. Veronica was the only one at the table, so I plopped down next to her. I listened, waiting for my family's typical morning chaos, but the house was quiet, so I asked, "Did they leave already?"

Veronica nodded, scrolling through her phone at the head of the table, already halfway through her chorizo-and-egg taco. "Mami is dropping her off and then going to Grandma's, so I'm taking the morning shift. You're on your own for these invites." Veronica drained her coffee cup and stood, taking her plate to the sink.

"I'll take your shift if you—"

"Nope." Veronica gave me a two-finger salute and a Cheshire cat smile before leaving the kitchen. The front door slammed with a finality that only Veronica could give to an inanimate object.

I huffed, even though there was no one left to sympathize with me, before looking at the stack of invitations that sat on the counter. Alyssa had ordered them custom off of Etsy, complete with coordinated envelopes.

As if the quinceañera herself had read my mind, my phone buzzed with a text:

> The addresses are on the fridge. Write, stuff, close, stamp. Try not to screw it up, bb lmao *kissy face emoji*

Oh, Alyssa. Ever prepared.

Feeling sufficiently used, I rooted through Alyssa's side of the room for the good gel pens, the glittery ones she tried to hide so no one could get them without her permission. I took everything to the living room, setting it all down on the coffee table to look at what Alyssa had gotten me into.

Looking at the dozens of invitations, I thought about calling Amanda; she was, after all, the most efficient person I knew. But I also knew what getting Amanda's help would mean, since it was the same no matter what group project or extracurricular duty we shared: Amanda would watch me do it for a few minutes before her control issues led her to anxiously take over and get things done her way, sure that the work would get done faster. I really didn't need that intense energy right now.

My phone buzzed again, a text from Dani this time:

Hey! Are we still on for this morning?

Oh no. I checked my texts from last night, and sure enough, a text had come in later on, while my phone was in Do Not Disturb mode. Dani, asking if I still wanted her to pick me up to volunteer at the debate competition for NHS. Fuck.

I texted her back.

I'm so sorry! I forgot and now I'm stuck helping my sister with quince stuff. Go without me

A moment later, a response came in, and my eyes widened.

That's fine. I was just gonna go to get extra hours, but I already have my hours for this month. Do you want help?

She really wanted to sit around and help me do chores? Well, alright then. I wasn't about to question a perfectly good opportunity to hang out with Dani.

If you're fine with addressing a zillion invitations, I'm your girl.

I smiled when she responded,

My favorite way to spend an afternoon. I'm on my way.

The twenty minutes it took Dani to arrive felt like two hours, and I had changed outfits three times, trying to strike a balance between "I'm cool and casual at home" and "I want to impress you with how nice I look even when I'm cool and casual at home." Artfully torn jean shorts and an off-the-shoulder T-shirt that I stole from Veronica seemed acceptable to me, but what if she thought I'd tried too hard? Was this going to be a train wreck? Should I cancel?

Too late. There was already a knock at the door. I took a deep breath to steady myself and went to open it.

Dani smiled at me shyly, waving in the doorway with that light awkwardness of someone visiting your house for the first time. "Morning."

Wearing a white V-neck and holding her little brown leather backpack, she looked like early autumn personified, and I was suddenly glad I'd spent so long on my outfit. "Good morning yourself. Thanks for the help. You really didn't have to do this."

"I know. I wanted to, so don't chase me off." Dani gave me

a sly half smile, leaving her shoes in the hallway as she padded over in her socks, following my lead and sitting beside me near the coffee table. "If you want me here, that is."

I shouldn't, but I did, and I was far too selfish to let this opportunity go.

"I just can't believe that someone would actually choose to do my little sister's bidding. Look at this mess." I swept my hand out over the table, piled high with envelopes and invitations.

"I'm great at errands. Put me in, Coach." She gave me jazz hands.

I smiled and handed over half of Alyssa's address list and a stack of envelopes. "How's your handwriting?"

And we were off.

"I never knew sparkly pens came in so many colors," Dani commented, looking in amazement at the twenty-four pack spread out on the table. I had noticed her trading out her pen every couple of envelopes; it was cute, and my lips had twitched into a smile every time.

"Yeah, it's definitely Alyssa's affinity for all things glitter. God help the carpet in our room when she makes cheerleading next year."

"You guys share a room?"

I nodded. "We just have one floor, so we're kind of cramped here. Veronica moved into the spare room when she got into UCAS because she said she needed the space to study, but I think she just wanted to have sex with her boyfriend without me or Alyssa walking in."

I wasn't ashamed of my house; it was small, but it was cozy. I'd lived here all my life, and my mom worked really hard to keep the lights on. It wasn't a glamorous life, but it was ours.

Still, I was self-conscious whenever any of the group came around the apartment, always making sure not to let them linger longer than necessary. I had been to all of their houses, and they weren't anything like ours. For starters, they all had houses, like freestanding houses, and none of them ran two businesses out of them (if you counted Veronica's under-the-table haircuts, which I did). Two parents who worked, even if they were divorced. In the case of Amanda, it was often a cruel form of torture to have her around, with her designer bags and Tory Burch flats.

"I get that," Dani said, licking the envelope she had just stuffed and pressing the seam with her finger to seal it. Pausing, she amended that with, "The space situation, not the sex."

"Yeah?"

Dani nodded. "We don't have a lot of space at our house either. My older sister moved out because she and her boyfriend were gonna have a baby. My mom was really torn up over it because Ale was still pregnant when she moved out, and she really wanted her and the baby to keep living with us, but I think she just needed to be on her own. My sister's apartment is this tiny studio on Sunshine Strip, but when you walk in, you can feel how happy she is. Like it's in the walls, almost."

"I didn't know you were an aunt. How old is your sister?"

"She's twenty, so it's not like she was that young when she got pregnant, but it still threw us off a bit." Dani smiled. "But Ava is so damn cute that after a while it didn't even matter that she was technically an accident. She just turned one. Do you want to see pictures?"

I grinned. "Of fucking course I do."

Dani straightened, her eyes lighting up as she immediately reached for her phone, pulling up her camera roll and swiping through. "I get a new picture like every hour, so you're in luck. Prepare for absolute cuteness."

Dani held her phone out to me. Ava really was precious,

all dark curls and chubby legs full of rolls, but it was the pride and adoration on Dani's face that really caught my attention.

I could stay there forever, just staring at the light in Dani's eyes.

The process of prepping the invitations went by quickly with both of us working on them, and when the last of the envelopes was stacked on the coffee table, ready for my mom to take to the post office, I wrung my hands in my lap a bit. Would she want to go home now? Did she want to hang out? How could I ask her? "Um, so I guess that's it."

Dani nodded, leaning back on her hands and looking around. "So this is your domain, huh? I gotta say, I expected more of you. Vans and beanies and Polaroids left everywhere."

"Do I look like a hipster with a Polaroid camera? What is this, five years ago?" I chuckled. "Most of my stuff is in my room anyway. My mom would kill me if I left any of my 'devil clothing' out here." Wait, did her bringing this up mean . . . "Did you wanna see my room?"

Dani smiled and stood up. "In spite of your lack of Polaroids, sure. Show me where the magic happens."

I tried to ignore the backflips my stomach was doing as I led Dani down the hall. I hadn't shown it to anyone new in a long time, and I felt exposed as I opened the door, her gaze sweeping across my room. She stepped inside, and I followed.

Dani was slow and methodical as she explored the room, looking at the jewelry and loose change strewn across my dresser, the titles crammed onto the shelf in the corner. "I'm sorry if I'm snooping."

"It's not snooping if I intentionally invited you to look at all the random crap in my room."

Dani examined the posters of boy bands, bubblegum pop singers, and Disney stars on Alyssa's side of the room. "You're not a fan of posters, I see."

I shook my head, cringing. "Not after my *Twilight* phase. Never again."

Dani looked over, amused. "Team Jacob or Team Edward?"

I scoffed. "Pssh, Team Bella. Kristen Stewart was my bi awakening."

Dani bit her lip, grinning. "At least yours was a real person. I had a crush on Kuvira from *Legend of Korra*."

That made me cackle. "You fell for the fascist."

"Did you even watch the show? How could you *not*?"

I sighed. "You're not wrong. I think I had a crush on every middle-aged woman in the show, and Korrasami was my *shit*. I read fanfiction about it *all the time*."

Dani laughed. "Maybe you read my awful fanfiction. There is no worse combination than a repressed queer with an internet connection."

I grinned. "Well, now I need to know your AO3 username. I have some reading to do."

"That will absolutely not happen," Dani said cheerily, turning her attention to the pictures hanging above my desk.

I had hung up some of my favorite musician photos for inspiration, for the moments when I got so far into editing that I thought I'd never find the heart of the photo ever again. Performance photos of Halsey, Kurt Cobain, Black Veil Brides, Alanis Morissette, Beyoncé, and more—all taken by photographers who knew how to photograph them on stage no matter how high-powered the performance was. "Why do you have these?"

"Inspiration. I want to do that someday, take pictures for

bands and stuff," I said. I pointed at a photo of Blessthefall's lead singer hanging from the rafters of a crowded venue.

"That. I wanna do that."

Dani smiled. "Why?"

"Because . . ." I swallowed, and my voice came out clearer and more confident than I thought it would as I continued, "Because these pictures are so important to kids who can't go to shows, who can't afford to or live in places like the Valley that don't get big acts like cities do. The pictures and the videos—hell, even the IG Stories or TikToks . . . all of those things help kids like us be there even when we can't, ya know? And I want to give them that. I want to create that experience for them."

I bit my lip when I finished, waiting for her response. I was waiting for her to tell me I was being ridiculous, or that it was too far away and girls like us couldn't have dreams that carried us to distant lands on silver wings, but she just nodded. "Is that why you want to go to NYU?"

"It was, originally." The words escaped before I could call them back, and I wanted to call them back, but I could only watch as they settled on Dani.

She furrowed her brow and tilted her head, then sat down on my bed. "'Was'?"

"Is. Was. I don't know." I bit my lip. I didn't want to voice this, but Dani wasn't around for the origin of this dream, and it felt wrong to outright lie to her instead of just letting her believe something that had once been true. "I wanted to, but now . . . it just feels like too much sometimes. The idea of leaving all of this"—I gestured around, at my room but also at the whole life that existed in this tiny apartment—"and starting over somewhere else, leaving my family and everything that could happen . . . not to mention NYU would leave me with a shit ton of debt that I can't exactly pay back as a photographer, and I don't want to do that to my family."

Dani winced. "Yeah, I get that. I really do. My family isn't exactly rolling in money either." She paused. "Do you ever feel guilty for having expensive dreams?"

The knot in my chest loosened just a little bit, knowing that someone else also felt that way. I sat down next to her. "All the time. If I'm leaving just to create more art, I could do the same thing here."

Dani smiled. "Exactly. I got into art because I started making etchings of leaves and flowers I found in my backyard when I was, like, six. How the fuck is Rhode Island supposed to give me that? I'm going to leave my family and miss my niece growing up for what, connections to fancy art dealers?"

I grimaced. "Yeah, that's ultimately what it comes down to. Climbing the fucking ladder, talking to snobby people with connections who could introduce us to other snobby people who might be able to get us where we wanna be. Wherever that is."

"Sometimes I feel like the shittiest person ever, like I'm betraying where I come from for a chance at the 'big time.'" Dani held up air quotes, rolling her eyes as punctuation.

Hearing how I felt coming from the mouth of someone else made this confusion feel lighter somehow, even if it didn't make things any more clear. Maybe that was enough, knowing that someone else felt this too.

Still, I stared at the floor as I said the next part of what I felt, wondering if she'd judge me. "I know it's my decision to make, but sometimes I wish it wasn't. I think that's why I let everyone else believe it's what I want because then I can place the responsibility of the decision on someone else and blame it on them for putting pressure on me, even though I know it's ultimately my choice and my cross to bear, I guess."

I snuck a peek at her, looking for judgment on her face, but I didn't find any, just a faraway look like what I'd said had taken her to some distant place in her head. "Maybe that's okay, since we still have some time to make the choice. We can run from it for a little bit, as long as we come back. Even if coming back is hard."

"Try *impossible*." I shook my head. "Can we put the blame on the fact that this system of education forces us to make huge life decisions at eighteen, when we haven't even actually *lived* a life?"

"I think that's a perfect place to put blame." She smiled and gestured at the door. "Come on, let me buy you a raspa. I saw a stand next door that's calling my name."

We sat on the curb outside with our raspas, the afternoon sun warm on our skin as we watched the cars pass by on the road, the heat waves shimmering off the pavement.

"These definitely aren't as good in Harlingen. Why does this taste so much better?" Dani commented, her mouth full of her Tiger's Blood Piccadilly. "It's cool that you have this right next to your house. Have you always lived here?"

I nodded, stirring my raspa around. I'd gone with blue bubblegum this time, adding gummy bears at Dani's insistence that no expense be spared. The flavor turned my mouth blue and was so sweet that for a moment I forgot that the world was more than just sugar, sunlight, and pretty girls. "Since before I was born. It was my dad's family's store."

"Where's your dad now?" Dani was looking down at her raspa, but I could hear the curiosity in her voice.

I poked at the ice in my cup. "The afterlife, I guess? Wherever that is. He died when I was three."

Dani frowned. "I didn't mean to pry. We don't have to talk about it."

"No, it's okay."

And it was. I didn't get many questions about my dad because he'd been gone so long that it was just par for the course, like the humming of fluorescent lights over your head. It was like that with everyone in our group. Amanda's parents were workaholics and high-functioning alcoholics. Jordan's parents were happy but always working. Matthew's parents had a messy divorce. My dad was dead.

I didn't know what made me want to tell Dani everything, but I did. I had never actually told anyone this part of my history because it had happened so long ago that my friends already knew about it, and there was no need to bring it up. I'd always been grateful for that, in a weird way, because it meant I never had to confront how fucking *sad* it was that this was a part of my life story.

But Dani hadn't heard the sob story that was my life, so this seemed like a good place to introduce that.

"My dad got stopped by a state trooper and didn't have his license near him. He reached back to get it, and they shot him through the window."

The words tasted like copper as they rolled out, and I watched Dani's face anxiously, looking for any sign of criticism or judgment. Even in the Valley, where most people were Chicanx, there was still colorism and racism and classism, people who wanted to justify the senseless slaughter of a man who wasn't armed, wasn't fighting. I felt sick just thinking about it, feverish with my anger.

Dani didn't miss a beat. Not looking away, her face flickered with rage, the feeling reflected in her eyes. Her mouth twisted into a snarl, but when she reached for my hand, her touch was cool, gentle. "That is absolutely heinous. Disgusting. I'm so sorry, Maggie."

My whole body seemed to sag in relief. "Thank you." I didn't know what else to say really, so I just squeezed her hand and didn't let go.

I needed to change the subject. "I know we make fun of you a lot, but do you miss Harlingen?"

Dani appeared to be thinking, idly mixing the pickles into the ice of her raspa. She took her hand away from mine to do it, and I missed it, mourned it almost. "Sometimes. I miss the way it used to be in Harlingen, when I had friends and things didn't suck socially. I didn't really like all the attention and all the extra stuff that came with cheer, but I liked to dance and tumbling was always fun, so it was worth everything else. I just wish I could've spent more time on my portfolio and less time fighting with my ex-girlfriend."

I nodded to show I was listening but didn't say anything. I wanted to know more, and questions were just unnecessary barriers. She continued, chewing a spoonful of her raspa. "It just got so convoluted, being in the spotlight all the time, knowing that every time you walked into a room, someone in there hated you or thought something about you that wasn't true. I felt bad because the uniforms and stuff were really expensive, but my mom knew how unhappy I was, so she was really glad I quit."

"You can always try out for cheer next year. I know it'll be only senior year, but it's still something."

Dani gave a wistful half smile. "No, I think I'm done with that part of my life. I joined cheerleading for my ex, and I never had as much time for art as I wanted. I never got to go to concerts. It was fun to perform for a bit, but . . . this is enough."

"'This'?" I asked, raising my eyebrows.

"This." Dani smiled, holding my gaze as she said, "Hold on, you have—here."

Dani reached out and took hold of my chin gently. A muscle in my jaw jumped when she did it, but she didn't seem to notice. She just held it, swiping her thumb along the corner of my mouth. I put my raspa down on the step, sandwiching my hands between my knees so Dani wouldn't see how hard I was trembling.

"There," Dani mumbled, holding up her thumb, which held a blue droplet of syrup. "Got it."

"Thanks." I couldn't feel my lips. Dani's touch lingered on my skin.

"Anytime." Dani smiled, tucking her hair behind her ear with lithe fingers.

I almost swore when the door to the store opened and Veronica called, "Hurry up, the beer shipment got here and I don't pay you to sit on your ass."

"You don't pay me at all," I yelled back before looking at Dani. "I guess you should go. Looks like I'm on duty now."

Dani grinned. "The grind doesn't stop. Want help?"

*From you? Always.*

---

That night, I pulled up the photo I'd snuck of our raspas, blue and red, beside each other on the sidewalk, a few drops of syrup covering the pavement below. The ice glittered like gemstones in the afternoon sun, and the sugary treats seemed to glow in the pale gold light.

I thought of our conversation, of how easily I'd opened up to Dani, and wrote:

D makes me wanna tell her secrets. She makes me wanna tell her stories of my dad. When I talk about him, it feels like fucking torture. But when I talked about him with her, I felt like I wanted to keep going and tell her the stories Veronica and my mom had told me: like how he whistled when he made pancakes or how he cried when he listened to bachata because it reminded him of my mom. I want to tell her everything, and the worst part is I know I can't tell her anything about how I feel. Until I'm sure. Until I know I won't screw it up.

**Matthew:** @maggie @dani are hanging w/o us
**Amanda:** Personally, i think it's rude that you sent that raspa pic to the group chat. SO JEALOUS
**Jordan:** BUY ME ONE
**Maggie:** Mind your business
**Dani:** Y'all have known maggie for longer than I have, i'm tryna catch up

---

**Jordan:** Are you and dani scouting locations for your next photo?!?
**Jordan:** Or was she trying on dama dresses? *side-eye emoji*
**Maggie:** MIND YOUR BUSINESS.
**Maggie:** Don't jinx it.

---

The next day before church, I blearily padded into the bathroom, yawning. Rubbing the sleep from my eyes, I stood at the sink and turned the water on, reaching, eyes half-shut, for my toothbrush. I found it, as well as something papery.

An aquamarine Post-it note was wrapped around the base of my toothbrush. It read *Pick an escort or you won't be able to be my dama b/c I killed you*. There was even an elaborately detailed drawing of a sugar skull outlined with a heart.

I rolled my eyes and discarded the note. If Alyssa could put half as much attention into her schoolwork, she would have been accepted to Harvard by now.

After brushing my teeth, I opened the medicine cabinet to look for my face wash, and covering the brand logo was a green Post-it. *Don't ignore me, hoe*. It was followed by a doodle of a skull and crossbones in sparkly purple ink.

I sighed and reached for my moisturizer. Another note, purple this time. *COUSIN LEONARDO*. Below the message was a gravestone that said *Here lies Maggie*.

Huffing, I turned and shouted through the closed bathroom door. "I get it!"

"Obviously not!" was Alyssa's reply.

I looked in the mirror, trying to will myself to answer my own questions. It was too early in the morning for this shit, and I still had Amanda's cousin's birthday party after church. I couldn't afford to lose my shit before the day had even started.

---

Amanda's cousin Adri lived on the outskirts of San Benito with her husband, Damian, and their daughter, Myra, in a small old house painted mint green. Today was Myra's third birthday, so naturally, when we pulled up to the tiny house, there were already about half a dozen cars outside, spilling out of the driveway and filling the spots beside the curb. Someone had parked their truck on the lawn, the doors open so that Tejano music could pour freely from the speakers. At least a dozen children played in the open space off to the side of the yard, while the older relatives chatted at white folding tables under makeshift tarps to protect them from the sun.

"Are you sure it's okay for me to be here?" I asked, scanning the tables. Amanda's youngest cousins had brought a few of their friends; the group of skaters and emos were loitering off to the side of the party, shoving each other and laughing. They were at Amanda's cousin's quince last year, but I couldn't tell them apart if my life depended on it.

"Of course it is—you're basically family. Besides, you're my stand-in plus-one since Jaime and I are fighting. You're my new date." Amanda turned to wave at her parents, who had gotten a ride from a pair of Amanda's tías (who were sober, so Amanda's parents wouldn't have to be), seated across the room.

"Wow, I feel so special and not at all like a consolation prize."

Amanda threw an arm around me and put a hand on my hip, tugging me into her side. "You know you're my number one. Now let's go look for food."

I tensed, not relaxing into her the way I normally would, because her relatives were staring now, eyeing her grip on my waist, and if this were a war, I'd have arrows jutting out from between my ribs for sure. Amanda didn't seem to care though, just marched bravely forward and tugged me along while my toes curled in my socks, like my feet were getting ready to start running.

It was easy for Amanda to play gay around her family.

With her string of boyfriends, no one would question her sexuality—not out loud, and certainly not in front of her. But it wasn't safe for me because it wasn't playing and homophobia wasn't a fucking joke. If she wasn't going to be my girlfriend, I wasn't going to be her stand-in boyfriend.

I shook out of Amanda's grasp as subtly as I could as we reached her parents' table, but Amanda didn't notice, turning to chat with her tías.

The ice chests outside held only beer, so I had to enter Adri's house to look for water for the table. In the tiny kitchen, lit only by a dim bulb and the afternoon light coming through the windows, Adri was loading Capri Suns from the fridge into an empty box to take outside. Pushing a strand of purplish-red-dyed hair out of her face, she jerked a thumb wordlessly in the direction of the fridge as she picked up an empty box of Capri Suns next to the trash and opened the ice chest. Indeed, it was eighty percent Michelob Ultra and twenty percent Capri Suns.

I nodded my thanks and grabbed an armful of cold bottles. I was shutting the door with my hip when Adri said, "So, my cousin's gay now." Adri was looking at me expectantly, like she'd asked a question, the box of Capri Suns tucked under her arm.

I swayed a little as I stepped back, the words stopping me in my tracks. "Um, no. She's not—we're not—I'm just here because her boyfriend couldn't come."

Adri raised her pierced eyebrow, scanning my face. Was she dissecting the memory of what she'd seen, analyzing the affection Amanda had showed me for clues? I had certainly done it enough times to make the same face she was making: that confused, white-lady-doing-math-GIF face.

Adri must have decided I was being honest because she shrugged. "Pinche Amanda. Okay. Whatever." She stopped on her way past me and pulled a Capri Sun from the box, handing it to me. "Here. For energy. With whatever you've got going on with my cousin, you're gonna need it."

Adri swanned away, and I looked helplessly down at the juice pouch. Along with it, Adri had also dropped doubt into my palm. Now other people were beginning to notice the strange amount of PDA that Amanda was bestowing on me. We had never ever been mistaken for dating until after homecoming. If this affection meant something, I needed to figure out what it was. Now.

But first, IG.

Checking to make sure no one was coming inside, I rifled through the kitchen drawers for a black Sharpie and drew a big heart around the little opening for the straw. I stabbed the straw into the pouch at an angle, right in the center of the heart, and took a picture of the juice pouch, placing it on the counter in the direct path of the pinkish-orange sunlight.

Dramatic? A bit. But it was an art assignment, after all.

Things with A are growing more and more painful the longer it goes on. The edges are becoming sharper, and the lines are even more smoky. What does it all mean, and will she even be willing to have a conversation about it? How much longer will I be able to wait?

# 8

Like any good Libra, I woke up on the morning of my birthday with both dread and delighted anticipation. I loathed and loved my birthday, and it was a weird balance of wanting attention and not wanting anyone to look at me.

But ultimately, it wasn't my choice whether or not I got attention.

The door creaked open as I was rubbing the sleep from my eyes, and Veronica's head emerged, backlit by the hall light. I could hear my mom shuffling around in the kitchen making coffee and opening the fridge, sounds of the house waking up. I stayed quiet as she crept over to Alyssa's bed and jostled her awake. There was some grumbling, but Alyssa got up, and together they came over to my bed.

Veronica prodded my shoulder. "Move over, birthday girl."

Alyssa didn't bother asking me to move. She just clambered over me like a monkey to wedge herself between me and the wall. I scooched closer to her so Veronica could lay next to me, squishing into my side. "Damn, you're both getting too big for this."

"Hush. You're going to do this every year regardless."

I could hear her smile in the dark. "Yeah, you're right."

"Tell the story, Vero," Alyssa mumbled, already fighting sleep with her face pressed to my shoulder.

"Yeah, V. I wanna hear it."

"Okay, brats. Here goes." Veronica waited a beat, as though gathering her memories. "Maggie, you were inconsiderate as fuck because you were a whole two months early."

I pouted in the dark. "Since when is being early inconsiderate?"

"It is when it's one in the morning during the worst thunderstorm of the season." Veronica shook her head, but I could hear her smile as she continued, "You picked the worst possible time to come out. I had to stay with Grandma, and they basically just grabbed me from my bed and tossed me into the car like a sack of potatoes."

Alyssa giggled. "You make it sound like you were kidnapped."

"I practically was, dude. Just left on Grandma's porch with my Ninja Turtles backpack and a coloring book." Veronica paused again, and this time, her voice was subdued, sad. "You were really small because you were so early, but Mami said you came out quick. It took you a while to cry when they pulled you out, and Papi said it was the longest minute of his life."

I heard this story every year, but every year, this part still put a lump in my throat. "That's really sad," I said, and my voice was scratchy with more than just sleep.

"Yeah, it was." The smile came back to her voice, though, as she said, "But then you cried, really loud, and you haven't shut up since."

I smacked my hand against her stomach, and she groaned but then laughed. "Mami said that's how she knew you were a fighter, and that's the only way she got through the three weeks you were in the hospital. I remember knowing something was wrong and wondering where you were, and I don't think our parents were around together that whole time. One of them was always with you."

"Sorry."

Veronica's hair got into my face as she shook her head. "Don't worry about it. I got over it. Eventually."

I laughed. "You weren't an only child anymore."

"*That* was harder to get over. But when you finally got home, I got over it. You were home, and all I remember is thinking that you were still so small and that meant I had to protect you always, with everything I had."

"Vero," I whispered, my eyes stinging.

Veronica continued, her voice a murmur. "For seventeen years, that hasn't changed, and I don't think it ever will, no matter how big and strong you get. I'll always take care of you, no matter how many birthdays you have."

For a while, we were all quiet, the gravity of her words setting in. "I'm really proud of you, kid. For everything you've accomplished, no matter what. I think I'll always be proud of you though, even if all you know how to do is tie your shoes."

"I don't even think she knows how to do that," Alyssa said. "She just ties the laces in a knot and shoves them in her shoes so all the laces are horizontal and there's no bow."

I flicked Alyssa on the head, and she whined. "It's a look, loser. And you do the same thing, so you can't even talk."

"She's right, Al," Veronica agreed, reaching over and squeezing my hand. "Happy birthday, kiddo."

"Thanks, sissy." I wiped away the tear that had slipped out. "Now I'm all emotional and the day hasn't even started."

"It's your birthday and you can cry if you want to," Alyssa

said. "It's like the old-ass song that Veronica likes that no one our age has ever heard of."

"Ugh, one day you'll both get older and regret everything you've ever said to me." Veronica shook her head and smacked my side, rolling out of bed. "Now get up and come get your birthday pancakes before I eat them all."

After I'd gotten ready for school and eaten breakfast with my family, I grabbed my bag and followed my family downstairs. "Who's driving me? Can we stop at Stripes for snacks before class? A reminder: It's my birthday, so no one can say no to me."

Veronica smirked as we got down to the store. "You'll have to ask the person driving you."

She nodded to the front of the store, where a familiar red car was parked outside, and my insides were suddenly filled with bubbles, like a soda that had been shaken up. Bouncing on the balls of my feet, I looked back at my family, all of them grinning, probably at how much I looked like a Chihuahua right now.

"I'll see you later?" I asked.

Veronica smiled and rolled her eyes. "Get home early. We're gonna celebrate before the game."

I hopped a bit in place. "Got it. Now can I go?"

Their laughter propelled me across the tiles, and I floated out the door to see Amanda getting out of the car, a huge smile on her face. "Birthday girl!" she shouted, opening her arms wide.

I flew into them, grinning into her shoulder. "Hi, Amanda."

"Ugh, did you get taller? Not fair." She pulled away and looked me up and down, and my insides trembled under her gaze.

I rolled my eyes to shake off the unsettling feeling of being scrutinized. "Shut up, of course not. You're just seeing things because now I'm older than you."

Amanda scoffed. "Ugh, whatever, I hate you so much." She straightened, her eyes lighting up. "Wait, I have something for you! Well, a lot of somethings, but this is the first one."

Before I could ask, she hurried back to the car and threw open the passenger door, rummaging around. Popping out, she hurried over to me, holding out her hand with a flourish.

A plastic crown lay in her palm, silver and embedded with cheap pink gems, but somehow it was the prettiest thing I'd ever seen, glittering in the light of the morning sun and made brilliant by her bright grin.

"Now you're officially the birthday princess," Amanda declared, lifting it and placing it on my head, snugly setting it around my beanie. "It might fall off, just pretend it doesn't."

"Amanda." Her name rode out on the rest of the air in my lungs. "This is—"

She laughed and shook her head. "Nope, that's just present one! You'll get the rest during the day." She held open the passenger door with a bow. "Now get in before we're late. We're going to Starbucks. That's present two!"

I grinned as I got in. Somehow, attention didn't feel quite so daunting when Amanda was the one giving it.

Amanda had always been the best at birthdays, for the entirety of our friendship, but this year, she had gone the extra mile, which I quickly noticed when I got to Art and a bouquet of helium balloons sat in my seat, a big 17 hovering over Jordan.

"Present three," Amanda announced as she leaned against the doorway, smiling at me, my eyes widening.

"How did you even do this?"

Jordan waved. "That was me! She made me pick the balloons up and I had to promise not to suck the helium out of them until I asked you first."

"If there's even one missing, Jordan, I swear to God—"

I tackled Amanda in a hug. "Thank you. I can't wait to cart them around all day and get way too much unwanted attention."

She squeezed me back. "How else will they be reminded that you're special?"

"I'm sure you'll never let them forget."

I pulled away to see her eyes on me, amused, and the intensity of her hazel gaze was too much. I was too aware of her arms wrapped around my waist, the heat of them comforting, and she gave me a soft smile, tugging on the ends of my hair. I hope she didn't notice the way I shivered at her touch. "I'll see you later, okay? Watch out for the rest of your gifts. I'm not done spoiling you."

I blushed as she left, and I was still red when I made my way to my seat, the other students calling out "Happy birthday!" left and right. I waved at them, saying thanks as I sat, taking the bundle of balloons and setting them down next to me.

Jordan was giving me a grin. "Happy birthday, dude! Nice crown, by the way. Did your girlfriend give you that?"

"She's not my girlfriend."

"That's not what it looks like," Jordan pointed out, flicking one of the balloons. "Oh wait! I also have something for you."

He rummaged around in his backpack. "I had some leftover money from my small business, so I got you this." He extracted a red beanie that looked exactly like the one I had on, just without the holes in the hemline from wear.

I took it, turning it over in my hands and marveling at the softness. "Jordan, this is so nice." I gave him a smile. "Thank you, buddy."

Jordan beamed. "I'm glad you like it. I was getting tired of watching you pick at the threads in yours. This way, your aesthetic is intact and you have a hat that doesn't look like Swiss cheese. Everyone wins."

"Don't knock it. This hat is older than you are. Show some respect." I shoved his shoulder, and he laughed.

Before he could respond, Dani took her seat across from us. "Happy birthday, Maggie!" She waved. "I wish I'd known. I would've made you a card or something."

I shook my head. "No worries. I'm sure I'll have enough to cart around with this stuff." I nodded at the balloons. "Amanda can go a little too far sometimes. She's a Leo."

Dani nodded. "You're a Libra, right?"

"Yeah, if you can't fucking tell by the everything about me."

Jordan nodded. "Indecisive, overthinking ass."

I glared at him, and he pressed his lips together. "Quiet down over there."

"You know what would make me shut up? A balloon."

He plucked the string of the smallest balloon and gave me pleading eyes, so I relented and nodded. "That'll just make you squeakier, not quieter, but fine."

Jordan was already undoing the balloon from its string, and Dani stared at him. "You're an Aquarius, aren't you?"

Jordan nodded as he sucked in some helium. I turned to Dani. "What are you?"

"Gemini, actually. Don't judge me."

I shook my head, holding up my hands. "I can't judge you. We've got air sign solidarity out here. We can't lose."

Jordan took the balloon out of his mouth and squeaked, "We're like the three musketeers."

Dani giggled and so did I, and I took the balloon from him. "Let me show you how it's done."

Dani, Jordan, and I spent the period inhaling too much helium and not doing any work, and my cheeks hurt from smiling. I had coffee and a crown, great friends, and balloons that floated on air the way my heart did, and knowing Amanda, the day could only get better.

And it did. Every period, there was a little gift waiting for me in class. I didn't know how she did it without me noticing, especially in the classes we were in, but it was magic. Whether it was a candy bar, or a stuffed animal, or a little trinket referencing inside jokes we shared, it paled in comparison to the smile that grew on Amanda's face as she watched me receive each gift, and her happiness at seeing *me* happy was the best present of all.

Well, besides the notes that accompanied each item.

*No one makes me as happy as you do.*

*You're so special and you don't even know it.*

*I'm so excited for the rest of our lives.*

*You're goofy and fun and the most wonderful friend.*

*I'm so happy we met in this life.*

By the end of the day, I had sixteen presents, my backpack bulging and heavy, and I caught up with Amanda after my last class at the pickup area near the band hall.

"Why are you spoiling me like this?" I asked.

Amanda laughed, sweeping her hair up into a bun on the top of her head. It was neat without her even trying, and my eyes lingered on the bare stretch of her neck, the delicate way she fanned herself with her hand. "Oh, Maggie, you still don't get it."

Her hands reached out, and she grasped my shoulders. I could only stare as her hazel gaze held me in place. "You're my best friend, easily the most important person in my life probably *ever*. Never forget that. Okay?"

I swallowed around the sudden lump in my throat, nodding. Amanda let go, stepping back but still smiling. "Good. Now, go home and eat something. I expect my best photographer to be on her game tonight, birthday or not."

I blinked, brought back to the present by the reminder of the football game I was supposed to be shooting tonight, even though my knees were now so wobbly I probably wouldn't be able to take two steps without collapsing. "Oh, oh, yeah, that's—that's probably a good idea."

"You'll get your last present during halftime. Don't keep me waiting," she said.

I smirked at the very idea of that. As if I'd ever been able to resist her.

At home, over the birthday cake Mom had picked up from HEB, she clapped her hands. "Okay, so now for your present!"

"Um, you got me too many things already," I pointed out, gesturing at the pile of gifts on the coffee table: a new pair of Converse, a My Chemical Romance hoodie, a new strap for my camera, *and* new headphones. We weren't exactly rolling in cash as a family. What more could they possibly give me?

Veronica shook her head, already headed down the hall to retrieve whatever it was. "This is different. Consider this gift an investment in your future," she called, out of sight.

She returned with a purple gift bag, stuffed with white tissue paper. I took it and set it on my lap, glancing around at my family. Alyssa and Mom were both grinning, their eyes glancing between me and the bag in anticipation.

Veronica settled into her seat, the picture of calm, but I could see the excitement gleaming in her eyes. "Well, what are you waiting for? Open it."

Still suspicious, I dragged the paper out, tossing it down beside me on the floor unceremoniously as I dug to reach the bottom of the bag. My fingers collided with something soft and purple, and I picked it up, my eyes wide.

It was another hoodie, a soft purple one with very familiar white lettering. *NYU* stared back up at me, and my stomach dropped and tightened. I looked up to see my family grinning at me from all angles, and I suddenly felt dizzy. "How—how did you—"

"I ordered it online," Alyssa said, bouncing a bit in her seat.

"We knew you'd probably get a ton of college gear because that seems to be all that the rich kids at those fancy colleges wear"—my heart squeezed at that—"so we wanted to make sure we got you started early," Veronica explained, smiling with a softness that I rarely saw from her.

"Do you like it?" Mom asked breathlessly, her hands clasped together and her eyes wide.

I gripped the fabric, searching for a price tag but saw that it had been removed, so I couldn't even do the exchange math between dollars and guilt. I bit my lip and released it, pasting on a smile and trying to mean it. "Yeah, I love it. Thank you so much. I can't wait to wear it."

The three most important people in my life beamed, and I prayed my smile looked genuine. These hoodies weren't cheap, I knew, but they'd wanted to support me so much that they'd shelled out for this on top of all the other gifts. I felt lower than dirt for having kept this from them for so long because now they'd actually spent *money* on the white lie I'd been telling them.

How could I take it back now? I needed to either buckle down and decide on NYU or tell them about my indecision, and both felt impossible, especially now.

Veronica drove me to the game, and as we rolled down Sam Houston, she said, "So. Those were a lot of gifts Amanda gave you. Even for a rich person."

Her face was passive, but that meant nothing since she had the world's best poker face, so I asked, "Yeah. Why do you ask?"

Veronica shrugged. "No reason, just that I know you guys have been a lot closer these days. You'd tell me, you know, if anything happened between you?"

"Is this the talk?"

"I'm basically your pseudo-dad. Of course this is the talk."

I nodded. "You have the right level of emotional constipation for the position of stand-in dad."

Veronica rolled her eyes. "Thanks. I'm touched. Seriously, though, I've always wondered whether you and Amanda were gonna be an item."

My heart leapt. Other people had noticed this too? "Is that only you thinking that because I'm bi, I can't be just friends with anyone now?"

Veronica shook her head as she rolled to a stop at the light before Williams Road. The road was a blur of headlights, bumper-to-bumper traffic in all directions, heading to the stadium. "You know we're past that. I just want to make sure that you're not getting yourself into something you can't handle . . . and that you know you can talk to me if you do."

She was studiously not looking at me, focusing on the traffic, but I heard the solemnity and care in her voice even as she tried to remain neutral. I smiled. "I know, sissy. And I will."

"Okay. Well. Good." Veronica cleared her throat. "Now help me find a parking spot when we get closer because it's the least you can do after making me drive in this traffic."

Luckily, the game against La Feria that night was a loud distraction from the problems that had been on my mind all day, and I lost myself in the yelling of the crowd and the grunts and thuds coming from the field as I roamed around the tarmac, taking pictures. The sky was black, the floodlights unrelenting, and I wove between coaches and cheerleaders and strewn duffle bags as halftime approached and the changing of the guard commenced, football players filing off the field as the props for the band's performance were brought on.

I took pictures of the band as they filed in, keeping an eye out for Amanda, but I didn't see her until they'd set up the podium and she was climbing onto it. Her uniform was spotless and wrinkle-free, her high ponytail neat, and she caught my eye from the top. She winked, and the flutter of her eyelashes was stronger than the night breeze brushing my skin.

I was enraptured, clutching the chain-link fence that separated the bleachers from the sidelines, as the band launched into their halftime performance. I had to switch my breathing to manual so I could remember to take in air as I watched Amanda conduct. The wave of her hands was steady and forceful, each flick like the beat of blood beneath a bruise.

Before I knew it, it was over. The band was marching off the field, but Amanda hadn't gotten off the podium. She seemed to be talking to someone below her, and I watched as she gestured in my direction. A gaggle of cheerleaders blocked my view, saying hi to me as they passed, and I offered them a quick smile, craning my neck to look for Amanda.

As the cheerleaders passed, I could see Amanda, no longer talking to whoever it was, and I was caught off guard when she looked directly at me, her eyes blazing with postgame adrenaline.

"Maggie?"

I looked down to follow the voice, and one of the freshmen from the percussion section was standing there nervously. It was Willow, who I vaguely remembered played the xylophone, and she thrust something out to me. It was a bundle of something, and it crinkled in my hands when Willow handed it to me. "They're from Amanda. She told me to give them to you. Happy birthday."

Then she was gone, hurrying back to her section, and I stared down at the bundle in my hands, which I now realized was a bouquet of huge purple and gold flowers with green stems. They were made of butcher paper; she must have stolen it from the art room at some point when I wasn't with her. Suddenly, there was no air left in my lungs, warmth flooding my body, but I felt lighter than ever, floating above the ground. When I looked up, searching for her, she was right where my gaze had last settled on her, on the stand staring at me.

Amanda's ponytail was now messy from her previous movements, a few tendrils of her hair fluttering in the night breeze, and her cheeks were flushed. Her eyes were steady on mine, and even from this distance, I could see the way they twinkled in the stadium lights. She grinned, a beautiful and brilliant thing stretching across her face, and very dramatically reached a hand up to her lips, bowing a bit as she blew me a kiss.

The force of it slammed into me, making my chest explode with butterflies, and like a cheeseball, I mimed catching it in my fist, unable to do anything but stare at that megawatt smile as she winked and looked away.

I was a fucking goner. I had no idea until then how badly I'd wanted this, but now I knew. The fizzy feeling from this morning had only intensified, and I felt like I was space-walking my way through the rest of the game, the bouquet of flowers clutched in my fist. I barely took any photos, too busy staring at Amanda, and I was only brought back to earth a few minutes before the end of the game by a text.

Meet me in the parking lot after?

This was usually our routine at football games I photographed, just a little catch-up before we went our separate ways for the weekend, but my heart pounded, remembering the kiss she'd blown me. I couldn't help but hope . . . I texted back *of course* and counted down as the long football minutes ticked away.

After the game had ended, I beat Amanda to the student parking lot, standing in our usual spot on the side of the athletic building, out of sight from the crush of cars and spectators that filled the lot. I leaned against the wall as band students walked the asphalt path from the stadium to the school, the sun-warmed brick calming my pulse as I waited.

Like any good leader, Amanda appeared after the last of the band had passed, her backpack slung over one arm as she crossed the green space between the road and the building. Her face was dewy with sweat, her baby hairs flying in the humidity. She was still wearing her rumpled drum major uniform, and her ponytail was loose and hanging over her shoulder, on the verge of coming undone.

She had never looked more beautiful.

It was moments like this when it felt useless to try and fight these feelings. Here was my gorgeous best friend, the person who knew me better than almost anyone, glowing with pride at a job well done. She had spent an entire day making my existence brighter than ever before. My heart had been taken hostage by this dazzling, ferocious girl, and I was helpless, dazed in the light of her smile.

"Hey you," she said breathlessly as she reached me. "How was the game?"

What game? Oh right. Football. That's what I was doing here. "It was good. Got some good shots, so the football spread will be good, at least."

How many times could I say "good" until it lost its meaning?

Amanda leaned her shoulder against the wall beside me, her smile tired but satisfied, and I mimicked her pose to face her. "I'm glad. I really do appreciate it. I don't trust half of my photographers the way I trust you."

"They're not even half as good as me, so . . ."

Amanda laughed. "That's true. So how did you like your birthday?"

"I loved it. I . . . I can't believe you'd do all this for me. I mean, I know you go hard . . . but this year felt different. I mean, seventeen gifts, Amanda." I brandished the flowers. "Like how did you even—"

"You'd be surprised what you can do with fifteen minutes and a YouTube video." Amanda shrugged one shoulder, giving me a surprising smile. "Would you make fun of me if I said something super cheesy right now?"

"Definitely." My pulse picked up speed, and I held my breath. I couldn't let something as unimportant as oxygen ruin this moment.

"Oh good." She bit her lip, then released it. "Every single year, I love you more. We just . . . we click so much more every year, like we're growing up but also growing toward each other? And going to school in New York, well, it scares me—"

"It does?" I had never heard her say that out loud before. Maybe I could finally tell her how I felt.

She nodded. "It scares me, going so far from everything we know, but knowing you'll be there with me, it makes me feel like I can do anything. *You* make me feel like I can do anything."

She took my hand, her palm soft and her fingers tangling in mine. "It's you and me, Maggie. Until the end of time. So I wanted to show you that, in my gift to you this year."

My body filled with warmth, and I couldn't contain the smile that flooded across my face. I squeezed her hand. "You did. You really did. And you . . . you make me feel the same."

She did. Amanda made me feel special and brave, like I could take on the whole world with her next to me. Maybe I could actually do this NYU thing, take on the city and take on the debt, if it meant I could keep her close to me. I remembered what Mrs. Lozano said, thinking about my future and what I wanted, and all I could think about right now was how much I wanted *Amanda*, no matter how much heartache it caused me.

Amanda's eyes dropped to the NYU hoodie I was wearing, and the corners of her eyes crinkled when she grinned. Her free hand came up and toyed with the drawstrings. "I like this. It looks good on you."

Her eyes flicked up as she twirled the strings between her fingers, and she was so *close*. I could count the flecks of gold and brown in her eyes, and she was still smiling in that soft, fond way that made me feel like I was soaring through the sky on silver wings. It would be so easy for me to lean in, ask if it would be okay if I—

Amanda's eyes caught on something behind me, and she smiled and dropped my hand to wave. "Babe!"

"You did great tonight, babe." I stiffened as I heard the crunch of gravel behind me, and then the clap of someone's hand on my shoulder. "What's up, girl?"

I bit back a curse. "Hi, Jaime," I gritted out as he came to stand beside Amanda, wrapping an arm around her shoulder.

I watched him tug her closer and kiss the top of her head as he turned to me. "Happy birthday, Maggie."

"Thanks, it *was*." Until *he* got here anyway. "So, um, I should probably get going."

I hated that I couldn't be around her when he was here. His existence loomed over my relationship with her, a dark cloud I couldn't ignore, and I could already feel the storm of doubt and misery inside me that brewed when he was near.

Amanda nodded, saying, "I'll text you later?"

"Yeah, sounds good."

"Happy birthday, Maggie," she said, giving me one last smile.

I held on to the image, committing to memory the feeling of her hand in mine and trying to ignore the way my body missed her as I walked away.

That night, I took a picture of the bundle of paper flowers, lying on its side in the light of my lamp, and readied another post, drumming my fingers against the table. Was it possible that Amanda might feel something stronger for me than just friendship? I was too deep in this to deal with the uncertainty any longer. I needed to make a move, and do it soon.

A, you made my birthday the best it's ever been. When I'm by your side, I feel like I can take on the world. I know you'd stand with me through anything, and nothing could stand against the two of us. It makes me want to throw away my fear and take on the challenge that is NYC because you'll be there with me. Could this connection between us be real, and is it enough to get through such an uncertain future?

# 9

"Excuse me, friends," Amanda announced on Monday at lunch, clapping her hands. "Now that Jordan is almost done abandoning the lunch table, it's time to talk about weekend plans."

We were eating lunch in the back of the AP Physics classroom, crowded around a lab table. Jordan wasn't sitting with us because he was in the classroom part of the room, finishing up a chess game. Mr. Velazquez, chess wizard/physics teacher, was the faculty advisor of the chess club, so he let the members eat lunch here under the guise of practice.

Eating lunch while hunched over the lab tables was less disgusting than sitting on the floor in the main hall, so, naturally, we tagged along with Jordan.

Jordan checked his opponent and turned in his chair to face us, glaring at Amanda. "Chess is a game of strategy, finesse. It takes time."

"In the words of April Ludgate, 'Time is money, money is power, power is pizza, pizza is knowledge.' Stop wasting it." Amanda waved her hand like she was batting away a pesky fly. "We haven't hung out on a weekend in forever, and I have the perfect opportunity—"

"It's y'all's fault that we haven't hung out," Matthew said, pointing at Amanda, Dani, and me. "If some people weren't high-freaking-achievers with twenty million extracurriculars—"

I held out a fist to Amanda and Dani, who smacked their knuckles against mine with matching smug expressions and said, "Nerd squad unite. It's all right, Matthew, you can follow my IG when I'm a tour photographer. I'll even put you in close friends if you're nice to me."

"I don't know about you, bro, but I'm seeing some snobs in the room right now," Jordan commented.

Matthew took his bag of Doritos out of the center of the table, passing them to Jordan. "Snobs don't get to eat my snacks."

"Eat my ass, Maldonado," Amanda snapped before resuming her neutral expression and clearing her throat. "As I was saying, I have the perfect opportunity for a hang. My parents are having a cookout at our place, and there's gonna be a bonfire, so they said I could invite y'all."

"You already know that I'm in. I love fire." I grinned. I loved Amanda's parents' parties because it was always fun to see grown adults get drunk and act like children.

"I'm down," Jordan said. "Your dad makes the best fajitas. I'm taking home leftovers, just so you know."

"As you should. Dani, are you in?" Amanda asked her, but there was a hesitancy in her voice that would've been oblivious to everyone else. I had known her the longest, so I could read her face like a book, and I was confused as to why it looked like she didn't really want to invite Dani at all.

Thankfully, Dani didn't seem to have noticed. She just beamed at the inclusion. "Well, I've been tempted with fire and fajitas, so how can I say no to that?"

"Hey, how long have you guys been there?" Mr. Velazquez asked, looking up from the intense chess match he'd been having with one of the seniors. "No eating in my lab. You're going to grow a third head."

I made a face at him. "I've cleaned your supply closet before. You don't have any chemicals here. This isn't even a chemistry classroom."

"Fair enough. But you still shouldn't be eating in here."

The bell rang, signaling the end of lunch, and Amanda grinned. "Too late."

AP English and AP US History were across the hall from each other, so Jordan and I turned left into History while the rest of the group went to English. Jordan rolled languidly down the aisle on his skateboard and dropped into his seat in the back, and I took the seat next to him, plugging my phone into the outlet. Mr. De La Cruz hadn't entered the classroom yet, so Jordan turned to me, eyes wide and expectant, and folded his hands on the desk, looking like some kind of skater therapist.

"You and Amanda out here looking *reeeal* gay on your birthday. And I heard you went out with Matthew a few days ago."

I shushed him. "Don't talk about this now."

I nodded to the left, and Jordan followed my gaze. "Oh. Right."

Tori was chatting with Letty and Jackie a row away, and the last thing I needed was for Tori to have a problem with me after the Matthew issue was done and dusted. "Could you be any louder?"

Jordan winced, his voice dropping to a whisper. "Sorry. So have you made any more headway on, ya know, the project?"

I kept my voice low, safe from eavesdroppers. "The Matthew thing has petered out."

Jordan raised an eyebrow, smiling. "Really?"

"Yeah, finally." I sighed. "I mean, I know I have a tendency to fuck up over and over again, but I'm pretty sure this is permanent."

Jordan clapped me solidly on the shoulder, jostling me, and I grunted, swatting at him. "That's huge, dude. I'm proud of you."

Suddenly, a group of guys from the varsity football team, who had AP English this period, not History, crowded around Jordan.

"Hey, man, you got the stuff?" Ricky, the running back, said, throwing a furtive glance at his backpack.

I raised an eyebrow at Jordan, who ignored me in favor of opening his backpack and showing it to the guys. "I got M&Ms, Snickers, Skittles, and Corn Nuts. Everything is a dollar."

I craned my neck to see what looked like a whole concession stand in his backpack, and as the guys brandished wads of cash at him, I whispered, "What the fuck, Jordan?"

Jordan smiled smugly as they left with their spoils, tucking the dollar bills into the pocket of his backpack. "I told Coach Navarro yesterday at the game about my little errand-running venture, and he let me take the boxes of snacks from the concession stand that were about to expire. One man's trash—"

"—is another man's new guitar. Genius."

Jordan nodded confidently and kicked his feet up onto the basket of the desk in front of him. Jessie Robles turned around and glared at him, and he swallowed and took his feet off the desk.

There was movement in my periphery, outside the classroom door, and I turned to see Amanda outside. I was about to wave when Jaime appeared beside her.

They were arguing; I knew the signs. Amanda's face was flushed, her forehead creased with lines, and Jaime was gesticulating wildly, running his hands through his hair and looking frustrated.

Amanda looked away, chin clenched tightly, as though she were about to cry, and Jaime shook his head, looking exasperated, as he left to walk into class. I looked away to make it seem like I hadn't been staring, but Jaime was heading our way. I cursed Jordan's money-making brilliance as Jaime stopped in front of him. "You got Starburst in there?" he huffed.

"You bet, man." Jordan held open his backpack. "Everything okay?"

"Yeah, it's fine. Girls, dude. Whatcha gonna do?" Jaime turned to me. "Your girl is something else, you know that?"

"We both are, so no sympathy here."

Jaime shook his head. "Don't know how much more of this I can take. She's so hard to please."

"Amanda likes Skittles. That should please her," Jordan suggested, and I glared at him. "What? She *does*."

"You're right," Jaime agreed. "I'll take two."

As he left, I narrowed my eyes at Jordan. "Whose side are you on?"

"Yours, you dick. But I'm running a business here." Jordan squinted in thought. "On the bright side, though, you might have a chance if she and Jaime are on the outs."

He wasn't wrong. A spark of hope had bloomed in my chest, and I couldn't help but think of the way Amanda had looked at me under the streetlights of the student parking lot on Friday, her baby hairs floating in the wind and her grin wide, the way she'd felt pressed against me under the stars. *Every year, I love you more.*

The quince was approaching, and Amanda and Jaime were

more fragile than ever. Maybe it was finally time to make a decision.

---

"You have to put all the older milk in front of the new ones we get in," I instructed Dani from behind the counter. "That way the older milk doesn't just keep getting older."

Dani had driven me home, and when she saw that I had a shift at the store, she had volunteered to help put away some of the shipments that had piled up during the day. I certainly appreciated the help, but mostly because I got to watch Dani's brow scrunch up in concentration as she looked at the invoices and carefully counted every product in the boxes. It was endearing, the care she put into even the most mundane tasks.

"Have you been doing this your whole life?" Dani asked, carefully arranging the milk in the fridge.

"Mmm, pretty much—since I was, like, three and could hand things to my mom without dropping them. Before that, my mom would stick me in this tiny playpen behind the counter." I smiled, remembering the stories my mother and Veronica had told me. "Veronica would stand on a step stool and run the register whenever I needed to be changed. My mom once changed me in under thirty seconds, that's how good she got at work-life balance. My mom was the original girl boss before it became a tool of white feminism."

"Iconic," Dani agreed.

I ripped open another box of menthols, wrinkling my nose as the formerly tightly packed odor wafted out. I checked the invoice before unlocking the case and stacking them up inside.

"When we got older and Alyssa was born, it was easier," I said. "Mom could actually get a break at the end of the day when Veronica got home from school and would go and nap for a bit with Alyssa."

Dani was quiet, and I looked up to see her looking at me with a calculating expression, as though I was a math problem she was trying to solve. "Seems like a lot of responsibility for two kids."

"Um, yeah, I guess it was."

I had never seen it that way, but now I thought about the years of learning math by helping my mom balance checkbooks, watching Alyssa anxiously as she toddled around learning to walk on freshly mopped floors, teaching her how to read using the shipments of the San Benito News that showed up on Thursdays. With Veronica working part-time at the store after classes at UCAS and me watching the register the rest of the time, our mother at least got to be a part-time mom instead of a full-time shop owner. No one had ever questioned the fact that Veronica and I had been raised as little adults.

I had never really thought much about it—not until now, when someone had actually said it out loud.

Dani misunderstood my silence. "Sorry, I didn't mean to overstep—"

I shook my head quickly. "No, no, you didn't. I was just surprised is all. Alyssa was the only one of us that really got to be a kid because the rest of us were raising her and running this place. And it wasn't hard, really. It just felt like everyday life, ya know?"

"I guess it could've been worse." Dani shrugged. "You could've been born into one of those families with a prank YouTube channel."

I smiled. "A grocery store is probably the least insidious family business."

The little bell tied to the front door rang out, startling

us both, and Veronica and Alyssa walked in, Alyssa racing behind the counter with barely a "Hi, sissy" as she grabbed the bag of Funyuns she had stored on the shelf behind me.

"Hey, don't be rude," Veronica scolded, setting her backpack down on the counter. "Say hi to—it's Dani, right?"

Dani nodded, standing up straight, and Veronica repeated, "Say hi to Dani."

Alyssa, mouth full of Funyuns, waved and garbled, "Hi to Dani."

I got hit with a wave of onion breath and tugged on her ponytail. "Ew, don't be rude."

Alyssa swallowed and then opened her mouth, breathing hot, smelly air in my direction. "Don't tell me what to do."

"That's nasty, staahhpp." I batted my hand at her as she crowded me against the counter, showering me with Funyun breath.

Veronica was holding in her laughter. "Both of you are so fucking childish."

"Ay, watch your mouth," I heard, and all three of us turned to see Mami descending the stairs. When she got to the bottom, she saw Dani there and wrinkled her brow, putting a hand to her chest. "A la madre, I don't remember giving birth to you."

Dani laughed, and I was surprised when instead of shaking my mother's hand, she gave her a hug. My mother was surprised too, freezing before hugging her back with a warm smile on her face. Turning back to us, she asked, "¿Quién es?"

"Me llamo Dani. Soy una amiga de Maggie."

My mother looked back at her, surprised and, it seemed, a bit impressed. I couldn't blame her; I had a barely functioning understanding of Spanish, and none of my friends even had that. "Hablas español."

Dani looked sheepish. "Estoy aprendiendo. It's slow."

"Do your parents speak it?"

"Yes, but they put off teaching us until a few years ago. I've been stunted, I know."

Mami shook her head. "Yes, I've failed my own children. They have terrible accents."

Veronica, Alyssa, and I had heard all this before, and we launched into our own excuses:

"You never taught us—"

"I *know* Spanish, my accent just sucks—"

"I'm learning Spanish at school! Yo soy Alyssa y yo quiero tacos!"

My mom gave Dani an exasperated face. "See what I deal with?"

Dani was trying not to laugh. "At least they're funny."

Mami smiled softly. "They're wonderful."

Alyssa frowned. "You're a sap, Mom."

It was incredible how fast our mom's face could go from wistful to withering. "Did you pay for those chips?"

That night, as Veronica and I cleaned up the kitchen and Alyssa did homework at the table, Veronica said, "I like Dani."

"You've only seen her twice," I pointed out, scrubbing a pan with steel wool at least half as old as I was.

"I like her too!" Alyssa echoed.

"You've only seen her once!"

"It's all about the vibes," Alyssa insisted. "The feeling you get around people. The *vibes*. Plus she did a nice job with my invitations. But mostly the vibes."

"Stop saying *vibes* like that, you sound like a creep—"

Veronica looked at me, begrudgingly amused. "See? The vibes don't lie. Seriously though, she was nice. Are you dating her?"

I spluttered, dropping the plate I was holding into the sink and splashing soapy water on myself. "I—what—*no.*"

"She looks at your butt when you're not looking," Alyssa pointed out.

My face was on fire. "She does not," I mumbled.

"Whatever you say, Mags." Alyssa shrugged, returning to her work. "For someone who's so smart, you sure don't think things through."

# 10

The bonfire at Amanda's house was scheduled for Saturday evening, but Veronica was going to CJ's and Mom would be working, so that afternoon, I texted Amanda to ask if I could be dropped off a couple hours earlier. The response I received made me feel warm despite myself.

**Amanda:** Yeah duh. Jaime's being an asshole. I could def use some alone time with you. Girls day out? *kissy-face emoji*

It couldn't possibly mean anything, but that kissy-face stirred something low in my belly. I remembered my dream about her, the way she felt in my arms, her kiss on my neck. Could I make this a Hail Mary trial date?

I waved at my mom as the car pulled away and let myself into the house. The front door was never locked, and we'd been friends long enough that Amanda's parents regarded me as a second daughter anyway. They had told me so themselves once, but they were also drunk at the time. Either way, I planned to make the most of it.

I kicked off my shoes and left them next to the door.

Amanda was on the black leather recliner, her long skinny-jean-clad legs kicked over the side. She waved at me with her foot, not looking up from her phone. "Hey."

"Whaddup?" I greeted, flopping down over the arm of the couch next to her.

Amanda frowned at her phone before tossing it to the side with a huff. There was steel in her gaze when she finally looked up at me, her jaw clenched tight. "Can we just get out of here for a minute? I don't want to see a boy ever again."

"I call bullshit on that, but sure, let's go."

Amanda was craving "heartbreak ice cream," so we went to the Sonic in Harlingen. It was five in the afternoon, and the heat was at its boiling point.

I looked over at the trees that lined the edge of the cliff that dropped down into one of the countless trails leading to McKelvey. Practically sitting in a basin, there were little hidey-hole pathways throughout Harlingen that led down into the trail, congregating along the river that cut through the center of it all. I wondered if Dani had explored all of them—

The crackling of the speaker and the monotone greeting of the Sonic employee on the other end made the vision of Dani scatter like a reflection on a river suddenly disturbed, and Amanda called, "Yeah, can I get an Oreo cheesecake shake with hot fudge? And add extra fudge."

She turned to me. I wasn't hungry, but did that matter when it came to ice cream? "Peanut butter shake."

Amanda parroted my words into the speaker, and the employee gave her the total before the speaker clicked off. She rolled her eyes. "My order was so obnoxious. Now even this Sonic guy is gonna know that I'm having relationship problems."

I bit the inside of my cheek. Of course, even on a girls' day, all Amanda wanted to talk about was Jaime. "What are y'all fighting about *now*?"

Amanda gave a disgusted scoff. "Ugh, we actually had a real conversation the other day, and I thought we had had a breakthrough. We finally decided to see how this plays out long-term—yeah, I know, *duh*—and then today he blows me off all day. I know he's been online because he watched my story—you're in it, by the way, of course."

I could only nod as Amanda barreled ahead. "And, like, I *know* he's in McAllen visiting his grandma and can't really text, but his *ex* is from McAllen. What am I supposed to do with that information?"

"Um, realize that he's there to visit his grandma and he's not going to ditch his whole family to see some ex from a year and a half ago? You should be happy—he gave you what you wanted: long-term talk and corny stuff like that." I tried to keep the irritation out of my voice, but it didn't matter anyway. Amanda was too busy blowing up Jaime's phone to respond to me.

A Sonic employee arrived with our shakes, and I was relieved to stop assessing this and enjoy my ice cream. Amanda waved off my attempts to hand her money. "Stop. This was my idea."

I nodded. Fine, I would just pay her in advice—even if the last thing I wanted to do was help her work things out with someone else. "Have you tried telling him how you feel?"

Amanda pursed her lips, pulling the cherry off the top of her shake. She plucked the fruit from the stem, then twirled the stem between her fingers. "I just don't want him to think that I'm going to go all crazy and super clingy."

"But you *are* crazy, and you're going to *get* super clingy if you don't work this out," I warned, stirring the whipped cream into my milkshake. I took a sip; it was too thick, so I decided to dig into it with the plastic spoon that came with it.

"Maybe." Amanda shrugged. She reached out to smooth a strand of my hair that had fallen out of the sloppy French braid I'd done that morning, tucking it behind my ear. Could she feel the way I shivered at her touch, gentle and warm against my skin? "But enough of that. I promised you a girls' afternoon, and here I am talking about a boy." Amanda stuck the cherry stem into her mouth, staring out at the road as her mouth worked. Her lips pursed and opened almost sinfully, and my hungry eyes wouldn't stop staring.

"It's fine. This is basically what a girls' afternoon with us is like anyway." I tried to tie my lips into the bow of a smile and prayed that Amanda couldn't tell the edges were frayed and falling apart.

Amanda pulled the cherry stem, now a neat, tight knot, from between her full lips, which were puckered in a kiss, and my brain felt as if I had just stuck a fork into a wall socket, my skin buzzing with excess energy. My mind was wild with the thought of her lips pressed against mine, pressed against my neck, my chest, my hips. I swallowed a few times and forced myself to look away, toward the empty field across the street. I focused on that instead of on the way Amanda's tongue had peeked out to meet her fingers, the stem bright red against her pink lips. Staring out at the field, I tried to focus the lens of my brain, trying to convince it that the subject in my vision was my friend, not my girlfriend, not someone who loved me the way I loved her—no matter how much I wanted her to.

But the picture was saturated with bias, with hope, and I didn't know how to keep my own perspective from sullying the image.

When we had finished our shakes, Amanda said, "Let's go to the bridge." I smiled and nodded. Just like old times.

We parked by the little field I'd been watching and walked down the dirt path that led into the arroyo's basin, where the main asphalt path was. We dodged joggers and kids on bikes, following the road until the foliage lining the edges of the path turned to stone and began to steepen and we reached the train tracks. Staring up the dirt hill littered with grey rocks, we made our journey upward, stumbling over stones and using our hands to steady ourselves as the hill got steeper.

Amanda reached the tracks before I did. I quickened my pace to catch up with her, the rocks shifting precariously beneath my feet and feeling like marbles. Suddenly, one of the rocks I was holding slipped from its spot, and I flailed, my stomach getting that swooping feeling as I stumbled back, yelping. Not missing a beat, Amanda whipped a hand out and jerked me back up.

The momentum of Amanda's sudden pull sent me stumbling forward. Unable to find my footing in time, I fell face-first into her with a strangled "Fuck."

Amanda was quick, though, only rearing back the tiniest bit as she wrapped her arms around me and steadied me against her. Heart hammering in my chest, I pulled back to stare at her, her arms so steady that even though we were still in a precarious position on the edge of the tracks, I felt safer than I had in a long time. Our noses were inches apart, her hands splayed on my back. I was frozen, unwilling to be the first to pull away. How could I? It felt like lying, like giving up, like caving in when all I wanted to do was be closer to her.

My eyes dropped to Amanda's lips, and her hands slipped down to my waist; she still hadn't released me. She didn't move to step away, and I pulled my gaze from her perfect pink mouth back to her eyes, which were searching mine.

I was still, afraid to stay but afraid to move. I waited, as always, for her to make the first move. Her eyes were contemplative; what was she thinking about? They roved over my face, and I didn't know what it meant. Amanda bit her bottom lip, and I wanted to surge up to catch it between my own, to see if that cherry had left its taste—

But Amanda released me, stepping back shyly, and visions of cherries and lips and hands on heated skin vanished, leaving me empty in a way I hadn't expected.

"Thanks," I said numbly.

Amanda just smiled and said, "Of course," before gesturing back to the bridge behind her. "Our kingdom awaits."

The train tracks near the park had long since been abandoned, although the bridge was still standing, weather-worn but still sturdy. The tracks themselves sat on a bed of rocks, suspended over the trail, and when we got to the middle, I peered over the side to the path below, to the road where we had just come from. People were passing by, walking, biking, and skateboarding back and forth. I waited for someone to look up; I didn't know why, but I wanted them to.

They didn't, and I turned back to Amanda, leaning against the railing. "It's beautiful," I said, gesturing to the view. You could see all the trees and paths, the water in the distance. Even the wisps of clouds felt insignificant here, in this haven in the sky.

Amanda stared at her phone as she sat, cross-legged, on one of the wooden slats. "It's the same nothing that it always is. All brown and green and boring."

I gave the horizon one last long look before sitting in front of Amanda, crossing my legs. "You're cheery."

Amanda looked up from her phone, setting it aside. "Remember when we first came here, before freshman year?"

I did. That was the dark summer, when Amanda's grandma died and Pinot Grigio became her mother's therapist. Amanda's house was in shambles then, yelling and breaking dishes a daily occurrence, so even though she didn't have a license, she always managed to show up at my house at any hour of the day, asking to hang out. The Valley's endless summer became a curse during those three months, a prison sentence we were all waiting out. The palm trees and perpetual sunlight made the Valley look like paradise to outsiders, but only we knew that longer days meant prolonged grief, no rest from the day's little tragedies. The nights were never long enough, and joy rarely came in the morning.

That was when we found the bridge, tagging along with Veronica and CJ to the park. They would sit at one end of the bridge while we sat at the other, all of us seeking the oasis of being suspended, secluded, in the air. For a moment, we got to hover over whatever issues had driven us there, seeking solace.

"Yeah, I do," I said, wondering where she was going with this.

"Things are so different now." Amanda laid down on the plank, and I took the plank next to her. The wood was warm from lying in the sun all day, and it was comforting. I laid on my side to stare at Amanda as she gazed at the sky. "But still the same, ya know?"

"Um, I guess? Say more right now."

The John Mulaney reference made her laugh, and my anxiety eased a bit as she rolled onto her side, propping herself up on an elbow and pillowing her head in her hand. "My parents worked their issues out, sort of. I met Jaime. You came out.

But I feel just as close to you as I always have. That hasn't changed."

I smiled, turning to her. "We have each other still. And I think that's all that matters, knowing someone is gonna be next to you for a long time."

For forever, if I could help it.

Amanda's eyes were calculating then, narrowing in thought. "Do you . . . why don't I feel this way in my relationship? Why don't I rely on him like I do with you?"

*Because I know you. I love you with everything in me. I could give you what you need, if you let me.* I didn't say any of that though. Instead, I said, "I don't know, maybe it's because we've known each other longer?"

"Not that much longer." Amanda bit her lip, suddenly shier than I'd seen her before. "Do you think . . . do you think it's because you're a girl? Like, did you trust Trish more than Matthew?"

I scoffed. "I didn't trust Trish as far as I could throw her, and for good reason."

"But seriously," she pressed. "Was it different with a girl?"

I turned to the sky, thinking back on both of my past relationships. "It was, and it wasn't. I was with Matthew first, and that felt one way, but getting with Trish was . . . interesting. Like, my heart knew it had feelings for her, but my brain had to catch up."

Amanda's brow wrinkled. "How?"

"Well, it was like my brain was still super heteronormative and trying to convince me that we were just friends, and that's why it felt different than it did with Matthew, but that wasn't the reason." I shook my head.

"So what was the reason then?"

Amanda's gaze was intense, and I swallowed a bit, feeling

like I was trying to describe the sun to someone who had lived their whole life underground. "I think . . . every person you love feels different to you. Like they leave their own unique set of fingerprints on your heart, pluck different chords on your heartstrings. That's why none of them feels quite the same as the others."

"Huh." Her eyes flicked up and down my face, and I couldn't tell what she was looking for. "Can I ask you something?"

"Yeah, of course."

"It might sound weird," she warned, sitting up facing me.

I sat up too, and my body buzzed, her words making the hairs on the back of my neck stand up. "You know I can handle weird."

"You can, can't you? You always could." Her lips quirked up in a soft half smile. "I've never kissed a girl, or anyone but Jaime."

My own lips twitched, and the words slipped out before I could contain them. "Do you want to?"

It was a joke (mostly), but Amanda didn't laugh. Instead, she bit her lip, giving the smallest, shyest nod. "Is that . . . I told you it was weird."

My mouth went dry, and my tongue felt like sandpaper, rough and useless. I swallowed around it, my voice small and shaky. "Well, I told you I can handle weird."

Her intense gaze didn't move from mine, and she looked so *beautiful*, lit up by the pink-and-orange sky behind her. "It doesn't have to mean anything or change anything. Just a kiss, you know?"

The walls of my chest felt like they were crumbling at that, but the hope in my brain flared still. After all, I hadn't been completely sure I was bi until kissing Trish had confirmed it for me. Maybe a kiss would do the same for Amanda.

"Yeah, I mean . . . you need to figure out how it feels. So you know."

"So I know," she whispered, her gaze dropping to my lips and then snapping back up to meet my eyes as she leaned in.

All I could see was her. Her soft skin, her glossy pink lips, and those hazel eyes that had always stopped my heart and restarted it with every look, every wink, every flutter of her long eyelashes. My chest squeezed, and my eyes slid shut as her lips touched mine.

Her gloss tasted rosy, and the press of her warm mouth against mine rooted me to the bridge. Even suspended over the world, her touch steadied me, and my head fell forward as she pulled away, chasing the tether that had formed between me and her and planet earth.

There was a pretty pink blush on her cheeks, and she smiled. "Thanks. That was . . . interesting."

*Interesting?* What did that mean? I opened my mouth to ask, but then Amanda's phone rang, making us both jump. She took it out of her pocket, squinting at the screen. "It's my mom, hold on."

I listened as she assured her mom that we'd be back soon, and I wondered if we were going to talk more about this, but as she smiled at me over the squawk of her mother on the other end of the line, I wanted to stay here in this moment, where nothing was happening between us now but maybe, just maybe, anything could.

---

Back at Amanda's house that evening, I was still shaken up from our kiss, but I tried to pull myself together. There was a party going on, after all.

The bonfire was already raging in the backyard when

Matthew's truck pulled up to the front of the house, Dani and Jordan popping out of the back seat.

"Let me at the fire!" Jordan called, pumping his fist in the air.

"He's been talking about it the whole way here," Dani filled us in. "Not gonna lie, it was quite worrying."

"Sounds like Jordan," I said. Her outfit caught my eye: a green sundress with little flowers and an overlarge worn denim jacket with flannel patches on the elbows. "I like your outfit. Very girl-in-an-indie-band."

"Thanks, I think." Dani laughed.

Amanda was quiet, and I snuck a look at her to see her glancing between us, her eyes narrowed the tiniest bit in suspicion. She met my eyes, and they widened slightly like she'd been caught doing something she shouldn't. She quickly turned to Matthew, breaking away from my gaze. "Maldonado, for once you don't look like a bum."

Matthew glared at her, his hair wet and his navy blue button-down snug across his shoulders. "For once you don't look like a stuck-up—"

I clapped my hands together. "Okay, shall we go to the back before someone starts a fight?"

"I can't deal with violence before food," Jordan added, flinging an arm around my shoulders and gesturing to Dani to follow us. "Come on, it's time you reap the benefits of having a rich friend."

He wasn't wrong. Amanda's parents always went all out with their parties, and this one was no different. The air was filled with the scent of carne asada and chicken cooking on the grill, and norteño music poured from the speakers of Amanda's dad's suped-up Ford. It wasn't loud enough to drown out the raucous laughter of Amanda's tíos around the barbecue pit, or the cackling of her tías as they goaded each other into yet another round of shots at the plastic folding tables spread out beside the bonfire.

The heady nature of the purple sky helped my chest unwind from the events of this afternoon, and the smell of smoke was actually comforting, like anything was possible if the air was hazy enough. As we sat around the bonfire, I caught Amanda's eye through the dancing flames, and she gave me a soft smile that felt like a secret between us. She jerked her thumb at Jordan, telling a story about his latest money-making errand bathing a Belgian Malinois with severe anxiety, and we shared a laugh.

Maybe this could be a thing, if we let it.

But that was before Jaime rounded the corner of the house, crossing the grass toward us, and Amanda caught sight of him. Her face lit up, her eyes rivaling the fire between us as she leapt up and rushed toward him. My stomach churned as Amanda's father greeted Jaime with a big grin and a slap on the back, her tíos shaking his hand as Amanda hung off Jaime's arm, smiling up at him like he was the cause of everything good in her world.

She had smiled at me a lot in life, but it wasn't until this moment, in the saturated overexposure of the firelight, that I realized she'd never smiled at me like that.

My chest seized. There were no words for the way the pain burned through me, setting my insides ablaze. I wanted to scream, wanted to cry, wanted to take off running and not stop until I reached the main road, but I was frozen, watching the irrefutable evidence that my best friend loved someone who wasn't me.

"Maggie?" Dani's voice cut through my hazy heartbreak,

and I forced myself to look at her, her eyes soft with concern. "You okay?"

I blinked and realized I had tears in my eyes, so I wiped at them quickly and looked away, standing up. My legs were shaking, and I needed to get out of there. "Yeah, um, just the smoke—I'm gonna get some air."

"Do you want me to come with you?"

The care in her voice made me want to cry again, and I really didn't want to cry about this here, *especially* not in front of Dani. I shook my head, taking a step back. "No, don't worry about it. I'm just—see you in a bit."

Without looking back at her, I turned on my heel and hurried across the grass, focusing on the dark side of the house that was farthest away from the bonfire. My body felt stiff as I reached it, and I leaned back against the brick, pressing my head into it. The slight pain brought me back to where I was, and I tilted my head up toward the sky, the motion-sensor floodlight blinking on above me and making it difficult to see the stars. I closed my eyes instead.

I could see her, and him, and the way she looked as she leaned in to kiss me. Conflicting images and their colors swirled in my head, giving me vertigo. I took a deep breath, and then another to try to steady myself.

"Maggie? What's wrong?" My eyes snapped open as Amanda rounded the corner. "You ran out of there like the devil was after you."

"Did I?" I couldn't keep the hard edge out of my voice, and for once, I didn't care if it hurt her or not.

"Ooh, scary voice. Come on, talk to me." Amanda reached out for my hand.

I jerked away as she made contact, the once-comforting feel

of her hand now burning like a branding iron yanked from the fire. "What is this, Amanda?"

Amanda's smile dropped from her face, her expression going serious. "What do you mean?"

"This." I waved my hand between us. "Amanda, you kissed me. You're my best friend and you kissed me."

She frowned. "You said it didn't mean anything."

It felt as if a fist was crushing my windpipe, my voice sounding strangled as I said, "No, *you* said that. I didn't say that."

Amanda crossed her arms, staring me down. "You said we could kiss. I just wanted to see how it felt, and you let me."

I blanched, my stomach twisting sharply at how cold the *you let me* sounded. "So you were just *using* me, without even considering how it might make me feel?"

"No, of course not. How the fuck was I supposed to know you'd take it like this? You told me it was okay!" Amanda insisted, reaching out to touch my arm. "Just slow down for a second—"

I pulled away again. My throat began to swell, and I cursed the fact that my body's primary coping mechanism for stress was tears. "Stop that. It bothers me."

"Stop *what*? I didn't even *do* anything!" she said exasperatedly.

"Just because I like girls doesn't mean you can touch me like that, doesn't mean you can kiss me," I said, crossing my arms. "It's confusing. How am I supposed to respond when I can't even tell what you mean by any of it?"

Amanda's brow furrowed. "What I mean? Maggie, we're friends. Best friends. We've always touched like that."

"No, we *haven't*, Amanda. We didn't touch like that before I came out to you, before you and Jaime started having problems, and you know it."

"What does *Jaime* have to do with this? Is this because you don't like him? Is that why you're doing this?"

"I'm not the one doing anything, you're the one who's always blurring the boundaries, and *no,* this isn't about Jaime, this never was. This is about you and me and how there are things you just can't do with friends. Like *kiss* them without meaning it."

Amanda's eyes narrowed, the hazel color looking almost grey with the ice in them. "Do you think I liked you or something, because I was very clear—"

"No, you weren't, and you haven't been." I exhaled exasperatedly, pinching the bridge of my nose. If this was *clear,* I didn't want it. I was done arguing with Amanda about physicality and sexuality in the dark while her boyfriend stood feet away laughing with her family. I meant absolutely nothing to Amanda other than being a best friend she could constantly blur the line with, who she could push around because she knew I would always be there.

Not anymore. "All you've been doing is toeing whatever invisible line you think keeps you straight while being able to do whatever you want. Just because I'm your 'best friend' doesn't mean you get to toy with me whenever you like. If you're gay, fine. If you're straight, great. But leave me the fuck alone while you decide."

Amanda was all-out glaring at me, the frost in her eyes chilling me to the bone even as a wildfire raged inside of me. "You need to go. I'll make up an excuse for you to the others. Just go home."

The lump in my throat was suffocating me, but I still managed to croak, "Fine."

When Amanda had stomped back to the bonfire, I blinked back tears and started walking, crossing the large yard until

I reached the front of the house. I started walking down the perfectly paved road, out of the neighborhood where I'd never belonged anyway. I pulled out my phone. "Hey . . . yeah, no, I'm fine, just . . . can you please pick me up?"

Veronica was rolling up to the curb right as I reached Sam Houston, walking past the large stone Liberty Estates sign. "What's going on?"

I wiped the tears from my cheeks, sniffling, as I yanked open the car door. "I'll explain later. Let's just go."

# 11

When we arrived home, I did the first thing I always do when I come home upset: I got into the shower.

I passed Alyssa watching TV in the living room and tossed a muttered "hey" at her as I fast-walked to the bathroom, hoping she hadn't seen the tears that had escaped on the ride home. It was useless. As I undressed, I heard Veronica say to Alyssa, "I think we have a situation."

Exhaling shakily, I turned the water on and stepped into the shower.

Under the stream of water, the noises from the outside world were muffled, and I felt a bit better. I stood there for a long time, sometimes crying, sometimes not, just letting the hot water wash this horrible day off of my skin.

I took my time, washing and conditioning my hair. I even exfoliated and shaved. When I ran out of things to do in the shower, I steeled myself and shut the water off, missing it already.

When I got back to my room, it was empty, and I dressed quickly. I already knew where my sisters were waiting. I found them sitting on Veronica's full-size bed, an array of brightly colored bags of snacks gathered between them. I didn't even bother with a greeting. I simply plopped down on the bed in front of them, pulled a Twizzler out of the bag, and chomped into it with abandon. Alyssa propped her chin in her hands, waiting for me to speak, and Veronica looked at me expectantly.

So I began, because I was tired of being all alone in my mind.

I told the whole story, start to finish. I told them about Matthew and Dani and Amanda. I worked my way through the context of what had happened tonight. Veronica and Alyssa were riveted, and I was surprised at how quickly the words spilled out of me, flooding the space between us and swirling around the snacks. It had been hard to keep this secret from them, and for a moment I wondered why I had.

And then I remembered: They were both far too smart for my bullshit.

"You've done some weird things," Alyssa said, "but this is by far the weirdest."

"For real," Veronica said, nodding. "Why in the world would you post your thoughts on the freaking internet?"

"You're old, you don't understand. See, this is why I didn't tell y'all, you're being so negative—"

"Because we're telling you the truth, duh," Alyssa said, raising an eyebrow. It was kind of crazy how much she looked like Veronica and me in that moment. Our mother had passed on some strong genes when it came to shade.

"I get it though. You wanted to figure things out without ruining the friendship," Veronica said, thoughtful. "I've seen worse things done for less."

"I put my bid in for Dani," Alyssa said, wrapping herself up in her galaxy-printed blanket so that only her face could be seen. "She was nice."

"I'm not taking bets. I want to not have this problem," I complained. "Veronica, tell me how to fix it."

"I'm not telling you a damn thing . . . mostly because I don't even know how to go about this." Veronica shook her head. "I've never liked three people before, especially not my best friend who freaking *kissed* me."

"CJ was your best friend," Alyssa pointed out.

"Yeah, but at least he knew he liked girls. Amanda doesn't even like girls and she took advantage of you." Veronica scowled.

"I told her it was okay," I muttered.

"That doesn't give her a free pass to do whatever she wants," Veronica said. "Yeah, consent is verbal, but it's also not. Read the room, Amanda."

"I wanted her to kiss me though. I wanted her to feel something for me, and maybe . . . I don't know. So I just let her."

"You jumped off the cliff and hoped she'd catch you before you hit the ground," Veronica murmured, her mouth twisting into something soft and sad. "Maggie, you're worth more than that. A lot more."

"You need someone who holds your hand and jumps with you instead," Alyssa said. "Not lets you splat on the ground like Wile E. Coyote. Like . . ." Alyssa lifted one of her hands, making a fist, then bringing it down heavily onto her other palm. "Kaboom."

I raised both of my eyebrows. Veronica kept her poker face for a few seconds before she burst out laughing, both me and Alyssa following suit.

The force of my laughter knocked me over onto the bed, and I stayed there, pressing my face into the blanket before dragging myself back up. I ran a hand through my hair, absentmindedly yanking out the tangles. "Jesus Christ, what am I going to do about the quince? All this shit and I still don't have a date. At this point, I don't even wanna think about asking

Dani because I'm too fucked in the head about it, and I can't bring her into this mess. I just kinda wanna hide in the hollow trunk of a tree and sleep for a thousand years."

Alyssa pursed her lips. "Well, we already got the dress, so that last bit isn't happening."

---

Later, when I couldn't sleep, I tiptoed out of my room for a bowl of cereal, hoping that mindless munching on the couch and scrolling through my phone would trick my brain into falling asleep. Before I could enter the kitchen, though, I caught sight of one of the photos on the wall in the living room.

It was a picture of me and Amanda, taken after our field day in eighth grade. We'd been partners in the three-legged race. We'd won, of course, but we had also tripped over our third leg at the finish line, landing smack on our faces. Our knees were bloody and bruised, but we had applied the Band-Aids we'd been given into the shape of our initials to celebrate our win. The photo was of us sitting side by side on a picnic table, arms around each other's shoulders, scraped knees with bandage initials: an *M* on my left knee and an *A* on Amanda's right.

I took a picture of the picture, tinted it pink, and hit Post.

> My fairytale, stereotypical, every-gay-movie-ever trope came crashing down, as it always does. She admitted to me she's having problems committing to a future with Jaime and I was so delusional to think that any affection she showed me right now was real. I'm supposed to be better than this, aren't I? More evolved or something. Can you age past naivety, or was that just a thing with young romantics?

---

My bedroom door creaked open early the next morning, pulling me out of a nightmare. Amanda was in it, and Jaime, and Matthew, but I couldn't say what happened. I just woke up with this vague sickly feeling, tears in my eyes and fear clutching my chest until I took in my surroundings, relieved to see that I was in my bedroom, alone, besides my mother, who was currently tiptoeing across the floor.

I sat up a bit as she perched on the edge of my bed. "Hi. Why are you in here so early?"

"Veronica went to get tacos and pan dulce for breakfast. I just wanted to come in and see you." Mami ran a hand over my hair, and I leaned into it, smiling. "You know that your dad used to have hair like this?"

I nodded. "Thanks for the tangles, Father." I rubbed my eyes, yawning. "Sorry I didn't come say hi to you when I got in yesterday. I didn't want to wake you."

My mom shrugged. She was already fully dressed, earrings on and lipstick applied without a smudge. Why was I such a mess when my mom was always serving looks? Why couldn't I have inherited *that* and not my father's curls? "I was already awake. I was watching *Golden Girls* on Hallmark."

"So you *did* hear me come in then."

"I heard y'all talking, yes," she said. "The walls aren't as thick as you think. Are you all right, mamita?"

I drew my knees into my chest under the sheets, wrapping my arms around them loosely. "Yeah, I'm fine."

"Is it Matthew? I never liked him," Mami insisted hotly.

"No, Ma. Amanda and I just got into a fight."

"Ah, la fresa." She scowled. "What happened? Is she your girlfriend?"

"*No,* Mom. She has a boyfriend."

"Your prima Imelda had a boyfriend before she became a tortillera."

I grimaced. "Ew, stop. I hate that word. You're going to ruin tortillas *and* Imelda for me."

"Pues, it's true." My mom shrugged. "Well, you've had fights before. Remember the spelling bee?"

"*Why* do you have to capitalize 'renaissance'? It's a technicality—"

"You made up after a week, right?"

"Yes, but Mommy, I don't think it'll be that easy this time. This isn't a spelling bee, it's real life."

She chuckled and shook her head. "That's why it won't all fall apart because of a 'technicality.' So try not to worry about it. Now let's go. We're going to the pulga today."

I repressed the urge to roll my eyes. Why did moms always think that 'Try not to worry about it' was helpful advice? What she said finally registered as I glanced down at the time on my phone. "Is *that* why we're up so early? What about church?"

"We have to pick up the centerpieces. This woman is only available at the pulga." Mom shook her head. "I've already prayed about it. Now hurry up and get dressed. Junior is driving us."

Of course it was more quinceañera planning; this was the only thing that even came close to God for my mother. Ever the perfect Catholic, she always closed her store on Sundays, and Sunday breakfast was a long, languid affair, complete with homemade flour tortillas, so I should've known something was up when she said Veronica and Alyssa were picking up tacos. You had to pry Alyssa out of bed with a crowbar without food as an incentive.

When I got to the kitchen, CJ and Veronica were unloading the food, and Alyssa was sitting at the kitchen table with her quince binder, adding notes with her colorful pens.

Veronica nudged her as she set the food down on the table. "No strategizing during breakfast."

Alyssa pouted but gathered her things and dumped them on the coffee table as CJ brought over the ottoman to sit on. "I need to figure out what makeup I'm going to wear or my whole life is over."

"Don't worry about it, tiny G," CJ said, putting Fritos in his barbacoa taco and considering it carefully. "My sister had blue eyeshadow, really pink blush, and red lipstick because my mom is stuck in the eighties, and she still looked cute. You'll be fine."

"You'll look nice with anything you put on, mamita," my mother asserted confidently, putting salsa verde on her taco. Taking a bite, she nodded approvingly but added more before saying, "All my girls are beautiful."

"You got that right." CJ nodded, giving Veronica a smile and a wink.

Veronica flushed and smiled shyly, ducking her head to bite into her taco.

"Then how do you explain our ugly attitudes?" I asked, chomping into my taco. I had to remember to thank whoever had remembered my Stripes order; you just couldn't beat beans, cheese, and bacon.

"We don't always understand God's work," our mother mumbled cryptically before sighing. "Dios, He tries so hard."

"I just want to take a lot of selfies and look good in them. Otherwise, what's the point?" Alyssa complained through a mouthful of egg and chorizo, then swallowed loudly.

Veronica eyed her with a raised brow. "To have a quince and hang out with all your friends?"

"You don't get this, you're too old. Likes on Insta are food for my self-esteem. Why do you think I'm so confident all the time?"

"Because you're Mom's favorite kid, so she gives you twice as many compliments as she gives the rest of us?" I suggested. Veronica nodded.

Our mother squinted, glancing around the table. "Well, right now Junior is my favorite because he's not annoying me."

CJ beamed.

---

The pulga is what RGV natives called the flea market. The best one was in Brownsville, and it was just a collection of folding tables under tarps on a big patch of land off South Padre Island Drive. After circling the lot for fifteen minutes, CJ was able to secure a spot near the entrance. "Praise Jesus," he joked, relieved. Veronica nodded.

"Always," our mother said seriously.

"Where is this lady's stand again?" Alyssa asked as we ventured out into the parking lot. There was no asphalt, just a large dirt patch serving as a parking lot, and it stretched out endlessly. The tents shimmered in the heat, flickering majestically in the distance.

And it was majestic, in a way. Where else could you buy piñatas, a new lawnmower, and a chameleon as big as your head, all for incredibly low prices?

"She's somewhere in the middle."

We began to meander through the aisles. Tables laden with fruit, tools, and toys were crammed up next to each other. Merchants called to us from every direction, offering a low price on jewelry, dresses, and counterfeit purses. It seemed to go on for miles, stretches of magic and wonder, the smell of deep fryers and the sound of bartering punctuating our every step.

I started taking photos of things I saw and sending them to Dani just because I thought she'd appreciate the artistic potential. I mean, who wouldn't appreciate an artful close-up of a chameleon that someone had inexplicably posed on a bike, the parts of which had all been replaced with parts from other bikes, making it look like Frankenstein's monster? The chameleon's little foot was stretched out, one of its toes pointing off in the distance. *Pulga ET?* I texted along with the photo.

A fruit stand organized by color so it made a rainbow, a fish tank with an axolotl smiling at me through the glass, a display of several types of flowers arranged in the shape of a heart. I made myself stop after that because I worried that sending multiple texts made me look desperate, so I just prayed that the photos would be well received and forced myself to pocket my phone.

A few stalls later, Alyssa complained, "I want pizza. Or spiropapas. Or both."

"There's a food truck at the end of the next aisle," Veronica suggested.

Alyssa pouted. "I don't want to walk."

"I'll go," CJ volunteered. "I need to look at the skateboards anyway. Mags, come help me carry the food?"

I blinked, my hand wavering as it reached toward a pair of faux Doc Martens on the table next to us. "Um, yeah, sure, I guess."

CJ took a different turn than we normally would to get to the spiropapa stand.

"Where are we going?" I asked.

"Taking a little detour. Your sister needs a new pipe for—um—"

"You can say she smokes weed. It's okay. I do too, Ceej." I grinned. As cool as CJ pretended to be, with his leather jacket and flannels and all-black leather Vans, he was still the same square he'd been when he and Veronica had gotten together back in Veronica's junior year of high school.

CJ shushed me, casting a wary glance at the nearby stands. "What if your mom has friends here? Your mom knows everybody. Anyway, you're going to help me pick a color."

We went down a few winding aisles until we found a stand selling glass pipes for five dollars. CJ looked them over. I watched him. "Did Veronica tell you?"

CJ looked up at me over the glassware, nodding. "Of course she told me. We tell each other everything. We tell each other when our poops are weird colors. That's what a healthy relationship is, little G."

"Veronica shits?"

"Shitting? In my family? It's more likely than you think," CJ parroted the meme, and I smiled.

Normally, people in our area stayed with their first loves. Whether it was for safety, financial stability, or just lack of options in this tiny proud place, usually first love was last love. There wasn't much room for talk of soulmates and romance when you had kids, a house, and a life in the balance.

But CJ and Veronica didn't have any of that, and yet they were still together. Not because they had to be, but because they wanted to be. It seemed to be so *good*: They had fun together, CJ treated all of us like his own family, and he looked at Veronica like she was the queen of his world.

I wanted that. But what if CJ and Veronica won the love lottery and now there wasn't anything left for anyone else in this town?

I said as much to CJ, who nodded thoughtfully as he picked up a blue-and-white-speckled pipe and inspected it carefully. He put it back and picked up an orange-and-red one. "I don't think that's how it works, bud. There's enough love to go around."

"I've only ever been with Matthew and Trish, and we all saw how badly I screwed those up."

"It was never entirely your fault," CJ pointed out, examining the array of bongs. "Love is both people working to make things right. So really, you're both to blame."

I grimaced. "Yeah, I know. Thanks for supporting me—I'm really glad we had this talk."

"Hey, none of that, ya snot." CJ held up a blue-and-green pipe. "What do you think of this one?"

I leaned in closer to examine it. The colors were swirling around each other. It reminded me of peacock feathers. "It's pretty. Veronica would love it."

"Dope. Anyway . . ." CJ shook his head. "I don't know what Amanda is doing, or how Dani feels, since I know next to nothing about queer girls except that what you see in porn is *not* real—"

I grimaced. "Ew." I was a fucking hypocrite though; all *I* knew about women-loving women was from porn, Tumblr, and CW shows that killed them off as soon as they could.

The woman running the stand gave CJ the Latina mom glare that could turn your blood to ice, pointing down at her toddler son, who was running his Hot Wheels along the edge of the table.

CJ handed the woman a wad of bills before gesturing for me to follow him as he walked away. "I just overpaid that woman because I thought she was going to kill me."

"You have a big mouth," I said as we walked back to the aisle we'd come from, heading to the food truck at the end of it.

"Yes, but that's beside the point. As I was saying," CJ said, pocketing the new pipe. "I've seen you with Amanda, and I've seen you with Matthew. I haven't seen you with Dani, but from what I've heard, you and her seem to have something that's not as complicated as what you have or had with Amanda and Matthew."

We reached the food truck, CJ ordering quickly in Spanish. He turned back to me, giving me a soft half smile. "Look, I know how much you want that happy ending. But you can't keep looking at the things that made you sad and expect them to make you happy just because they're familiar and you don't know if you're going to get that with anyone else."

I looked down at the ground, then back up at CJ. "What if I don't know how to love a new person?"

CJ shrugged, then smiled. "Then learn. You have time."

Faces swam in my head, Amanda and Matthew and Trish. People I'd hurt, people I hadn't known how to love right. "How do I figure it out?"

CJ chuckled sympathetically. "Time. And no matter who you're with, if they're worth their shit, they'll wait for you."

"Did Veronica wait for you, or you her?"

"Both. Always both."

Our order was called out. Along with the spiropapas and pizza, options for Alyssa, CJ had remembered to get fruit with Tajín for my mother and nachos for Veronica. CJ was quiet as we walked back. "Before Veronica, it felt like my whole life was spent looking for something. With Veronica, I found it. And you will too. You just have to be patient with yourself as you learn how to keep it."

We got back to the group at a stand selling phone cases and bootleg DVDs. Alyssa ran over, making grabby hands for the food, and CJ gave it to her. She squealed, taking a bite of her pizza.

Our mom brandished a large, weirdly shaped garbage bag, and CJ, knowing his cue, took it from her. "Look, I bought a new weed whacker so we can finally get the sides of the house."

"You mean so CJ can get the sides of the house," Veronica deadpanned, but the amused smile on her face betrayed her tone.

Mom blinked at her oldest daughter. "Yes, that's what I said. Weren't you listening to me?"

"All right, we gotta go meet the lady," Alyssa said. "Do we have everything we need from here?"

CJ slung an arm around Veronica's shoulders, and she patted his hand gently. "I think so."

As we began walking, CJ and Veronica fell a ways behind, but I could still hear them as CJ said, his voice soft and low, "Look what I got you."

When there was only silence, I turned back to see Veronica giving CJ a tight hug, the pipe in her hand. "You remembered. Thank you," I heard Veronica say, and she pressed her lips to his.

I faced forward again. This was private, and Veronica would kill me if she caught me looking, but damn if it didn't make me take CJ's words a bit more seriously.

When we got home from the pulga, sweaty and covered with dust but satisfyingly exhausted, I took a shower, then headed straight to my room. My family was in the living room, Mom announcing she was going to take a shower and Alyssa pleading with Veronica to take her to Christina's house. I rarely got a moment to myself in this shared bedroom, so I lay back on my bed, shoving earbuds into my ears and opening my messages.

Dani still hadn't read my messages, a fact I knew because she always kept her read receipts on and now the Delivered tag was staring at me judgmentally. She usually answered my texts within the hour, but it had been three since I sent them, and still no reply.

Maybe it was too early to start worrying, but the last twenty-four hours had me on edge, and I couldn't help but feel like something was wrong. I opened up Spotify and pulled up Phoebe Bridgers's discography, shutting my eyes and letting the sound drown out my doubt.

My love life may be falling apart, but at least there's a song for that.

# 12

The first cold front of the season arrived the week after my fight with Amanda, and the poetics of that change in weather wasn't lost on me. Fall had officially arrived in the Valley—all sixty degrees of it. I was grateful for my *Captain Marvel* hoodie, especially because I could *feel* Amanda's cold shoulder down to my bones. When I passed the yearbook room, she was already at the standing computer station, buzzing around the students, who were working on their layouts. Her eyes met mine as I passed, lingering for just long enough to let me know it wasn't a fluke before promptly passing over me like I was a piece of government-issued school furniture. My hands shook with the shame of the dismissal, and I stuck them in the pockets of my hoodie to hide it. I forced my chin up and entered the art room.

Amanda was the one who'd hurt me, not the other way around. I had nothing to be ashamed of.

Dani and Jordan were at our usual table, but as I got closer, Dani's eyes flicked up to me and back down. I raised my hand to wave, but she just muttered something to Jordan and turned away, picking up her stuff and moving to the back of the room where the charcoals and paper were.

I tried to catch her gaze as I sat down, but she avoided my eyes, sitting down and turning away from me. The unread text messages from this weekend burned a hole in my pocket, and I asked Jordan, "What's that about?"

Jordan shrugged. "She just said she needed to work on her project. I don't know. It's probably not, like, personal or anything."

"Yeah, sure." I wasn't convinced, but I let it go. One worry at a time. "Amanda kissed me. Or I kissed her. Whatever. It was unclear."

"What?" Jordan squeaked. His hands flew to his beanie, and he tugged it down past his eyebrows.

Mrs. Lozano called the class to attention, so I turned away from Jordan to face her, thankful for the interruption. As she talked, I tuned her out, Jordan's barely contained anticipation vibrating next to me. Mrs. Lozano dismissed us to work on our projects all too soon, so I reluctantly looked back at Jordan, dreading facing the inquisition that was heading my way.

"What happened? Tell me everything!" Jordan said as soon as I turned to face him. His eyes were wide.

I shook my head. "I just . . . I was so delusional, J. We were hanging out before the bonfire, and she just wanted to see how it felt, and I . . . I let her because I thought . . . I should've known better. She doesn't like me, and she never will."

Jordan's smile was sad. "I mean, I get it. It's not every day that your straight best friend who you've been crushing on asks to kiss you. What else are you supposed to think?"

"I let her do it, J. She told me what she wanted, told me why she was doing it, and I . . . I didn't listen. I wanted to kiss her, and I wanted it to mean something, and she told me it wouldn't, but I still hoped that maybe . . ." I hated the sound of my own voice, the way it cracked, how fucking clear it was now that I was saying it. "I consented, but it was like I gave my consent to a completely different situation and then got my feelings hurt."

"Sometimes we don't really want to believe someone when they tell us who they are. Especially when it goes against everything we want."

"This is total Libra behavior and I hate it. I hate me."

Jordan reached over and patted my head. "Well, at least you have one more part of your project wrapped up. Now that just leaves Dani, right?"

"Yeah, but I think . . ." I glanced back at where she was sitting, her head ducked over her sketchbook. "I think maybe that's in jeopardy. She didn't respond to my texts all day Sunday and she didn't even look at me when I came in."

Jordan shrugged. "Maybe she's just busy. Besides, I think she's coming to the show on Friday, so you can talk to her then."

I blanched, feeling my stomach drop. "Fuck, Amanda was gonna be my ride to the show since there's not a game this week." I bit my lip. "Can you—?"

Jordan rolled his eyes, then smiled. "Of course I can pick you up, you fucking mess."

I flicked his head, and he whined, batting away my hand. "Shit. Just for that, you're paying for gas."

---

The Las Palmas Race Park in Mission would always hold a special place in the hearts of everyone in the Valley who had a taste for punk, metal, and the like because of the now-deceased Never Say Never Festival that used to be held there.

I had only gone once before it shut down, with Amanda and Jordan—and without my mother's knowledge—when we were thirteen. We were far too young to be there, but for those six hours, that didn't matter as we braved the throng of moshers and the walls of death that opened up randomly in the crowd like the noisiest splitting fault line.

The grin on Jordan's face as we pulled into the dirt parking lot told me he was remembering this too. "This is the big time, Mags. *Shit*."

I patted him on the shoulder as he showed his pass to the security guard so we could be let into the back lot reserved for the acts. "You've made it, my friend."

"You don't understand. Legends have walked these grounds. Heroes. Gods." Jordan pointed at my camera as we got out. "You better take a ton of those for posterity. What if we tank and this never happens again?"

"I don't think that'll happen, but okay." I nodded solemnly, shouldering my camera bag. "I respect my mission."

Matthew was already there, helping the drummer unload the van, and so was Dani, oddly enough. Her back was turned, her long hair swept up off her neck in a messy bun, and I was greeted by the sight of her sinewy biceps flexing under the strain of the crash cymbals and hi-hats she was carrying.

I tore my eyes away before she could turn around and catch me gawking. My gaze landed on Matthew, who was setting his keyboard up on the side to make sure it didn't get damaged. "Hey, Matthew. Nervous?"

"Only every fucking time, but being here certainly doesn't help." He pushed his hair out of his face and gestured at the big stage in the middle of the race park, which was being set up for the first act. "If we fuck up, we're doing it in front of that band from Pharr that made it big, and basically everything we've worked for is fucked."

Key of Reason was the second act, right before the main band, River Rats, who started in Edinburg a few years ago and were now a cult favorite throughout Texas. I hated to agree with Matthew, but he was kind of right, and it seemed like the other two band members knew it, judging by the constipated looks on their faces as they huddled around the van. The drummer had a nervous habit of rubbing his sticks together like he was trying to sharpen them, and now he looked like he was attempting to set them on fire with how fast they were going.

"You'll be fine," Dani said, appearing by Jordan's side and holding out her fist for him to pound. He did, and the cool indifference in her gaze as she looked at me chilled me to the bone. "Hey."

"Hi." She'd looked away before the word was even out of my mouth, and the cold left me shaken. She seemed to be more interested in the drum kit than she was in me. What had I done that had made her so mad?

I had to talk to her, and this show would be the perfect opportunity. Surely she'd hang out with me while the band was backstage and the first act was going on. We were the only ones we knew here. It'd be weird if we didn't hang out.

Apparently, Dani didn't care about that because as soon as we'd gotten all the equipment backstage and they'd started the preshow playlist, she was gone, disappearing into the crowd that was gathering at the foot of the stage without a word to me. I set my jaw and, for the first time ever, left my camera in the van. The first act hadn't even started, so I'd come get it later before they went on. First, I had to track down this girl and make things right.

I'd never been the kind of person to go looking for a fight, but I couldn't leave this alone. I didn't want to. Dani had disappeared into the left side of the crowd, and I teetered a bit as I watched her enter the tightly packed mass.

But I'd always been the first one into a crowd whenever I went to a concert, never afraid to throw elbows to get to the fence at the front, so it didn't matter that I didn't know what game she was playing. I knew the arena, and that was enough.

It was like wading through a punk edition of *Where's Waldo*. Looking for high-waisted shorts and a Joy Division T-shirt was nearly impossible, and every time I got a flash of chestnut curls, I'd follow it until it inevitably disappeared. As the set time for the first act crept closer, the crowd started buzzing with excitement, and their rising anticipation made my adrenaline spike.

Finally, I found her near the front, but when she turned around and saw me approaching, she pushed her way through the crowd and disappeared again. I clenched my jaw. What the fuck was her problem?

Maybe I should've given up, but my brain had dug its nails in, and it wasn't letting this go. So I chased her.

Every time I got close, she'd manage to evade me, and it only got harder after the first act came on. I didn't even catch the name of the band, could barely hear the music or the crowd singing along over the sound of my heartbeat in my ears, and the only thing that mattered was the girl I was currently role-playing *It Follows* with.

I had managed to catch her in the middle of the crowd, and suddenly the tangle of bodies in front of her solidified into a single curved line, and the yelling and thrashing of people just beyond told me everything I needed to know. A mosh pit had opened up, the concert equivalent of a Mario Kart banana thrown in her path.

Dani skidded to a stop in front of it, and she hesitated. I took the opportunity to get closer, and I smirked. I may have been sweaty and tired and bruised from all the people I'd been pushing past, but it had paid off. I was only a few feet from her, and there was nowhere for her to run to.

But Dani turned around to see me standing there, and a tiny smug smile flickered onto her face. My stomach dropped as she turned back around and pushed her way right into the mosh pit, disappearing past the human barrier into the no-person's-land beyond.

"Fuck!" I yelled, the people nearby squinting at me briefly before going back to their business, and I hesitated for a moment. I hadn't been in a mosh pit in a long time, since it was ill-advised to take an expensive camera into it, but nothing was stopping me now, just my own fear that maybe I'd gone soft and lost my edge while hiding behind the lens.

But it was time to stop cowering outside the frame.

I steeled myself and pushed my way in easily.

If anyone was surprised by a curvy five-foot-tall kid bursting into a circle of burly college-age guys and tattooed and pierced leather-clad girls who looked like they ate girls like me for lunch, they didn't show it. They just immediately pushed me to the side, and my body revved up at the familiar feeling. I shoved back, grinning, and jumped along with the music, shoes hitting me in the shins and elbows flying into my ribs. It was heaven on earth, this pocket of chaos, and it was almost enough to make me forget my mission.

Almost.

Craning my neck, I immediately picked out Dani, bouncing a few feet away from me and letting herself ricochet off the bodies around her. I pushed my way over until I was only a few feet from her. Her jumping happened to spin her around to face me, and her eyes widened when she saw me standing there. She stuttered in her movements then, stilling immediately, and it was almost comical, how frozen she was amid the shoving that threatened to knock her off balance. Staying still in a mosh pit was probably suicide, but I stopped moving too.

"Why did you—why would you follow me?" Dani asked, aghast.

"Why wouldn't I? I wanted to talk to you." I raised my voice to be heard over the crowd. "Why are you running from me?"

Dani said something else, but I couldn't hear her over the crowd, and I yelled, "What?!"

She got shoved a little more aggressively, stumbling over her feet, and so did I. "I can't talk here! Can we—" Dani motioned back to the outside of the mosh pit, and I nodded jerkily.

When we made our way back out, through the back of the crowd, we were both too winded to speak. I put my hands on my knees, panting into the ground. "I'm too old for this. Why did you make me do that?"

"You didn't have to follow me," Dani pointed out, wincing as she prodded at a dark red spot on her thigh where a bruise was sure to form.

"Why in the world did you think I wouldn't?"

Dani glared. "I didn't think you cared that much what I thought. It's not like I'm—we're—whatever."

She averted her eyes, and I frowned. "Why were you running from me? Like legit *running away*."

"I wasn't running. I just wanted to get a good spot in the crowd."

"You had a good spot," I pointed out. "You were, like, two rows from the front at some point. It was pretty impressive, actually."

Dani rolled her eyes, crossing her arms. "Look, I just thought that maybe we shouldn't be hanging out as much as we've been. I'm sure your girlfriend wouldn't appreciate it."

I raised an eyebrow. "What girlfriend are you talking about?"

"I heard you and Amanda talking at her house."

My stomach plummeted to my feet, like an elevator with the cables cut. "You . . . you heard that?"

Dani's face was sharp, smooth marble, cool and calculated. "If you had something going on there, I didn't want to interfere. So I thought we should put some space between us."

"Amanda is not—yeah, we kissed, but that was just Amanda being Amanda and pushing boundaries. We're not *dating*," I said.

"You kissed though," she pressed.

I didn't know why Dani was being so pushy about this. It wasn't like she'd expressed interest in dating me, so why did she care if someone else did?

Fuck it. Might as well tell her the truth—at least, as much of it as I could.

I sighed. "Look, if you must know, Amanda wanted to see what it felt like to kiss a girl, and like the clueless bisexual I am, I let her kiss me because I used to have a crush on her and I always wanted to know what it would be like to kiss her." I kicked the ground. "So yeah, I let it happen, so thirteen-year-old me could have her answer as to whether or not Amanda and I could've worked out. And we can't because she's straight and also because she's a dick who plays with my feelings and I don't really even like her as a friend right now so . . ."

I chanced a glance at Dani, and her face had softened a little. It was still unreadable, but at least the ice there had thawed somewhat. "Oh. That's . . . complicated."

"Yeah, you're telling me," I scoffed, but then I just exhaled. "So if you want to judge me or whatever, you can, but the bottom line is Amanda and I aren't dating and there's nothing going on between us. So this"—I gestured between her and me—"whatever it is? Not an issue."

I watched Dani's face carefully, and the knot in my stomach loosened when she cracked a sheepish smile. "Well . . . then I kind of overreacted, huh?"

She rubbed the back of her neck, cringing, and I couldn't help but smile. "Yeah, a bit, kinda. Why did you . . ."

Dani shrugged, flushing a bit as she tilted her head and fluttered her lashes. It was unfair how pretty she looked when she was embarrassed, because I was finding it really hard to stay mad at her.

"I'm sorry. I guess it was just self-preservation."

I nodded. "I get it. What were you protecting yourself from?"

Dani pursed her lips, her brown eyes boring into mine. "Something that could hurt me if I let it. This whole time, I've not wanted to feel anything for anyone, but now maybe I do, and I—I don't know what to do, and I'm scared."

The air inside me stilled. I tried to switch my breathing to manual, and the focus on inhaling and exhaling gave me a moment to figure out what I was going to say. "Well, I'm scared too, so you're not alone there."

"Well . . . maybe we can be alone together sometime?" Dani offered, a coy smile on her lips.

I didn't know what else to say, and I needed words right now. I needed her to say what she was feeling, to be direct with me, but after everything that had happened today, it didn't feel like now was the time. I didn't want to ruin the fragile peace we'd made, so I just nodded, a promise to continue this conversation at a better time.

A short, round brunette with an undercut ran through the gap between us, startling us both, and hurled herself into the audience. The people in the back lifted her up easily and tossed her onto the waiting hands of the crowd, carrying her, screaming, to the front.

Wide-eyed, I turned back to Dani, and her eyes were wide too, gleaming. Her spine was ramrod straight as she bounced on her heels. "Do you trust me?"

"Um, yes?"

"Do you wanna crowd-surf with me?"

I had never crowd-surfed before, and I bit my lip as I lost sight of the girl who'd just been launched into the crowd. It was concert tradition, but I'd always been too chickenshit to try it.

But looking back at Dani, all the breathless hope on her face, I couldn't help but remember that I had just followed her into a mosh pit. I'd probably follow her to hell if she asked me to. Being with Dani had felt like I was in constant free-fall, so was crowd-surfing really that different?

"Fine," I relented. "Let's do it."

Anxiety was already making my legs shake, but when she took my hand to pull me to the crowd, it fit so well in mine that I almost forgot I was scared shitless. God, I really was a sucker for a pretty girl.

A guy in a beanie and a blond gym bro looked at me expectantly as we got closer to the back of the crowd, and I stepped forward. I panicked when I felt Dani let go of me, but then she stooped down to weave her fingers together, looking at me intently. She nodded toward the guys. "Use them for balance." Then she gave me a comforting smile, lifted her woven hands, and said, "Use me to fly."

So I did.

The swoop in my stomach was dizzying as I was tossed up into the air, stumbling into the crowd's waiting hands. I wasn't prepared for how unstable it felt, the way the crowd staggered under me just a bit. I was about to scream, to demand to be let down, but then I looked up. A sea of hands stretched out before me, endless, and seeing the band from so high up, the lights swirling and the lead singer going hard on the mic, I was able to get the widest, clearest picture of the concert, the sun setting in the background.

I wasn't even mad about not having a camera to capture it. This fleeting moment felt like it should stay that way. Brief, flashing, fantastical.

The human conveyor belt beneath me jolted, and I was pitched forward, roving over the crowd. All I could do was enjoy the ride and pray I wouldn't get dropped.

The stage drew closer, and I might as well have been riding a real wave, I felt so high. Laughter bubbled up inside me, effervescent as it left my mouth. I looked over to see Dani a little ways behind me, looking much more steady than I did. She waved a hand, grinning, and I waved back before the crowd dipped a bit, and I had to face forward as I dropped into the waiting arms of a security guard.

"Out you go," he said, dropping me on my feet without pretense. I stumbled off to the side in a daze, clumsily following the line of people who were leaving. I was giddy, lost in a haze of fading adrenaline, as I whirled around looking for Dani. "Maggie!"

I turned around, pausing to let Dani catch up with me.

She was sweaty and looked just as wrecked as I felt, and our smiles were the same. I should have been self-conscious, worried about my sweat-slick face or the redness in my cheeks, how disastrous my hair must look right now. But Dani looked at me with nothing but awe in her eyes, and despite my insecurities, I had never felt so beautiful.

"How'd you like it?" Dani asked, breathless.

Her eyes were shining with excitement, which was *really* distracting, but I managed to answer honestly. "I loved it. Thanks for . . ." Moving to San Benito. Being my friend. Making it safe for me to be brave. Making it safe for me to be me. "Thanks for being here."

Dani brightened. "Of course."

I was still breathing heavily, so keyed up and excited, and suddenly the distance between us felt like too much. I wanted to kiss her, but it didn't feel like the right time. I was sweaty and gross and pretty sure that one of my bra straps had come undone, but I didn't care, I just wanted her closer.

Holding her gaze, I held out my arms with a giddy smile, and she grinned, stepping into them and wrapping her arms around my waist. We were closer than we'd ever been; this was the first time we'd hugged. I had thought it would make me feel nervous, especially being all sweaty from running around, but all I felt was her warmth, the comfort of her body. My body relaxed against hers, the press firm enough to make me feel supported but soft enough to make me feel safe.

Was this the moment? Maybe the adrenaline would help me overcome my—

The security guard glared and told us to move it, popping our little bubble of bliss, but Dani took my hand and smiled. I'd taken Jordan's keys before the show so I could have a safe place to keep my camera, and as we walked back to the parking lot to get it, hands swinging easily between us, I couldn't believe how natural and *normal* it felt to be here with her. Even holding her hand was less nerve-wracking now, comforting where before I'd been nervous to touch her, unsure what lines I could cross. Now I wondered if there were lines at all, or if there was just a green light telling me to go for it. As Dani gave me another soft smile, knocking her hip against mine when she told a joke, the risk of rejection was ebbing in my mind.

Could I really do this—launch myself into the fray of a new relationship, risk everything for a chance at happiness with this girl who had carved out a space for herself in my life without thinking twice? Could I take that leap?

Looking back at the crowd, I couldn't help but think that in some ways, I already had.

Later that night, back at home, I posted a picture that I took of Dani's bruised knees next to mine.

Knowing that D was affected by the conversation she overheard between me and A has made me rethink everything she's told me in the last few months about not wanting to be in a relationship. Without M and A in the way, there's nothing stopping me from pursuing D except her not wanting a girlfriend, and with the way she talked to me today, part of me thinks that might not be the case anymore. Tonight at the concert, even though it took some chasing, she opened up to me a bit. Maybe a little more bravery could come in handy, if I could only find the words to tell her how I feel.

# 13

The joy I got from experiencing the concert with Dani was almost enough to forget the rest of the trouble that awaited me, but it all came back to me when I came downstairs the next morning and saw Amanda's car in the parking lot.

Veronica eyed the car warily as she came up beside me. "You can always just slip out the back door, and I can drive the car around so you don't have to confront her."

The idea of sneaking out and ignoring Amanda was tempting, but when I had confronted Dani yesterday, we'd been able to resolve things. I needed to talk to Amanda about how I was feeling, and I needed to be open to whatever she had to say right now. I needed to meet her halfway. "Nah, it's fine. You go inside. I need to deal with this."

Veronica nodded and left. I adjusted my backpack so I wouldn't slouch and walked over. Amanda got out of the car, coming around to sit on the hood.

"Hi," she said, looking sheepish.

"Hey." I nodded. Amanda was hunched over, her hands in her pockets and her leg bouncing up and down like she had had too much coffee. This was the most uncomfortable she had ever looked.

"I suck at this."

"At what?"

"Apologizing."

"You're off to a great start."

"Thanks. So . . . I'm really, really sorry. I was a total bitch to you, and you didn't deserve that."

She patted the spot next to her on the hood, and after some hesitation, I sat down. "I was a dick to you too. I'm sorry that I . . . I didn't even try to tell you I was mad before I just exploded."

Amanda shook her head. "You were frustrated, and you had a right to be. I shouldn't have . . . just because you agreed to kiss me didn't mean it was okay. I shouldn't have asked in the first place. Just because you're bi doesn't mean I can cross those kinds of boundaries like that."

I bit my lip. I had to know. "So why did you then?"

Amanda sighed. "If I admit something to you, will you promise not to judge me?"

I gave her a half smile. "As long as you promise not to judge me for anything I tell you right now."

"It's the least we can do, I guess." She exhaled and said, "Well, I . . . I guess I'd kind of been feeling a little jealous of how much you and Dani were hanging out. I knew she was gay, and she likes all the same music that you do, and she's good at art, so you had a lot of things in common with her."

"Oh," I breathed out. That explained her weird behavior around Dani. Amanda had always been a jealous person, but I thought that just applied to Jaime, not me.

"Yeah. I had never felt that way about you before, and it . . . it made me wonder if I felt something for you, like more than friends." Amanda flushed as she looked at me. "So I thought that maybe I could kiss you and find out, and that if I said it didn't mean anything, it would be okay. And it wasn't."

Huh. She'd been conducting an experiment of her own with me, hoping for some kind of clarity, just like I had been. I had thought I would be crushed knowing that she didn't have feelings for me, but instead I just felt relieved. Our fight on Saturday had shaken me awake, had pried my feelings for her from my chest. Knowing that she didn't—couldn't—have feelings for me had helped me make sense of my own emotions.

Amanda had been my plan for the future this whole time, friendship and romance and big-city dreams all wrapped up and tied with a bow—it was mine for the taking. I'd been holding on to the fantasy of her for too long, like it was a childhood blanket I carried around with me because it made me feel safe, but I needed to let it go if I ever wanted to learn how to move forward with my life.

"I had just never felt such intense jealousy in a friendship before. I thought it had to be romantic, ya know? Like I was only allowed to feel jealous over someone I had feelings for." Amanda's brow wrinkled. "Is it weird that I felt jealous, and still feel jealous?"

I frowned. "Heteronormativity likes us to think that the only meaningful relationships we can have are romantic, but, Amanda, our friendship has always felt just as special as my relationships with Matthew or Trish. I think I was confused because of that too. That's why I let you kiss me when I shouldn't have. I needed to figure out what this was, and my feelings got hurt and I was more confused than ever."

"Me too. Things with Jaime haven't always been super steady, and I just . . . I thought nothing would ever change between you and me, but to be honest, I think they have, ever since you came out." She cringed when she saw my face and was quick to correct herself. "Oh god, that sounds like I'm blaming you, but I'm not! I just mean . . . I wasn't sure if I was allowed to feel as close to you as I did if you were bi, and that's not fair."

"Nothing has to change because I'm bi."

Amanda shook her head. "No, it absolutely does, and that's okay. I can't just ask to kiss you the way I would someone who is straight because you're not. The boundaries have to be redrawn between us because certain kinds of touching mean different things to me than they do to you."

I bit my lip. She was right. "I think . . . I just wanted you to keep treating me the way you always had because I was scared that if we changed at all, you wouldn't want to be close to me anymore."

Amanda smiled sadly. "I felt the same way, but I can't just keep acting with you like you're straight because that denies who you are, and I don't want to do that because I *love* who you are, all of it. I refuse to act like you're anything less than everything you are."

My throat tightened at her words, at the fervent care behind them, and I managed to squeak out, "Boundaries. Yeah. I'd like that." I cleared my throat, trying not to cry. I loved my best friend *so much*. "For what it's worth . . . Dani could never replace you because I don't feel the same way about her that I feel about you."

Amanda smirked, and I blushed. "You want to kiss her as not an experiment, right?"

I rubbed the back of my neck. "Um, yeah, I do."

Amanda laughed. "Believe it or not, that makes me feel better. Good to know I'm not gonna be replaced."

I chuckled. "The best friend position is filled, but I have

an opening in the girlfriend department, so . . . hopefully she applies."

"You're such a nerd—I love you." She rolled her eyes and smiled. "But, like with Matthew and Trish, the same rule applies: If she hurts you, I will end her."

I grinned. "I wouldn't expect anything else. Just so we're clear though . . . you're my best friend, no matter how much our relationship changes."

Amanda's voice was small and nervous. "I know feelings are weird to talk about, and we're both too evasive for our own good, but . . . can we keep talking about boundaries as they come up? I just . . . I just want to do this right."

Relief warmed my chest like the first sip of coffee on a cold morning. "Yeah. Yeah, I'd really like that."

"Good." Amanda smiled. "Is it, like, counterproductive or something if I ask you for a hug?"

I smirked. "I'll allow it."

Amanda threw open her arms, and I stepped into them. The hug was tight and familiar, and for the first time, it wasn't ruined by thoughts of *what does this mean?* or *why is she doing this?* The longing I had felt before had also vanished, leaving in its place something bright, shiny, and new.

The feeling of friendship, unhindered and uncomplicated. The way it was supposed to be.

"Can I take a picture? I want to remember this as the moment when we both fucked up because I'm glad it's not just me." I said it jokingly, but really, I just wanted to get the perfect closer for her chapter of my project.

Amanda rolled her eyes and smiled, positioning herself on the hood of her car. It was one of the things I liked about Amanda—she was always prepared for a photo shoot. "Fine, Avedon. Do your thing."

"The fact that you even know who that is makes me incredibly happy. Now hold still."

For anonymity, I took the picture from behind Amanda's head as she stared off in the direction of the morning sun. I made sure the car was in the first third of the frame and Amanda, hands in her pockets and curls reflecting the emerging light, was in the last two thirds. After I took the picture and prepared to edit it, I stopped. The sunrise gave Amanda a purply pink glow, her face obscured and turned toward the future. It was sweet and a little nostalgic, but unmistakably Amanda. I left it alone and just wrote the caption, knowing what I needed to say.

> There is nothing in this world that I want to come between A and me, especially not weird feelings. A few days away from her has given me enough space to really think about what I want, and it's nothing that she can give me. I fell for her when I was first discovering myself, when I was new to this bi thing and didn't understand what it meant to love girls, but since then, it's changed to an entirely different kind of love. And I have never been more grateful.

# 14

That morning, I rushed into Art on time for once, with Amanda snickering at me the whole time. I was high off our conversation that morning, the swell of validation in my chest at the idea that she and I would be okay. It was like some emotional milestone had been reached, and my heart had the green light to go after what it wanted. There was nothing stopping me from telling Dani how I felt, and now that I could see that happily ever after in the distance, there was nothing that could stop me from going for it.

Dani laughed, straightening up from where she'd been hunched over her sketchbook as I slid into my seat. "Someone's got energy today."

I smiled brightly, unable to contain it. "Yeah, I guess I do."

Jordan, who I hadn't noticed in my haste to get to Dani, spoke up. "Well, I'm gonna talk to Lozano real quick. Don't miss me too much."

He raised an eyebrow at me as he stood up, and I smiled at him, hoping he could see the gratitude in it. As he walked away, I turned back to Dani, whose eyes were glittering as she waited for me to speak. "Do you want to hang out?"

My foot wouldn't stop bouncing up and down, and she smiled at me. "Yeah, of course. With the group, or just—"

I shook my head quickly. "No, I mean . . . just with me. Like a date," I added promptly to make sure there was no confusion.

Dani's eyes widened, her lips parting. "Oh," she breathed out.

It couldn't have been more than a few seconds between that and her response, but they could've been a year for how agonizing they felt. I was starting to wonder if I'd gotten this whole thing wrong, but then her lips split into a full-blown grin. "Magdalena Gonzalez, are you asking me out?"

"Well, I sure am trying to. If that's not clear."

More silence, and I watched as she bit her lip, considering. "Do you have any more confused friends who are going to try and kiss you?"

The irony of it caused me to let out a gasping laugh. For once, I could be honest as I said, "Nope. Sorry to disappoint you if you needed a reason to run from me."

Dani's mouth dropped open, and she blushed. "This is already a mess, and we haven't even gone out yet."

"Aha, so you admit it!" I pointed a finger at her. "You want to go out with me."

Dani rolled her eyes, smiling, then grabbed the hand I'd thrust out, shocking me as she wound her fingers through mine. "I only run away from things I actually want to run toward, so . . . yeah."

I smiled, squeezing her hand. "Well, there's a lot to unpack there, so . . . are you free after school?"

Her answering nod made me want to crow with victory, but Mrs. Lozano was calling the class to attention, so I settled for just grinning like a maniac and holding her hand under the table.

After class, Mrs. Lozano called me to her desk, and I trudged over hesitantly. "Am I in trouble?"

Mrs. Lozano shook her head, laughing. "No, you're not." She opened up her desk drawer and pulled out a Manila folder, setting it down in front of me. "I was just thinking about your predicament the other day, and I did a little digging."

At her nodding, I picked up the folder and opened it. Inside, there were printouts on different universities in Texas: Texas State, University of Houston, the Art Institute of Austin, and others. I looked up at her again. "What is this?"

"These are some colleges in Texas with good photography programs, and even better financial aid possibilities." Her eyes were soft, and she smiled. "I know you had questions about money, so I wanted you to have some info on that. Check the back."

The first half of the documents had information on Texas schools, but the other half were from colleges out of state: NYU, Stanford, UCLA, RISD, SCAD. My eyes widened. She'd included information on their financial aid programs as well. "Mrs. Lozano, this is way too much—"

She waved a hand. "Pfft. It literally took, like, twenty minutes, and that's including printing time. It's my job as a teacher to make sure you have as many options as possible for any kind of future you want."

I bit my lip. "What if I still don't know what I want?"

Mrs. Lozano's smile was kind. "Then it's even more important to have all the information. Just think about it. Now get." She jerked her head in the direction of the door. "If you're late, just tell them to call me and I'll yell at them about time being a construct used to enforce rules of professionalism rooted in white supremacy."

The rest of the day, all I could think about was the folder in my backpack. In Spanish, the only class I didn't have with any of the group, I looked at the printouts until my eyes blurred, my brain filled with a haze of numbers and percentages and class information. Could I really go to any of these schools? I had the grades and extracurriculars to back it up, but did I have the money, the will to do this?

Mrs. Lozano was right that having more options was helpful when you didn't know what you wanted, but in some ways, it left me with even more questions.

I resolved to put all thoughts of college out of my mind as I headed to Mr. Treviño's classroom after the final bell to find Dani. I looked in through the window to see the students milling about, packing up and chatting with each other. From the front of the classroom, Dani's eyes met mine, and she winked. I grinned.

"Maggie, hey," she greeted a few minutes later when the bell rang and the students poured out of the classroom. Dani's smile was radiant, and it was contagious, my lips quirking up to match. "Are you ready to go?"

I nodded. "Your place or mine?"

"I realize I've never actually asked you to come to my house before. The store just felt like more neutral territory since I didn't know if you felt the way that I did." She bit her lip, shifting her weight a little. "So maybe you'd like to come over?"

I realized she was right. I hadn't been inside her house before, only seen the outside of it when we dropped her off after hanging out with the group, but now, to see the inside as, well, not as her girlfriend, but as more than a friend . . . "I'd really like that."

Dani lifted her chin up a bit, smiling and gesturing toward the student parking lot. "Then let's go."

As Dani pulled into her tiny driveway twenty minutes

later, I was suddenly struck by nervousness. I had just finished texting Veronica to let her know that she didn't need to pick me up and wiped my sweaty palms on my jeans, hoping Dani wouldn't notice.

"Here it is, my castle," Dani said as we made our way up the broken sidewalk to the bright red door, seemingly freshly painted whereas the rest of the house's deep blue color was fading. I had to step over several tools that had been left in the yard. "Sorry, my dad is constantly starting projects and not finishing them, so his stuff is kind of everywhere."

"My dad was like that too, which is why the back porch looks like a Lowe's threw up on it. He died and left us with all his old shit. Inconsiderate ass." I couldn't help but smile though, as I remembered how happy my mom said his projects made him.

Dani laughed as she fished her keys out of her pocket and unlocked the door. "Your dad and my dad would've been friends. They could've bonded over annoying us."

The first thing I heard once we were inside was the babbling. And then the *Doc McStuffins* theme song.

I followed Dani down the narrow entryway to the living room. The room was bright, with the big windows in the back doors letting in the afternoon light. In the middle of the floor, a curly-haired baby toddled around on a large blanket, gumming some foam blocks and babbling that strange baby language that only parents could ever seem to decipher.

"Don't you have your own house?" Dani called out, stepping over an old Vera Bradley diaper bag on the floor.

"I came to do laundry. Nice to see you too, sister dear." A taller girl came into the living room and embraced her before peering at me over Dani's head, then stepping to the side. "Who's your friend?"

"Ale, this is Maggie," Dani said, gesturing at me.

"Mm-hmm, you've told me about her." I smiled and stood a little straighter despite myself. Dani had been talking about me. At home. To her *family*. I felt like I was under a microscope as Dani's sister gave me a very obvious once-over.

Dani seemed to see it too and frowned. "Maggie, this is my big sister, Al-ex-an-druh."

The dig seemed to work, and Dani's sister's untouchable facade cracked a bit when she glared at Dani. "It's *Alejandra*, Ale for short. Daniela is just annoying like that."

Dani and Ale looked almost exactly alike, except for the height difference and the fact that Ale's hair was darker, and the similarities in their features were almost amusing to look at. Ale settled on the couch, and the baby on the floor immediately crawled over to her, pulling herself up using Ale's jeans and teetering against her legs. "This is Ava, my spawn."

Dani settled on the floor beside the blanket, cooing at the baby. She pulled her into her lap, giving her a squeeze, and the baby grunted in response. "Hi, Ava, how are you? You're getting so big."

"The pictures don't do her justice," I said, taking a seat next to Dani on the floor. I waved at Ava, who threw an arm out in my direction. "That's a good try!"

Dani laughed. "Ava, this is your tía's friend, Maggie." Dani held the baby up. "Say hi."

Ava stuck a fist in her mouth before squealing something indistinguishable around it. Dani looked at her in a playfully disapproving way. "We're going to work on that."

I smiled. "She's perfect."

And Ava was, with waves like Dani's that were the same color as Ale's and the same eyes they both had. This family had great genes, apparently.

"Thank god you're here. I came to do laundry, and Mom isn't out of work yet, so doing this with Ava is a damn nightmare." Ale breezed down the only hallway in the house, turning the corner and disappearing from view, calling, "Fill your madrina duty. How was school?"

"It was good," Dani called back, setting Ava back down on the floor. Ava crawled to the corner of the blanket with her stuffed animals, picking up a deflated-looking puppy and sticking its ear in her mouth.

We played with Ava while Ale grilled me between loads of laundry, peppering me with questions about school and extracurriculars and my family. Dani seemed resigned to this, letting her sister interview me until a certain smell permeated the room and Ava began to whimper and then cry.

Dani swiftly passed Ava off to Ale, standing and motioning for me to follow. "Well, I'm out."

Ale smirked, rifling through the diaper bag and pulling out a changing mat. "Coward."

I followed Dani down the narrow hallway, pausing to glance at the pictures hanging on the walls. There were sets of both Dani's and Ale's school photos from kindergarten to now, and photos of family, including two people who I took to be Dani's parents.

Dani's room was small but bright. It was cluttered with books and clothes, but the blankets, sheets, and the rug were all blue and purple. Dani took a seat on the rug, and I sat beside her, dropping my backpack down.

"Your sister was nice," I started.

Dani surprised me by laughing. "You don't have to lie to me. I know she can be a little much with new people in my life. Ever since the drama with my ex, she's been a little overprotective."

"Veronica was the same way after Matthew and I broke up.

I feel like it affected her just as much as it affected me, so now she has trust issues with everyone I bring around." I bit my lip, wondering if this was the right moment to ask. "So what was the story with your ex? If you don't mind me asking."

Dani gave me a half smile, leaning her head back on the bed. "Ah, so I guess it's time for that conversation. I mean, I guess it's only fair, since I made you follow me into a mosh pit because I couldn't deal with my shit."

"It was my choice. But yeah, if there's something you'd like to share with the class . . ." I gestured around her room, giving her a smile that I hoped was encouraging.

Dani sighed. "Well, I wasn't exactly honest with you."

"What do you mean?"

Dani looked down, wringing her fingers in her lap. "I didn't cheat on Melissa, but that doesn't mean I was innocent."

"What did you do?"

Dani was quiet, and then: "Our relationship had gotten really toxic. I had let her take all my time and attention. I dropped all my extracurriculars to join cheer with her. I didn't know how to react when she cheated on me because I had built my whole identity around her. I didn't know how to tell her that or even begin to deal with it, so I didn't. I just left."

I stared. "What? Like you didn't—"

"I didn't tell her I was breaking up with her." Dani's voice was small, and I had to lean in closer to hear her. "I left a box of her stuff on her porch and blocked her number. I avoided her in the hallways. I couldn't fucking deal, so I was a little *bitch* about the whole thing."

I had never heard her use the word with such venom, the self-loathing dripping from her words. I didn't know what to say, and my first reaction was: "Yeah, that was kind of shitty of you."

I cringed. *Nice going, Maggie. Way to be sympathetic.* But Dani just let out a snort. "You're telling me. So she assumed I'd found someone else and didn't have the decency to break up with her. And she was right about that last part."

"So she told everyone," I said. "And they all crucified you."

Dani nodded and fell silent. I had thought, all this time, that Dani was so smooth and so experienced and had all the answers. But I supposed that Dani might be bad at this too. "She's a shithead, and you didn't deserve that."

"Maybe I didn't. But it's what happened." Dani just sighed and gave me a sad smile. "I'm just trying to learn from it and not repeat the same mistakes. I think that's the only good thing about messing up. You learn not to do that same thing. You make a mess, you clean it up, and then you hopefully don't do it again."

"Or you fuck up again and again until you learn your lesson." As I did, but this wasn't about me, so I kept quiet.

"I didn't know how to be in a relationship. I still don't. What I told you was true, that I wanted to focus on myself when I moved here, but a part of me also just wanted to avoid relationships altogether because I was sure I'd be bad at it." Dani was quiet, and her voice was small but steady. "But I'd like to find out if I can be better now, with you, if you'd like."

I smiled and took Dani's hand in mine. "I'd really like that."

Dani gave me an apologetic smile then. "I was so suspicious of you after what I overheard between you and Amanda, and I just . . . I was beating myself up for letting myself catch feelings and getting hurt in the process. So I ignored you and ran from you like a coward, just like I did with Melissa. And I'm sorry."

Ah, that made sense now. "I forgive you. I can't say I wouldn't have done the exact same thing in your shoes."

Dani nodded, squeezing my hand. "I don't wanna do that with you. I wanna talk about things, and be honest about our feelings, and just . . . communicate, you know?"

A stab of guilt hit my heart as she said "be honest," and I didn't know why. It wasn't like I was lying to her about anything. Not telling her about my project and the full extent of how I realized my feelings for her wasn't the same as lying, right?

Dani's face was so open and so vulnerable, those big brown eyes so trusting, that I wanted to give that back to her. It could destroy everything, especially now that I knew how deep her trust issues ran, but could I let this continue without coming clean?

The throb in my chest told me I couldn't, but I didn't have the words to tell her now, so I just said, "Yeah, I want that too."

At least that much was true.

Dani smiled and released my hand, running her fingertips over the back of it before reaching for her backpack. "Enough of this feelings crap. Wanna do homework?"

A welcome distraction, but I still groaned. "Ugh, fine."

We worked in easy silence for a while, and I was surprised at how comfortable I felt, in my socks, my books spread out across the floor, as though I'd been hanging out in Dani's room my whole life. I liked watching Dani draw; a little wrinkle formed between her brows, and her eyes were intense and focused, fingers smudged with graphite. I kept looking at her and losing my train of thought, so after I'd fought my way through my physics homework, I resigned myself to doodling on my shoes, filling in the white lining along the edge of one Converse with my red Sharpie.

"Can I draw something?"

I looked up to see Dani looking at my shoes. "You want to?"

Dani nodded. "Yeah, I've seen the lyrics you have and think I have something cool to add. If that's okay with you."

My fingers fumbled for the collection of Sharpies in my backpack, unable to gather them fast enough. Once retrieved, I dropped them in front of Dani. "Sure, yeah, of course."

Dani took a few of them, and I pretended to scroll through my phone as she worked, pausing occasionally to push her hair back behind her ears.

I was becoming increasingly unnerved by how much I wanted to do that myself.

"There," Dani said a few minutes later, blowing on the fresh ink. "How's that?"

On the toe of my shoe, she had drawn a tree, branching out over the open space. There was a small sketch of what looked like a girl sitting in the branches.

"I noticed the lyric from 'Roots' on the other shoe and thought it would be fitting," Dani said, gesturing. "*I don't care if it's boring or fun—*"

"*I grow toward you like branches to the sun.*" My eyes widened. "You like the Alice Aesthetic?"

Dani flushed. "I hadn't really listened to them that much before, but I knew you liked them, so I gave them another chance. The new album's great, but I think *Martyrs and Mayhem* was honestly my favorite. What about you?"

I probably looked like I was glitching or something, but I just couldn't stop staring at her drawing. The prettiest girl I had ever seen, with the most patient heart of anyone I'd ever met, had looked up a band I liked without me even suggesting it, and she had *liked* it. And wanted to discuss it. Fuck. Why did it feel like she'd taken that Sharpie and written her name on the insides of my chest?

I watched her refine the drawing a bit, the words lingering on my tongue: *I was really confused and messed up when we met and I had weird feelings for three people before I was able to decide on you.*

Yeah, I wouldn't want to date me after that.

---

That evening, over fries and too-thick milkshakes at Whataburger, Dani smiled at me across the table. Even under the harsh fluorescent lighting, she looked gorgeous; it wasn't fair. How could I sit across from her and *not* think about kissing her?

The fact that this was an official date had no bearing on the event itself; it felt like it was just us as we always were when we hung out. We still talked about music we liked, artists whose talents we envied, and which brands of gummy bears could rip out fillings (Haribo—it actually happened to me, so I had the data to back this one up), but now I got to hold Dani's hand across the table and openly stare at her. Dates, it had turned out, were just friend hangouts with the volume turned up.

And kissing hopefully, but I had no idea how to approach *that* yet.

All night, I'd been gazing at Dani, trying to find a way to tell her about the quince, but every time I tried, the words stuck in my mouth like a fly caught in a spiderweb. Suddenly, I understood Matthew's fear of letting Tori meet his family. I'd only just asked her out a few hours ago; how could I ask her to my sister's quince, ask her to stand in front of one hundred of my relatives during one of the most high-stakes, high-pressure traditions of our culture?

Williams Road was darkening with the approach of night. I stared at the setting sun through the window, craving fresh air. I turned back to Dani and said, "Let's go somewhere."

Dani gave me a bemused smile. "We *are* somewhere."

I blushed because, yeah, I certainly hadn't been clear. "Yeah, I meant let's go somewhere we haven't been to together yet. I wanna go somewhere new with you."

Dani grinned. "I know just the place."

With Dani beside me, the darkness surrounding McKelvey Park felt inviting instead of suffocating, like a world of possibility lay in the shadow of the jungle gym. The crescent moon gave just enough light for us to see, and the play structure was steady under my hands as I climbed it, settling on the top landing.

"I know it's not new to you," Dani explained, "but I've never brought anyone here before, so it feels new to me."

"Why haven't you brought anyone else here?" I whispered, watching the way her baby hairs fluttered around in the breeze.

Dani pursed her lips in thought before she said, "I don't know. I started coming here when I was with Melissa, and it was just so pretty and so nice to sketch that I didn't want to taint that with any of her mess. And she wouldn't really get it anyway." She laid her hand gently over mine and gave me a shy smile. "But you take pictures, and you're so good at it, and you see things in such a beautiful way that maybe . . . maybe you'll love this the way I do."

The warmth of her hand spread up my arm, my veins flooding with the feel of it, and I smiled as we dangled our legs over the side of the play structure, staring out at the hillside lined with trees. Looking out over the sloping path, the streetlights reaching every crevice and the moonlight shining over everywhere it didn't, I might as well have been sitting at the top of the stratosphere. This place begged for a picture, but at the same time, I just wanted to live in this moment without rushing to capture it. My breath escaped in a whoosh as I said, "I think I do."

We were only a few feet off the ground, but in this jungle gym hideaway with the kindest girl I'd ever met looking into my eyes, I was standing at the top of the Empire State Building in a storm, the lightning buzzing all around us, lit up but safe, shining and electric from the inside out.

She turned to look at me, and I could feel the charge between us, the gentle begging in my soul to be closer. As I stared at Dani's pretty pink lips awash in moonlight, I felt that swoop in my stomach, that desire to close the gap between us. Dani held my gaze, squeezing my hand a bit as she leaned closer, slowly, like she was waiting for me to meet her. I could feel the ghost of her breath, begging me to give in, and I leaned in—

The scream of the iPhone's signature ringtone cut through the moment, startling us, and we both immediately checked our phones. No point in sharing a kiss if our mothers killed us for not answering our phones. It was Dani's phone, and she answered, giving me a sheepish, apologetic look. "Hey, Mom . . . yeah, I'll be home soon . . ."

I was both disappointed *and* relieved to be interrupted. The more time I spent with Dani, the harder it would be to lose her if I screwed up. Her kiss would open the floodgates and set free all the secrets I was trying to keep, and I needed to take control of it before it hurt both of us.

I needed to tell her, but on my terms.

That night, I posted a picture I'd taken of the trails, lit up gold in some spots by streetlights but pitch black otherwise. I wanted to make this right, to deserve that perfect place Dani wanted to share with me, but that meant being honest, and being honest meant possibly destroying this fragile thing we'd built for ourselves. I didn't want to let her go, but if I let our relationship rest on a lie, I didn't deserve to keep her. I had to tell her, even if it tore everything apart.

I could've stayed with D in that playground hideaway for thousands of years without end. She makes me feel new, like even with everything I've done and all my mistakes, I can still be capable of caring for someone well, that I could love well. But I can't do that with these secrets I'm keeping. If I want her to trust me, I need to be someone worth trusting.

---

That Monday was Halloween, and I couldn't help but feel a little ridiculous, listening to Chloe x Halle on the speakers behind the counter on the steps to the apartment in my Halloween costume, drinking a Monster, and waiting for Jordan to pick me up for school.

"Halloween is the devil's holiday," my mother mentioned casually from behind the register as she typed a few numbers into the Excel sheet she used to balance the books. She'd been repeating this proclamation every few minutes or so.

I rolled my eyes, which I'd also been doing periodically. "Maaa."

"Yeah, Mom, it's just candy. And her costume isn't even scary; it's nerdy," Alyssa said, coming in from the backyard where Veronica had been working on Alyssa's Halloween hairdo.

I pulled off my headphones as I stared at her hair, which was in two buns sprayed with silver hair glitter. "Says the girl in space buns."

Alyssa sniffed. "My friends and I are going to the Halloween dance as space fairies."

"Sooo aliens?"

"Space fairies."

I nodded. "Cool." Alyssa pulled a Mexican Coke out of the

fridge and popped the top with the bottle opener attached to the counter. Our mother eyed her suspiciously. "Did you pay for that?"

Alyssa lifted her chin proudly and dropped a dollar and a quarter into Mom's waiting hand. "Now I did."

Veronica narrowed her eyes at Alyssa as she watched the exchange. "Where did you get that? Did you keep the change when Mom sent you into Stripes to pay for gas this morning?"

"*No.* For your information, I packed one of the brownies that you made yesterday and some kid at school paid me five dollars for it."

"You charged a kid five dollars for a brownie Veronica made from a box?" I asked.

"He's not the brightest." Alyssa shrugged.

"Hey, so I know you barely let my friends in, but can I please tell Matthew he can bring Tori as his plus-one? I kinda feel bad for the whole 'trying to steal her boyfriend' thing, so I wanna make up for that." I cringed.

Alyssa laughed. "LMAO, I'm dead. Whatever, that's fine. Who are you asking to escort you if Matthew's out and so is Amanda—*ohhh,* I get it!" Alyssa grinned. "Dani?!"

I nodded, grinning. "I want to ask her, yeah."

Hopefully. If she doesn't hate me after I tell her about my project.

Alyssa raised an eyebrow and nodded, understanding. "I like her. Get her measurements before you start making out." She gave me a thumbs-up.

"I never liked Matthew," Mom said.

"We know," Alyssa and I said in unison.

"I'm just reminding you." Mom smiled at me. "But I like that Dani." She hustled off as some teens came into the store, chattering loudly and wandering through the candy aisle. Her business required her to pay attention to other delinquent children over her own delinquent children.

The bell attached to the door rang out, and Jordan skated into the store. "'Sup, Gonzalez ladies?"

"What are you?" I asked. He looked like himself, beanie and hoodie and skateboard and all.

"No skateboarding in my store," our mother called from the back. Jordan hopped off immediately.

"I'm Aladdin. Duh," Jordan said, his arms spread as if to say *See?* He was indeed wearing a bright red beanie, a purple hoodie, and a red belt looped through his khakis. "I even got this!"

He pointed at his belt, where he'd hung a key chain with a tiny stuffed monkey that looked like it had seen better days.

"Did you put a rug on your skateboard?" Alyssa said, staring down at the board.

Jordan picked it up and brandished it. It was covered with a brick-red welcome mat, hastily cut to fit. "Yes."

"Huh." I stared at it, squinting. "Well, all right. I rate it a seven. Good job."

"Magda, what are you?" Mom asked, staring at my costume.

I threw my arms out to show off my costume. I'd attached cutouts of question marks to a T-shirt dress and put on a pair of cat ears. I had Veronica paint whiskers on my face too. "I told you. I'm Schrödinger's cat."

"Dope." Jordan nodded. "Pretentious but dope."

"I just don't get it," Mom said.

She had also been saying that for the past hour.

I sighed dramatically, heading for the door. "C'mon, Jordan, let's go find people who will appreciate my costume."

"Long shot, but okay."

As he drove, his phone pinged in the cup holder, and he asked, "Check that, would you? I'm expecting something."

I nodded, picking it up and peering at the screen. It was a Cash App notification, and I raised my eyebrows. "Why is Fernando paying you twenty-five bucks at seven forty-five in the morning?"

Jordan lifted his chin, grinning proudly. "The basketball captains are going as the Aladdin cast, and Alfredo backed out, so they needed someone to fill out the role for the athletics costume contest. *Ergo*, me, your friend, neighborhood errand boy, saving the day." He gestured down at his costume as he braked at a red light.

Suddenly, his slapdash costume made a lot of sense. "You're not even *on* the basketball team, or on any sports team."

Jordan put his hand on his chest as he turned back to the road. "How dare you cheapen my love of the sport. Just because I'm not a player doesn't mean I don't respect the craft and athleticism that's involved in basketball."

"Name one position."

Jordan fell silent, and then he said, "Fuck you."

I laughed. "That's what I thought." I checked my whiskers in the mirror. Smudge-free, even after breakfast. Veronica was *good*. "So guess what?"

"What?"

"I went on a date with Dani." I couldn't help but grin, especially when Jordan gave a hyena-like shriek.

"This changes everything! So is your project, like, done-done?" Jordan gasped, accidentally jerking the steering wheel as he turned to gape at me. "Are you going to ask her to the quince? She'd look great in a dress! Or would she wear a tux? I don't want to assume—"

I gripped the sides of my seat as the car lurched around

with his excited motions. "Oh my gosh, please slow down and stop shaking. We haven't talked about any of that yet, and I . . . I don't know how to ask her."

Jordan frowned, slowing down and steadying the car once more. "How about 'Dani, will you escort me to my sister's quince?' When you come down to it, it's the same request you'd make of any friend."

I shook my head. "But she's not just any friend. She's my—my—well, we haven't actually said what we are yet. But whatever it is, she's that. And I—I don't—I feel weird about asking her that when there's still so much I haven't told her."

Jordan's eyes widened at the road. "Wait, do you mean . . ."

"I . . . I think I should tell her about the project."

His mouth opened and closed like a fish, and he said, "Um, I think that's a bad idea. There's such a thing as being too honest."

I scoffed. "That's not a thing. She already has, like, *debilitating* trust issues. I told you about what happened at the concert. If I keep lying to her by omission, it's going to destroy her."

Jordan nodded solemnly. He'd swooned when I told him about the mosh pit and crowd-surfing and spent the next few days in class poking at my bruises while I scowled and swatted at him. "But isn't that all the more reason to not tell her?"

"She's gonna find out anyway. It's not like I've ever been good at hiding things, especially from people I . . . care deeply about." I sighed. "I don't think this is gonna work out well if I keep the secret, and I . . . I don't want to start our relationship based on lies."

"Well, are you going to tell Matthew and Amanda too?"

That threw me off a bit, but then I remembered what I'd told Amanda, about how friendships required just as much work as romantic relationships, needed the same amount of honest communication, and deserved the same respect.

Amanda had been vulnerable with me when she admitted her jealousy, and Matthew had confessed his own issues. Dani had opened up to me too. The only one not being fully transparent here was me. "I think I have to, J."

"Look, I know this is, like, the mature thing to do and everything, but I hate it."

"Me too, J. Me too." I remembered that I'd also implicated Jordan in this, so I said, "I don't have to tell them you knew. You'll just have to act surprised when they tell you."

Jordan sighed dramatically. "I cannot tell a lie. You know this. My face is an open book, and my business is based on one hundred percent transparency. People trust me. I can't have my company's reputation sullied by falsehoods."

"You know Matthew is probably going to kill you when he finds out you kept this from him, right?"

Jordan winced as he pulled into the school parking lot. "Yeah, well. I'll just lay low after you tell everyone so he knows but he can't tell me shit. It's what every successful business would do in the face of a publicity scandal."

"Atta boy. Now you're getting it."

# 15

The next day, I woke up with this awful sense of foreboding that made me feel like I couldn't breathe deeply enough. I couldn't hold the secret of the project in my body any longer, and I needed to let it out as soon as possible.

That morning at school, I walked around in a trance, trying to figure out the words to say that wouldn't leave me lonely and friendless.

*I couldn't untangle the threads of you in my life, and I needed to get it all out in a way I understood . . .*

*There wasn't enough room in my heart for all of you, and I was bursting at the seams . . .*

*I didn't know how to explain what I was feeling to myself, so I used what I saw outside of me to try to figure out what I saw inside myself . . .*

*I'm sorry I couldn't handle this quietly . . .*

*I'm sorry I couldn't keep this to myself . . .*

*I'm sorry.*

*I'm sorry.*

At lunch, we were hanging out in the physics room again, waiting for Jordan to get out of chess. Apparently, Mr. Velazquez had had enough of our loitering and zeroed in on me and Amanda.

"Overachievers! If you're going to insist on eating in my lab, I need someone to get supplies out for tomorrow's lab. I'll give you extra points on your test."

Amanda's head jerked up at the mention of extra credit, and mine did too. I sucked at physics, so any leg up I could get was sorely needed.

Mr. Velazquez handed us the lab instructions. "Easy enough," Amanda said as we walked to the back of the room. "Ping-Pong balls, those paper towel tubes we brought in last week, scales."

"I just don't know what any of this has to do with physics, but whatever."

As I followed her into the back room, I couldn't help but realize we'd be completely alone, in neutral territory. She could walk away from me if she was mad, and she hadn't driven me to school this morning, so I wouldn't be left stranded if she hated me.

This was as good a time as ever to tell her, so I fought past the nausea and panic and pulled out my phone as we ventured deeper into the room.

"I'll get the scales from the cabinets," Amanda said, unfolding the step stool, "since you're short."

"You know what—"

"Oh quiet, it's not an insult, just a fact."

"I still hate it." I pouted as I pushed the cart we were using deeper into the room. I found the Ping-Pong balls and set them on the cart, and as Amanda rummaged around in the cabinets, I took the profile off private in case she'd want to look at it later without me around.

The pictures weren't loading because there was no signal,

and I held my phone up, hunting for one. I found one bar in the corner of the room, and I stood on tiptoe, trying to chase it, putting my hand on the cart for balance. I just needed to show Amanda the profile, so it would be enough to load the grid, if I could only get another bar—

Under the force of my balancing act, the cart gave way. If I'd had more common sense, I would've realized it had wheels and was therefore unlikely to stay still, but instead, my clumsy ass went crashing to the floor and the cart went sailing across the small space, whacking into Amanda.

"Ow, Maggie, what the fuck—" Amanda grabbed hold of the counter, steadying herself, which was more than I could do, because I'd fallen onto my side and sent my phone sliding to rest at the foot of the stool. My heart rate spiked as Amanda looked down at me, wide-eyed, and scrambled off the stool. "Oh my gosh, are you okay?!"

"Yeah, I'm fine. Don't worry." I propped myself up on my hand, pulling myself onto my knees even though my right one was bruised. I grimaced but started in the direction of my phone.

To my horror, Amanda had bent down and scooped it up. "It's all right, I got it. Are you—Did you get hurt because you were checking *Instagram*?"

She looked down at the screen as I got to my feet, wincing as I rubbed my hip. I started for her, praying the profile hadn't loaded. "Hey, privacy—"

"Did you start a new profile for your pictures? These are really great—wait, what are these captions?" Her eyes darted around the screen and she fell silent.

The quiet was deafening, and I froze in place. "Amanda . . ."

Her head came up slowly, and her eyes were hard as she looked at me. "Who is A?" Her voice was cold, flat.

"Amanda—"

She gave a humorless laugh that sent chills all along my arms. "Don't *Amanda* me. Are you . . . Who are M and D?" she asked, still looking through my phone.

"Give it back." My voice was high and shaking. I reached for my phone, but she jerked it away, still looking at it.

"What is this? Why are you talking about us like this? What the fuck, Maggie?" she spat, tossing my phone into the cart.

I grabbed it, looking down at the picture she'd opened. It was the picture of us that I had taken after our fight about the kiss, the caption an angry rant about her. "Amanda . . ."

"Tell me the truth, Maggie. I know that might be hard for you," she snapped.

"I . . . I had feelings for you." The words were rough, like shards of glass scratching the sides of my throat on the way out. "I was confused, and I—I had weird feelings about Matthew and Dani too, so I . . . I just wrote it down. And . . . and I used it as my art project."

It hurt to add that part, especially when her already cold expression had turned indignant.

"So you took pictures without our permission and posted them on the internet for the world to see, for a *teacher* to see, without telling any of us about it? You put personal details about my life on your finsta."

My stomach clenched and turned, my hands numb and shaking. When she laid it out like that, it sounded horrible. "Amanda—"

"Guys? What's going on? What was that sound?"

Forcing my gaze away from Amanda, I turned to see Matthew, who had spoken, and Dani, both of whom were frozen in the doorway. I followed Dani's eyes from me to Amanda and back. "Um, I—"

"Ask Maggie," Amanda interrupted, her eyes slits as she

backed away and headed for the door. "She has a lot to say about you both, apparently."

She stomped away, pushing past Jordan, who had appeared behind Matthew and Dani.

"Hey, what—Maggie? What's happening?" His eyes flickered around, from my pale face to Matthew's and Dani's expectant looks. His eyes widened, lighting up with understanding. "Oh shit," he said quietly.

I looked between the three of them, and I took a breath, handing my phone, open to the profile, to Dani. "There's something I need to tell you . . ."

Matthew and Dani both looked at the phone, and the few minutes of silence were painful as their faces changed. "So you . . . you . . ."

I bit the inside of my cheek, then released it. "I'm saying that for the last few weeks, I had really confusing feelings for the three of you and—and I used this profile as my project for art so I could figure it out."

Dani was silent, and every tap of her finger against the phone felt like it was slamming against my brain. Matthew craned his neck to look over his shoulder, and I couldn't see either of their faces, could do nothing but wait for their reactions with suffocating, soul-crushing dread rising in my chest.

After a long, long minute, they both looked up. Dani's face was ashen, her lips set in a hard line, and the hurt and rage in her eyes pierced me like a spear to the chest. Matthew's narrowed eyes passed over me to settle on Jordan. "Did you know about this?"

"Please leave me out of this." Jordan gulped, shoving his fists in the pockets of his hoodie.

"Did you *know*?" Matthew demanded, brandishing the

phone in his face. "That this whole time she was taking pictures to make posts for her weird art project?"

My eyes flickered to Jordan's. Somehow he was still asking for my permission, even though I had dragged him into this mess. I nodded, allowing him to get himself into even more trouble.

Jordan looked back at Matthew and sighed, shrugging. "Yeah, dude, I knew. We just talked about it."

"Behind my back—"

"Hey, stop it," I snapped at Matthew. "It's not his fault."

"Of fucking course not—it's yours." Matthew's glare burned into me like a brand. "You just had to tell the whole fucking internet about all my fucking flaws and our relationship problems? Here you were practically begging me to trust you while we were dating, and you turn around and do this the second I let you in? *Anyone* could have seen this!"

My mouth felt as if it had been rusted shut and I wrenched it open like a bear trap that had snapped after years of dormancy. "It's—it's not—I never wanted—it was private. I never wanted you to find out. I didn't want you all to hate me. I just wanted to work through my feelings without anyone—"

"Without anyone getting hurt? You knew this would hurt us. Hurt—*hurt me*." Dani was trembling, a coil of barely contained rage, and her eyes were glassy with unshed tears. I had seen Dani hurt before, suspicious, but never angry, and now she was absolutely *livid*. "So what? You chose me? What kills me is that you liked me, but you still had to make a whole project before you could figure that out. You had to choose me over two other people. How do you think that makes me feel, to be one of a *set*?"

Through shaking lips I mumbled, "Dani—"

"Not only that, but you told the world I'm damaged goods

and have trust issues? Nice. At least now I know what you think of me. Thanks for being honest about that, at least." With one final burning look, Dani stood up and headed back toward the classroom.

"This was really fucked up of you, Maggie. Just so you know." Matthew gave me one last glare before turning around and leaving, ignoring Jordan as he went.

I was left with Jordan, tears welling up in my eyes, and he gave me a weak smile. "Well. You did it."

Yay me.

After school, Jordan drove me home. We didn't talk. He kept glancing at me out of the corner of his eye at every stoplight, but I didn't want to look at him, didn't have the strength to pretend everything was okay. The window was cold against the side of my head as I stared idly at the purple-grey clouds blocking the setting sun. I pretended I was floating through space, zooming past planets and stars, to a universe where this hadn't happened, where I didn't have this heart, and it hadn't made me do this incredibly awful thing.

When we pulled up outside the store, Jordan turned around in his seat. "I'll talk to you later, yeah? You'll text me?"

"Yeah, I will." I didn't want to talk about this now, but I would inevitably blow up his phone later. I knew myself enough to know *that*.

I lingered outside the door. My mother was at the counter, separated from me by only several feet of tile and a thin metal screen. She would no doubt pepper me with questions in both English and Spanish, and right now I didn't have the words to explain myself in either language. I rounded the house and snuck off to the backyard.

On the back porch, Veronica was doing a princess-type of bun on Alyssa, winding strands of hair around a curling iron.

Alyssa waved. "We're hoping this one is the one!"

Veronica looked up just as I stepped into the circle of light, and she quickly set her curling iron on the stool beside her. "Oh god."

Alyssa gaped. "What happened?"

My eyes immediately began to well at the question, and I tipped my head back, hoping the tears wouldn't fall as I tried to compose myself. I couldn't speak, an ocean of shame filling my throat. I heard some shuffling, and then someone burrowed into my side. I looked down at Alyssa, who had her arms wound around me, and up at Veronica, who had never been as comfortable with physical affection but had slid an arm around my shoulders regardless. I let myself lean on Veronica, my eyes sliding closed for a moment; it was sometimes a blessing just to be held.

Later, over leftover spaghetti, I told them what happened. Veronica, ever the pragmatist, was also working on Alyssa's guest list and seating chart, but every time I spoke, she made sure to give me all her attention, her steady dark eyes always focused on me.

When I finished, my sisters just stared at me.

"I know this isn't the right time, but—" Alyssa started.

I glared, raising an eyebrow. "So don't."

"You don't know shit," Veronica said to Alyssa, who frowned.

"Ha!"

Veronica whipped her head around and pointed at me. "You either. You don't know shit."

"Ay, why the hell are you cursing?" None of us had heard the door open, but our mother had walked in, followed closely by CJ, who waved sheepishly.

Alyssa rolled her eyes. "Maaa, everyone does it—"

"Don't roll your eyes at me, Alyssa Ann. I didn't raise

everyone else. I raised you, and I didn't raise any of you to talk like that." Mom frowned. "What would your papi say, if he heard you talking like that?"

"Papi had a sailor's mouth too, if I remember correctly," Veronica pointed out.

"Mentirosa. I'm going to shower. Junior—" Mom turned to glare at CJ, who pursed his lips guiltily even though he hadn't been in the house long enough to have done anything wrong. "You better be out of this house before my girls are in bed. I better see you leave."

"Yes, ma'am," CJ stammered. He was always loud and boisterous when he wasn't in the hot seat, but under our mother's gaze, CJ was just as powerless as the rest of us.

Mom wandered to her room and shut the door, and CJ took a seat at the table, kissing Veronica on the cheek and taking her hand. "So what's going on, triple Gs? Y'all look like you're having the best time ever."

"CJ, I don't think I'll be able to go out right now—" Veronica started.

"I figured when I saw you guys in here looking like the world was ending. So what are we talking about?" CJ gave me his full attention, folding his hands in front of him.

"Maggie's project got found out," Alyssa filled him in.

I grimaced.

"Whoa," CJ breathed, eyes wide. "So now what's going to happen?"

I shook my head, toying with the last clump of spaghetti on my plate. "I don't know," I admitted quietly. "They seemed really mad."

"Just give them some space. They're just mad right now. They'll calm down eventually, and then y'all can talk about it," CJ suggested. Veronica nodded.

My chin wobbled, and I pushed my plate away, crossing my arms in front of my stomach and sinking down into my seat. "What am I even supposed to say? Hi, I'm Maggie, and I'm such a disaster that I needed a school project and a fucking finsta to figure out who I liked? And that decision didn't even matter in the grand scheme of things. How am I supposed to make any actual big decisions in my life if this is the only way I can do things?"

Figuring out my feelings had been hard enough, and I'd been focusing so much on that because I didn't want to think about the decision I was avoiding about college. Now that I had come clean about that, I could no longer ignore the fact that life was full of decisions like this—and I wasn't prepared for any of it.

Veronica gave me a sad smile. "At least you figured it out, right?"

"At the expense of my friendships!" I wailed. "What other things am I going to mess up because I can't get my shit together?"

My relationship with my family, for one, once they found out I had doubts about the future that they so passionately dreamt of for me.

"You didn't mess it up," CJ said. "Just say you're sorry, and give them time."

"I don't think it's going to be that easy this time. You didn't see their faces."

"No, but we know you," Alyssa said quietly, and I looked up at her, surprised at the solemnity in her tone. "I don't think any of them want to lose you."

"Why am I so bad at this? Is *everyone* just bad at making decisions and relationships and big life decisions and no one told me?" I said, throwing my hands up in exasperation.

Veronica pointed at me. "That one. You got it. But I think you're on the right track."

"How?"

Veronica smiled sadly, half her mouth turning up. "Because all this time, no matter what, you kept trying. You didn't give up trying to figure out what it actually was. Don't give up on your friends yet." Veronica reached across the table and took my hand in her own. It was calloused, warm, and soft.

That night, I couldn't sleep, so I tortured myself by scrolling through my photo library, laptop balanced on my stomach as I lay in bed, staring up at the plastic glow-in-the-dark glitter stars Alyssa and I had stuck on the ceiling years ago. It was a miracle of cosmic proportions that they hadn't fallen off. I turned back to my laptop, to the weird self-harm that was basking in the glow of old memories.

Matthew at the play, grinning at the camera. Jordan at homecoming, face screwed up as he aimed a pie at the vice principal. Amanda on the riser at band practice, always ready to lead.

And, of course, pictures of Dani.

A picture I took at the resaca. The picture of our bruised knees. Dani in the store, holding up two Funyuns to encircle her eyes. Dani smiling serenely on the curb in front of the store, tilting her head, her curtain of dark hair falling over her shoulder to let the light shine through.

We'd had a Snap streak going as well; tears pricked at the corners of my eyes as I stared at the little fire emoji next to our chat, trying to commit to memory the sight of the only connection we still had, now turning to ash.

# 16

The next day at school, my friends didn't so much as look at me all day. The only one who talked to me was Jordan, and even he was more subdued than usual, my bad mood rubbing off on him. He didn't try to engage me in conversation about what had happened, but I knew he was expecting me to say something from the anxious look in his eyes every time I caught him looking at me. I knew he meant well, but I just didn't have the energy to go into it at school, of all places.

His too-pure-for-this-world heart, though, was still kind enough to try and distract me. *I gotta run an errand after school. Wanna come w/?* he texted during last period.

I could tell I must have looked really pitiful when I left for school this morning because my mom didn't question me as much as she usually would when I texted her to ask if Jordan could drive me home, and I was grateful for that.

I headed off the line of questioning Jordan was about to begin when I got in the car by asking, "So what are we doing tonight? Dog-bathing? Cat-feeding?"

"Nope." His smile was coy as he pulled out of the parking lot. "You wait and see."

When we arrived at a mini mansion in Resaca Shores, one

of the more well-off neighborhoods in San Benito, I felt out of place the minute we pulled into the driveway. "How much are you making for this job?"

"Way too much for what the job actually is," Jordan said gleefully, twirling a set of keys around his fingers as he got out. "Let's go. There are hungry mouths to feed."

The glow was the first thing I noticed when we crossed the threshold.

The house was dark, and it was your typical rich-person house, with immaculate tile floors and high ceilings, but what set it apart was the far wall of the living room. Set against it were huge fish tanks, three rows of tanks stacked on top of each other like they would be at a pet store, filling the entire bottom half of the wall.

"Shit," I breathed, drawing closer to it. The blue light had a pull to it, the water reflecting it like the brightest of diamonds.

Jordan beamed as he came up beside me. "Impressive, huh? The owners are out of town, so they paid me a ridiculous amount of money to feed them for two days. They're super temperamental, though, so they gave me a list of how much to feed them, and what."

Jordan went over to the side of the tanks, where a small white cabinet sat. He opened it to reveal half a dozen different canisters of dry food and a couple that looked to contain live feed. "Ah, a bounty," he marveled.

My eyes were glued to the tanks, roving over the fish. There were three tanks filled with bioluminescent fish alone, one with what looked to be a mini-shark, another with a pufferfish family, and one with what seemed to be the entire cast of *Finding Nemo*. I didn't know a ton about fish, but this person really seemed to know what they were doing. "What the fuck kind of hobby . . ."

"Rich people really be out here being rich and having time for luxurious collections." He waved me over to the cabinet. "Now get over here. I didn't bring you here to stare. We have clients to feed."

We had to consult the list Jordan pulled from his pocket to make sure we didn't fuck anything up, but between the two of us, we were able to get done in half an hour, the fish a captive audience. They stared at us, gawking and trailing along behind us suspiciously as we crossed back and forth in front of them.

It was surprisingly draining, so when we were done, Jordan and I just sat on the floor in front of them.

"How were you brave enough to do this?" I asked him.

He pulled his gaze away from the crab he was making faces at and looked at me. "What do you mean 'brave'?"

I watched the tanks, the fish dancing in the water as they tried to get the last bits of food. "Fish are super temperamental. How did you know you weren't gonna screw this up and, like, kill one of them?" I would've been an anxious mess the whole time, petrified to make the wrong decision about how to feed them or when.

Jordan shrugged. "I mean, I'm worried about it, yeah, but it's still really cool to do it. I gotta try, especially if I want my hundred dollars. I don't really need it—"

"Wait, what? You got the money already?" I gaped at him, probably making the same face the fish were.

"Yup, I'm gonna go pick up the guitar tomorrow." Jordan beamed proudly, his smile gleaming in the turquoise light.

"Dude, that's awesome! Why are you still running errands then?"

"Because money is money, and it gets me out of the house. I get to do a lot of cool stuff, like this." He waved at the fish tanks. "How awesome is this?"

I smiled at the axolotl that was lurking in the tank near my head. Maybe it was just my imagination, but it seemed like it was smiling back. "This is really cool."

"Plus, I'm doing my project on it, so that helps."

I raised my eyebrows. "I thought you were doing it on the after-school program."

Jordan shook his head. "Nah, I was, but then I realized that I was spending even more time on stuff like this than I was spending on the after-school program, so I started drawing pictures of that."

He pulled out his phone and showed me photos of his drawings, comic-like illustrations of a doodled superhero walking dogs and delivering groceries. There was even a drawing of him feeding fish, but in the tank with a snorkel and swim fins. "This is Everyman, and he goes around helping people."

"That makes your errand business way cooler, honestly."

"Nope, it's just as cool. It just makes everyone else see how cool it is."

I smiled. "That's amazing, J. I'm really impressed."

Jordan swept his arm around in an exaggerated bow. "Thank you, thank you, I'm rather impressive, yes."

Seeing his project reminded me of my own, and I fell silent, looking down at my hands. With the light bathing us both in blue, I felt like I was underwater, in that neutral space where even gravity worked differently. Maybe that's why I felt safe enough to talk about it. "I fucked up, J."

Jordan patted me on the shoulder. "You sure did, buddy."

"Do you think I'm selfish?"

Jordan squinted. "Is that a trick question?"

"No, really. Did I handle this all wrong? How did I completely screw this up?"

Jordan thought it over. "Well, it seemed like a good idea at the time, but the execution left something to be desired."

"Yeah, you could say that." I scoffed and tilted my head back, staring at the tiles in the ceiling and trying to find a solution in them, as though they were tea leaves. "I just wish I had someone, anyone, else to blame except for my lying ass."

"So fix it," Jordan said, shrugging in my periphery.

I lolled my head to the side pitifully to glare at him. "I'm literally doing the only thing I can do right now, which is nothing."

Jordan didn't back down, even though I was attempting to look as intimidating as possible while making the least movement. "That's not true and you know it."

I exhaled in frustration, resting my elbows on my knees and dropping my head onto my hands. "Well, what do you suggest I do, J? They're not going to talk to me."

Jordan shrugged. "You don't know that. You haven't even tried to apologize yet."

"What am I supposed to say? *Matthew, sorry I tried to seduce you while telling the internet about our relationship problems? Amanda, sorry I threw away our friendship for a chance to date you?* Or, or Dani—"

Bile rose in my throat. "Oh god," I choked, rubbing my eyes with the heels of my palms. "She's never going to forgive me. The only thing she wanted here was a fresh start, not more drama. I didn't even think about how this would affect anyone else; I just thought they'd never find out. But god, look what the fuck happened—"

I felt a pat on my back and gave a watery chuckle, wiping away a few stray tears. "Look at me, fucking crying like I am the victim here. I'm the one who hurt people, I shouldn't be . . ."

"It breaks both ways," Jordan murmured. "It always does."

I eyed him. "When did you get deep?"

"I watch a lot of TV, but that's not the question." Jordan looked at me seriously. "The only way to make it better is if you let it out."

"I don't wanna cry right now—"

"That's not what I meant." Jordan appeared to be thinking about something before amending, "Well, not entirely. You should still cry, but that's not what I meant exactly. You need to talk to them. Tell them how you're feeling."

"They won't listen," I muttered. My voice sounded small.

"They will if you're honest. I think you owe it to them now."

I sighed. "Yeah, I do. But how?"

Jordan shrugged. "Dunno. You're gonna have to figure that out yourself though, 'cuz I'm not helping anymore. I can't handle the stress of keeping secrets, and Matthew punched me in the arm yesterday for keeping secrets from him. I would really not like another bruise, *thankyouverymuch*. I'm too delicate for this crap."

---

My mom was waiting for me outside the store when I got back home. I thought I'd been pretty good at hiding my feelings during the day, but she took one look at my slumped shoulders and said, "We're going to get tacos."

I straightened up in my seat as she turned off Williams Road and got onto the expressway, heading toward Brownsville. When my mom said "tacos" and turned in this direction, I knew we were heading to Mari's.

Mom grew up on the outskirts of San Benito, the rural area on the way to Brownsville and running along the border wall, which she called el ranchito. The houses and trailers out there were smaller, and the roads were broken and littered with potholes that made driving through the neighborhoods feel like commuting along a piece of Swiss cheese. The area was one of the poorest parts of town, but my mom said it still held all the best parties when she was growing up, and having been to quite a few of Josh Ortega's kickbacks, I could believe that. Still, my mom avoided the neighborhood, citing a desire to be as far from her "rebellious youth and bad decisions" as possible, which *sucked* because Mari's, which was my favorite taco place, was right on the edge of her old neighborhood along the border fence.

The tiny stucco building didn't look like much from the outside; then again, not many good restaurants in the Valley did. But they had my favorite tacos, and my mother knew that, so when I told her "thank you," her tiny smile told me she understood just how much I meant it. The place had a little drive-thru window, which wasn't uncommon at snack stands like Mari's, places that served nachos and chicharrones with Tajín and Hot Cheetos with cheese, things you could eat on the way back from work or school before you'd go eat actual dinner at home. As Mami ordered at the drive-thru, her Spanish flying past me too fast to catch, I tuned out, staring past the trees behind Mari's to the field beyond.

The Rio Grande Valley was practically a country of its own.

We picked up a couple dozen tacos al pastor and bistec and little baggies of salsa verde and roja, onions, jalapeños, and cilantro. Mom pulled out of the drive-thru but lingered in the parking lot just a bit, and I saw her glancing at me out of the corner of her eye. When she said, "Magdalena, mírame," I knew I couldn't hide it anymore. I turned to her, already feeling the weight of the situation pressing against my teeth. Mami was staring at me sympathetically. "What's going on with you these days?"

"My friends are mad at me."

"Why?"

"I messed up." My mother looked at me expectantly, and I sighed, recounting the events of the last few days along with their context.

When it was over, I bit my lip, scanning my mother's face for a reaction. There was no anger or disgust, just a light curiosity. "I don't know what to say. This is an interesting situation you got yourself into."

I scoffed quietly. "You're telling me."

"Well, I would say talk to them, but you're smart enough to know that already." I nodded. "So I'm just going to say that it's okay."

"Okay to what?"

Mom smiled softly. "To mess up. To not know what to do and make bad decisions because of it, and learn from what happened. To run away sometimes, as long as you come back."

I sighed. "Even if it means losing your friends forever because of a half-baked plan that went wrong?"

"Even so." My mother tapped tasteful dusty pink nails along the steering wheel. "I miss your papi."

Where did that come from? Her words and the sad, faraway look in her eyes made my chest feel tight, and for the zillionth time today, a lump formed in my throat. "What makes you say that?"

"If he was here, he'd know what to say. He taught me what I know about love, and I did the same for him in my own way." My mom shrugged. "We'd always wanted to provide an example for you girls, and it's hard to do now."

I patted her hand, and she gave me a small warm smile. "You did, Mami."

"I could explain it better if he was here. He had a stronger way of loving than anyone I know. I see so much of him in you—how intensely you love, how caring you are."

"Was he a good husband?"

My mother's smile widened. "Yes, the best. He gave me much more than I thought I'd ever find in a husband, in a partner. We loved each other, but trying to keep the store up put a lot of stress on us. We had to fight to make things work. We had to have fights in order to talk through those things."

"You never told me things were hard between you two." I sorted through the haziest memories in my head, looking for a trace of any problem they'd had and coming up short.

My mother shook her head. "I never wanted you to know. Veronica knew a little bit, since she was older. But we did a disservice to you for not letting you see it."

"How?"

Her eyes were soft and just a little sad, but her smile was genuine. "So you could see that a real marriage, real love, is work. That couples fight, they don't like each other sometimes, but they keep trying. It's a fire you keep tending, even when you can barely see any sparks. I wish we had shown you that it's normal to go through hard times. It's important to fight. To mess up. That's how you learn how to do things right."

"I didn't know that," I said, picking at the little bundle of foil on my lap. I could feel the heat of the tacos inside trying to burn my legs through my jeans.

"How could you? You're seventeen. All you know of the world is from movies and that little teen show you watch about the white kids who have sex all the time."

"Mooom, it's called *Riverdale*—"

"I know what it's called, and I don't like it."

I giggled, and my mother smiled and took my hand. "You're not expected to know how to do this yet. You learn as you go.

But you have to keep going, to keep making it better and keep learning from it. Even when it looks hopeless. It may not feel like you're getting anywhere, but as long as your fights are productive and you learn from them, your mess-ups can be just as valuable as your successes."

"What if you do everything you can and it doesn't work?" My voice was that of a child, the child that I was, really. The drive-thru line was filling up now, so my mom started the car again and pulled back onto Military Highway, heading home.

She squeezed my hand as she drove. "Then it doesn't work, and that's okay too. Sometimes things fall apart and we don't know why. The only way is to go through it, to try, to fight. You have time to make this right, Maggie. Just try again."

Her eyes looked like mine. I had no choice but to believe her.

---

**Maggie:** Hi

**Maggie:** How are you?

**Maggie:** Omg that's unnecessary
i know how you are.

**Maggie:** Dani please talk to me

**Maggie:** At least let me explain. Please.

**Maggie:** Dani?

---

Talking to Mom had helped, but I still didn't know what to do, so I was still, as usual, a sad sack the next day at school after another day of my friends avoiding me—Amanda's eyes glancing over me, Matthew turning away whenever I entered the classroom.

Worst of all was when I ran into Dani before lunch.

Jordan had chess, and I really didn't want to be around anyone else, so I'd taken my sandwich and shoved it in my backpack, wandering around trying to find an empty doorway to hole up in.

That's when I saw Dani in the hallway outside the yearbook room.

We both froze, staring at each other. Backlit with the afternoon light that was coming from the back door of the hall, Dani looked as rough as I did, darkness under her eyes, her shoulders slumping wearily. She opened her mouth and then closed it, as though the words sitting on her tongue had failed her.

I tried. "Dani, I—"

Dani shook her head. "I can't. I just . . ."

And then she walked away, down the hallway. I took a step to follow her, saying, "Wait—"

But she didn't turn back. My heart felt as heavy as her steps, sinking like a stone in the ocean of my chest as she got farther and farther away, finally disappearing from sight.

Her retreating back was all I could think about the rest of the day, and when Veronica drove me home from school, I went straight upstairs to shower and hide in my comforter cocoon.

"You've been moping around since all this happened. I think it's time to get up now."

I could feel Veronica's eyes on me from where she stood in the doorway, but I didn't look up from my Sudoku game. "I don't think so, thanks."

"Look, I know it sucks, but I really need you today, okay?" Veronica said exasperatedly.

I reluctantly sat up, squinting at her. "Fiiine, what's happening?"

"I have to study for a test today, and Mami and Alyssa are going to deliver the damas' dresses."

"And how does this affect me?"

Veronica gave a frustrated sigh. "Geez, you're being a brat right now. I need you to run the store tonight."

"Why?" I whined. "It's not my night."

"I don't care. I have a test, and you haven't really been helping with the quince stuff lately, so this is a great time to make up for it."

"I did the invitations and the photos," I snapped hotly.

Veronica leveled me with a cold stare. "Yeah, and you haven't done anything since then. I don't need to tell you how much Mami does for you, and this is the *least* you can do for her and Alyssa right now."

I was instantly flooded with shame, and the rush increased when I replayed the last few weeks in my head. I'd been so absorbed in my own drama and edits for my project that I hadn't even noticed how much quince prep had taken over the house, the rolls of turquoise ribbon and boxes of party favors suddenly making the room feel ten times smaller, pressing in on me until they were all I could see. I thought about my conversation with Jordan. If I was going to fix things with my friends, maybe I should fix them with my family first. "You're right. Get out so I can get dressed."

I pulled on an Asking Alexandria hoodie and a beanie, resigning myself to an afternoon and evening of silence. I took my place at the register with an old crossword puzzle book and a pen with a chewed-up cap. The first hour or two went by fairly quickly, with customers coming in and out purchasing beer and cigarettes and chips. I practiced looking composed, joking with the customers as I rang them up, but when the little bell above the door signaled their exit, the smile slid off my face like melted ice cream, my muscles aching from holding its unnatural shape.

My art project was due the next day, and I didn't have an ending to it that didn't make me out to be the villain in my own tragic love story. I didn't have a date for Alyssa's quince. I probably didn't have any friends anymore, other than Jordan, and I was tired from a school day spent avoiding my friends and wondering what they were saying about me. *Oh Maggie Gonzalez, the slutty, thirsty, desperate bisexual! Of course this happened—what else are bisexuals good for? Aren't all bisexuals cheaters and liars? Maggie obviously didn't want to choose, so she just went after all of them. What a fucking slut.*

My eyes stung again, a warning, and I rubbed at them, willing the tears away. But I remembered what my mom had said, about making mistakes and learning from them, about being allowed to be a mess sometimes as long as you came out better for it.

If my friendships were going up in smoke, I was at least going to make something good out of the ashes.

I opened up Google Docs on my phone and began planning my final write-up for the project, the last great hope for my project *and* for my friendships.

# 17

The final photo for my project was a shot of the group after Matthew's play, a selfie I'd taken at Wingstop. But I'd edited the photos to have red-permanent-marker-style hearts around Dani, Matthew, and Amanda's faces, like a kid would draw around a photo of their crush in the yearbook.

I spent hours that night writing and rewriting the final essay for the project, the one I hoped would save all my friendships while also helping me not fail Art, considering I didn't have a neat and tidy solution to the problem I'd set out to solve. This had been the hardest part of the assignment, I'd realized: trying to find the right combination of words to express how deeply sorry I was, hoping that it was okay to stumble and trip over them as long as they were honest. Open. Full of love.

*I started out my project kinda selfishly. I wanted to know if I was bad at love. It's the question I asked myself, always, especially after my relationships would crash and burn.*

*I thought that because I had always been bad at love, I always would be, so I took precautions. I stayed away from dating and love and whatever, but it just caught up with me that much faster. When I realized I was feeling all sorts of ways about my friends and also someone totally new, I used this project to try to express what that felt like to me through photographs. To be stuck over people from the past as you're falling for someone new—I thought something was wrong with me. I needed to find out what, and in the process I broke my friends' trust in ways that were especially dickish.*

*I disregarded my friendships because I thought for some reason that my pursuit of romantic love was more important, and it wasn't. No matter who it's with, you need to treat all the relationships in your life like they are precious, worthy of all the respect and care in the world.*

*I figured out my feelings at the expense of my friends', and I'm really sorry for that. Even though this project doesn't have a perfect happy ending, I've accepted that no one's love story actually does. A happy ending is not the end. It's the beginning. I'm still learning how to be a good friend, a good daughter, a good sister. And that's okay.*

*The truth is, we're all figuring out how to love, and it's not just romantically. We're figuring out how to love our friends and our family, how much is too much, what to give and how much. We're all messing up, we're all natural disasters waiting to tear up our own lives. But we're trying, and we'll never stop trying to fix ourselves, and I think that's what counts.*

I turned in the project in Art the next day using the computers in yearbook to drop the photo and Word document in Mrs. Lozano's Google Drive before first bell. I sent the files to Matthew, Amanda, and Dani as well, my last hopes buzzing in my fingertips and making them shake.

When I got to Art, Mrs. Lozano gave me an encouraging

smile, as though she knew I'd had other uses for the files. "I hope your project gave you the results you were looking for."

Not yet, but I was working on it.

When I got home from school, I jumped at the chance to help cover the store when Mami and Alyssa left to pick up the tuxedos and get extra party favors. I was still me, and crap at customer service, so an hour into my shift, I was bored out of my mind and couldn't even bring myself to put on my customer-service voice when the little bell rang. My words sounded bitchy even to my own ears as I said, "Welcome, let me know if you need help."

"You're lucky I wasn't a real customer; you'll never make it in retail."

My head snapped up, and sure enough, Matthew stood in the doorway, holding a Taco Bell bag. "What're you doing here?"

"I was a dick. Can you talk?" he asked, giving me a sheepish smile.

He didn't look like he was here to yell at me, and he'd brought Taco Bell. How could I say no?

I was quiet as he took the food out and set it on the counter. He took advantage of the silence and said, "What you did with the write-up was really brave, and really, really honest. And I was able to kinda process everything, and I'm really sorry about going off on you without hearing what you had to say first."

"I'm the one who should say sorry. I *am* sorry. About everything, about not being a better friend, or a better girlfriend. And I'm sorry to Tori too."

"I talked to her, and she's not mad or anything. She kind of suspected that you had something going on, but your advice that day at the park was super helpful, so I think that kind of gave you credibility in her mind."

I smiled. That was comforting to hear, weirdly enough. "I'm really sorry about blaming you for our relationship crashing and burning. It was my fault too. I was just not ready to stop being angry at you, and I didn't know how else to deal."

"It's fine." Matthew gave me a sad half smile. "You weren't the only one still dealing with their feelings. We *did* leave things in a weird place when we broke up, and my family was a mess then too and still is a mess. Dating Tori was a completely new thing that had me kind of shaken up. I wasn't sure how I felt sometimes. It wasn't just you."

He paused, raising his eyebrows. "But you liked all of us. And we were all on some kind of dating game show in your head?"

"No, I mean, it's not . . ." I cringed. "I guess essentially, yeah."

Matthew smirked for the first time since we'd sat down together. "So was I eliminated first or—?"

I flushed, disgruntled. I pulled my beanie further down over my ears. "You lost points first just by the fact that you're my ex, so . . ."

Matthew gave me a wry grin, shaking his head. "How am I supposed to compete with Amanda 'Miss Perfect' Guevara and Dani 'Pretty New Girl with a Mysterious Past' Mendoza if I don't even know I'm competing?"

My smile faded at the thought of Dani and Amanda, then wobbled precariously before falling away completely. Matthew turned somber then, murmuring, "Have you heard from them?"

I shook my head, trying to will away the knot gathering in my throat. I had hoped to hear from them by now, but I hadn't. I took a bite of my quesarito, hoping it would push down the fear that was rising in my belly.

"I talked to them," Matthew admitted. "I felt like I had to, since we were all in the same boat, really."

I grimaced. "The same boat caught in my natural disaster."

Matthew chuckled. "Yeah, that's a good way to put it. They just need some space right now. That's all I was able to get from them. I haven't heard from them since you sent the essay though, so . . ."

"I figured." I sighed, biting my lip. "I just want to talk to them. Make things right." Looking at Matthew shyly, I asked, "So are we cool?"

Matthew's eyes were soft, and there was no joking in his voice as he said, "Yeah. We're good. Soooo . . ." He gave me an expectant look. "Dani?"

"It doesn't matter," I said, staring at my shoes. Bad idea. That damn tree stared back up at me, the stick figure of a girl sitting so hopefully in the branches, about to touch the sky. "Maybe it was possible before, but she's not going to like me, not after this."

Matthew shrugged. "You don't know that."

I shook my head. "How can she? I don't blame her if she never wants to talk to me again. It's not like I was ever really good at this anyway."

"What?" Matthew asked.

"This." I gestured around us, as if a wave of my hand could somehow encompass the entirety of my status as a romantic failure. "Love, dating, whatever. I'm bad at it. I'm a complete fucking mess. Look at what happened with us."

"To be fair, I was pretty bad at it too back then, and now. But I don't actually think that matters all that much because we're supposed to get better at it. No matter how bad we are at this, we're going to get better. But good or bad, you deserve a happy ending."

Matthew gave me a sad smile and patted my shoulder, gripping it tight. It was comforting, hopeful, even if I still had more hearts to win over. I lifted my chin to the sky, told the clouds to sweep me off my feet and carry me through the rest of my apologies. I'd need divine intervention for this, certainly. "It'll be happy, but let's hope it's not an ending."

---

When Veronica got home from her class a half hour later, she came with news: "Mami and Alyssa are going to be home later than expected, so I'll take over for you if you go pick up the dress."

"Shouldn't she have already done that?" I asked, tapping my fingers against the counter as I completed a doodle of the fruit shelves in front of me that had been my still life model for the afternoon. "The quince is less than a week away."

"She had to add another layer, the skirt wasn't full enough, and one of the damas needed her dress altered last minute, so she wanted to wait to get both at once. I mean, until *you* could get both at once."

My militant party-planning kid sister. Of course she'd volunteer the worst driver in the family to transport precious cargo. "Okay, but if I crash your car because the dress blocks the back windows, you're gonna have to tell Mami it's Alyssa's fault."

I took Veronica's old yellow Kia to the Sewing Box on Sam Houston, where I had to toss the smaller garment bag containing the dama dress onto the back seat before piling the giant bag containing Alyssa's fluffy turquoise ball gown on top of it. I had to battle the end of the bag further into the car so I could close the door, and I didn't even want to know how many layers of tulle they had added to make Alyssa's perfect princess dress.

When I got into the front seat, sweaty and irritated, I looked back to see the garment bag blocking the back window now and groaned, reaching back to push it down. Running my hands over the fluffy bag, my hands slowed almost of their own accord, as though their attention had been pulled. I found myself twisting fully around in the front seat, unzipping the bag to reveal the blue satin of Alyssa's dress, beaded with tiny, precisely placed rhinestones in swirling silver-threaded patterns. The fabric was silky and smooth, light and airy. It looked delicate and elegant, but I knew just how much labor had actually gone into the dress: the research, the endless fittings, the countless alterations. It was just further evidence of how hard Alyssa was working to make this the best quince ever. Alyssa had carefully orchestrated every aspect of the outfit: the tiara, the white flats and the heels she would change into during the reception to signal her transition from girl to woman, the tiny diamond earrings. No detail had been overlooked.

If Alyssa could take on the most high-stakes mission of her life and nail every single part of it, I could take the single step required of me and actually reach out to my friends instead of hiding like a coward. I faced forward and put the car in drive. I passed the grocery store, barreling down Sam Houston.

The Liberty Estates sign welcomed me, the sign bright against the night.

Pulling up in front of Amanda's house, I put the car in park but hesitated, Amanda's house looming menacingly at the end of the driveway. Should I do this? I could always turn around now. Maybe it would be better to give Amanda her space—

The front door opened, and Amanda stepped out in cutoff

shorts, an old camp T-shirt, and flip-flops. She stood in the driveway, looking at the car. I took a deep breath and stepped out. She met me halfway down the driveway, arms crossed.

"I got your essay," she said by way of greeting, her voice not giving anything away. She held my gaze, a challenge.

Amanda had her guard up, but I wasn't here to attack. "Yeah. I just wanted . . . I just wanted to explain myself. I'm sorry that I didn't tell you how I felt. I wasn't thinking about Jaime maybe seeing it or . . . I was just—"

"Angry?"

"Yeah."

"I know I can trust you, Maggie. That's not it." Amanda shook her head. "I think I was just more hurt than anything else. You were keeping all these secrets from me too. I know why you didn't tell me about your feelings for me. But everyone else? Maggie, I'm supposed to be your best friend. I'm supposed to be the one you run to for that stuff."

"You *are*." The word tore itself from my chest because it was true. That was why I'd squashed it down as long as I could; I was crap at keeping secrets from Amanda, and that didn't change when one of the secrets *involved* Amanda. "It was all just too complicated, and I didn't want to deal with it, so I didn't tell anyone until Jordan."

Amanda was silent, staring at me expectantly. She knew me too well; she knew I had more to say. "About the post . . . I just, I need you to know that I don't like you like that. But you keep me grounded. Our whole lives, our friendship was steady. And when everything started to change . . . I just didn't want to have to change too drastically. Pretending I had a chance with you felt like trying to pin things down, make them stop moving. I just didn't know what was going to happen, ya know? What if we grew apart?"

She shook her head. "Maggie, that could never happen. At least, I won't let it. And, Maggie . . . I went back and looked at the other posts. Was that why you didn't tell me about NYU?"

Ah, yes. She'd seen that. "I just . . . I didn't think you'd understand. You don't have money problems, and . . . I didn't want you to think I was flaking on you."

She shook her head. "Maggie, I don't have money problems, yeah, but that doesn't mean I don't understand that you do. I know this shit is expensive, and I would never think you're flaking just because you can't pay for it. No one should have to pay this much for school, and I'm just lucky that I can afford it."

She reached out and took my hand. "No matter where you go to college . . . I want us to be us. I meant it when I said we're endgame."

I searched her face for any hint of a lie, but there was none. She really meant it. Suddenly I couldn't remember how I could have ever doubted her.

But I guess that was why this had to happen. I had to mess everything up in order to see how strong our friendship was, and now I knew.

"I don't know where I'm going or what I'll be doing," I said, "but I'd like to be your best friend while I'm figuring it out."

"Duh, Maggie." Amanda shrugged. "We're best friends forever. You get to annoy me and I get to annoy you at home and in various glamorous cities around the world until we're old and grey and we move back here because as nice as other places are, neither of us can live without Stripes or tacos for very long." I nodded solemnly. "And we'll have houses next to each other and our kids will teach each other how to make a bong out of a Gatorade bottle so they can be all vintage before deciding it's just easier to use a vape pen, and we'll pretend we don't notice. We'll have a great time forever and ever."

"You have this all figured out," I said, smiling.

"Duh. Someone has to keep their head on straight here."

The force of my affection for her slammed into my chest, propelling me forward, and I hugged her. "Thank you."

She froze for a moment, and I panicked briefly until I felt her hug me back just as tightly. "Anytime."

Amanda's arms dropped slowly, and I noticed her red-rimmed eyes and the shadows underneath them. I was sure I looked the same. Was this what friendship was, what caring was: hurting when someone else hurt, sharing their pain? Sharing their healing? Was that what love was, what my mom and Veronica had told me it was about?

"So wait, did you really like me that much?" Amanda asked.

"For a long time, I thought I loved you. When I fell in love with Matthew, it was like *BOOM* first love, and that made sense, but with you it was softer. More innocent, younger, I guess? But now with Dani . . ."

Amanda gave a small smile. "It feels different?"

I nodded. "First love is really earth-shattering. It flips you upside down and makes you feel like you're in a Nicholas Sparks novel. Everything is do or die, ya know?"

Amanda chuckled. "You're always so dramatic. It's not that deep."

I stuck out my tongue. "That's exactly it though. Since everything with you guys started to get complicated, it was like earthquakes all the time. But Dani makes everything feel really still. The ground is still cracked and settling, but it's healing. It's not so chaotic all the time, and things feel a little quieter, easier to deal with . . . am I making any sense?"

Amanda nodded. "Yeah, weirdly enough. She makes you happy."

I grinned. "She really does." Then I remembered. Dani wasn't mine, and after all this, she might never be. "Or at least, she did."

Amanda's brow furrowed. "Have you talked to her?"

I shook my head. "I don't feel like it's my place. Everything got so fucked up so quickly, and after everything that happened in Harlingen . . . she trusted me and I broke that trust. I feel like I let her down. I'm pretty sure she hates me now."

Amanda smiled, good-naturedly rolling her eyes. "Dramatic. You didn't ruin everything. I forgave you. So did Matthew. She can too."

"You forgive me?"

"Duh." Amanda opened her arms, beckoning, and I let myself relax as we embraced again. "Thanks for coming. I know it wasn't easy for you."

I laid my head on her shoulder. "No, but it was worth it."

---

**Amanda:** Y'all I have an idea

**Jordan:** Why'd you make a new chat? I thought you weren't mad at Maggie anymore

**Dani:** Am I still allowed to be here

**Amanda:** Hush we know you and mags are still gonna end up together. Don't play yourself. I made a new chat bc i'm plotting

**Matthew:** Oh god

**Tori:** Why am i here? What's happening???

**Amanda:** Can all of you just shut up for a minute and let me explain?

That night, I decided to make dinner while Veronica tended to the store, but the only thing I knew how to make was migas and eggs, so breakfast for dinner it would be. I was watching the leftover beans cook in the pan, scraping the bottom to make sure none were sticking, when Mom and Alyssa came through the door. I brandished my spoon accusingly at them. "You're home early."

"By like ten minutes," Alyssa said, laying the bags of bulk-size candy and supplies for her gift bags on the floor. "It took forever."

"Are you dirtying my kitchen?" Mom asked, peering at the stove suspiciously as she put her purse on the end table.

I threw my arms out toward the stove, displaying the bubbling pans filled with eggs and beans, the comal that was heating up for tortillas. "I made dinner."

My mother smiled bemusedly and followed Alyssa, who had made a beeline for the stove.

"It's not burned," Alyssa marveled, wide-eyed.

"Did you make migas and eggs?" Mom asked, taking no care to keep the shock from her voice. "Breakfast for dinner."

"They're not as good as yours, but the tortilla pieces are crispy like you like, and I figured you guys would be hungry after the errands, so . . ." I shrugged, staring anxiously at the two of them.

Alyssa smiled. Mom rubbed my back, smiling softly. "You didn't have to do that."

"I know. I wanted to." It was the least I could do, and honestly, I felt damn good doing it. Like I wasn't a waste of space. Like I was capable of caring for other people in a way they wanted, in a way they needed.

That night, we ate and commiserated about our long days. Veronica talked about a bleaching job gone wrong in class—"Her hair was the texture of overcooked spaghetti, I am not even kidding"—and Alyssa recounted their day full of errands. "Traffic in Brownsville sucks, but I got to see Mami swear in Spanish at some guy, so that was cool."

Listening, I offered, "I can help. Ya know, with anything that's left to help with."

Alyssa tilted her head. "Yeah?"

I nodded. "Yeah, I was looking through the binder earlier"—I motioned toward the gargantuan quince binder on the counter—"and I figured you might need help since there's still stuff to do."

My mother beamed with pride, and even Veronica looked begrudgingly impressed. Alyssa just tapped a finger to her chin. "The lady messed up the centerpieces, so you can help me replace all the ribbons."

Spending hours fixing someone else's mistake sounded like a task one would take up as a vocation in hell, but it had felt good to cook for my family, and good to help them out as the quince stuff was starting to snowball.

Honestly, it would also be nice to think about something that wasn't the trash fire of my love life.

After dinner, Alyssa and I sat on the living room floor surrounded by cardboard boxes full of botched centerpieces.

"Okay, so this is what we have to do." Alyssa carefully unwrapped the lavender ribbon off the centerpiece she was working on before measuring a scrap of aquamarine ribbon from the roll she'd bought at Michael's, cutting it after determining it was the right size. "And then you wrap it and tie it. See? Easy."

"Huh." I stared at the centerpiece, moving it around as I examined the bow. "Okay, I think I got it. Let's go."

The next half hour passed quickly as lavender ribbon piled up around us. The sound of blades cleanly slicing bits of ribbon had a quiet rhythm, and we toiled away.

Slowly, with Alyssa occasionally reaching over to adjust something that I was doing, the centerpieces went from lavender to aquamarine, matching Alyssa's chosen color scheme. Right when I was starting to feel like the mice Cinderella had roped into making her a whole freaking dress, I figured I'd done enough work to avoid the lecture she was sure to give me and decided to just spit it out: "So I don't think I'll have an escort to your quince. I guess you figured that out by now, though."

"Of course you'd wait until the last minute to tell me." Alyssa rolled her eyes, looking more and more like Veronica every day, but her good-natured grin was all her own. "Don't worry, I got it handled. Don't you worry . . ."

I chuckled at my dramatic baby sister before falling quiet.

"I'm sorry things got so fucked up," Alyssa said.

"You and me both." I sighed. "I screwed everything up."

"So? We all do." Alyssa shrugged. "Try again."

"What?"

"Fixing your problem is going to be as easy as fixing this." She held up a shorn piece of lavender ribbon for emphasis. "Okay? It just takes time."

"Yeah, but you helped me with this."

Alyssa smiled. "I didn't say you had to fix it alone. Yeah, you have to do the apologies and stuff yourself, but you know I'll always be here."

I smiled, pulling her toward me and kissing her on the crown of the head even as she squirmed. "When did you get so wise?"

"When you became a bisexual disaster. Someone had to pick up the slack."

I grinned. "I *am* a mess, aren't I?"

"Duh." Alyssa eyed me cheekily. "But I think Dani likes it."

I turned red. "Shut up."

"She likes you."

"Not after this."

Alyssa reached out and took my hand, sweeping her thumb back and forth over the top. "You smile more when she's around. You even giggle. You're not all doom and gloom, even with your eyeliner and your flannels—"

"Hey, watch it—"

"When you're around her, you look younger, like you're starting over again. Like you're just beginning." Alyssa squeezed my hand. "She'll be back. Just watch."

"How do you know?"

Alyssa smiled. "Because in the movies, the girl always gets the girl."

"This isn't like any movie I've ever seen."

"That's because this is better. It's real."

# 18

The next day was Friday, the day before the quince, and I still didn't know for sure whether my friends would be coming or not. Since Amanda and I made up, things had been back to normal at school, at least this morning, so maybe they would be there? Even Dani had been hanging out with the group again as of this morning. She still wasn't talking to me, but at least she made eye contact sometimes. What else could you expect, when you take someone's trust and shit on it?

When Amanda and I approached the arts wing (on time), Dani and Jordan weren't in the classroom or in the hall, and I raised an eyebrow at Amanda as we both lingered outside the room. "Where's everyone?"

Amanda shrugged. "I don't know. Jordan probably got stopped for his skateboard again." She opened her Kanken, rummaging around. "I think I left my calculator in yearbook."

I shrugged. "I lost mine so much I stopped taking it home."

"Imma go look." Amanda hurried off without looking at me, and I frowned as I went into the art room, taking a seat near the front. I had thought Amanda and I had been cool, but she'd been distant all morning, texting behind my back and not talking much. Had something happened in the hours since we'd made up that made her hate me again?

If that was the case, *she* was apologizing to *me* this time, goddammit.

After a few minutes of scrolling through my phone under the table, I heard the low murmurs of the other students increase in volume, and then something bumped into the leg of my chair. I looked down to investigate and saw a very familiar skateboard rocking lazily on its wheels beside my seat. "Jordan, wha—"

I whipped my head up to snap at him, but my retort died on my lips when I saw him. He was standing in the doorway, ramrod straight with a shit-eating grin on his face, a giant aquamarine *Q* hanging from his neck by a piece of twine. "Huh—"

Then the rest of my friends filed in one by one, each with two different letters, and they arranged themselves in a line in front of me. I scrambled to keep my jaw from dropping when Tori brought up the rear, holding a question mark (honestly, mood). She gave me a barely there but genuine smile, looking me full in the face for the first time in what felt like ages.

"Ayyy, you spelled it wrong!" someone shouted from the back of the room, and I bit back a laugh when I realized that Amanda and Matthew were switched, spelling out *QUCEIN?*

"Fuck, Matthew, why'd you fuck it up?" Amanda hissed, pushing him out of the way.

"Not me, you!" Matthew muttered accusingly, glaring at her as he stumbled off to his correct place.

"Fucking figures—"

"Um, guys?" I asked, drawing their attention. They all perked up, wearing *QUINCE?* proudly as they looked at me, as though just remembering I was there.

Jordan cleared his throat. "Hello, the last few weeks have been weird, but we'd all really, really like to come to your sister's quince. If we're still invited. I mean, I knew I was still invited 'cuz I haven't done anything wrong ever—"

Tori nodded, waving her question mark. "*Anyway*, but some of us were actual assholes."

Matthew interrupted, "Can relate."

"But we'd really like to come. I even have an outfit picked out," Amanda mentioned.

Tori spoke up, unexpectedly gentle, but maybe this was what she was actually like. "If you'll have us, of course."

Looking at my group of friends, bouncing on the balls of their feet with their letters, my heart filled with fondness until it felt like I was drowning in it. Tears filled my eyes, and I tried desperately to blink them away. "Of course you guys are invited."

The group broke formation and cheered, Jordan pulling me into a side hug. I was passed from person to person, and even Tori gave me an awkward pat on the back, the rest of the class clapping reluctantly, even if they didn't know what the hell was going on and really didn't give two fucks. The group hurried to take seats at our usual table, laughing and talking over one another, and in the melee, I almost forgot about the one person who was missing.

I forced myself to relax, taking a deep breath and trying to put myself back in this moment. After all, I had my friends, and we were going to the quince together. Whatever happened from here on out was just an after-party.

---

My friends had forgiven me, but it felt like there was still one more missing piece of the puzzle that I needed to own up to.

That night, over bowls of caldo de res at the kitchen table, I let the steam of the soup melt the chill of nervousness in me as I said, "Can I tell y'all something?"

My family paused their eating, except for Alyssa, who slurped loudly before asking, "Did Dani get you pregnant?"

Veronica pinched her, and she yelped, reaching over and tugging on a strand of Veronica's hair.

"Girls! Behave yourselves. We don't hurt each other in this house." Mom glared at them until they murmured apologies to each other, then turned to me, schooling her face back into its formerly serene expression. "Mijita, what's going on?"

Her eyes were kind, and my sisters were patiently waiting. I swallowed before saying, "I . . . I'm not sure I wanna go to NYU."

Mami's brow furrowed as my sisters' eyes widened, and she asked, "What? If this is about the money—"

I shook my head. "It's kind of about the money, but it's also about . . . I don't know if I want to be away from y'all for that long. Away from my home, you know? Flights would be really expensive, so I wouldn't get to come home that much. I've been thinking about it for a while."

Veronica tilted her head to the side. "Why didn't you just tell us you weren't sure? We could've talked to you about it earlier."

"I thought you'd be mad at me. Are you not mad at me?" My voice cracked, small like a child's, and I couldn't breathe as I waited for their answer.

They were all quick to shake their heads. "Magdalena, we just want you to be happy, to have whatever future you want," Mom said. "You told us that was NYU, so we wanted to support you. We didn't mean to push you, but . . ."

"We wanted you to have everything that we didn't have because it seemed like you wanted that too," Veronica continued.

"So is it, like, official? You don't want to go there? Not that we want you to," Alyssa quickly added, "but just, what do *you* want?"

What *did* I want? "I don't know. I'm not saying I don't want to go there, it's just . . . I don't know right now, and I want it to be okay that I don't know. You know?"

I waited, watching their faces, but it wasn't long before Mom reached over and squeezed my shoulder, her eyes—my eyes—apologetic. "Of course it's okay, mamas. You have time, and whatever you decide, we'll support you. I'm sorry we didn't make that clear before."

"Yeah, Maggie," Alyssa chimed in. "I was going to miss you a lot, so I want you to stay, *but* I was also looking forward to having you out of the house so I could be the favorite child—"

Veronica rolled her eyes. "You're already the favorite. Mom lets you get away with everything."

"Wrong! You're the favorite, V, and you always have been," I whined.

Mami sighed dramatically, putting her hand to her forehead. "Right now, I don't like any of you, so you're all wrong."

Alyssa looked to Veronica for translation. "Does that mean we're all the favorite?"

"By default, I guess." Veronica shrugged.

"That's like the family equivalent of the participation award," I pointed out.

"A participation award is still an award." Alyssa grinned and clapped her hands. "Go us!"

---

**Dani:** Are you sure this is okay? What if she doesn't react well?

**Alyssa:** Trust me I'm the BEST at big gestures. It'll be great. *sparkles emoji*

# 19

Finally, it was Saturday: Alyssa's birthday and the day of her quinceañera.

The flock had arrived. I could hear them, the chatter of my tías like seagulls as they thundered up the stairs. Their steps shook the walls as they banged through the front door, my mom greeting them just as loudly. I heard purses being thrown around, the rustle of plastic bags.

I gave a muted groan, ducking my head under my pillow and yanking my blanket over me. I hadn't agreed to a wake-up call, but it made sense. The group chat we were in with all my tías and their kids had been popping off for months, with everyone coordinating their own part of the day; most of the cousins, us included, had muted the shit out of it after Alyssa's quince had been announced, and for good reason. Every time Mom wasn't working or running around with one of us, she was texting. She'd even figured out how to use GIFs. The one of the penguin with its wings out while "COME AT ME BRO" flashes below it was a particular favorite.

I peeked out of the blankets; Alyssa hadn't moved a muscle, just continued snoring with no mind to the fact that her cavalry had arrived. The door opened, and Veronica tiptoed into the room. "Wassup?"

Veronica pointed at the bed, and I understood. Together we crawled under the covers, sandwiching Alyssa between us. Alyssa stirred, her bed head poking out of the covers. "Stop, it's not time to get up yet."

Veronica smiled, and even in the low light, I knew it was the soft smile that she reserved only for special occasions and other moments of productive nostalgia. "But it's your birthday."

Alyssa stilled before slowly turning onto her back, looking at both of us. "It's my birthday," she whispered in awe.

Veronica nodded. "So your birthday . . . you were right on time, unlike Maggie."

I pouted, but she just continued, "It was the middle of a fucking Saturday, and I was in the store with Mom, and then her water broke all over my jelly sandals."

I winced. "Ew, that's nasty."

Veronica flicked my head. "Childbirth is a beautiful and sacred process."

"Yeah," Alyssa said. "Go on!"

"Well, Mami and Papi started running around like chickens without their heads, and they called Tía Lupe to come stay with me, but she was at work until five, so basically I had to stay at home by myself for two hours with this one." Veronica nudged my shoulder.

"I bet if you went to a doctor, they'd probably tell you that's why you have anxiety," Alyssa said, stroking her chin like she had a beard.

Veronica paused. "Huh. You know what, you're probably right."

"We love therapy with Alyssa," I said. "What was I doing while she was being born?"

"You ate and napped, so basically the same things you do now." Veronica laughed. "But anyway, Al, your birth was kind of hard because it was a C-section, so y'all had to stay in the hospital for a while. After that, Mami had to go back once to fix the incision because it wasn't closing and it got infected."

"Ouch. I feel like I should apologize for that," Alyssa said, wincing.

"Nah, she'd probably just say something sappy about how your big head and the weird position you were at inside of her meant you were special, which I don't think it does but whatever. You weren't my kid." Veronica shrugged.

"Moms are so weird." Alyssa shook her head. "Maggie, what do *you* remember?"

"Not that much, honestly, but I remember that you were a really tiny baby," I added to the story the best I could. "You also cried all the time, so that's basically the same as it is now."

"Rude. Sorry I'm not afraid of my own feelings like the both of you are."

"She's right, V," I sighed.

"I'm not apologizing for being the canary-in-the-coal-mine eldest daughter that wasn't taught how to express emotion." Veronica shrugged. "Alyssa, you're the last great hope of the family as far as emotional maturity goes."

"Less pressure for us, so thanks for that," I added.

"Anytime," Alyssa said fondly. "Hey, guys?"

"Yeah?" Veronica answered.

"Thanks. For everything. The party stuff but also for helping Mami raise me and stuff."

My heart swelled, and I squeezed my little sister tightly, kissing the top of her head. "It was a team effort."

"And we're a great team," Veronica said. She patted Alyssa's thigh. "Come on, let's go. Time to get up."

I nodded, sitting up. "Time to make quince magic happen."

We went our separate ways to throw on clothes before going to the living room. CJ was already sitting on the floor by the coffee table, surrounded by bags of candy and a stack of cellophane bags. It was barely seven thirty, last time I checked, but he already had a plate full of eggs, beans, and tortillas, and was shoveling food into his mouth. "How long have you been here?" Veronica said, pecking him on the temple as we passed him.

CJ grinned at her, taking a sip of coffee from the chipped souvenir mug Mom had brought from some long-forgotten trip to Nevada. "I came early because I knew there would be breakfast."

"There always is," Alyssa said, her eyes lighting up as she raced into the kitchen. "Granny!"

I followed her. Grandma Lupita stood at the counter, mixing sugar into her coffee. Alyssa smothered her in a bear hug; she was already half a foot taller than Granny was, and Granny teetered under the weight, laughing. "Ay mijita, happy birthday. You're getting so big. ¡Que chula!"

Alyssa thanked her, and Granny hugged me too. Pulling back to scrutinize me, she frowned and asked, "Did you comb your hair? Where are your earrings?"

"She's right, kid. How dare your ears be naked at seven thirty in the morning," my Aunt Ana said, pinching a hot tortilla off the comal between long acrylic nails, dropping it onto a plate, and passing it to Mom. Our mother was beside her, scooping eggs and bacon onto plates and handing them to my little cousin, Amber, who was waiting by my mother's side so she could load her with plates and send her off to the kitchen table. Veronica went over to greet Amber's parents, my cousin Imelda and Vanessa, her now-legally-wedded-wife-and-mother-of-Amber-but-we-don't-talk-about-it-in-front-of-Granny, who were sitting at the table sipping their coffee.

As soon as my sisters and I got our plates, we carried them out to the living room; the kitchen was way too hot from all the people crammed in and the stove running full steam. Veronica plunked down next to CJ on the floor, and Alyssa and I sat on the other side of the coffee table. CJ was already on his second plate, no doubt because Chicana aunts *loved* their sons/nephews/grandkids/niece's longtime boyfriends.

"Freeloader," I said, pointing at him with a piece of bacon.

Alyssa popped a few personalized M&M's into her mouth from a bag on the floor and shrugged. "That's all right. I'm putting all y'all to work. Everyone's gonna earn their food today."

Alyssa wasn't kidding; there was an endless list of tasks to accomplish still, which would keep the whole family on their toes. There were teenagers to pick up and deposit at the store, little cousins to corral in our room with a set of cheap old Legos, Barbie dolls long since stripped of their polyester clothes, and the *Despicable Me* trilogy, and scuffles between tías to mediate. I stuffed bags full of table favors and sprayed more hairspray that morning than I had in my entire life.

When Alyssa's hairstyle was done—the last hairstyle Veronica had tried had ended up being the one, and Alyssa now wore a bun with pieces pulled out and perfectly curled, framing her face—she and I cornered Veronica on the porch. Veronica looked at us suspiciously. "What?"

"Your hair needs help," Alyssa pointed out, fingering Veronica's flaming-red locks. The dye was now faded and starting to look patchy; Veronica had been taking care of our needs for the last two months and had obviously neglected herself in the process.

Veronica batted Alyssa's hand away, arching her brow and standing up. "I don't have time to do my hair right now."

"No, but we do." I pulled on a pair of black gloves, and Alyssa came up behind me, already wearing gloves as she mixed the dye.

Veronica's face was passive before, but now it was verging on murderous as we forced her back into the chair. "I swear to God, if it's uneven—"

"Relax." I waved her protests off, handing Alyssa the conditioner. "I've learned from the best."

I didn't stop moving until Veronica's hair was its trademark bright red, and after helping Alyssa into her dress and getting Veronica to zip up my own, I left my little sister in Mom's capable hands and barricaded myself in the bathroom to do my hair.

As I curled it with my straightener, the mirror told me I hadn't changed much in the last two months, at least not on the outside. Part of me expected to see the past few weeks on my skin, in acne scars in the shape of tears or dark pools under my eyes where bad memories swam, but I didn't.

Holding eye contact with my reflection because maybe I would respect myself more that way, I promised I would talk to Dani tomorrow, after this quince business was over and I had time to plan what I wanted to say. I had to, or I would end up saying something ridiculous and rambly, something along the lines of *I know we just met but I think I'm falling in love with you and I'm really sorry I'm a trash disaster I promise I'm not as promiscuous as I seem really I've only had eyes for you since this whole thing began and I really wanna hold your hand again and maybe I'll even be brave enough to kiss you this time*.

Whatever. I'd edit it later.

---

I was lost in thought sitting in the limo with Alyssa and her friends on the way to Our Lady Queen of the Universe Church as they screamed and joked around in that way ninth graders did, talking loudly over each other and laughing uproariously. I wished my friends were here, but it wasn't *my* quince (thankfully), so they were all meeting us at the church.

I was the lucky one who got to chaperone these barely-not-kids in a tiny contained space.

Alyssa was absolutely radiant in front of the church, the rhinestones on her aquamarine dress sparkling in the sun.

I had seen her in her dress earlier, but in all the chaos of preparation, I hadn't had the chance to really look at her. In full makeup, the afternoon sunlight glinting off her tiara, Alyssa looked like a queen. Her hands were on her hips as she and Mom, in her mother-of-the-quinceañera dress and shawl, worked on getting the court into correct formation for the procession into the church.

I, as a sulky and insecure fifteen-year-old, had thought these traditions were meaningless and extravagant, but watching Alyssa actually enjoy this whole process made me think that maybe I'd missed the point. It wasn't about "becoming a woman," or whatever our cisheteronormative society decided signaled womanhood. It was about, for one day, feeling like the most important, most confident, most incandescent person in the entire universe.

And I loved that for her.

Matthew pulled into the parking lot then, and I made sure Veronica didn't need any help with the court before heading over to his truck, smiling all the way.

Amanda was doing her best to slither out of the truck as gracefully as possible in a tight but tasteful cocktail dress. She glared at Jordan as he stood off to the side trying not to laugh. "Shut up, you ass, you try navigating this little-penis-complex vehicle in heels."

Matthew came around the side, holding hands with Tori. "Your mom didn't call it little last night." Tori screwed up her face in disgust but let out a little laugh.

Amanda flipped him off, and Jordan looked around. "Can't we all just be civil for one day?"

Honestly, I didn't care what barbs my friends threw at each other; we were here, together, our weird little family intact, except for—"Is Dani . . ."

"Is Dani what?"

And then she was there, coming around from the other side of the truck, and I was so relieved to see her face that it took me a while to notice what she was wearing.

It was the dama's dress. The one I had helped Alyssa pick out. The one that I myself was wearing. The turquoise beading, the bow at the waist, even the matching kitten heels.

On Dani.

Dani was glowing, her skin shining against the golden afternoon. Her dark chestnut hair was pinned back, framing her face and cascading down her shoulders in gleaming curls. Her smile was nervous but genuine, her hands twisting anxiously in front of her. "Hi."

"You're wearing the . . ." I trailed off vacantly, eyes wide. I couldn't even finish the sentence out loud. Dani. Was wearing. The DRESS.

She bit her lip. "I didn't know if this was okay, but I knew you didn't have an escort and. . . ." She paused, taking a breath before continuing, shy but sure, "I haven't told you how much your presentation meant to me. So I gave you a big gesture instead."

A big gesture. She had gone through all this effort, for me. She must have had to get in touch with Alyssa about the dress since it fit her *perfectly*, and the idea of all the hoops Dani must have jumped through had all rational thought fleeing my brain. I couldn't find any words to say or the ability to pick my jaw up off the floor. "I—"

"Hate to interrupt this little reunion, but some of us have things to do and places to be," Veronica announced, striding over and pointing at Dani and me. "Mostly you two. I don't particularly care where the rest of you sit, but if you don't leave now, you'll end up having to sit in front of cousin Leonardo, and he and the tíos are already drinking, so it's only a matter of time before shit goes sideways."

I winced and turned to Dani. "Can we do this later maybe? I have so many questions."

Dani smiled. "And I have answers. We'll talk."

The promise in her words rang loud in my ears, and it sounded a lot like hope.

Alyssa texted me and Veronica that she needed a last-minute hair touchup, so I reluctantly left Dani with the rest of the court, where CJ was staring down the chambelánes as he gave them a threatening lecture on appropriate conduct. At the back of the church, as Veronica added more hairspray to Alyssa's updo and Mami pinned a wayward curl back into place, I took the moment to demand, "How does Dani have that dress?"

Veronica gave a sly smile. "It was Alyssa's idea. Mami and I just pitched in for the extra dress." Mom nodded, shrugging coyly.

Alyssa waved cheerily. "Hi, I'm a rascal. You were really sad, and I didn't entirely believe Dani wouldn't ask you out. So I got it just in case. And *then* Dani came by the store to talk to you, so I convinced her to wait until the quince for a surprise!"

I frowned. "You just let me marinate in my misery . . . for a surprise?!"

Alyssa grimaced. "My plan had some holes, yeah."

"We just want you to be happy, mija," Mami added. "And she makes you happy. It was an easy choice."

Happiness bubbled up inside me as I looked at my little family. Flinging my arms around Mom, my voice was thick as I said, "Thank you."

"Oh god," I heard Veronica mutter, "here she goes again being emotional and dramatic. It's just a dress, not an engagement ring."

I waved her over. "Stop talking shit and just get in here."

Veronica laughed and joined in, Alyssa bringing up the rear as she threw herself on top of us, all of us teetering, but not falling, under the weight of her dress. I felt our mother's laughter, the tremble against my skin, and as always, I couldn't tell where I ended and they began, love unfolding around me in a warm haze.

"What did I miss?"

I peeked out over Mom's shoulder to see that Dani had entered the room, a warm smile gracing her face as she took in the sight of all four Gonzalezes in a bear hug. "I just have the best family," I blurted, blushing a bit as I gave the group one more squeeze before extracting myself to stand next to Dani.

"Well, that's not a surprise to anyone." Dani held out her arm for me to take, beckoning me with an eyebrow wiggle. "Shall we go find our places with the rest of the court?"

I laughed, linking arms with her. "You sure know how to treat a girl like royalty."

Like all Catholic traditions, the ceremony was long, with Alyssa reciting her Bible verses fluidly in English and Spanish. The minutes flew by though, because I kept looking over at Dani, and when I caught her looking back, we both blushed. I was more entertained than I'd ever been in church before.

Outside after the ceremony, it was decided that CJ would be taking a few of the gargantuan centerpieces in his truck, but Alyssa had given us strict orders not to risk putting any in the bed, so Veronica had to put the rest in the trunk of her Kia. She tossed the keys to me. "Go slow. Be safe. And stay out of my back seat."

Veronica glared at me and Dani, and I wanted the ground to open up and swallow me, but Dani just laughed. "Wouldn't dream of it."

Alyssa and her friends decided they wanted to entertain themselves by walking around the mall unsupervised for an hour (an excuse to show off that was not subtle, but none of us were going to call her out on it, lest we get hit with the "I'm the birthday princess and I get to do what I want" speech), while the rest of us would get the reception hall decorated. Veronica giving me the Kia had been a calculated move, and I was eternally grateful for the privacy as we took the scenic route to the Las Palmas reception hall on the border of Harlingen and San Benito.

"Why . . . how . . . ?" I started, shaking my head as I trailed off, unable to keep a coherent train of thought.

"I'm not gonna lie. The fact that you liked Matthew and Amanda at the same time as me hurt. I really thought that you were just another person trying to mess with me or something."

My face burned, and I forced myself to keep looking at the road, even if my stomach was turning. I had to let her say this. What I did had consequences, and I couldn't shy away from that.

Dani continued, "I didn't know whether I was going to forgive you, and I certainly didn't want to see you, yet . . . And then you sent me the write-up."

I bit my lip. "What did you think?"

In my periphery, Dani took a deep breath. "I took a more careful look back at all the other posts and then started to piece it together. I saw how your thinking started to change about me, and how you stopped posting about the others when we began hanging out more."

Screw this driving shit. We were making good enough time, and it wasn't like I was a horribly vital part of the process. "Can I—I don't want to have this conversation not looking at you. Can I pull over?"

"Yeah, sure."

I pulled over onto the shoulder, parking and looking Dani full in the face for the first time since we'd started driving. "I really just wanted the profile to be private. I didn't think anyone was going to see . . . I just didn't know how else to deal with what I was feeling. It's not an excuse for what I did, but it's the reason."

"Yeah, I know. I was mad about it, but then I kind of had to sort through what was anger and what was hurt." Dani gave me a sad smile. "Yeah, what you did was kinda shitty, but I know what it feels like to not want to deal with your feelings and then have them blow up in your face anyway. There was a lot more to you and Matthew and Amanda than just run-of-the-mill feelings. That much history would fuck anyone up, and then there was me and all my shit . . ." Dani sighed. "I get it. I'm fucked up too."

"I've been really fucked up inside for a long time," I said pathetically.

"Maybe so, but it's not fucked up to not know how you feel. You wanted to be sure about how you felt, and yeah, maybe you could've gone about it differently. But, Maggie . . . you make me feel more comfortable being angry or being uninhibited than anyone else has."

Dani reached over to hold my hand over the console, her skin warm and soothing, and I couldn't help but relax with her touch, weaving my fingers with hers. "You make me feel that way too. Like I don't have to worry that you're going to hate me if I make you mad. I get to be as messy as I want, as sad or as irritated as I want, and it's okay because you would still like me. I don't know if you still—"

"I do," she interrupted. "I do still like you."

Relief crashed through my chest, knocking my lungs loose from the death grip my anxiety had on them. "Okay. Good. Good. That's . . ."

"Good?" Her lips twitched.

"I mean . . ." The words were jumbled in my mouth, tripping one over the other as they struggled to escape from their cage. I held my breath to steady them before exhaling slowly. "I'm so bad at feelings. Like, really bad. And even worse at voicing them. But I like you. I really, really like you."

Dani smiled. "Yeah?"

"I was really messed up about Matthew from our history and Amanda because of other stuff," I said, rushing a bit. I took a deep breath before continuing because this next bit was important. "But I wasn't messed up about you. At all. I knew I liked you. I knew I wanted to get to know you. I didn't know where it would lead, or—or what it would *mean*, especially in the context of everything else. But I knew I wanted *you*. It was that simple. It *is* that simple. And I screwed it up."

Dani looked at me for a long time. "You didn't screw it up," she said slowly.

I blinked at her. "What?"

"Ever since I met you, I felt calm around you. Even when you hurt me, even if I had no reason to, the only one I wanted to talk to about how hurt I was, was *you*." Dani squeezed my hand tightly, her brown eyes unrelenting in their intense gaze. "Even when I was mad at you, you still felt safe to me."

I was afraid to breathe, to ruin the calm that had settled in the car, but that was ridiculous, so I took another deep breath, feeling safe that she wouldn't leave if I stopped for a moment to collect myself.

"If you planned this"—I gestured at the dress—"why didn't you *talk* to me?" My voice was broken as I thought of how awful I'd felt when Dani couldn't so much as look at me.

Dani ran a hand through her hair, exhaling softly. "I didn't plan it, not until I'd decided to forgive you, so it was just a couple of days."

"Okay, well, *still*, why didn't you just tell me?" I asked, an edge of annoyance creeping into my voice. "Do you know how bad I've felt? Dani, you couldn't even *look* at me. I thought I'd lost you forever."

"Because that's what I *do*!" she burst out exasperatedly, though the sadness in her eyes told me her frustration was not at me. "I run. I did it with Melissa; it's how I naturally react. I run, and that's how I am, and I know I told you I wouldn't do that, but bad habits are hard to break." Dani sighed. "But I didn't want to be that way anymore. I wanted to talk to you, and hear you out, and . . . I was coming to find you, the day before the quince proposal. I went to the store."

"Uh-huh." I raised an eyebrow, waiting for her to continue.

A small smile bloomed on Dani's face. "Alyssa was there. She told me what she'd planned, and I thought it was a good idea . . . But mostly I was afraid to talk to you."

Her voice was small and sheepish, and I asked, "Why?"

Dani shrugged. "I have never been good at communication. Thus, me just ghosting Melissa, and me running from you that day, and then me ghosting you. I didn't know if I was ready to hear what you had to say, or knew what I wanted to say . . . It was scary. I'm sorry."

I understood. I hadn't exactly been the shining example of bravery lately. "I forgive you. If you forgive me. We're all learning, I think. And . . . and I'd like to learn with you. If you'd like."

"In the last post on the finsta, you said you liked me. That you wanted to learn how to love me." Dani bit her lip, eyes wide and questioning. "Did you mean it?"

I blushed—it might as well have been a permanent stain today—but I nodded firmly. "I did mean it. I do mean it."

Dani gave a small but dazzling smile. "Well, if it wasn't clear before . . . I really, really like you. And I'd like to be with you now, even though we both are probably way too emotionally immature for this. I'd like to try, with you."

Dani's gaze dropped to my lips, and I mumbled, "I'd like that too."

"Unless of course there are other people involved—"

I gave a wild, relieved laugh, and in a moment of boldness, I reached up to stroke Dani's face. "Only you. Always you."

Dani smiled and leaned closer, and this time, I met her halfway, closing the distance between us.

Finally.

The car seemed too small to hold the universe that unfolded between us in that moment, ready for exploration. Warmth poured into me when Dani's lips touched mine, and every cell seemed to be leaping, buzzing with energy. I didn't know where to put my hands, and the steering wheel was really harshing my vibe right now, but I leaned over the console and held her wrists, sliding my hands up her arms to cup her face. Dani threaded her fingers through my hair and tugged lightly, and I surged forward, deepening the kiss.

Nothing had ever felt this good. Ever.

Dani pulled away, seeming reluctant. "I think they might be waiting for us," she whispered breathily, lips swollen and eyes bright.

"Well, I've been waiting for you," I said before I could stop myself, blushing again and tucking a strand of hair behind my ear.

Dani smiled shyly and gave me a soft fluttering kiss, and my insides sang. "Well, now you have me. And we have time. Just not now."

I wanted to mention that the back seat seemed to have a vacancy, but there would be time for that later; after all, Veronica would definitely make good on her threat. Besides, Alyssa would kill us if we were late and holding her centerpieces hostage.

---

Las Palmas was the reception hall where both Veronica and I had held our quinces. It was sprawled across a large plot of land, looking more like a house than a reception hall. The palm trees and the gazebo bar outside were wrapped in strings of white lights, and the hall's low ceilings gave it a more intimate feeling. With the help of my friends and family, the hall had transformed quickly into a turquoise and soft white dream.

Alyssa's effortless grandeur meant the party was a Gatsbyesque dream. Alyssa was in her element, her friends oohing and ahhing over her decorations and personalized candy. After the shoe ceremony, she strutted around like a peacock, even though she was wobbling like a baby deer in her new heels. I knew she would take them off later and go barefoot, but it didn't matter.

My baby sister was growing up.

Cumbia blared through the room, and the drunker people got, tíos and tías laughing uproariously after too many shots of Crown Royal and too many Coronas, the more they danced. My friends were getting tastefully tipsy at their table, and my mother was buzzing around the room, a social butterfly just like her youngest daughter. I had switched out my heels for the new white Converse Mom had given me for the occasion. New shoes were a blank slate, and my eyes were drawn to them as Dani and I stood up to dance. Even though the song was way too upbeat for it, we swayed together in the center of the floor under the lights. Neither of us knew how to dance to pop music, but it was enough to have her in my arms, warm and full and so very real.

It was almost overwhelming, how beautiful this night was. The music, the twinkling lights, the love and camaraderie in the room. I was strangely nostalgic for it, even if the night wasn't anywhere near over. Maybe that was what made it special, its ability to be missed beyond the parameters of time. Dani pulled away to smile dazzlingly down at me before looking around at the circle of family and friends gathered around the dance floor. "I really want to kiss you here, but . . . is that okay?"

I knew what she meant. Historically, it was hard being queer in the Valley, especially with family, but I was one of the lucky ones who had a (mostly) accepting family that was pretty good about not being shitty and queerphobic (to my face anyway). As for anyone else who might be here, well, I really didn't give a fuck. "Yeah. More than okay."

Dani smiled and leaned in, and I surged up to meet her. Under the swirling lights and the trembling bass from the cumbia, I felt that kiss down to my bones, reverberating through my cells, and the din of the party fell away. For a moment, it was just us, connected irrevocably in our corner of time. The world was quiet and still in a way it had never been before.

Dani sighed into my mouth, her hands coming up to hold my face, and I had never felt more at peace.

"Ewww, gross, get a room," I heard, and I pulled away, forcing my eyes open to see Alyssa's friends at her table, gawking.

Alyssa squealed, lifting her toronja Jarritos bottle in a toast. "Now you can't say I never give you anything!"

I flipped her off, and Alyssa grinned and stuck out her tongue.

Later that night, Dani went to get me a drink, and I leaned back in my chair, watching as Alyssa whirled around the darkened dance floor, spinning with the lights as she danced with her best friend Christina. I smiled when Alyssa grabbed her by the waist and tugged her close in a way that was practiced and familiar, hands gripping her hips just a little too intimately.

Alyssa was looking at Christina the way Dani had looked at me ever since we'd met.

"She gets that from you, ya know," Veronica said, leaning closer to me. She was watching our mother, who was flushed and giggling from too many glasses of wine, as CJ led her in a clumsy two-step to the Spanish version of "Achy Breaky Heart."

"What do you mean?"

Veronica gestured toward Alyssa and Christina, off in their own little world, before taking a sip of her Cuervo and Sprite. "She never would have been brave enough to do this if you hadn't gone after what you wanted."

"And messed everything up in the process."

"Yeah, but at least you tried. And you fixed it." Veronica shrugged. "That's really all there is to it. It's pretty simple: If you're trying, you really can't be bad at love."

I was silent, watching Veronica, who smiled as she turned back to the dance floor. If I hadn't been listening so closely, I would've missed the quiet awe in her voice as she said, "Her bravery is yours."

Alyssa looked over at us suddenly and waved with a huge grin, still holding Christina's hand. I blew her a kiss as Veronica lifted her glass.

The night spun around us, and the stars in the Valley had never seen so much life.

# 20

That wasn't the happy ending. This was.

May came quickly, catching me by surprise. My alarm went off, far too early on a Saturday morning, but I rolled out of bed fairly quickly and dressed for the day. I didn't feel like straightening my hair, so I threw a beanie on over it and stopped to look, as always, at the last picture I had turned in for my art project. I'd hung it on my bedroom wall, and it was of all my friends after the quince, sitting on the steps outside the venue, Amanda laughing and Matthew grinning, Jordan wide-eyed and pointing at something off-camera. Dani and I sat on the bottom step, pressed together to ward off the cold night. She had her denim jacket on over her dress, and I was wearing the flannel my mom had packed for me. My head was on her shoulder, her arm around my waist, and I'd outlined her face in a red Sharpie heart. The photo had a big 100 scribbled at the bottom, along with a note from Mrs. Lozano:

*Love this! Your write-up was so moving. You executed this assignment perfectly, and it showed your growth as an artist, a person, and a friend in the process. Thank you for teaching us all that it's okay to be a little messy sometimes. I can't wait to see what your future holds.*

I smiled at the paper and flew down the stairs.

CJ was ringing up customers at the register, and my mother was doing the heavy lifting at the fridge, stocking it with sodas. "What can I help with?" I offered, coming over.

Mami shook her head, smiling, and handed me the car keys. "No, mamita, I'm all right. Just drive safe."

"Yeah, Maggie, get out of here! It's my turn to help Mom." Alyssa beamed as she took over, and Mami looked on the verge of tears as she slid the box over to her and stood up to join Veronica at the counter.

Veronica turned to glare at me as she came in from the back porch, shears in hand, her belly protruding from under her designated hair-dyeing smock. She was five months' pregnant and even crabbier than she'd ever been, but her eyes had never looked softer. CJ came down the stairs and handed her an orange juice, and she took a big gulp. "You try creating a human life on nothing but cheeseburgers and orange juice."

CJ grunted. "I told you we can't have any more cheeseburgers. We're going to end up with heart disease. I'm cutting you off. We gotta find a better source of protein than that."

"The baby and I *like* cheeseburgers," Veronica muttered darkly, but she smiled when CJ put his hand on her belly, rubbing it gently.

Veronica and CJ had grown even closer over the past few months, something I hadn't known was possible. I knew CJ was ready to lock it down, as he'd been asking her to marry him almost once a day since they'd found out she was pregnant, but Veronica just said it was too much, too fast, so CJ was patient.

Veronica would be ready someday. I knew that much. It was just a matter of when.

"Has anyone seen . . . aha!" I snagged my Converse from the rug by the back door and sat on the stairs to pull them on. I looked at the doodle that Dani had first drawn that day in her room, but it was the other shoe that made me stare.

It was a doodle of a girl in a tree, identical to the first, but next to it was half a heart made of tree branches, the other half on the other shoe. I smiled as I finished tying my shoes and stood.

"Love you, guys. If you want anything from Lali's, text me!" I called over my shoulder, then disappeared out the door.

Heading down Sam Houston, I didn't have to go far, but I still felt myself driving a little faster than normal, bouncing in my seat with excitement. Pulling up in front of the house, I got out quickly, leaning against the passenger-side door. Waiting.

And then Dani was there, locking her front door and turning, her green sundress floating around her knees and her hair in a messy bun. When her eyes landed on me, her smile opened unabashedly, and she started forward.

I would have thought that the awe I felt at seeing Dani walking toward me would have faded by now, at almost seven months in, but if anything it had just gotten stronger. Each step seemed too slow, and I couldn't contain myself, rushing to meet her halfway up the drive.

"Good morning," she said when we were face-to-face, her shy half smile warm. Her eyes were on mine, that burning gaze somehow tearing me apart and stitching me back together all at once.

"Hi." I slid my hands around her waist, pulling her closer. I couldn't look away from those wide eyes, so full of light.

The butterflies swarmed but they calmed when Dani's hands

came up to cradle my face. As giddy as Dani made me, something in her touch soothed the hurricane that forever raged inside me.

When Dani kissed me, I tasted rain and spring and summer, galaxies collapsing and beginning at the press of our lips. She breathed life into me, and I gripped her closer. I wasn't great with words; I was more of a picture person, after all. I'd find better ways to tell Dani every day that she gave me the universe in a kiss, the stars with a glance, the ocean with her words.

At Lali's, I ordered too many pancakes and got a stomachache, and Dani laughed at me while she devoured a tower of bacon. As far as lives go, ours was pretty mundane, but as Dani grinned and wiped a drop of syrup from my lips before going to pay the check, I couldn't help but think that maybe that wasn't such a bad thing. I had all the stardust I wanted in this little town, and I wasn't sure if I'd find anything quite as magical out there.

When we left the restaurant, leftovers in hand at Jordan's request, and arrived at the resaca, I told Dani so. "Do you think the outside world is really all it's cracked up to be? Like the East Coast and all that."

Spring was beautiful in the Valley, the vegetation just starting to heal after a harsh freeze this winter. It was fresh outside today, and the breeze felt good on my skin, so I left my flannel tied around my waist as I settled next to her at our picnic table.

Dani hummed thoughtfully. "I don't know. Maybe we'll find out when we get there." She shrugged. "Or maybe we won't go, and it won't matter."

"Veronica is having a baby, and that . . . that changed everything. My entire world feels like it's going to change, and if I leave, I'm not going to be here for any of it."

Dani's eyes were sad, and she put her chin on her fists, balancing her elbows on her thighs as she stared out at the water. "I get that. Ava is getting older, and I just don't know if I want to be away for that long. I'm scared too, Maggie. I'm more confused than I've ever been."

"Me too." I bit my lip. "Is it . . . is it okay that we don't have things figured out right now?"

Dani nodded. "I think so. This whole thing, it's a big mess, but . . . I think we can figure it out together, ya know? Be confused together."

She pressed a kiss to my temple, so gentle and kind, and my breath caught in my chest. I wound my arm around her and hoped she knew how much I loved her as I pulled her closer to me.

We hadn't said *I love you* yet, but now it was just a matter of who would be brave first, and it didn't matter, really. We knew what we had.

"Hey hey hey, what up?" Jordan boomed, startling us as he popped up behind us. Beside him, Amanda grimaced at the noise and Matthew smacked him on the shoulder as they both approached the table.

"They were having a moment," Matthew scolded.

Jordan slid into the seat across from us, immediately reaching for our leftovers from breakfast. We twisted around to face them all after sharing a smile that seemed to say *to be continued.*

He shrugged, cramming three strips of Dani's bacon into his mouth at once. "We're best friends. They can have their moment in front of us."

"Weren't we going to meet at Starbucks?" I asked. "In fifteen minutes?"

"We have each other's locations, remember? I figured this

would be easier." Amanda shrugged, shoving Jordan over and taking the seat next to him.

"You're a creep," I complained.

Amanda waved me off, and Matthew just shrugged. "Where y'all go, we go. We're a collective third wheel."

Dani laughed, her hand settling on my lower back. Her thumb snuck under my shirt, rubbing circles into the skin there and causing me to lose all ability to think in straight lines. "The more, the merrier."

"That's what I said," Jordan garbled through a mouthful of pancake.

"So what are we doing for prom?" Matthew asked. "Tori wants to know if she should rent a limo."

"Jaime doesn't even wear pants in winter, so I doubt I can wrestle him into a tux . . ."

"You haven't even asked me to prom yet," I accused Dani, obnoxiously nudging her chin with my forehead.

Dani ran her hand up my side playfully, and I squirmed, pressing further into her side. "I have plans for you, don't you worry. You deserve the best promposal."

Dani kissed my cheek, and I grinned. The ends of my hair danced in the spring breeze, and mist from the fountain floated on the air, giving us some relief from the heat. In just a couple weeks, it would be sweltering, but for now, the sun was kind, and the leaves of the tree above us were lending us shade, and that was enough for now.

# ACKNOWLEDGMENTS

To kick this off, I need to thank the beautiful people of the Rio Grande Valley for letting me spill our secrets and tell our stories. Everything that I am is made up of everything that you are. Thank you for being the main characters of every story I want to tell, and a special thank you goes to the city of San Benito for letting me be the main character whenever I come back home. ¡Puro pinche 956!

There are too many family members I want to name, so I'll start with the ones responsible for my existence on the planet: my parents. Thank you for everything that you've done for me and Monica. I wouldn't be the person I am today without your love and care.

To Monica, my little sister, my companion in chaos: I hope I'm as cool as you when I grow up. I'm so proud of everything that you do, and I hope this book makes you a little proud of me too (especially since I've cried to you about it a lot and you should at least get bragging rights out of it).

To Nick, my partner: Thank you for keeping me fed, hydrated, and caffeinated during the process of writing (and re-writing) this book. Thank you for keeping the house running while I was drowning in words, and for reminding me that bathroom breaks exist and I should take them when necessary. Thank you for being the only person in the world that I'd want to go on this wild ride with. I love you to the moon and back and straight on till morning.

The person I will be thanking until I'm blue in the face is Lauren MacLeod at Strothman Agency. Thank you for being this book's—and my—biggest cheerleader and the best agent a writer could ask for. From the start, you saw what this book could be and never let me forget it. There aren't words to express how grateful I am to you for all the drafts you read through and your kind and patient responses to every late-night email I sent you when I was spiraling in self-doubt and existentialism. Thank you for making a messy, snarky Chicana from Texas into a novelist.

To Kat Brzozowski, my absolute dream of an editor at Feiwel & Friends: Thank you for using your special brand of editorial magic to make a story I wrote at my cramped kitchen table into something bigger than I could've ever imagined. You're a star, and I'm so happy to be in your orbit.

Thank you to Jean Feiwel for opening the door to me and a world of other Chicane writers to come. Thank you to the wonderful team at Feiwel & Friends, including Kathy Wielgosz, Liz Dresner, and Celeste Cass. I want to give a special shout-out to Nicole Wayland, whose marginalia kept me laughing while I went through your copyedits.

To Zeke Peña, who is responsible for the life-affirming awesomeness that is the cover: Thank you for bringing Maggie and the Valley to life in a way I could have only dreamed of. Your art helped me see the place I knew in an entirely different light, and I'm grateful for the dimension your work gives the story.

Thanks to any and all extended family who let me bring

my laptop to write at family functions while chiding me gently for working so much.

Thank you to the friends that let me ignore them while I worked on this and welcomed me with open arms whenever I poked my head out of my writer's cave.

Thank you to my fandom friends for reminding me that I'm not a terrible writer and that not everything has to be perfect in order to be meaningful. IYKYK.

Lastly, thank you to my therapist and my psychiatrist, without whom I—and by extension this book—might not exist.

Thank you for reading this Feiwel & Friends book.

The friends who made

possible are:

**JEAN FEIWEL,** Publisher
**LIZ SZABLA,** Associate Publisher
**RICH DEAS,** Senior Creative Director
**HOLLY WEST,** Senior Editor
**ANNA ROBERTO,** Senior Editor
**KAT BRZOZOWSKI,** Senior Editor
**DAWN RYAN,** Executive Managing Editor
**CELESTE CASS,** Assistant Production Manager
**ERIN SIU,** Associate Editor
**EMILY SETTLE,** Associate Editor
**FOYINSI ADEGBONMIRE,** Associate Editor
**RACHEL DIEBEL,** Assistant Editor
**MALLORY GRIGG,** Senior Art Director
**LIZ DRESNER,** Associate Art Director
**KAT KOPIT,** Associate Director, Production Editorial
**KATHY WIELGOSZ,** Production Editor

Follow us on Facebook or visit us online at fiercereads.com.

**OUR BOOKS ARE FRIENDS FOR LIFE.**